TOR BOOKS BY FRAN WILDE

Updraft
Cloudbound
Horizon

To Kim
watch the clouds!

CLOUDBOUND

FRAN WILDE

TOR

A TOM DOHERTY ASSOCIATES BOOK
NEW YORK

CLOUDBOUND

Copyright © 2016 by Fran Wilde

Edited by Miriam Weinberg

A Tor Book
Published by Tom Doherty Associates
175 Fifth Avenue
New York, NY 10010

www.tor-forge.com

Tor® is a registered trademark of Macmillan Publishing Group, LLC.

The Library of Congress has cataloged the hardcover edition as follows:

Wilde, Fran, 1979–author.
    Cloudbound / Fran Wilde.—First edition.
        p. cm.
    "A Tom Doherty Associates book."
    ISBN 978-0-7653-7785-2 (hardcover)
    ISBN 978-1-4668-5821-3 (ebook)
1. Single women—Fiction. 2. Conspiracy—Fiction. 3. Flight—Fiction. I. Title.
    PS3623.I5355 C58 2016
    813'.6—dc23

2017288038

ISBN 978-0-7653-7786-9 (trade paperback)

Our books may be purchased in bulk for promotional,
educational, or business use. Please contact your local bookseller
or the Macmillan Corporate and Premium Sales Department
at 1-800-221-7945, extension 5442, or by email at
MacmillanSpecialMarkets@macmillan.com.

First Edition: September 2016
First Trade Paperback Edition: September 2017

Printed in the United States of America

0 9 8 7 6 5 4 3 2 1

for Tom and Iris

PART ONE

DISAPPEARED

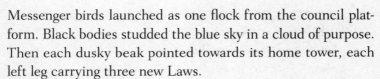

Messenger birds launched as one flock from the council platform. Black bodies studded the blue sky in a cloud of purpose. Then each dusky beak pointed towards its home tower, each left leg carrying three new Laws.

The city's councilors watched them go. "Let this be enough."

A junior councilor, still wearing her wingmarks proudly, murmured, "On their wings."

The birds flew northwest from Naza, southeast to Bissel, and to all the towers between and beyond. They used the city's winds to ease their passage. They flew past tiers where families gathered, waiting for news. Where mourning flags flew, new madder-dyed silks fluttering among faded rose rags.

More than half the kaviks crossed the city's center, where the Spire, cracked and groaning in the wind, stood empty. Flaps and cackles broke the morning's eerie silence as the birds diverted around the walled tower, avoiding its gates, its gaping mouth.

The kaviks bore the bone chips tied with spidersilk thread at their black ankles as their ancestors had, curling their claws against the clatter of bone chips. They made no comment except for a curious tilt when recipients lifted the cords from their legs. A caw for food, which was often slow to come. Puffed feathers as they listened to the new Laws, and the altered Laws, whispered, then sung. Kaviks remembered the words. They remembered everything: the Laws of this generation, the Laws of those that came before.

∽ GROWTH ∽
No tower may use scourweed to elevate
their tiers above any other. No citizen may possess
or store it, stem or seed.

∽ SPIRE (revised) ∽
None enter the Spire, night or day,
unless council-sworn or with council-say.

∽ ESCORT (new) ∽
No Singer-marked or Singer-sworn may fly
between towers unguided.
They will their host towers abide and be cared for
without complaint or reprisal.
Wings they may borrow, but may not own,
lest the city be again divided.

1

CODEX

As children, we learned early that the clouds were dangerous.

Turns out the city wasn't all that much safer.

Between three towers, the council platform hung suspended, its thin profile on the horizon the only thing protecting the city from itself now. Councilors paced, barely visible at this distance, preparing for their morning votes, while I peered at them through sharp cracks in the Spire wall. I wanted to be out there, in the open sky, leading. Making Laws, rediscovering our past, keeping tower from fighting tower. Not here, accompanying Kirit Skyshouter on a cloudtouched expedition into the Spire's remains.

But Kirit and I dangled from tenuous ropes in the Spire's dim afternoon light anyway. We swung within the cracked walls and over the deep gaping center of the Spire because the council and my mentor, Doran Grigrit, had asked it of me.

"No one else can find the codex, Nat, and few want to go in the Spire as it is. She's offering to help," he'd said on the council plinth earlier that morning. "The Singers knew how the city grows, why it roars. How the towers rise. We're on the verge of a new age, with new discoveries, but we need to retrieve as much knowledge from the past as we can, before the Spire cracks further and our opportunity is lost. None of the other Singers have been near as helpful in this effort, not since the new Laws. Take her in."

And here we were.

I hummed a verse of a popular song.

The Spire cracked as a Shout rose up,
freed the city, freed us all.

"Knock it off, Nat. I'm trying to count tiers." Her voice was rough, even when she spoke. The healers said it could stay that way forever.

"That's Councilor Densira to you, Skyshouter."

These days, children sang of Kirit the hero. She was that. She was my wing-sister too, and would always be. But she had faults, and a stubborn streak, and her friends stood a fair chance of getting killed. I knew all about that. Worse, she'd been acting strangely in the past few moons, since the fever. Distant. Obstinate.

"What deal did you cut with Doran?" I said, then sneezed. Bone dust everywhere, even so many months after Spirefall. A cold east-spun wind whistled through the cracks running the Spire's outer wall. The stuff silted the dim light.

She didn't answer. Singers hadn't been keen on helping the council or the towers much lately. A fair number of towers hadn't wanted to help the Singers in a while either. And no one was sure whether Kirit was Singer or Tower any longer. Probably not even Kirit herself.

I took my eyes off of her for a moment to squint at the carvings we swung near. Panels depicting winged battles, sky-mouths attacking with grasping tentacles and rows of glass teeth, tower fighting tower. Singers and their carvings. Their tattoos. The city was well and done with all of that.

Life was better lived in the open towers, not in this walled one. Out in the sky. Not trapped in the Gyre's echoes at the

Spire's center, where I'd nearly died not that long ago. Where Kirit had nearly killed me.

And where I'd tried to kill her in turn.

I sneezed again and the rope swung.

"Quiet, Nat!"

She made it sound like I was sneezing on purpose.

"It's the dust." I kept the irritation out of my voice. The city's hero wouldn't be able to blame the newly elected junior councilor from the northwest quadrant for botching her search. I wouldn't give her any reason to complain.

Besides, I was curious. My mother, Elna Densira, had spoken of the codex with a mix of reverence and fear since Kirit and I were children. She'd said the pages contained our city's survival in numbers: lists of what towers needed shoring up, a record of appeasements. I wanted to see what the city's roars and rumbles over time looked like. I couldn't imagine the heft of it.

We had nothing like that in the towers. Too heavy to carry up, too hard to maintain. Only the Spire and the Singers could keep records like that for generations. But instead of sharing their knowledge, they secreted it away. They practiced crimes against the city in its name.

We knew that now.

After Spirefall, searchers had cut carvings from the Spire walls and sorted through rubble, but the codex eluded them. Then more tiers collapsed, and rumors of rogue skymouths in the Spire began. Most wouldn't go near the Spire now, even if the new Laws didn't forbid it.

If I helped bring the codex back today, that would make me, if not more of a hero, more of a leader, despite having only nineteen Allmoons.

Kirit continued her descent on the gently swaying rope and

I followed, inching down the rough fiber. The silk of my foot-wraps caught on a splinter.

What remained of the Gyre's winds were hollow sounds: bone shards knocked from balcony edges that skittered and bounced down the walls, the flap of a whipperling struggling to stay aloft and in the light, my breath coming fast as I lowered myself down the rope. Once a place to fight for the right to speak, the Gyre resonated now with ghosts and loss.

I gripped the twisted fiber and sinew rope tightly enough that my knucklebones showed hard and pale beneath my skin.

"I wish you'd brought newer ropes," Kirit said.

"Complaining? Not very heroic, Skyshouter." So many songs praised her deeds, her words, her sacrifice. She should know the city had bigger troubles than old ropes.

"If I'd had access to supplies, I would have brought my own ropes," she snapped, looking up.

She always hated when I teased.

In the sunlight, the web of scars across her scalp and face from her burns gleamed silver. I bit back my frustration, and felt a twinge of regret. I swallowed that back.

"Council gave us these." Most of the council had. Three councilors actually, from three separate towers and three different quadrants. These days, that represented a lot of cross-city cooperation. When Doran Grigrit, my mentor; Vant Densira, my tower leader; and Hiroli Naza, Lead Councilor Ezarit Varu's apprentice, first told me what Kirit wanted to do, I'd balked. I'd been tracking runaway Singer fledges since Spirefall and working to address the unrest that was blowing through the city. Important things.

But curiosity won out, and my sense of honor. Lead Councilor Grigrit trusted me to keep an eye on Kirit, and not give her any special treatment. Meantime, Vant had asked me to grab as many Lawsmarkers as I could find on the way, as a service to Densira. We needed those.

"I wouldn't tell Ezarit you're going, or with whom," Vant had cautioned.

Fine by me. Ezarit had enough power to drop me into the clouds if she wanted, even without full control over the council. I was merely a junior councilor. If she had no power over her daughter's doings? That was her problem, not mine.

The bone walls creaked and the dust increased. I imagined myself falling again, wings torn, down the Spire's depths. A feeling I could generate all too easily. And yet? I didn't feel fear here.

Maybe I'd agreed to return in order to prove that to myself. To prove it to her. That I was not afraid of the Gyre, or the Spire, or Kirit herself. Neither afraid nor angry enough to cloud my judgment as a city leader. That was important to know, especially now.

The rope groaned and I paused, looking for the sturdy gallery tier the artifexes claimed still existed. Kirit hadn't stopped. She wouldn't ever stop, not without a solid bone wall right in front of her. "The ropes can take it, but the walls can't, Kirit. Time to pick a tier and get going."

She stayed on the rope. I bristled despite myself. "We shouldn't even be in here. No one else is allowed in. Soon no one will be."

"You can go back to chasing Lawsbreakers if you want." Still descending.

"Not today." She was always like this. I braced for more argument. "You said you'd be quick. Let's just hurry." Besides, Doran Grigrit had hinted there'd be extra tower marks in it for me if we returned with what Kirit sought. "If something happens to the city's hero on my watch, I'll never rise beyond it."

Surprising me, she laughed, but the sound had a brittle edge.

"And I'll never rise beyond it if a city councilor gets hurt in my presence."

She was right. The songs that called her Skyshouter would quiet further, while those calling her Spirebreaker or worse would become even more popular. I didn't want that for her. She'd suffered enough. We all had. She was gaining my sympathy, but she kept talking. "Elna would have my wings for it. And Ceetcee and Beliak too."

Her bringing Ceetcee and Beliak into this, much less my mother? Clouds.

"This is city business, Kirit. If you care so much about what Elna thinks, you should visit." She didn't know anything about us anymore. We'd sent whipperling notes that Elna, who'd helped raise Kirit, was completely skyblind. That Ceetcee would be a mother before next Allsuns. There'd been no reply. Meantime, Ceetcee and Beliak helped me care for Elna as she learned her way in a darkened world. They were caring for me too. And I them.

"Seriously, Nat. You can wait safely up top. I'll be right there. You have enough Lawsmarkers, you don't need to salvage any more. You'll barely be able to fly home with that." She'd missed my point completely and was eyeing my salvaging satchel. The word "safely" burned.

"Always seem to need more these days." I tried to keep my voice light, but this was harder than I thought it would be. We had so much unsaid between us. "I can carry more than you think."

Deep in the Spire, an enormous crack sounded, then tapered off to a rip like battens piercing silk. Echoes of bone striking bone reverberated as a piece of a tier tumbled into the depths. Over this sound rose a rush of wings. Gray- and brown-bodied wild dirgeons and two midsized gryphons shot up from the Gyre in a cloud of beaks and feathers. My favorite messenger bird, a whipperling named Maalik, burrowed into my robes with a squawk.

"Watch out!" The escaping flock surrounded the ropes and rocked it. Scratched us in their passage and were gone in another cloud of bone dust that left us coughing and struggling to cling to the swinging rope.

I held on tight, but Kirit slipped, her feet scrambling to wrap the line again. She grabbed too late for the rope with her knees and dangled for a moment from her fingertips. Her wings, half open for safety, buoyed her in the Gyre's breeze, and I struggled to keep my balance as the rope swung wildly. The gallery wall we'd anchored to creaked.

"Easy!" I whispered through gasps for clear air. Whether I spoke to me or to her, I wasn't sure. Below us, the dark pit rippled with shadows.

If I had to, I could dump the satchel I carried into the Gyre and grab her before she fell too far. I hadn't found anything I couldn't bear to lose yet.

Except Kirit. I couldn't let her fall. Birdcrap. I shifted my grip on the rope, readying to help if she needed me. Her Spirefall injuries hadn't healed well.

"I've got it." Her voice was level, tightly controlled now. Still her arms shook as she gripped the rope. She turned her face away so I couldn't see her discomfort.

She hooked a ledge with her good leg and climbed over a solid-enough-looking gallery wall. "I wanted to search this tier next anyway."

Maalik cackled and climbed to my shoulder, pinpoint claws never breaching my silk robes. He tested my earlobe with his beak, gently. *Yes, bird. Still here.* "Some help you were."

Tossing my spear, bow, and carry bags onto the tier, I followed her. The Lawsmarkers I'd found, plus a few metal scraps, clacked and screeched as the bags hit the floor.

Searchers had turned through the rubble. But scavengers had been here too. The signs were all over. The cages far below, broken during Spirefall, had been pulled to pieces to remove the precious wire mesh inside.

Rubble began to shift and slide as Kirit made her way into the alcove. Bone dust billowed, and she coughed again. "Too much dust," she muttered. "You were right."

At least I was right about dust. Maybe now I could find out why she'd been distant. Ceetcee would want to know why she hadn't answered our messages. "How's it downtower at Grigrit? Dusty there too?" I remembered cleaning a downtower midden once with her, so long ago. I wrinkled my nose at the memory.

She grunted. "Damp. Doran's kept us on the lowtower's dark side. Cold there."

She could have had a hero's quarters once she recovered from her Spirefall injuries, but she'd chosen to live downtower. That must have made her very bones ache.

"Are you maybe a little cloudtouched?" My joke fell flat. I kept going. "Who'd want to live that far down by choice?"

"Singers and fledges don't have a choice," she snapped, but kept sifting rubble. So much for conversation. It didn't look like she knew what she was looking for, that was for sure.

"If the council hadn't taken the Singers' wings," Kirit began again, "I could have used Wik's help here. And Moc and Ciel's."

In previous searches for the codex, Wik had provided nothing, especially under guard. But I didn't say so. "The Singer twins?" I shook my head. "They don't listen. Won't stay in their classes. If we brought them to the Gyre, they'd probably turn scavenger and disappear."

"Nat."

"What? It's been going around." She blinked at my tone, and I bent to hide my dark expression, gathering my weapons from the tier floor instead. Once we'd been closer than friends. Almost siblings. But even then, we'd teased and squabbled. Things were harder now.

"Scavengers aren't hurting anything," she finally said, avoiding a bigger fight.

"They're thieves." She caught my look and frowned. I frowned right back. "I have responsibilities now, Kirit. All Lawsbreakers weaken the towers. Scavengers are Lawsbreakers. They cause disorder that we can't afford. You'd understand if you were on the council." I sounded like Doran and Ezarit when I said things like that. Strong. A leader.

Kirit had been offered a seat straight off, and her choice of mentors. Council had even kept the seat open while Kirit endured her Spirefall wounds and the resulting bone dust infection that nearly took her leg. After Allsuns, when she'd finally recovered enough to hear the offer, they'd asked again.

And she'd said no.

The city needed her, her family needed her, and she'd refused. I hadn't. Nor had Ezarit and Doran. Hiroli hadn't, even though she'd lost her family in Spirefall. She still wanted to help fix the city. In council we learned to debate, worked to keep towers from splitting off or severing bridges, tried to govern without the Singers, even defended towers from raids and riots. It was hard work, and we gladly did it. But not Kirit.

A verse of The Rise came unbidden, the melody learned from years of repetition, the words those she'd tried to teach me in the Gyre.

> The city rises on Singers' wings, remembering all,
>   bearing all;
> Rises to sun and wind on graywing, protecting,
>   remembering.
> Never looking down. Tower war is no more.

The city was coming apart: each tower for itself. As the songs warned.

"Hurry, then," I said. But she dithered, turning this way and that. Searching. "Kirit, really. If you don't know where to look, let's end this. Whatever you want from Doran, there's got to be a better way to get it. I have a vote to prepare for." I hadn't meant to say that last bit.

"Vote? More Laws? Because of the riots?" She must have heard the rumors. There'd been market riots over food, over fair trades. Over Singers walking past. The most recent on Varu, two days ago. There'd been so many skymouth losses during Spirefall, and too much anger from survivors.

"You'd know if you were on the council, instead of making expeditions like this one." It came out sharp and fast. Maybe I'd meant it to. I wanted to fight with her about this—her responsibility—about everything.

Even here, in the Spire's ruins. Especially here.

She met my gaze for a moment. Her shoulders squared. "There haven't been any riots on Grigrit," she said. "Doran runs a tight tower." But then she sighed. "Let's do what we're here for, and argue about that later. The codex should help. And then you will tell me who's getting new Laws this time."

All of them, I wanted to say. *All the Singers. Including the Nightwing Wik. We'd get Rumul too, if we could find his body.*

But we'd been sworn to secrecy until the council was ready. It was our one chance to unify the city, and the timing had to be right.

"Nat," she said again. She reached out a hand, silvered with two Singer marks, and seared with the wilder lines—marks made by skymouth tendons acrid on her tawny skin as she'd fought Rumul to the death. The fight that had eventually cracked the Spire.

I was caught between taking her hand and revulsion. Not at

the appearance of her hand, but at the thought of all she'd done. The Spire had cracked, and the skymouths hidden inside— hidden by the Singers in order to protect the city—had escaped. Many had died. She'd fought then too, and me beside her; Spire and tower fighting together until all the monsters had been captured.

Now she was a hero, but increasingly unwelcome. The city had found its path without her. But Doran had trusted her enough to come here, with an escort, saying, "She's earned another chance, Nat. Her decisions lately notwithstanding, she defended the city once."

Her fingers hung in the air, inches from my arm. Then they trembled and she pulled away. Her brass-flecked eyes, much like Ezarit's, but framed by silvered scars, seemed to plead with me. Then she bowed her head. "I'm sorry, Nat. I'm sorry for your anger."

"You have to pick a side, Kirit. You can't be tower and Spire both. Not anymore."

"If *I* can't be both, who can?"

"Why would you want to? They were monsters. You knew that when you fought Rumul. Before that too." Anger, bubbling up. Singers had killed my father in order to keep their terrible secret. They'd tried to kill me.

Not they. She. Kirit.

"It's not that simple!" Kirit threw up her hands. Dust curled in the disturbed air currents. "Some worked against Rumul, from the inside. Why are you repeating rhetoric when you know the truth, Nat?" The tower creaked again. "Many fought for the towers."

I knew it wasn't that simple. My father had tried the same a generation before.

On my wrist, a faded blue silk cord held a single message chip. One of my father's carvings, found after Spirefall. "They moved too slow. Too many died," I said, each word sent after her like arrows. "You should be angriest of all."

I reached out then, to the Kirit I'd known since childhood, to Kirit Densira, not Kirit Skyshouter, but my hand grasped air. She'd already turned away to search more of the dim tier, and a large alcove nearby.

From the tier above, a floor had collapsed into a pile of rubble in the alcove. A carved stool stuck crookedly from beneath shards of ceiling and wall. Several more cracks ran across the floor where we stood.

"Rumul's office was above," she whispered, turning in place. Getting her bearings.

My wrapped foot slid over the bone floor, testing the seams. The wreckage signified that the floors—tough outgrowths of bone at each new level—could sunder and break without warning.

Working in secret before his death, my father, the artifex Naton, had riddled the Spire with holes. I was glad he'd drilled Rumul's office as thoroughly as he had, but I wished I didn't have to walk through it now.

I looked closely at the fallen ceiling, and the small patch of sky that showed through another hole in the wall. Those weak points had helped us bring down Rumul. *And the whole Spire too, releasing the monsters within.* Now the same weaknesses threatened our safety.

Kirit shivered like she was still feverish. "Did you hear that?"

"Hear what?" Kirit's ears were sharp, even after her illness. Secret Singer training. Echoes. Eerie stuff. Flying at night was good, but the sharp hearing? Disturbing.

I peered into the Gyre. "Just bone chips falling from where we hit the walls, probably," I said. "Don't go thinking everything's a skymouth!" I made tentacle-finger gestures and a face to go with them, wide jaw, tongue wagging. It must have looked awful, but suddenly I was afraid too—of the Spire collapsing, of the clouds far below, of a skymouth lurking, uncaptured and invisible, below—and I didn't want Kirit to see it.

I was a city hero, just like her, at least to some. And a city councilor. A junior councilor.

"No time to be afraid," Kirit whispered. She picked up the pace of her search, pulling shards of bone from the rubble.

The slop rope we'd descended swung and smacked against the wall. A sudden breeze? The soft scratching sounds could have been my imagination. Then a screech echoed up the Gyre that made my skin crawl. Kirit turned, eyes wide.

"Only bats," I said. *Please be bats.* But a dark shadow circled the lowest visible tiers, far too big for a bat. As it moved, its tail swung and flicked. A beam of sunlight hit it from above. Feathers glistened on broad wings. A long beak stitched up and down as it sniffed the air. I edged back, pulling Kirit with me.

Clouds. Those feathers are the size of my arm.

"There were songs," I whispered. "Old ones. Of things living in the clouds that carried away the dead." *Let's fly, Kirit. What's down there is wrong; it is danger.*

Words from an ancient song echoed in my ear, in an old friend's voice:

> *They eat the stars.*
> *They crack the bones.*
> *They . . .*

Peering over the gallery edge, I struggled to remember the rest of the words. But all was dust and darkness.

Ceetcee, Beliak, and I had studied with the old windbeater, Tobiat, while I was being punished for attacking the Spire. Weighed down with so many Lawsmarkers, including Treason, I could barely fly. I couldn't hunt. The day Ceetcee—whom I

knew from wingtest—landed on my lowtower tier with fruit for
Elna? I'd waved her off with a wary "We don't need that." But
she'd stayed, had even coaxed Tobiat uptower. When Beliak
brought two geese he'd shot, and work for us to share—winding
sinew and fiber into ropes for bridges—I began to feel part of
the city again. Not a Lawsbreaker. Productive. Tobiat had sing-
songed at us while we worked.

Tobiat had been sharing what history he knew, it was clear
now. Singers had kept the city's stories to themselves for generations. Verses from "The Bone Forest" and "Terror of the
Clouds." "Corwin and the Nest of Thieves." After Spirefall,
scavengers had found carvings far downtower that had matched
his songs. But Tobiat had died in the market riots at Viit, and I
was already forgetting what he'd taught me.

Doran was right. Each new violence cost us stability, good
people, knowledge. Even though the council was preserving Tobiat's legacy, his trove of songs, for the good of the city, it wasn't
the same.

"Must be a gryphon," Kirit said, shaking me out of my
thoughts. She sounded hopeful. Gryphons were sharp-beaked
and aggressive. "Or a trick of the light. Come on."

"That's far bigger. Worse than a gryphon. That could be a
bone eater."

She'd heard the songs too, of course. Right from the Singers
themselves. Shook her head. "They're cloudbound. Never seen
this high."

"Maybe not when the Spire had skymouths hidden in the
Gyre," I said. In talking with Doran and Hiroli about the towers,
and how fast they used to grow—which was Hiroli's project—
we'd compared rumors. That skymouths in the clouds had
battled gryphons and bigger birds. That they'd won. "Maybe
they were keeping the bone eaters in check." My voice was little

more than a whisper, quiet against the scratching sounds below. I closed my eyes against the vision of a giant mouth opening wide while invisible tentacles wrapped Kirit, pulling her away.

"If there are bone eaters this high," she said without looking away from the rubble pile, "the city has bigger problems than the Singers."

The memory of Spirefall, and of almost losing everyone I cared about, was still too fresh. Ceetcee had fought that day. Beliak too. I took a calming breath and let it spool out from between my lips. "Now we really have to hurry," I said, pulling her with me towards the slop rope. "Up and out."

But she pulled back, then slipped my grip. Headed towards the rubble.

"If it's not a gryphon, it's something else," she said. "A bone eater won't want living bone. Otherwise the towers would have been food long ago. We'll be fine."

"Unless it's dining on Singer skeletons from Spirefall." Typical tower talk, these days. But she froze. She didn't turn, didn't yell at me. I wished she would yell. Ceetcee and Beliak certainly would have. Ezarit too. Sometimes I was an idiot.

But I could try to fix my mistakes. "That wasn't your fault, Kirit," I said quickly. Maybe I only made things worse. "Tell me more about what we're looking for."

No Singers we'd questioned would describe the codex well enough to anyone from the towers. Bone tablets, they'd said. Big ones. There were a lot of those.

Kirit held her scarred hands up, an arm span apart. "Most pages are this big. Marks carved on both sides. We need . . ." She stopped to think. "The pages charting the city's roars"—she meant the destructive, roaring quakes—"the Gyre challenges, and"—she paused, swallowing hard—"the appeasements."

"You mean Conclave." When Singers had fed Lawsbreakers

to the clouds after a roar, it was not called an appeasement. It was called a Conclave. "Use the word if you're going to think it."

"Yes. That. They're marked with numbers of Lawsbreakers and kinds of Laws too." So many Laws. So many ways to break them. Again I felt the ghost weight of Lawsmarkers around my wrist. The Lawsmarkers I'd gathered uptower bumped against my side.

"Forget the challenges." The fewer pages we had to find, the faster we could be out of here.

"No. The city needs to know how many times Singers had challenged Rumul and the leaders before him. To know that not everyone agreed. To see differences among the Singers. Between Rumul's allies and Wik, for instance."

"It won't do any good, given the city's current mood. They're guilty of not doing enough, at the very least."

"Even Wik? You fought by his side. And he yours. And me?" She stared at me.

I felt another twinge of regret. "You were taken to the Spire against your will." *But in the end, she'd sung Singer vows.* The only reason she didn't need to heed Escort, the new Law, was because she was the Skyshouter. "You ended the Singers' reign."

She was right about one thing. The city had bigger problems now. And the city was about to call on her to renounce the Singers. To denounce them all, even Wik. I was forbidden from telling her; we needed her help first.

She bit her lip and stepped through the ruins of Rumul's office in silent disagreement, ignoring sounds from the Gyre that were now loud enough that I could hear them too.

Her silence rankled. "You know I'm right. The people have every right to be angry over what happened in their midst." *You have to know I am angry too.* "I fought by your side. And Ceetcee, and Beliak. All of us, together."

At home, Beliak had given me extra pitons, a sack of spiced

apples. Meantime, Ceetcee had worried about the Spire's stability, and Kirit's. About her behavior lately. "She's been through
so much. Give her a chance," Elna had added.

I was trying. Despite how frustrating Kirit was. And how
stubborn.

"We care about you, Kirit," I said as gently as I could. "All of
us worry. Let's hurry."

"If you care, quit distracting me. Keep an eye on the Gyre
and whatever's down there," she said. Gruff rejection. I took another deep breath and complied.

Trying to watch both the Gyre's depths and Kirit as she
navigated the rubble was a tough task. After a while with no
movement from below, I decided she must have been right
about the gryphon. I joined her in the alcove.

"I'm trying to think like Rumul," she said. That gave me
chills, but she added, "He might have put the codex and other
valuables somewhere out of the way." She hadn't told me to get
back to my post, so I drew closer. "They brought it to the Spire's
roof during the last . . ." She paused, but I waited her out. The
gap in her sentence spread.

Conclave.

It was only a word, I knew. But her not saying it, while she
wanted me to forgive the Singers? Not all right. Making her say
it would give me some satisfaction at least.

"You can't pretend you're above all the Spire's horrors by not
saying that word." Ceetcee would swat me if she ever found
out I was talking to Kirit like this. "Speaking a truth brings it
out into the open. You know that as well as I do. Say it."

"Conclave" was an important word. But Kirit remained silent.

"It's part of our history, and part of the city's survival. Everyone knows what happens when the city roars unappeased," I
said. Towers cracked and broke. People died. Monsters escaped.

"After that—after Conclave—Rumul must have hidden the

codex." The hook she used to test the rubble knocked loose a tumble of bone. I heard a quiet sob. "You haven't seen a Conclave, Nat. They were horrible."

She was right. I'd never seen one. I couldn't imagine what they were like, but I'd lost my father to one. I was about to reply when a sharp sound echoed off the walls. A clatter and a raucous screech.

"What's the bone eater doing?" Kirit smoothed her robe.

"I thought you said it wasn't a bone eater."

She didn't reply.

I stepped on the pile and levered myself up, hoping my legs wouldn't wobble. The pieces of floor and ceiling, the wreckage of Rumul's worktable, shifted and settled. I moved again, holding my breath. At the pile's edge, closest to the wall, I spotted a faint glint of brass peeking from a knotted and torn package of gray silk. Metal. I reached for it. Metal was worth many tower marks.

The floor beneath me creaked as I neared the Spire's ruined wall.

"Nat," Kirit whispered.

"The artifexes promised this tier was still safe. Ceetcee too." Especially Ceetcee. I put as much confidence into my voice as I could. "Promised" was a very strong word for what she'd said. "Hoped" was closer.

My ears picked up sounds that none in the city ever wanted to hear. Cracking sounds, from deep within the walls.

Kirit heard them too of course. "Nat, get back!"

Backing up, I knocked loose a pile of small tablets. Carvings excised from Spire walls. They rattled to the floor. One broke, exposing another layer of carvings. More secrets.

"Nat," Kirit whispered again. The cracking noise grew louder.

"What?" I asked, sharply. I wanted to get the brass.

The Spire's outer wall crackled over the wind. Then the thick noise of bone ripping from bone filled my ears. The far edge of rubble where I'd stood moments ago disappeared. In its place was blue sky, a cloud of windblown dust. The new hole in the wall ran down to the tier floor. There, existing cracks darkened, then widened near my feet. I backed away fast, the tier below me already visible. More rubble fell away.

The surface beneath my feet began to move. I slipped.

"Kirit! Run!" I turned and scrambled, but the crack was too wide and I fell into it, riding a wave of dust and bone. The Spire echoed with the sound of debris falling hard to the next tier. In the dust cloud, I grabbed for anything solid as I slid, and caught my bone hook on something that hadn't moved, hadn't fallen in. The edge of Rumul's worktable, wedged at an angle in a crack.

My feet swung free above the lower tier. The bone hook, strong enough to carry a flier beneath me, held true. "Kirit?" I said, over the roar in my dust-filled ears. My face and arms were caked in bone dust. What was left of the pile we'd been searching was a jagged mess below me. I stifled a sneeze.

Our spare rope dropped down the hole beside me. Kirit, breathing hard, slid down the rope. "We're going down. It's too unstable up here." Her voice was calmer now. Whatever else, Kirit could think straight in emergencies.

She dropped to the floor. Using one hand, I grabbed the rope, while holding fast to the bone hook with the other. When I was ready, I let the bone hook go and swung the weight of my body onto the rope, then through air that sparkled with tiny shards of bone to the tier floor. Once down, I eased to my hands and knees, not trusting my legs yet. Beneath my aching hands, bone dust and metal glittered. I clutched at the shiny bit of brass that had caught my eye above. Squared corners, etched, my fingers told me. I dropped it in my satchel. The metal had poked from a silk-wrapped packet above. Where was that packet? I crawled forward, searching. Kirit could have the codex. I could sell the brass.

Kirit caught me searching. "Scavengers are Lawsbreakers, huh?"

"We're on council business, with permission. This isn't scavenging." I might have grinned.

"You haven't changed so much after all," she said. She sounded happy about that.

"I've changed," I said, readying my arguments. But they all fell away as a shadow blocked the light from the Gyre and the hole above my head. Kirit and I turned together as an enormous bird blacker than night blocked our exit.

2

BONE EATER

A rattling hiss from deep within the dark expanse raised the hair on my arms. The bone eater bent over me, serrated beak parting. Its purple-black tongue covered with sharp spines tasted the air. Saliva dripped on the floor, on my arm; it burned when it hit my skin. With a screech, the bone eater lifted one of its claws above me, each talon a sharp curve the size of my head. Its dark tail whipped around on the floor for balance. I froze. The creature blocked our escape, left no space to hide.

We'd been taught to fear skymouths, Singers, clouds. But the bone eater, long lost to time and myth, was what now stood before us, ready to attack. As the talon descended, I swore. The Spire's walls would *never* be the last thing I saw in this city.

I sat up fast, dodging to the left of the claw. I hit the bone eater with my bow.

Kirit screamed.

Once, she'd stopped attacking skymouths with that scream. But the bone eater's inner eyelids came down pale over its dark eyes, and its beak did not veer away. Its claw scraped the floor, gouging bone, then rose high again above us both.

This time, when the claw dropped, I ducked. Sharp talons missed me and snagged Kirit by the robe. Dragged her across the floor. I tucked and rolled beneath the beast's legs, my wings clattering on debris. When I got my feet under me, I nocked an arrow. The bird shifted to glare at me through its legs. Slowly, it began to turn, dragging Kirit. She struggled to reach her knife.

I shot once, then pushed myself to my feet and ran for the Gyre. Behind me, the bone eater clacked its beak and screeched. I'd hit it.

Kirit scrambled free.

"Clouds, Kirit, you can't shout everything down," I yelled. "Find something to throw at it!"

The bone eater lowered its enormous head and charged me.

I unfurled my wings and leapt from the gallery. The bone eater jumped after me, miscalculating the distance. Its head scraped the tier's ceiling, it was so big. I swung a small parabola around the Gyre's void, and the bone eater overshot me.

With a screech, my whipperling, Maalik, dove in to distract the giant bird: a gray wisp against the bone eater's black expanse. *No, Maalik. Get away.*

Before the bone eater could turn and attack again, I locked my wings and nocked another arrow. Took aim and let fly, striking its neck. The creature screamed, snapped at the shaft sticking from its feathers, and vanished into the darkness.

I circled the Gyre again. I'd hunted for much of my life. I knew the bird wasn't dead, but it wasn't coming back up the Gyre fast either.

Neither was I. Without the windbeaters below, there wasn't enough of an updraft for me to rise back to the tier where Kirit waited.

She'd noticed me struggling to find a gust. "Wait there."

"Ridiculous thing to say, to someone on the wing, slowly sinking." But the tension had drained from our voices. I heard her laugh.

"True."

The rough rope the council had sent us with hit the gallery

railing closest to me, and I grabbed hold. Dragged myself hand over hand back up to where Kirit had lashed the line to a grip. Above my head, Maalik flew in worried arcs around it, up, up, up.

"We have to warn the towers," Kirit panted.

I nodded agreement. Finally, she was talking sense. Then something caught her eye and she darted around me, to where Rumul's worktable had fallen. *Birdcrap.*

She got down on her hands and knees, then her stomach. Spreading her weight, she reached for something I couldn't see. I listened for more walls cracking, but heard nothing. Finally she stood up, holding another mildewed, silk-wrapped packet, about an arm's length across. It looked heavy, but thin. Two pages at most.

The packet clicked and shifted in her hands. Broken.

"That won't do you much good cracked." *Come on, Kirit.*

She frowned. "It has to. But it won't be enough."

"Come on, now, before that thing comes back," I said.

Bigger problems, she'd said. We definitely had much bigger problems now.

But she was turning, studying the walls near the floor. "We need the rest of it."

She didn't listen. Ever. "We're done here."

"We're not done." She knelt near a solid-looking part of the tier wall. "Here." A relieved sigh. "We need as much of the codex as we can find. Rumul must have hidden the most important pages in the one place he knew no Singer would touch." She pulled aside the trash that had piled against the wall—rags and pieces of broken dishes. A pile of dusty, gray feathers.

There, at knee-height, two codex-sized pieces of bone pressed against the wall. New bone grew around their edges, turning a strange color. Gray, not the yellowish white I remembered from when Densira rose.

Kirit yanked at the first tablet. It didn't budge. She drew her knife, but hesitated, the blade point above a small gap between wall and page.

"I'll do it," I took the knife.

"You don't understand," she said. "This is forbidden."

"By whom? Kirit, we make the Laws now." I put the knife edge between the wall and the page. Pried the bone tablet away with a crack, revealing a deep cut in the tower's wall. Deeper than any carving I'd seen in the Spire. The bone within was spongy and smelled strongly of something I couldn't place. Almost like new bone, but sour. Thick. "Clouds, what is this?"

"Heartbone," Kirit said. "This is the lifeblood of the city." She looked at the second plate, then grabbed hold and pulled. "Or it was. The color is fading. It's dying." Her voice wobbled. The page tore from the wall, leaving exposed, sickly heartbone.

I handed her the page. "I'm sorry," I said. How did you mourn a tower? Even one as malevolent as this? "Peace to the Spire." I touched my eye and pointed up, the gesture that marked the passage of a citizen.

She watched me and said, quietly, "Thank you." Tears pooled in her eyes but didn't fall. She let me grip her shoulder, and put her hand over mine. For a moment, we were simply friends once again. A friendship scarred and wounded, perhaps, but still friends. And it was enough.

The sun passed beyond the Spire's apex, and we were in shade once again. She looked down at the pages she held. "Birdcrap." Rooted through the shards in the silk packet.

"What's wrong now?" I was eager to leave this place.

She pointed at the top of one tablet. "The broken one says Challenge." A long line of date marks that I recognized and symbols that I didn't ran down the page. She shifted to show me the other page. Hesitated, then pointed. "Conclave."

"There's nothing about tower growth here. Doran wanted that."

I couldn't turn my eyes from the Conclave page. The lines spoke for themselves. Lawsbreakers. Grouped in tens, then hundreds. My eyes itched and my vision blurred. Finally, Kirit tucked the pages into her satchel, though they were almost too big for it. She couldn't secure the cover properly. Three whole pages, broken pieces of more.

"Kirit, it has to be enough. The bone eater is going to come back, or its friends are."

She nodded, sadly. "It will have to be enough."

How did the song with bone eaters in it go? Terror of the Clouds? I tried to recall Tobiat's exact words again. *They carry the dead away.* But what did they do to the living? I didn't want to find out.

We ascended the last tier together and stood side by side on the Spire's lip. "Here," Kirit said. "Conclave happened here."

The way she said it, I knew she meant my father's Conclave. His mark, scratched somewhere on that terrible page. We'd been infants when it happened. "It wasn't your fault."

I took her hand again and stood next to my oldest friend in the city as the sun slid towards the cloudtop and the horizon. The wind had cooled even further, and below us, the doomed Spire settled and creaked. All around it, the towers of my home stood like beacons against the dark, their tiers open to the setting sun, filled with green gardens and colorful banners. I took a deep breath, feeling like I'd escaped from a prison.

Kirit wiped her eyes, then checked my wings. "No holes," she said, finally. "You were lucky."

"You were, too." I readied myself to fly. But she stayed me, her hand on my arm.

"Tell me about the vote." She'd remembered after all.

Doran had advised me not to tell her. Said it was for her own good. But now? How could I not? "Tomorrow," I said. "Or the next day. There have been too many roars. And now a bone eater this high in the towers? It's bad luck. The city needs appeasement. The remaining Singers will be tried for their crimes against the city. Those with the most Lawsmarkers will be taken," I pressed my lips together as she stared at me. "And there will be a Conclave." The first since Spirefall.

Her jaw dropped. "Thrown down. My mother agreed to this? You agreed to this?"

"There are enough votes to overrule your mother," I said slowly. It was what Doran had said when I'd helped count the projected votes. "But she does not yet know." Doran's instructions again. Ezarit was too personally invested in this. Worse, no matter how much I admired her, Ezarit was a whipperling leader, ready to listen, interested in compromise. We needed a hawk. A gryphon.

Kirit paled. "We have to tell her," she said. "We have to stop this."

"You cannot, Kirit. You're not even council. You're not supposed to know."

Kirit could never control her emotions. Her jaw tightened and her expressions passed through rage and dismay to sadness and resolve. "But you knew. You agreed to it."

I dipped my head in acknowledgment. Convincing councilors to vote now wasn't something I was ashamed of. The towers wanted action. Expected this of their leaders.

"You have no idea what you do. How horrible it is. These are people, Nat."

"They are Singers. They threaten the towers' integrity." I was sure of that. Each month that passed towards Allmoons, there were more riots and more tower attacks. The remaining Singers had been sequestered after the first riot. But the city's anger had grown. "There must be a Conclave. For the city's sake."

Atop the Spire, with the sky turning pink and orange around us, Kirit stared at me.

"You'll understand, when there's been more time," I said. "When the city is stable again. Maybe someday you'll be ready to sit on the council with us." I sounded like Doran, talking to other councilors, convincing them.

A flight of bats poured from the cracked Spire wall, startling us. They spun in the air, snapping at bugs. I heard Kirit draw a ragged breath.

"Then you'll send me down with them," she said, stripping her wings off and handing them to me.

3

HEART OF THE CITY

Kirit stared at me. She pressed her wings to my chest.

I grabbed at them, fearing she'd drop them over the Spire's side next. Grabbed her hand too.

This wasn't how it was supposed to go, not any of it. I stood there on the Spire, clutching at Kirit, but hearing Doran's words after I'd been elected to the council.

He'd come to find me at Densira. Brought a bolt of silk for Ceetcee, teas for Elna. We'd stood on the balcony, and I hoped he'd ask to mentor me on the council, as Ezarit had already asked Hiroli Naza. Doran's robes were richly quilted; his many tower marks were woven in his hair. And his laugh boomed reassuringly.

"Son," Doran said, "you were handed a bad game and a second chance. More than one. The Singers killed your father, impoverished your family. They did it to scare people. They used you to do it."

Yes, they had used me, and my family. Doran felt that, when Ezarit had known me all her life and hadn't paid it any mind.

"You screwed up, too, didn't you? My own kids screwed up once or twice."

I swallowed my pride. Some Laws had certainly been broken. They might have needed to be.

"You broke Laws. Not without good reason, but Laws nonetheless. Now you have another chance. Now you're a hero who saved the city from skymouths, from Singers. You could be a good leader, maybe even great, to unite the towers. To help us rise again, on our own this time." He looked at me quietly for a moment. I waited him out. He was a trader; he was pitching me hard. He cleared his throat. "To do that, we need invention, curiosity, and decisive action. We need to uncover the city's secrets, set them out for all to see. We can't flinch at the hard parts. Sound like you?"

Oh, it did. I said as much. He'd clapped me on the shoulder. "Tell your family you're apprenticing with a lead councilor, then. And tomorrow we start on the hard part."

"Like what?" I wanted to start right then.

Doran smiled, pleased. "That's the metal in you. But it's delicate too, like a good wing. You can't talk about this until enough of the council agrees with us. I'll show you how to get people to agree with you. This one will go over easy, but it gets harder after that."

"What will go over easy? If it's a question of safety, we do what we must."

"We need to cut ourselves off clean from the Singers. Kirit does too. She's had enough time to recover. She needs to help the city's leaders, if she won't become one herself. She's offering to help a little bit, but she's stubborn."

"That sounds like Kirit."

"Does it? I worry she might be affected by her injuries, her fever." He was concerned about her, about me. "She doesn't understand the tension in the city right now, that's for certain. We need to help her understand."

I'd said yes. I would help my mentor. I'd help my city. And my friend. *Yes.*

Now, atop the Spire, I wrapped Kirit's fingers around her wings. Made a warding sign with my hands. "Put these back on. It was decided. You're not guilty of anything."

My satchel shifted when I reached out to take her arm to let her know I wasn't judging her. The Lawsmarkers inside clacked and rattled. She pulled her arm away.

"I'm not guilty? Of letting skymouths terrorize the city? Of taking Singer vows?" Her voice rippled across the air in angry waves. "Who decided who isn't guilty? Who has done all this deciding in the city's name?"

Kirit, my wing-sister, wingless atop the Spire. Shouting. Irrational. Unlucky. She would fall, and I would be responsible. I said what I could to calm her.

"It hasn't been technically decided yet. There hasn't been a vote," I said. "But there will be, and the vote will carry."

The look in her eyes when I said that made me regret every word. But she put her arms through her wingstraps again, and angrily began buckling them. "What about the fledges? They can't help where they were born. Will you throw them down too?"

"I hadn't—wait. No! Kirit, wait." No one was talking about fledges.

"What do Ceetcee and Beliak think of this?" She stared at me, the wild strands of her hair flying in the wind, her scars stark on her anger-darkened cheeks. "What about Elna?"

They didn't know. None of them. It was Doran's idea, and he'd sworn me to silence. "I couldn't—" I ground my teeth hard. It had all happened fast, and I'd sworn, we'd all sworn. All the junior councilors, and some senior delegates. Vant had been all for it. "Kirit, I shouldn't have told you, even. I'll be punished."

"By whom?" she yelled.

"The fledges are safe. Those who listen and are acclimating, at least." I kept trying to make this better, and all I was doing was making it worse. But she had her wings back on and both hands free. Something I'd said had been the right thing. So I spoke again in a rush. Her safety was important too. "You'll have to renounce the Singers, of course. To keep your citizenship. Take a tower name again."

Wide-eyed, she gripped the front of my robes. Maalik launched off my shoulder with a noisy squawk. Her silver-marked face came close to mine, and I felt her breath hot on my cheek in the cold air. "Renounce? How can I possibly do that, when it's clear I—" As she shook me, a curl of her hair brushed a mark on her cheek. A dagger. "Doesn't the city have bigger problems than prosecuting Singers?"

"The Singers are dividing the city. The city is angry and needs to be appeased. Haven't you heard? It needs leadership. You don't understand." Doran's words. My heart pounded, this high above the clouds, my wings still half furled. Even with wings, if I had to dive after her, we'd plummet fast.

She shook me again. "Tell me everything. Help me understand what's happening, Nat. We get no news at Grigrit." She gestured to her carry-sack, to the codex pages. "I was trying to bargain with Doran for information and food for the fledges. But no one will tell me anything since I declined the council. It was not the most politic of decisions." She'd stopped shaking me. Looked up at me, her eyes wide. "Tell me what's going on. Once, not that long ago, I did that for you."

She was right. In the Gyre below us now, she'd told me Singer secrets.

All the fears I had about telling her the truth? She'd felt those. And more. I knew fully what she'd done back in the Gyre. Broken Singer Laws to save me. I'd been so angry with her that I'd forgotten.

I started to speak, but she spoke first, fierce and determined, misinterpreting my stunned silence.

"Tell me or I'll tell everyone about the trial, starting with Elna."

Elna. We'd tried to protect her from the developments in the city as much as possible. Anger flared. "She's ill, Kirit. You haven't seen her since Spirefall, and you'd tell her this?"

"If I had to. I am sorry to hear that she's sick. I had no birds, no messages. I'll come to see her. Is it a cough?"

I shook my head. How could she have missed the birds we'd sent? Had someone at Grigrit intercepted them?

"But, Nat," she continued, alarm increasing, "look at what we just saw. The Spire—I broke it so badly that the heartbone is dying. Tell me what's happening to our city."

My mouth went dry as I made the connection. Dying Spire. "Bone eaters don't eat living bone." Our eyes met, wide with horror. Parts of the Spire might already be dead. Yes, there were greater dangers than the Singers. We'd grown up near Lith, a blackened and broken tower that had fallen only a generation before, sending so many—families, artists, leaders—into the clouds.

"First we warn the towers closest to the Spire," Kirit said, her anger with me displaced by the threat. "If the Spire falls, it could damage their tiers. Or worse."

"Grigrit, Bissel, and Naza won't like this. They are wealthy and well-positioned."

"They *were* well-positioned, but not anymore. And they don't have to like it, Nat. They only have to prepare."

The city's center was at greater risk than anyone had imagined. The Spire was not merely unstable, it was dying. And if it fell, like Lith had before it, many more would die too.

Below us, in the evening light, flight classes wobbled on patchwork wings, returning to their towers' safety. A few oil lamps began to light up tiers on Varu, Bissel, Grigrit, warm glows among the bone spurs. A melody accompanied notes plucked on a dolin, nearby. The tiers were wide open. None had barricaded themselves behind shutters. No towers attacked one another.

It was a happy evening. The kind songs said the Skyshouter had returned to the city.

For a brief moment only Kirit and I knew the truth: that soon everything would have to change.

4

SINGERS' RISE

"We'll go to Grigrit first," Kirit said. "It's closest."

"Good. Doran will know what to do," I agreed. Kirit looked at me strangely, but Doran was my mentor, and a firm leader. He would move his people to safety, then help the city to act. If he did it quickly, I could return to my own tower sooner, and to my own family.

"Maybe Doran is part of the problem, Nat," Kirit said, her voice so low I almost lost it on the wind.

"Then why did you agree to help him in the Spire?" *How could I trust her if she didn't trust me, or my mentor?*

She shook her head slowly. "I am a ward of his tower, Nat. You don't understand. He's complicated."

Doran *was* complicated. He made deals and bargains, said good trades made good politics. I didn't always like his decisions, but he was willing to teach me what I wanted to learn: how to lead. And Doran looked after his tower and the city. He would act on our information. Kirit's suspicion didn't mesh with her willingness to help him search the Spire. Maybe everyone was right, that the fever had made her a bit skytouched after all.

"At Grigrit, you'll see how quickly he comes up with a plan," I finally said.

She bit her lip, but nodded agreement.

I unfurled my wings fully and caught Kirit giving them an

appraising glance in the last of the daylight. She'd landed after me when we met to search the Spire. She hadn't seen Liras Viit's latest design.

"Those are fancy," she finally said. Apologizing for talking down about my mentor? Rare for Kirit, but not impossible. More likely, she'd decided *I* was skytouched, and didn't want to waste time arguing. That was more Kirit's style.

She returned to tightening her own wingstraps: the only pair of gray Singer wings still allowed in the towers. Although not for long.

My wingsilk was hunter-shaded blues, rippled with brown. Though I spent most of my time now in the council, I still helped guard Densira and procure game; I'd maintained the right to wear the colors. "Doran's design. Had some made for Ceetcee and Beliak too." I didn't mask the pride in my voice.

Kirit clicked her tongue once. "You always wanted to hunt. You were good at it. Why become a councilor?"

"I want to help lift the city up, make it better. Keep the Spire from happening again." I paused, then asked the question that had bothered me for so long. "Why won't you?"

She shook her head. "Not yet. I won't be someone's rallying cry."

She launched from the Spire's lip, and I followed, quickly overtaking her on the strong evening breeze. I kept my eyes open for prey—it wouldn't hurt to bring some food home when I made it back. But the evening held only bug-chasing bats. What did she mean, "rallying cry"? She'd stopped the skymouths and the Singers. But she didn't want to take responsibility for what came after. "Responsibility isn't a rallying cry, Kirit! It's hard work." I said that to the windspill coming off her pinions. Then I felt bad. She hadn't chosen any of this. To demand she continue to be a hero when others would gladly step forward? That was cruel.

On the short glide to Grigrit, the wind felt like silk against my cheeks after the Spire's dust. My wings filled and, despite my concerns for Kirit, my heart lifted to be going home soon, once this task was finally over. Worry about the Spire dampened the freedom I felt when I flew, but the joy was still there.

By the time we approached Grigrit, the sky had darkened and stars pricked the eastern horizon. Kirit began echoing as she neared the tower, clicking her tongue rapidly on the roof of her mouth. Flying downwind of her, I could hear it, barely. The Singer technique for flying at night was still a sought-after skill. But enough had learned it that we wouldn't need the graywings' help anymore.

I kept silent, not wanting to distract her navigation. I could fly at her pinion without a problem, and I didn't want to risk her losing her satchel in a sudden updraft. But the night air remained clear. All around us, the towers rose dark against the dark sky. Oil lamps began to brighten Grigrit's high tiers, and others in the distance. So many lights crowding into the tiers here. So many people.

We circled Grigrit to the side that was trapped in the Spire's near-constant shadow. A few dim lights glowed in the shadows' depths.

Kirit spilled wind from her wings, and I followed, descending lower than I'd intended to go. I thought she'd agreed we'd talk to Doran. What was she up to? Doran's tier was at the top of Grigrit. We were far below that.

We skidded to a stop on the slick, narrow balcony allotted to Grigrit's five Spire refugees: two novices, the fledge Moc, a weighted Singer leader, and Kirit.

Maalik fluttered in behind us and took his usual spot on my shoulder after I furled my wings halfway, ready to take off again.

"What are we doing here?" I demanded. "We were going to see Doran."

"Kirit?" A fledge looked out from behind the patched sleeping screen. Her short hair was a spiky mess from sleeping on the secondhand mats they'd been given, which were rolled neatly against the tower wall.

"Did you eat already, Nadoni?" Kirit asked her, setting down her satchel.

My own stomach growled softly. I would be headed to Densira and a home-cooked meal, but for the Spire. "Kirit, really—"

She turned to me. Spoke firmly, but gently. "We can spare a few minutes. These fledges are under my protection. The tower has grown stingy with its food, and I want to make sure they are prepared and well enough to move if need be." She held my gaze with hers until I bowed my head, agreeing to wait. She sounded like Ezarit. The matter was urgent, but the fledges came first.

Two more heads appeared from behind the screen. "This is Minlin," Kirit said. "And you know Moc."

I gritted my teeth. The boy had been a plague on every tower agreeing to host him and his twin. Grigrit was his latest stop.

The fledges watched us shrug from our wingstraps. Moc's eyes were locked on the silk spans, the bone battens of my wingset. He seemed hungrier for them than for food.

"We're fine," Minlin said, her chin high.

"Starving," said Moc.

"We haven't eaten much since the dirgeon yesterday," Nadoni acknowledged slowly from the corner.

Near the tier's thick core wall, gristled laughter sounded. Lawsmarkers clattered together and then the laughter stopped and coughing began. Minlin paled, but didn't lower her chin or drop Kirit's gaze.

Kirit turned to me. "Do you have anything in your satchel?"

I had the last of Ceetcee's dried apples, spiced with sweet herbs. I pulled these out and shared them with Minlin and

Nadoni first, then Moc. He'd edged close enough that he could touch my wings. I furled them tight so he wouldn't get food on them.

My new wings had specialized cams and pulls that made them much more responsive to the wind than previous designs. They had to be stowed with care.

If my wings had been damaged in the Spire? I would never have heard the end of it from Doran. He'd recommended his own wingmaker for the design. I set them aside reluctantly. Kirit had shucked hers off as soon as she landed. On second thought: *incredible luck. They weren't damaged, and we retrieved the co-dex.* That was skyblessed, and I shouldn't forget it.

Nadoni sidled near Moc, eyeing my wings as if she could eat them. Hers had been taken too. All of the Singers' wings except Kirit's had been taken, while novices' wings had been replaced with fledge wings. The sets already leaning against the core wall looked like they had less control, less power than what Singer fledges were used to. I hadn't been part of that decision, but councilman Vant had explained that it would "help them fit in."

Taking their gray wings had been necessary. I'd figured replacing fledges' wings could dampen tower jealousies. Now it seemed cruel.

Doran hadn't argued the point. So I hadn't either.

"Risen, may I?" She asked so politely, I let Nadoni take my wings. My shoulders relaxed, despite myself. She placed my wings reverently near the pairs of patched, faded tower wings.

Moc handed me a small sack of stale-smelling water. "All we've got left. Market tomorrow."

"We have enough markers for fruit now," Kirit said, patting her satchel. My stomach rumbled at the thought of food cooking at home in Densira. "And better sleeping mats too, if we're careful."

The comforts of home I was used to were far away. I imagined Ceetcee tucking quilts around Elna to keep her warm. Settling in to watch the stars on our balcony. A pot of chicory ready to warm for the morning. We were all young still, save Elna, but it was a good place to be. I missed it now.

In the oil-light here at Grigrit, I could see that the tiny tier space they'd been assigned was indeed as cold and damp as Kirit had said. The fledges pulled the mats from the wall. Down dribbled from torn seams.

I pulled Kirit aside while the novices went to work on the dried apples.

"Why do you put up with this?"

She shook her head, the few sparse braids she'd been able to coax from her hair swinging around her brow. "How could I do differently when they have no choice?" Her eyes met mine, pleading for understanding. I nodded, trying. I would never go downtower again if I could help it.

"Why not try to bring them up with you? At least the fledges?"

"Moc," she said. "And Ciel." She didn't have to say any more. Of all the Singer fledges, the twins stood out, both for being twins and for what the Singers first tried to wave off as irreverent playfulness. Even from a distance, across the tier, I could see that Moc's wrists and shoulders were decorated with minor Lawsmarkers. And a few majors.

"Stealing?" That was a new one.

"I didn't!" He crossed the distance to where we stood in two long strides. He was much taller than when I'd seen him after Spirefall.

"Moc!" Kirit ended the argument before it began. Turned to me. "He wants to fly. He wants to help. He could teach tower fledges so much with the right wings."

Moc hissed under his breath. "And I tried, didn't I? They like trying to hear, and think my dives are funny. But these

wings"—he threw a hand towards the pile near the wall—
"didn't work right, and their parents caught us, and—" He held
out his left hand. Two more medium markers dangled from
his wrist. *Disruption, danger to tower.*

I frowned and cleared my throat. Caught Kirit's warning look
to Moc and stopped myself before lecturing him. I could see
she'd been trying already. "And where is Ciel?"

They both stared at me. Finally Moc spoke. "Summoned to
council two days ago to talk about learning echoing while young.
Didn't you see her? She was supposed to be back by now."

It was the first I'd heard of it.

"Someone else's project, probably." I wasn't sure who was
working with the Magisters on navigation, but Doran would
know where she was sheltering. The brass-haired boy's face
brightened at the fact I took his concern seriously. A relief to
see he did care for something besides my wings. "We'll get her
back to you."

"Thank you, Risen." He used the honorific without dissem-
bling. With a bow, he sat with the novices, like a proper fledge.
But the stealing. That was unlucky.

Kirit saw me looking and nudged me. Calling my attention
to the dark shadows approaching, blocking the purpling sky.
"Doran's guards. To see who's come to visit the Singers at this
hour."

"Doran knew where you'd gone."

She laughed softly. "Yes, but they can also count. Two return
after one left? Time to send the blackwings down."

The hunched form in the corner laughed again. A brittle
sound, sharp in the damp air.

"That Singer," Kirit explained, "has barely spoken since I
moved downtower, except to spit 'Lawsbreaker' at me. He likes
to laugh at us." The comment made the elder Singer laugh
harder, until his coughing began again.

In the oil-light, I could see the elder Singer now, weighted down with layer after layer of Lawsmarkers. It didn't surprise me. Across the city's towers, Wik and the other Singer leaders were similarly weighted, and several were under guard for their own safety. There was a water sack within his reach, and Nadoni walked to him and handed him an apple as I watched.

With a clatter and a loud laugh, Doran's guard landed on the tier balcony. "Singers!" she shouted. "Rise."

Kirit brushed apple bits from her robes. The novices and Moc stood too. I heard the elder Singer struggle to stand, clattering.

"You are welcome," Kirit said, bowing. She had begun to straighten when Doran Grigrit himself landed behind the guard and furled his dark wings. Kirit bowed lower instead. "You are welcome, Risen." The novices followed suit. I stayed upright.

Doran left the guard on the balcony, and strode into the tier until he nearly filled it. The man was a giant. His wings were the biggest Liras Viit had ever made. "Kirit Skyshouter, well returned! I'd expected you uptower. Had a meal prepared."

My stomach rumbled again.

Kirit kept her head bowed. I'd never seen her abase herself like that. It was chilling.

"You may speak freely," Doran said. "You are among friends."

When Kirit raised her head, it was obvious from her clenched jaw that she didn't feel friendly at all. I was stunned too, and a bit awed. In council, Doran Grigrit rarely deferred to anyone. But neither had Kirit, ever.

Politics, Nat, Ceetcee had told me. *If you want to rise in council, you must become savvier about politics.* Here, in this downtower tier, I was far from my depth.

Then Doran turned to me. "Well?"

I smiled, proud. "We found the codex." Kirit's jaw clenched

harder, and her hands curled to fists. Clouds. I hadn't meant to steal her glory. "I mean, Kirit found it."

"Excellent!" Doran held out his hands. "Let's see it."

Kirit put both hands on her satchel, which she'd kept slung across her chest after she'd removed her wings. "I'll share it with council in the morning. With the full council." She turned to me, eyebrows raised. "As we'd agreed."

We'd agreed on no such thing, but the tension in the room made me wonder what I was missing. I nodded to buy myself time to figure it out.

Doran seemed to billow in the dim light. Then he let out a calm breath. It was a technique I'd seen him use in council and had been trying to emulate. He was showing us patience, leadership. Despite deep misgivings. "Of course. As is proper, Skyshouter. Respect is so important. But let me suggest that you turn the codex over to a council representative now, for safekeeping."

If I'd had fire, I could have lit the air, Kirit was so tense. I knew Doran well enough by now to see he was being helpful but was running out of patience. He was pushing hard. And I'd known Kirit all my life. She would refuse as hard as she was pushed.

Doran extended his hand, reaching for the satchel again. For the codex. Kirit turned to me. "I will give it to a councilor," she finally agreed. She pulled the strap over her head, ruffling the down-thin hair near her forehead. Held out the satchel to me. "Nat will keep it safe tonight."

The sack was heavier than my Lawsmarker-filled bag, and more awkward. I held it carefully. This would suit Doran and Kirit both. As long as I could swap it back to Kirit to carry tomorrow.

"Fine," Doran said, the word tightly clipped and sharp edged. "When will you fly?"

Kirit met his eyes. "As soon as I see these fledges well provisioned at the market tomorrow. Unless you brought a meal down?"

She had defied him and was now questioning him. I'd never seen Doran so close to yelling. He was an astute politician, usually. But Kirit's challenge was too much for him.

Time for diplomacy. Or at least distraction.

"We have much to tell the council, and much that Grigrit needs to know as well," I began. "The Spire is dying, as Lith once did. Nearby towers should be warned that it could collapse at any moment." A new worry emerged. *Would the city hold Kirit responsible for this too?*

Doran nodded slowly, letting me distract him from his frustration. "This I suspected."

Kirit pointed over his shoulder, to the Spire's dark bulk in the distance. "And yet you let your people live in its shadow without preparations? What about the other towers?"

"I am making preparations, Skyshouter. Many are at work on the problem. You would know more if you had agreed to help lead the tower. Your job today was to find the codex."

"What preparations?" I asked, forgetting we weren't in private conversation. I'd not heard Doran mention any preparations.

The Councilor ground his teeth. I began to see why Kirit had stayed bowed. Doran at home in Grigrit was not appreciative of, or accustomed to, being crossed. He was much more malleable in council.

But at the same time I'd asked my question, Kirit said, "And I found it. You must keep your end of the bargain."

For the first time in a long time, I was almost completely in the dark. That seemed to happen a lot around Kirit. She'd mentioned a bargain in the Spire, although Doran hadn't brought it up when he'd first proposed I accompany her on the expedition.

But Kirit hadn't explained what the bargain was. I hated being a game piece. Honesty was the only way out. "What bargain?"

Neither of them looked at me. "That you did," Doran said. "But the council leadership won't know what to do with the pages."

"How do *you* know what to do with them?" I asked, but Doran gave me a look that said, *Let me work.* I knew that look from council. I'd obeyed it many times and watched admiringly as Doran maneuvered a situation to his advantage. Now my concern about whatever arrangement Kirit had tried to make with him deepened. "What was the bargain?"

Doran raised his voice. "Councilor Densira. This is not your tower. Nor are these your citizens."

He'd used the honorific, but I'd touched a nerve. Interfered with a plan. And it frustrated me that I didn't know what the plan was. No one spotted my discomfort. Doran had turned back to Kirit and was preparing to lecture her too. Kirit looked tired, her head bowing. I hated seeing that.

My fingers caught up the chip I'd tied to my wrist; I brushed the etched surface beneath my thumb. "With respect, Councilor Grigrit," I said. "Kirit Skyshouter is still under my protection, as she has not yet discharged her duties to the council. She must still help translate the codex."

Now I had their attention. Kirit's eyes were wide, but a small smile played at the corner of her mouth. Doran's glower deepened.

I'd stepped into trouble again without knowing what I was up against.

Doran calmed himself after several long moments. "You are correct, Councilor Densira. My thanks for the reminder. Will you accompany me to the balcony?"

He turned on his heel as he said it, his half-furled wings nearly clipping me in the process. I followed him out.

"You'd best keep an eye on the codex," he muttered as we left the relative shelter of Kirit's quarters. "And on your new friends."

"I did what you asked. I'll keep doing it."

He shook his head slowly. "For the city to survive, everyone needs to cooperate, not proceed according to their own wishes. The towers that have threatened to sever their bridges? The violence that has already taken the markets? We can't let that grow or destabilize the city. We need to rise above it."

"What about the Spire?" I asked. "What we saw—"

He waved a hand. "This is much bigger than the Spire, Nat. I've kept you out of much so that you can deny involvement if we lose. It's risky to do what I do—working for compromise behind the scenes—but the reward is faster action. Stick to your duties, don't lose sight of the codex, and it may all work out anyway. After the vote tomorrow."

I had more questions than before. "The vote still has precedence? Even with the danger to the Spire?"

I could barely see his face in the dark, but I knew Doran shook his head as if I were a fledge who'd wondered where the wind came from. He hadn't used that look on me since my first few weeks on the council.

"If the Spire falls—when it falls," Doran said, "the Singers will be blamed for that bad luck too. As well they should be. We'll have done our duty to the city by removing them. And if it falls after Conclave? It becomes a symbol of the city's new hierarchy. Let it fall. We'll keep safe the citizens in its shadow. I promise, Nat. I have a plan. And you are not, at the moment, helping me keep that plan on track."

I wasn't good at duplicity. My father's legacy to me was Spire walls riddled with holes in protest of something he thought wrong. Doran's tone increased the suspicion I might be a game piece in a greater plan. I composed myself carefully, so he would think I was cowed but still loyal. I wasn't sure what I was, really. "I'll try to stick with the plan, Doran. Though it would help to know more of—"

"Excellent. Thank you, Councilor." Doran clamped his large hand on my shoulder. Every inch of him, down to his fingers, was taut sinew. He spun me around. "You'll guard your charge tonight then, and see her safely to council in the morning."

With a push, I was back inside the tier. Seething. A moment later, with a flutter of silk unfurling and battens settling into place, Doran and his guard left the balcony.

Kirit rose from where she'd been sitting with the novices, her back to the elder Singer.

"Birdcrap, Kirit, what was that about?"

She put her finger to her lips. "Nat, I need your help." She leaned close to me. "Tomorrow, we need to find safe places for the fledges, then we must go to speak with my mother. Doran has not been honest with us. With any of us."

"Look, I know he is ambitious, but it's to protect the city. He wouldn't—"

She interrupted me. "You saw him tonight? That is the Doran who this tower knows. No dissent. Few beyond Grigrit understand how much ambition he has. Yes, he wants to unite the city, but on his terms."

"The market riots are destroying the towers. Tearing the council apart." How could she not understand the need?

The riot at Viit especially had left the market smoke-damaged, several dead, and many citizens unnerved. I'd searched the tier in the aftermath and could remember clearly the smell of burnt stalls, even moons later. When I'd finally found Ceetcee and Beliak barricaded in their market-tier quarters, we'd bundled their things into panniers, rolled their sleeping mats, and moved them into Elna's and my quarters at Densira that night.

At Allsuns, after the tower had approved our living arrange-
ments, we'd lit a mourning flag for Tobiat, the four of us feeling safer together. "Nowhere, not even Densira, will remain
truly safe without order, Kirit."

"You're right," she said slowly, weighing each word. "And we
need answers to heal the city. I thought I could bargain with
the codex in order to gain more time, to help Singers and the
towers work together to fix things. But hearing about the vote,
and seeing Doran's reaction tonight to the Spire news, I worried he might not keep up his end of the bargain."

"Why?"

"Have you noticed the new council guard?"

I nodded. "We need them, given the unrest. The riots."

"Perhaps. Some of them have fine wings for fighting." She
eyed mine. "As do you, but theirs are darker. Is the council
preparing for a fight?"

"Not that I know of. But when Singers have stirred up rebellious towers—"

She shook her head. "Doran's guards here are as well outfit-
ted, maybe better, and there are many more of them here than
a usual tower complement. I can't see it straight yet. But I know
now we're barely welcome here; we're becoming everyone's bad
luck. All of us. Tomorrow, we fly. After we find safe places for
the fledges. All four of them."

She was counting Moc too. And Ciel. I'd forgotten to ask
Doran about which tower Ciel was staying in. Tomorrow.

"Singer?" whispered the youngest novice, Minlin, suddenly
at Kirit's elbow. Not Spire-born. Minlin had been taken by the
Spire as an infant, from Viit. Now his former tower didn't
want him back. None of the northwest towers wanted to house
Singers, or their fledges.

"It's just Kirit now." Kirit put a hand on Minlin's head.

"Could you sing The Rise? I can't sleep."

The city's greatest song. Many times, Elna had used it to comfort us as children. But now there were two versions—tower and Spire. Both hinted at fighting and desperation that had threatened our ancestors' survival before the Singers pulled them from the clouds. The tower version was sung as a message of hope. The Spire version had reminded Singers morning and night of their united purpose—so they claimed—and sacrifice, how our history was only rosy because it was tainted with blood. That heroes sometimes fell alongside those who would harm the city.

Which one would Minlin want? "I'm not so great at singing quiet," Kirit said.

He giggled. "I remember. You sang it wrong once too—" He stopped, his eyes filled with tears.

"Shhh. It's all right," I said. "I'll help." We walked to where the fledges rested. Moc lay on his mat, grumbling at us.

But when we sang, I began the first verse of the tower Rise:

> *The city rises on wings of Singer and Trader and*
> *   Crafter,*
> *Rises to sun and wind, all together,*
> *Never looking down.*

Meanwhile Kirit began the Singers' Rise. Our words passed over and through each other, a jumble. Soon, Moc and Nadoni joined her song, their sweet voices honeying the burrs and sharp edges of Kirit's voice, and the Singers' Rise took hold.

> *The city rises on Singers' wings, remembering all,*
> *   bearing all.*
> *Rises to sun and wind on graywing, protecting,*
> *   remembering.*

Never looking down. Tower war is no more.
Always rising, never failing. The city forever.
Rising together. Rising as one.

As I let my melody drop, I remembered Elna's soft voice shaping the hopeful tower Rise—the only Rise we'd known then. Now everything was different. Songs were split in two, towers broken, families far-flung.

Throughout the song, the elder Singer kept silent. Then he spat on the ground. "Tower against Spire? No more. It's tower against tower now. You'll see."

5

BALANCE, GRAVITY, JUSTICE

When the sun rose above the cloudtop the next morning, damp air turned to vapor. The Singers' lowtower quarters steamed. I wondered whether I'd ever feel truly dry again. These quarters were the least habitable on Grigrit and far too close to the cloudtop. The tier's central core had grown too far out for the living space to be remotely comfortable.

Across the city, my family woke and prepared for the day. I could almost smell the chicory warming, hear Elna singing, see Ceetcee combing and braiding her hair. Instead, I sipped a spare mouthful of stale water at Grigrit.

A ladder dangled by our balcony. The bony overhang that ran an uneven circuit around each tier was narrower than those above because the core was so thick. We climbed carefully, our wings half furled, knowing that a fall could send us into the clouds: first Moc, then Minlin, Nadoni, Kirit, and me.

The market tier hummed with activity. I smelled fresh-roasted stone fruit from a stall and ached for it. The families who kept quarters on this tier had pushed their belongings together to make space for vendors. Even at this early hour, haggling and gossip rippled through the crowd. I heard vendors discussing the Singers loudly with their neighbors. When I drew close, they quieted, or shifted the discussion to the winds.

My stomach growled again. I hadn't gone hungry for this long, ever. Even when we were in the downtower of Densira as children, Elna and Ezarit had always made sure Kirit and I had enough to eat. Even when I hid from the Singers after I'd lost my fight in the Gyre and was nearly sucked into the clouds. Tobiat, Elna, and even, secretly, a rebellious Wik had kept me fed.

Now I reached into the small drawstring purse at my waist for markers. Handed one of the Spire markers I'd found the day before to the vendor lifting the first pieces of flatbread from a heating plate. She looked at the sigil carved on the bone disk, showed it to her partner. Both women shook their heads. No good.

The vendor selling fist-sized apples also refused the markers. I shifted the satchel on my shoulder. More unwanted Spire markers rattled against the broken codex pages inside.

"No one takes Spire anymore," Moc said, returning from another stand. "Last market, a few vendors took them still, but today, no one."

Long ago, downtower at Densira, Elna and I'd been short tower markers many times. Ezarit and Kirit too. My heart went out to Moc, a little.

"Dying tower, dead markers," I said. *Dead tower, dead markers,* if I was honest. Moc looked at me quizzically, as if I was being cruel. I reached in my small purse. "Can you use these?" I offered a Grigrit marker and two Densira markers. "Here."

"I have two from Naza, also," Moc added.

"Where did you get Naza?" Kirit sounded afraid to hear the answer. Moc had no wingmarks yet. Tower rules. No wingmark, no flying beyond the quadrant.

Naza was on the other side of the city. *Clouds, Moc.*

"A couple of council guards asked me and Ciel how to echo," he said, proud. "They paid in advance. That's why she went." His pride faded. "I couldn't go. Not with the new Laws. Not with these wings." He flicked at the fledge wings furled at his shoulders.

Kirit's ears pricked up. "Which guards? The ones that came for the old Singer now and then? They were rough with him. You should have told me."

Moc looked hurt. "I want to help. Or at least eat. I'm starving."

I had Densira markers as well. And council markers. "You don't need to use your money." Besides, the shopping was a cover for what Kirit and I needed to do before we left. Find safe havens for the fledges.

I used one Densira marker to buy the apples. Nadoni took the apple I offered and gnawed it down to the core. Moc seethed at Kirit's elbow.

"Still no word from Ciel?" Trying to take his mind off the snub.

Moc shook his head. "No birds from her in days."

"Did you fight before she left?"

He shook his head again, and this time, he did not meet my eyes. "And our last whipperling never came back." I'd given Kirit three of Maalik's fledges as a get-well present.

"All of them, gone?" The boy was beyond irresponsible. But perhaps the whipperling had returned to Densira . . . Fledges sometimes went to their birth tower by mistake. I let it go, for now. Moc was in enough trouble already.

Moc lifted the message chip on my wrist, tentatively. "A councilor with a Lawsmarker? What did you do?"

I pulled the chip away, annoyed. "It's not a Lawsmarker. It's an artifex's drawing." A message from the past. I may have spoken more sharply than I meant to.

Loud throat-clearing behind me made me jump. I turned to find Doran Grigrit, standing at the next stall with his arms crossed over his elegantly beaded robe. How much had he heard?

He beckoned us over calling, "Good to see you've returned,

Skyshouter. Welcome to Grigrit, Councilor Densira." As if we
hadn't spoken the night before. As if I'd never insulted him. I
tried to return his smile but worried my eyes were as cold as
Kirit's, next to me. "No worries of riots here." He looked proudly
over the safe space of the Grigrit market.

Kirit looked too. Her face indicated her doubt of his sin-
cerity.

We needed to get the fledges safely placed, then get out of
here. To the council. We had big problems. Was one of them
Doran Grigrit, my mentor? Was Kirit right? I wasn't sure. I hated
not being sure.

"I'll buy those Spire markers from you, Moc Grigrit. Ten for
each one of my tower marks."

Moc sputtered, tense. Because Doran gave him a tower
name? Or for the ridiculous barter. "Spire markers might be
worthless, but I can sand them down into something I could
sell. Like message skeins!"

Kirit grabbed Moc's arm in quiet warning. I sucked my
breath. Moc was playing the sharp edge of the knife when we
needed to fly away clean.

"Of course, if you have better things to trade," Doran continued, "we could get you and your fledges better quarters uptower."
He'd cast his voice loud enough for all the stalls to hear.

"I'm afraid we don't have anything to offer." Kirit's voice didn't
waver. Her hand gripped her satchel, knuckles pale on the strap.

She'd forgotten we hadn't switched satchels back. So had I,
almost.

"If you'd spend your time helping the city heal, rather than
herding refugees, perhaps you'd know which side to stand on
too," Doran said. His voice remained friendly, but he stepped
closer. Now a hint of amusement touched the edges of his
eyes.

We weren't going to get away clean, not at all. Nadoni and

Minlin circled around our bone-still trio like worried dirgeons. Their worn gray robes flapped in the market breeze.

I faced Doran again, trying to gauge whether he was maneuvering for influence or truly angry. "Let's discuss the Spire markers, before we draw a crowd?" Even on Grigrit, we were still Kirit Skyshouter and Nat Densira, who helped save the city. No matter what, that was still true. "If they are so worthless in the market, why would you want them?"

Doran laughed so sharply, nearby vendors peered over their tiny stalls, trying to guess what we'd done to provoke the towerman.

I took an involuntary step backward, blocking Moc's attempt to move between us and Doran. I hadn't heard the councilor speak with that much controlled anger ever in council. But then we had refused him last night. I'd defied my mentor. Kirit, her tower councilman. We'd lied.

Doran's eldest daughter looked up from where she and her mother filled market baskets with fruit and fresh bird meat. She quickly looked down again. Minlin and Nadoni watched us all, eyes wide as whipperlings; the apple in Nadoni's hand stalled halfway to her mouth.

"Councilor Grigrit." I held out a conciliatory hand. A gesture I'd seen Doran use many times on the council plinth. "I haven't been to market here before. Perhaps I don't understand how Grigrit barters. My question was not meant to offend."

The market's collective breath eased, and I heard conversation pick up again. I hadn't realized how much silence surrounded us.

A lifetime ago, before Spirefall, Doran and his family had delighted in betting and bargaining in the northwest quadrant. They'd come for the wingfights, and once, Doran told me later, to take Kirit back with them as a trading apprentice. Instead, Kirit and I had been punished by the Singers, a blow to Grigrit's honor. Doran empathized with the cruel way the Singers had treated us—he'd gotten a broken deal too.

I smiled at him with genuine respect. He'd helped me much on the council, and I still hoped he would teach me more. I hoped Kirit's impression was wrong. "I would be honored if you could show me what I don't yet understand."

He stilled. Raised his eyebrows at my contrition. At my reminder of our relationship on the council. Junior councilor to mentor. Then he tilted his head, agreeing. He handed Minlin and Nadoni a fistful of Grigrit marks and pushed them towards the stalls. "They should find apprenticeships. Small fingers do fine work," he muttered.

Then he turned back to us. "I'll show you what we do with Spire marks these days."

Those two novices had probably never bartered alone in their lives, I realized. We stood to lose all the dearly bought markers. Kirit noticed the same thing. "Moc," she said and pushed his shoulder, "go with them."

This time Moc didn't argue. The trio moved through the market as I turned Doran's words over in my mind. We'd bought ourselves a little time and kept up the ruse that we were provisioning the fledges before we left for the council platform. We had to fly soon.

Doran waved us towards where the market's host families' belongings had been piled. In the shadow of a bone spur, several men and women hunched over a square of silk decorated with a small city map.

The players had piled up tower marks on spaces in each quadrant. They rolled bone dice across the map's surface. When one cackled and knocked over a tower in a different quadrant, two other men swept up the marks. I could see that most of the towers were made of Spire marks, with tower sigils set atop: Mondarath, Naza, Laria, Harut.

"What is it?" Kirit was familiar with bird fighting and other forms of tower gambling that the Singers had disdained, but this game was complicated and new.

I'd played it on Mondarath, but never Densira. "I've heard it called Balance in the northwest. And Gravity in the east."

Doran's face grew fierce. "We call it Justice."

Another player spoke up, looking at Kirit. "See that center tower? That's where they're all trying to go. First one there wins."

The center tower was topped with a Spire mark.

"You'll excuse me," Doran said, clapping both Kirit and me hard on the shoulders. "I have a tower to run, and council vote to prepare for. I can't while time away over games." He put the Spire marks on the table, and he was gone.

Laughter erupted as another tower fell. The winner, a woman with her back turned to me, wearing dark, silk robes, crossed strands of glass beads, and tower marks in her hair, grabbed up the markers and shook them in her cupped hands. Her opponents groaned as she pocketed the markers. We could see, as we circled, how much strategy the Grigrit players had built into the game.

Without seeming to stare, each of the other players eyed Kirit's gray wings, her tattoos and scars. Her hair still spiky as it grew back.

"Singer," one player, a young guard with wingfighting scars on his cheek, greeted her. His fingers toyed with a bone-handled knife on the table. Another raised his chin to me: "Risen." The third spat against the tower's central core wall.

The fourth player, the woman, turned her head to the side long enough to look me up and down. "Councilor Densira, Doran says many good things about you. Hello, Kirit."

With a shiver, I recognized Dix, the former Magister from Viit. She'd dressed me down after my group flight, when I'd nearly fallen into the clouds on my wingtest. She'd been Kirit's mother's oldest rival, and had left the northwest after Spirefall. What was she doing here?

Dix wore different tower marks in her hair now. Southern ones. A mix of Grigrit marks and a silkspinner tower's chips. She smiled and held my eyes for a heartbeat. Then turned back to the game.

Kirit's hands clenched tight knots around her satchel straps.

We left as quickly as we could to search the market for the fledges.

❧ ❧ ❧

"Kirit!" Moc chased after us across the market tier. The two novices trailed behind him. "Did you see the wings?"

Kirit slowed and turned to where he pointed. I walked a few paces more, eager to be clear of this place, but returned when Kirit didn't move. A stand crammed at market's edge near the balcony held a neat row of furled wings in bright colors. Armatures and finger controls were set out for viewing. Liras Viit's familiar laughter rang out as he talked with a customer behind his worktable.

"Those are stunning, Moc," Kirit said.

They were beautiful. One design was a match for the wings I wore. Another, quite like what Doran's guards wore.

Moc couldn't tear his eyes away. As we watched, Liras pulled aside a cover and gave the customer two wingsets, both black. Not the deep gray of a Singer's night wings, but colored as if they'd been dyed by Lith—the broken tower that poked barely above the clouds.

The customer took the wings and walked away without handing over any marks. When her back was turned, Liras sank to his stool, his smile sliding towards frustration.

Kirit moved towards the stall, and I followed. What was she up to?

We passed a group of young mothers who pulled their children back from us, whispering, "Spirebreaker." I heard another mother murmur, "Cloudfood."

A cluster of young fliers bumped Moc in passing. Kirit reached out quickly to grab his shoulder. Bore down hard. The boy squirmed, but did not protest.

Where we stood in the market stalls seemed to become more crowded. Denser. Men and women our age pressed close. Someone jostled and called, "Skyshouter!"

Would there be a riot here after all?

Silently, five blackwings pushed through the crowd. Three men, two women, all with faces as expressive as bone spurs. They did nothing but reroute the crowd around themselves, but that was enough. The space between stalls in the marketplace became less crowded very quickly. The young mothers had disappeared with their children.

Kirit's life on Grigrit had been thus for many moons, since she moved downtower. This was what I couldn't see while I was judging her from my council seat.

"Skyshouter," a tall male blackwing said as we passed.

"Thank you, Hart Grigrit, mercy on your wings." Kirit bowed her head in greeting.

The guard cleared his throat. "Any more of these disturbances, you and your fledges will be confined to quarters. Towerman's orders, for the good of Grigrit."

She nodded again, gripping Moc's shoulder even tighter. "I understand."

I, however, didn't comprehend. "They didn't do anything!" I protested.

The blackwing shrugged and walked away with his cohort. Not his problem. Stunned, I rolled the incident over in my mind.

How much worse it would be for Kirit if she didn't renounce

the Singers in council? She surely heard the whispers. Still Kirit moved through the market crowd, unafraid.

"Liras!" she called.

The wingmaker, famed throughout the northwest quadrant for his skill, had set up a booth at Grigrit market. When he saw Kirit, his face lit up and he stepped around his wares to give her a hug. "You are a sight for cloudy eyes."

He bowed to me. "Nat, Councilor, how do you find your wings?"

"They are excellent," I said. "What are you doing here?"

"I go where the sales are. Doran has been kind enough to make me a place here." The stress returned to Liras's eyes. "How are your mothers?"

Suspecting Liras knew Ezarit had landed well after Spirefall—everyone did—I guessed he meant Elna.

But Kirit didn't realize that. "She's moved to Varu, to be close to the city center."

"Elna is as well as can be expected," I added. "Thank you." Liras tutted over us. I looked at his work. "These are fine wings. You are adding new techniques."

Liras smiled. "We've learned much from Singers' wings. And Doran found some old designs and combined them with inventions from his own artifexes. His guards and associates benefited, as you well know. He's quite an innovator."

Kirit made a face, as if to say, *Doran? He's many things.* Her grip remained tight on Moc's shoulder.

But I could see that if the city needed innovation, Doran would find a way. More than that, he could inspire others to find new ideas, new ways to look towards the future. That's what the city needed. And new gadgets and tools had been entering the southern markets lately. If Liras said Doran was a source, I wasn't surprised. "What other innovations?"

Waving his hand in a circle, Liras said, "Oh, so many things. Wind catchers, better condensers. There's talk of much more." Liras encompassed the whole city in a gesture.

I added items to the list of things I wanted to ask Doran after council. I wanted to get involved, and now that we'd retrieved the codex, perhaps I could. Once he calmed down.

Liras was alone in the stall. I'd almost left my respect and manners back on the council platform. "How is your family?" His daughter had been a Magister and a wingmaker. She'd flown with Kirit's group for our wingtest.

He bowed his head. "A skymouth, during Spirefall. I know you both did your best."

"Calli?" The horror in Kirit's voice shook me. She truly didn't know the city now, didn't know she shouldn't shout about its losses. I pictured the crimson banners, the faded flags on towertops: so many.

But Liras Viit—Liras Grigrit—bowed his head. "Calli's partner, Vida, and their little girl lived, but Calli is gone. I care for them now, my sons too. The boys are guards here." His expression blended sadness and pride.

Calli had been Liras's most talented apprentice, and a good friend to many on Densira. My heart splintered, stabbing at me from the inside. "I am so sorry for your loss."

"Your sons will do well on Grigrit," Kirit said kindly. "Doran runs a steady tower."

He nodded and ran his fingers over a pair of furled wings. "I do not know how I'll work, once the new fledges' orders come in. I've taken a large commission. I wish she were here." He looked at the novices trailing us. "Are either of your fledges good with wings?"

Minlin's eyes brightened with hope, as did Nadoni's. Yes, both of them were good. Singer-trained even. Moc poked at my side. "Me!" he whispered. His Lawsmarkers clicked together on his wrist.

My pulse raced, and I struggled to calm it. We had our solution, I hoped. Liras could take the fledges, and we could be on our way. *On to greater problems.*

Kirit pulled Minlin and Nadoni forward. "They're young, but talented. If you seek an apprentice."

Liras's slow smile came as another sharp tear to my heart. "I'll try out both, with a small wage, and food."

The luck didn't offset Calli's loss, but it was a start for all involved.

"Thank you," Kirit said. She nudged each fledge to respond as well. Then curiosity overwhelmed Minlin as he assessed the stall with a worker's eyes. "Why so many black wings?"

Liras's face closed like a trap. "Apprentices don't ask too many questions; they follow my lead. Understand?" Both fledges bobbed their heads, and I breathed a sigh of relief. Two fledges accounted for, though Minlin's question nagged.

Meanwhile, Moc fumed behind us.

"You didn't even try, Kirit!" he said.

"You've not been interested in wings, ever, except for flying, Moc." Kirit kept her tone light. "Besides, I need you to come with us."

Moc wasn't interested in playing along. "I need something to do!" In his desperation, he gripped Kirit's robe. People around us began to stare again. I heard the sense of betrayal in his voice. Left to his own devices, Moc would churn his frustration into trouble. I understood the cruelty of the elder Singer's laughter. The Laws already accumulating on his wrist.

Liras Grigrit watched us carefully, then led the two fledges into his stall. "Fly safe, Skyshouter. I'll watch these two until your return."

We bowed low to him in thanks, and he struggled to bow even lower in response. Then Kirit and I, with Moc wedged between us, walked to the tier's far edge. This side of Grigrit had a clear view of the cracked Spire and the northern towers beyond.

We were nearly away.

I was glad of it, though I didn't know why we had to take Moc with us. Doran's desire to hang on to the codex the night before had sparked my unease. Watching the tower citizens play Justice had fanned it. From the near-riot to small things like Liras's excitement over new inventions this morning, life in the southwest had grown more complex and dangerous than Doran had been willing to share. The wind had certainly turned against the Singers, but there was more to it, like a bad smell on a gust that hit for a moment, then disappeared.

Kirit was right: the contents of her satchel wouldn't be safe on Grigrit, or anywhere in the southwest. All of it needed to be in the council's hands, even the broken pieces.

But Moc? He was in a foul mood, and he'd be slow in the air.

Moc struggled to adjust his fledge wings. They were under-powered compared to what he'd been accustomed to in the Spire, but he'd had time to get used to them. If he'd applied himself. I felt selfish hoping he wouldn't slow us down too much. We couldn't afford to stop and rest on too many towers along the way.

Bone eaters, a dead tower. The riots. Postponing the vote. We had to hurry now.

"We'll fly towards Bissel and use the crosswind to take us to Varu," I said. Varu was where Ezarit was, and the other city council leaders besides Doran. "Perhaps, if Ciel has discharged her duties, we'll find her along the way."

The relief that colored Moc's face was painful to see. There'd been many changes for everyone because of Spirefall. I'd heard the songs—the ones about Kirit and the ones laced with worries about the city's progress. What I hadn't heard last night were many complaints from most of the Singer fledges. They'd lost their home and been thrown from their routines. They'd gotten in trouble, surely. They'd survived. But they'd kept trying to fit in; Minlin and Nadoni were good examples. I felt a rush of pride for them, mixed with hope that if they could make it, the city could too. And perhaps Moc could find his way.

As for Kirit? I didn't know. I didn't want her to fall.

Moc, Kirit, and I judged the winds from the market-tier balcony. The midmorning sky was a rich blue. A few bits of cloud had risen high enough to bring dampness to the higher tiers. The tower glittered with condensers, both the polished bone kind and several with thin metal linings. The metal reflected the sun in sharp sparks. Innovations. Grigrit was very wealthy in those, indeed. In the north, collectors were lowered to condense water inside the clouds and then retrieved. It was hard work.

I could hear the thin gurgle of water in the bone spouts nearby. Moc swallowed thirstily.

We readied for the long glide around Grigrit, then past Bissel to Naza. Did Kirit know that Bissel was where the council kept Wik? The Singer who'd fought beside us at Spirefall had been her teacher, once. She hadn't asked after him, except to use his name in argument yesterday. We were in a hurry, but Bissel was right on the way. If Wik had been among my friends or family, I would have wanted to see him one last time.

"Do you want to stop at Bissel? To see Wik?" I asked.

She swallowed and I could see her eyes fill. Yes, she wanted to stop. "He came to visit me while I was sick. He stayed by my side. I knew he was quartered close by, but Doran said if I went to see him, the towers would think we were plotting. Yes. I would like to see him."

Despite Doran's warning, it wasn't too difficult to stop for a moment. Making the offer had eased the gnawing sensation in my stomach; she should be able to see him before the vote. "We'll go."

I scratched a bone-chip message to Densira—to Councilor Vant, to Elna, Ceetcee, and Beliak—letting them know I would fly first to Bissel, then to the council plinth. Kirit added a chip marked for Ezarit on Varu. With both chips tied to his left claw, Maalik launched and flew to the northwest.

I leapt first, heading northeast, letting the guards see Moc was escorted, as was appropriate for his age, if not his skills. Couldn't have him earning more Lawsmarkers.

He followed, wobbling and cursing like an adult. He dipped before circling back up to my level, breathing hard. I grimaced in the shadow of my wing. He would slow us down.

Kirit leapt last, joining us in the air as we completed a waiting circle in Grigrit's updraft. Then we flew wide around the Spire, headed for Bissel.

Once he got his wings under control, Moc chattered between us. I flattened my own wings, spilling wind so that he could keep up.

"Can we watch the wingfights at Mondarath after we go to council? I heard they're letting Singers play. Macal, for one." He'd asked Kirit, but I answered.

Macal was Wik's brother and Moc's cousin. "Macal's a tower Magister, and a councilman. He's flown numerous wingfights." *And he'd renounced his Singer connections.*

"Sure, and if they let one Spire-born play, maybe more can fly."

To fly, to fight. I understood that impulse.

I saw Moc's desire clearly now. But Macal had chosen tower over Spire long ago. Most of the city hadn't realized he'd been Spire-born, until Spirefall. Still some spoke of him as if he'd stayed Singer. Mondarath had discussed removing him from the wingfights. How deep did the city's anger go?

My thumb brushed the old message chip's carved surface. That connection to the past helped my thinking. Would Moc and Kirit be any safer in the north than they were at Grigrit?

Kirit read the silence as skillfully as she read the wind. "Maybe later, Moc?" She whistled to me as a caution. But Moc continued, his voice ringing high above the wind, "Macal can use his Singer skills in wingfights now that people know. That's what I want to see. An actual wingfight outside the Gyre."

"Those skills belong to the towers now," Kirit reminded Moc. "Don't call them Singer skills."

Moc wobbled as the gust we rode guttered and then strengthened. He wasn't watching for wind shifts as he should. "Pay attention," Kirit scolded. He tipped a wing and flew ahead of us, frustrated, and we let him go.

The curve of Moc's wings wavered against the blue sky, and I began to calculate how he might adjust them for more control.

Which was why I didn't see anything when the wind disappeared from beneath us.

6

A HOLE IN THE WIND

My wing's silk spans guttered loudly and bellied in their battens. My ears popped as I flipped and spun. I dropped from the sky, Kirit falling beside me.

Flailing, searching for a breeze. Finding nothing. My gorge rising. Falling. I was falling again.

The clouds rushed up to catch me.

My wings were still locked, but nothing supported them. I panicked, my feet kicking wildly, which only made me spin faster. The clouds seemed to open like an eye, the sky and the towers flipped upside down, became teeth in a giant mouth, and we fell towards it, too afraid to scream.

In a glance on my next spin, I saw Moc falling above us, flailing. I could no longer see Kirit. I couldn't control my wings in the air.

My breath and my heartbeat grew loud in my ears. I'd fallen before, broken wings twisted around me, the sky blocked by splintered battens and torn silk. Falls were always filled with noise caused by wind whipping past. Now all went silent. The wind didn't roar as I fell through it. Each inhalation grew more difficult. I tried to recover by unlocking my wings and forcing them to a hard curve. I fought for any breeze. Spreading my ankles as wide as I could in my footsling, I hoped for more lift, a bigger foil for any available air.

Kirit flipped back into view, gasping for breath, almost crashing into me. For a moment, she struggled beside me, face ashen, lips purple. It felt as if a windgate had opened, as in my nightmares, and once again sucked all the air out of the Gyre, and me with it. But we were in open skies, not the Spire. Confused, I grappled the air between us too late, just as Kirit had once reached for me and missed. Then I tumbled away.

Nothing slowed our descent.

City and sky rolled white and blue around me. Moc screamed, breaking the silent void. I shouted for help with what little breath I had. Tiers rushed past, and the clouds grew close. Below me, then above me, a swirling void within the white pulled at me. The clouds rose over us.

I couldn't see Kirit again. My heart felt like it was about to fly from my chest, and I'd always been falling. I would always fall. What would Beliak and Ceetcee think happened? Doran?

My mother. My family.

Elna's heart would break. Two more she loved, lost to the clouds. I couldn't let that be the last thing she knew. Nor Ceetcee and Beliak, when we'd begun to form a life together. I wouldn't leave any of them like this. I flipped in the void, fought gravity. Tried to rise with every muscle. Every breath.

The light grew dim, then brighter, then dim again. My hair whipped around my head and spilled across my face. My new hunters' wings creaked ominously. I fell past the shadows of broken bone long hidden from the city; past gray tower trunks I'd known well above the clouds that here were strangers.

Useless wings! They churned the void without effect. My footsling tangled around my feet. My body spun, momentum pushing me into a new tumble that left me gasping and unsure which direction was up. All was white and gray and shadow. At the edges of my eyes, darkness began to close in. Now I could see no towers in any direction. Only cloud and my own flapping robes and wings. Pressure built in my ears.

I imagined a tangle of ropes stretched across the cloudlight like an old bridge. I thought I saw shadows in the distance.

My feet caught—or were caught by—something rough and damp. Soggy sinew and fiber wrapped one ankle and trapped the other leg at the calf. I could almost breathe, but all smelled of mildew and damp. Gravity pulled on me, stretching me painfully as it fought to keep me. And then my body jerked, my neck and shoulders snapping hard.

Was I dead? The netting spun, wrapping me, wings and all. I felt a breeze against my cheeks. Wind. I snapped hungrily at the clearer air.

Was I alive? I'd fallen through the clouds. I was supposed to be dead.

The netting had a familiar scent, heavy in the nostrils. Like muzz. My vision wavered. Did I hear laughter?

"Grab the fledge and the Skyshouter. Clouds take this one," the air whispered.

I'd seen small birds pretend to be dead when a larger bird hunted them. I sank as deep into the net as I could and acted as if the muzz had taken me.

The netting bounced and wobbled as someone landed near me, then took off.

Silently, I sang The Rise in my head, then other songs Tobiat had taught us, starting with "The Terror of the Clouds," fighting off muzz-sleep the whole time.

> *They crack the bones*
> *They eat the stars*
> *They carry—*

Once again the song's words slipped away, lost.

Another wobble on the net, and then turbulence. Shouting. Kirit's voice. Kirit trying to fight. The sound of tearing wingsilk.

I fought to roll over in the sticky net. Failed. I reached fingertips—all I could move—to my quiver. Empty.

My arrows had spilled in my fall. My bow tangled in the net, pinning me. If I moved too fast to free it, I'd follow the arrows into the void.

"Go after her! We need her and what she's carrying. Can't have gotten far with that rip in her wing." A familiar voice? The wind? The muzz muddled my thoughts. Kirit had fought her way free. That much I knew.

The netting bounced again as another flier—the last? I hoped so—launched.

They thought Kirit had the codex, not me. We'd never traded bags back. I'd lost her, and Moc; I could at least protect the codex. I lay still, my right hand gripping my father's carved chip. How long was long enough to lie here? How would I find Moc? Was Kirit hurt? My mind waded through the effects of the muzz, fighting sleep with questions, anger. I bit the soft inside of my lip, hard, shocking myself awake with the pain. Eventually, I could think again.

I struggled, working the sticky net loose enough to reach my bow and untangle it from the sticky ropes. Waved the arc of bone and tendon above and beside me, getting my bearings in the dim light. If I'd practiced echoing instead of singing for the past seasons and could echo as well as Kirit or Moc now, I might not have been so blind here.

Still, using the bow and with my eyes growing accustomed to what light there was, I gained a sense of my situation. I lay on my back in a flat net. Nothing above me but shifting clouds. The sticky net held me tight. I had to get free, to find the laughter's source. To find my companions. I set the bow back over my shoulder, turning instead to the short-handled glass-tooth knife the council had given me after Spirefall. Reached to the side and prayed for contact.

The knife caught the netting. I felt fibers begin to split beneath its edge. I sawed, my shoulder muscles protesting the angle. Finally, the net broke and I fell again.

But this time I fell into the wind.

I let myself drop into the clouds, hoping I wouldn't hit anything. Half furled my wings. Above me, the net's remains sagged: a hole where I'd been, but the rest spanned the gap between two thick tower trunks.

The wind rushed past my ears as I fell away.

When I'd built up enough velocity, I spread my wings and let them fill. Then I arched my back and dragged hard at the wing grips. I'd escaped the wind shadow, if that's what had caused our fall. And the net. I could avoid crashing cloudblind into the tower if luck stayed with me. Half a hunter's work was luck and patience. Even if I'd spent the last months arguing Laws in council, I would always be a hunter at heart.

I bumbled into an updraft that bore me higher into the gray, damp clouds. Around me, dark forms, thick trunks of towers. Bissel? Grigrit? I had no idea where I flew.

Was that the shadow of a ledge? Perhaps. I aimed for it, slowing my glide so that I wouldn't smash myself towerside if I was wrong. I needed to rest. To get my bearings. Then I'd figure out how to get above the clouds.

The ledge was barely that: a slim spur almost overrun by the tower's bone core. Still, I could stand on it and lean against the core wall. Let my legs stop shaking from the exertion. Breathe. Air filled my lungs, a breeze played with my hair.

Around me, the clouds were not a constant thickness. This was a surprise. From above, they'd appeared almost solid, a wall of white. Below, when a sunbeam broke through, I could almost see the next tower over. And then I could see it clearly.

The Spire's massive carved wall appeared in the clouds, then disappeared again, back into shadow and mist.

A low whistle nearly escaped my lips. It looked so close. No giving away my position, if anyone was nearby to hear. If I hadn't imagined the voices.

Then the clouds closed. No matter what I had imagined, I was on my own, below the city.

I peered again into the clouds, waiting for another break. My eyes ached with staring at the white. Mirages appeared: spots of distant glowing blue pulsed where I looked too hard. The damp began to get to me, and perhaps the shock of falling also. My legs shook and my teeth chattered. I could not stay there. Not without arrows. Not this close to the Spire, where bone eaters and who knew what else lurked.

❦ ❦ ❦

My time became measured in breaths. Too many to count. In staring at the white air, at the shadows within it, while thinking of my family far above. Elna, Ceetcee, Beliak. My growling belly. The damp.

I would go mad with it. I would have to fly soon, or try to climb. *No one returns from the clouds.* Wrong. I'd return. I'd prove everyone wrong. And I'd bring Moc and Kirit with me—if I could find them.

Patience rewarded, finally: a sunbeam wormed its way through the cloud wall, illuminating mist and edges so beautifully I gasped. The air was still chilled, but the Spire loomed before me, piercing thick heaps of clouds in its rise.

The breeze buffeting the ledge carried a thick smell, sweet like rotting apples, but heavier. I recoiled from its sudden slap on my senses, bumping my head against the tower core. Then the smell disappeared as quickly as it had come.

Within the clouds that surrounded the lower Spire, a large shape, darkly solid and slow-moving, was outlined crisply against the brighter clouds. My skin prickled, increasingly cold. I reached for my quiver again, before remembering it was empty. I couldn't make out tentacles or teeth, and the shape was wrong for either skymouth or bone eater.

I thought I heard the rhythm of voices again, far distant, blown on the wind coming from around the Spire.

What was the shadow? Why was it circling the Spire? Whose voices were those? Where had Kirit and Moc gone?

So many questions. I struggled to get my bearings. *Plan, Nat. Don't just react.*

Go up, as fast as I could? Or try to figure out what was happening, here below?

We'd fallen, impossibly, between Grigrit and Bissel, while taking the Spire on our right wingtip. Had we fallen straight down? It had seemed so. And when I'd flown up, it had been at a relatively sharp angle. Perhaps I stood on Bissel? I was obviously not far from the Spire, although I'd never been so many tiers down. Whatever made the slow circumnavigation of the Spire's walls must be close to the cloudtop.

Closer than I was.

Was it still morning? I couldn't tell by the sunbeam's angle, rapidly dimming as the clouds closed. I had to make my decision soon, or I'd find myself trying to fly cloudblind, or scaling Bissel with only the pitons Beliak had given me.

Logic said, *Return. Go to the council. Let them send a search party for Kirit Skyshouter and the Singer fledge.*

Curiosity said, *Investigate.* And rekindled friendship said, *Find them now.* I shook my wings open and launched into an upswirl of mist. Soon I caught a powerful windflow around the Spire and rode it.

The wind led me away from the shadow-shape. But if I was right, the gust would carry me back around the Spire. If I was lucky, I'd find a handgrip or wall carvings to cling to.

If I was unlucky, I'd end up deeper in the clouds.

Cold and damp chilled my skin as I flew around the Spire's wall. My cheeks, long accustomed to dry air, felt slick. My ears, long used to the city's noise, searched for sound.

It had been a long time since I'd been so alone. Since Allsuns, over a year ago, and then only for a short while.

The quiet of flying solo in the clouds, the mist my only companion, made me edgy.

Even when I was Lawsbound. Elna and Ceetcee, Beliak and Tobiat had filled my quarters with friendship, family. Before that, I'd had Kirit, always nearby, and our wing group, practicing our flight skills around our crowded tower. Shouting to each other from open balconies. The entire city was a family. We didn't sequester ourselves away from one another. That was something Singers did.

"Put myself into a bit of a tight spot," I whispered to my absent friends, my companions, my family. "I'll make it back."

As I came back around the Spire, I spotted a shadow below me and far forward. The sun's angle in the clouds chased the dark spot with ripples of light.

I trailed the shadow from three tiers above until it disappeared around the Spire. The mist and my hunters' colors cloaked me well enough, I hoped. Far below, at a break in the mist, a net swung in the wind, lopsided, and a hole cut in its webbing.

This was where we'd fallen.

I hadn't imagined it. What had happened to us?

Above me, another shadow loomed beneath the clouds, closer now. Unmoving. I passed beneath it: a bone spur and wire construction attached to the Spire with bone screws and pegs. It lined up with the shadow's path below.

My wingtip grazed the Spire wall with a skitter. *Pay attention, Nat, or fall forever!*

I tightened my fingers in my wing grips and shifted my body

weight, slowly easing my glide away from the tower. Before I'd gotten too far, I spotted the carvings that marked an upcoming handgrip—a safety precaution tower fledges were taught to fly for in emergencies.

I risked flying closer to the wall again. Unwrapping my fingers from the grips, I locked my wings, wrapped my elbows around the winghooks and readied myself to reach into the air. Wobbled and almost slammed into the Spire wall. Then I saw the handgrip: crusted and overgrown, but still usable. I grabbed, jerking my already tired shoulders so hard I nearly cried out. A small rodent—gray, with a hairless pink tail—scooted out of its hiding place in the grip, making me jump but not let go. The rodent began to climb away. I swung there, catching my breath, until I found a place to rest my toes as well.

Soon, the shadow circled below me. I could hear regular noises coming from it. Conversations, perhaps. Whistles. No birds, no animals that I knew, made noise like that, save one. There were people in the clouds, working the Spire's side. No one was going to believe me, should I ever return above the clouds to tell them.

Another break in the mist gave me a glimpse of the space between the Spire and Bissel. Distances narrowed far below, until the towers seemed to grow together. In the muted distance, other towertops stopped midcloud.

Those towers hadn't risen when the city did. Some had broken. We knew this from Tobiat's songs. Others stopped growing. The city grew past them. Forgot them.

Not everyone had forgotten.

The noises grew louder as, below me, the shadow's edges sharpened. Plinth-shaped, like the city council's meeting space, but smaller by half. And unlike the council's platform, this one was not suspended between the towers. This platform floated.

I stared, blinked and stared again. This was no cloudtouched dream. Below me, bulbous shapes rose silver above the plinth, visible only because the sunlight hit them cloudwise.

Skymouths. Hanging right below me.

My feet scrambled against the Spire's side, trying to climb away fast. In the cloudlight, the creatures' limbs dangled limp, trailing silver in the wind, and very visible within the cloud cover's shadows. I cursed at my fear, trying to drive it away.

These weren't skymouths, not anymore.

They were four filled air sacks made of skymouth carcasses. They supported the platform below.

These air sacks floated on their own, without wings. Tethered to the plinth, they wobbled in the wind, but without a skymouth's natural motions. The monsters' corpses hung in the cloud-ridden air, buoying the plinth's corners, while the platform's center sagged against several bone supports.

The skymouth air sacks had been filled to near bursting with gas. Rot gas? That was the only gas I knew that rose, but it was unstable at this volume.

On that plinth, figures worked. Gray robed, some of them. Others, wearing brighter colors at the plinth's far edge flickered and disappeared. On both sides, shadow figures moved wing-shaped oars the size of windbeaters' wings to steer the plinth around the Spire's trunk.

The shapes and colors resolved themselves as even more clouds shifted: gold hair, and black. Four figures who looked very small at this distance rode the platform as it circuited the tower.

My fingers wrapped the Spire handgrip, and my foot struggled to stay on its resting notch. Still, I felt as if the air had disappeared beneath me once again.

What I saw made no sense.

Spotting more grips below me, I descended another tier, intent on seeing more.

❦ ❦ ❦

On the Spire's mossy side, my blue and brown wings were barely dark enough to blend into the shadows. The light had faded again as moonlight replaced sunlight. I couldn't judge distances well in the dim, but I was much closer at least.

As I snuck up on the plinth, a brighter moonbeam sliced the clouds. Pieces of the whole structure appeared. A long boom swung from the plinth's center, holding a net aloft. Another net was undergoing repairs by two figures who were still small, even up close. Children.

Small fingers do fine work. Doran's words echoed through the last of the muzz.

Clouds chewed at the moonbeam and a scrim of mist obscured the plinth. The nearest skymouth skins seemed to shimmer blue-silver with reflected light. I could see them easier now.

Two fledges worked at the plinth's edge closest to the bone tower. Now and then, one of them knelt or lay down. A larger figure stood watch.

I strained my eyes, counting. Waiting. Four children worked the plinth.

Their guard focused attention on the Spire wall, and the work the fledges were doing there. The smell came again, close enough to be sickening. Foul air surrounded the plinth, the skymouth hides. I could see the sharp objects that the children had pushed into the bone tower's overgrown core as the plinth circled. Dark, moonlit liquid dripped from the resulting holes into goose bladders and bone buckets.

Flattened against the Spire, I remained unseen. I rested in a shallow divot, a sealed-over Spire gate from long ago.

The child workers attached spigots and buckets to the holes they'd made. They pulled other buckets and taps from holes that no longer dripped. The plinth continued to circle, slowly, as a guard struggled with the large wings to guide its turn.

Looking up, I saw a glow above the fledges still working the taps that quickly faded and went out. The clouds parted and a moonbeam caught on two metal assemblages connecting tower and plinth. I could barely make out the tendons that had been stretched between them. They looked like work my father might have done once—a mechanism that kept the plinth circling close to the tower.

Ceetcee and the other artifexes used similar but simpler tools to help them build bridges between the towers. But someone had modified this construction. Someone who understood tools. Another artifex.

The plinth made a turn, two large silk wingfoils swinging out with the same speed as windbeaters' giant wings had worked to churn up the Gyre.

Five more windbeaters' wings hung from the Spire, above the plinth, at the end of the bone and metal outcropping. The expanse of it stretched down the Spire's side, and bolts had been driven far enough through the bone wall that dark liquid seeped down the bone, pooling in old carvings.

Five foils, arrayed in a circle. Enough to spin a Gyre of its own, or the reverse of one. If someone could get it moving fast enough, they might make a hole in the wind. A hole big enough for a flier to fall through. I clutched the message chip on the blue silk cord at my wrist. Felt its solidity, its realness. *This happened. This was happening.*

I hadn't imagined the shadows. Nor the missing wind. I hadn't imagined the nets. I was neither dead nor skytouched.

Using handholds and the tier's narrow ledge, I followed the slowly orbiting platform as far as I could, until I came to another gate. This one half open.

A shadow passed between me and the moonlight, a flier descending fast, and before I could worry about rodents or what else might be behind the gate, I pressed myself into the crack.

The plinth below me dipped, then rose.

A familiar voice broke the night below me, not bothering with whispers. "You are working too slow. The city needs you to work faster."

I knew that voice. I'd heard it that very morning *Councilor Densira . . . Hello Kirit.* Dix. Talking to the small figures on the plinth as if they were garbage.

Another black-winged guard approached the plinth and whistled. Pulled a spindle from a satchel and attached it to skymouth-hide tethers.

"It's time," Dix said. The fledges hoisted more silk foils onto the spindle's sides. The guard extended it up with the turn of a crank and connected with the array on the arm attached to the Spire. The fledges, with Dix shouting at them, pulled hard at the spindle and set it spinning like a top. Fast. Then faster. The giant array whirled above their heads.

Wind buffeted my ears as the sky screamed open.

Small bugs and birds rained down, hitting the Spire wall and the platform beneath me.

A new set of child-sized wings plummeted from the sky, past the plinth. The second blackwing dove after them and moments later, dropped a freshly sky-plucked and struggling fledge onto the plinth.

The guard shouted, "Flying at night is forbidden, fledge."

Dix lifted another, small, wingless fledge by the arms up and over the plinth's edge. "You are unlucky today. The city can only feed hard workers. You see how easy it is to replace you," she said, her voice loud enough to be heard clearly. The fledge's legs kicked once, twice. Dix let go and the fledge fell, into the dark. I forced myself to stay on the wall, though every muscle jumped

forward when the fledge fell, wanting to go after it. I needed to
stay and watch. My gut ached with the choice.

The plinth groaned against the leash that bound it to the
tower's girth. The blackwing split the evening's silence with a
barking laugh.

Dix spoke again. "Eat."

There was little dissent from the children this time. The
plinth rolled with footfalls. I could hear whispering. "It tastes
bad."

"Just eat it. Who knows when we'll get more."

"I feel sick. I want to go home."

"Shh. They hear you, they'll do more than throw away your
wings."

Silence.

I touched the knife sheathed on my left arm. I couldn't cut
the plinth the way I'd cut the net. Everyone aboard would fall,
and I didn't have any way to catch them.

"I wish we could go back up."

"Won't be long, fledge. This tier's almost tapped out." Dix
again, her voice firm. Down here, she was in charge. But in
charge of what? And the tier was almost tapped of what?

Liquid dripped from the Spire's taps in a soft rhythm—drip
drop, drip drop. Again, the thick smell hit me and disappeared.
I remembered where I'd met that smell before: when Kirit had
revealed the cutaway in the Spire. The heartbone.

Shock made me reel, and I clutched at the wall. *The children
were draining heartbone from the Spire, at Dix's command.*

The Spire wasn't dying. Dix was killing it. Now I knew.

Dix and her cohort endangered all those in the towers: this
was Treason against the city. The greatest of crimes. While the
council above planned a new era, with great advancements,
the city was being fatally weakened from below. And no one
knew.

No, that was wrong; some had to know. Whoever created this, whoever allowed it.

Now everyone needed to know.

I had to speak. To tell the council. The city.

The lanterns on the platform above were extinguished, leaving only moonlight to cut the darkness. An adult spoke in stern tones. "Sleep. Don't roll off the edge. If you do, you'll have to hang there until I come to untie you."

Then silk whispered over battens, a wingset unfurling. Two dark-winged fliers dipped off the plinth and circled to find a gust. I pressed back into the windgate, hiding, hoping my cloak concealed me enough in the darkness and clouds.

Dix passed close by, but still well below me. The Spire's remains hid me well. I saw the tower marks woven, southern-style, in her hair as she swept around the tower's side to begin the climb up through the cloudtop.

A scree of mist obscured the plinth below, and I dropped closer, nearly reaching the end of the rope Beliak had given me. The clouds parted, and the moon brushed the platform, its skymouth husks, and its occupants with silver.

On the plinth below, I made out a shock of brass-colored hair. Moc. Beside him, an arm curled protectively around his shoulders, sat his twin, Ciel.

Though I scanned the platform and the Spire around it, taking in the mechanisms, the fledges, and the guard, my eyes couldn't find what wasn't there. There was no sign of Kirit anywhere.

7

ESCAPE

The platform below me continued its slow circuit while the fledges huddled in half darkness. Beneath their feet, only a thin span of fiber and silk kept them from being lost in the clouds. When I got close enough, I could see the pale creases in Moc's robe where his wingstraps had recently pressed, but the wingset itself was nowhere to be seen. None of the fledges wore wings.

The risk of it took me a moment to comprehend. My own complicity took longer to weigh on me.

Above the clouds, I'd figured the missing Singer fledges for runaways, another council headache. I'd shared my assumptions in reports, and the fledges had been written off. But at least some of those fledges were here. Dix had brought them below the clouds, conscripted them, and taken their wings, while the council and the towers remained unaware. Cold disgust curled in the pit of my stomach. Everyone thought the fledges had run away and were hiding somewhere, because I'd told them so.

Even Ciel, who I'd assumed safe on another tower, had been missing for days. If the city was a family, we'd let some of our youngest charges fall. All of us but Kirit.

Now the fledges I'd called runaways curled on the plinth below me. My hand went to my knife, thinking to cut their tethers. And then what? They couldn't fly. They looked too tired to attempt—wingless—an ascent of the Spire. And if we were caught? We'd all be thrown down.

To leave them here any longer was unthinkable too. Kirit wouldn't leave them. I couldn't either. But Maalik was gone, taking our message to Varu. I could not send for help. I had my knife, my bow, and a handful of pitons. Some rope. No arrows.

No hunter worth their wings would find themselves in a situation like this. No city leader either. I wasn't prepared. But I'd survived worse.

I squared my shoulders, feeling the wingstraps dig in. Pulled my hood low to shadow my face. Began to work my way down the Spire's grips and footholds. I'd bring them back to safety, and then the city would hear what they knew, and what I knew now: that Dix committed Treason.

First, I needed to take care of the guard.

He stood at the plinth edge, a boy several years younger than me. Black wings, wingmark still tied to his left shoulder. Since no one knew what took place here, his main task was to guard the fledges; his gaze was focused on them, not the Spire above.

I'd blended with the Spire's mossy walls on the lee side while I inched closer, my muscles aching from the tight grips and footholds. When I was close enough, I pushed away from the wall and flipped, a perfect arc. I tackled the guard and pushed him into the platform's thick hide. The guard yelled, but I pressed his face to the fabric. He struggled against my weight. Several fledges watched us, but didn't move. I grabbed at the rope I'd carried since the Spire, but I needed more hands to bind the guard. More rope too.

"Help me!" I whistled, trying to get Moc's attention, or Ciel's. Why weren't they moving? Their brassy-haired heads lifted, eyes scanning the darkness. I stuffed the guard's hood into his mouth and put my knee into his back. Gestured urgently at the fledges. "Moc! Ciel!"

So slowly I could almost feel the moon age above us, Moc's eyes focused on me. "Nat." His voice was dull. Ciel left his side and scrambled across the platform. She took the rope from my hands and tightened it around the guard's wrists. The guard groaned and struggled, but I kept him pinned.

"Get his feet too. What's wrong with the others?"

The girl looked exhausted, her hair greasy, her skin nearly gray. "They're not feeding us much," she said. "Just this. I throw mine away, mostly." She held out a square of what looked like rendered goose fat, only thicker and the wrong color. It stank like the Spire had.

Even as the guard struggled against my weight, I tried to comprehend. "They're feeding you heartbone?" I stared into the fledges' dulled eyes. *Was this a drug?* We were worse off than I'd thought—drugged, wingless fledges couldn't possibly attempt a climb, or be much help to me at all. Only Ciel seemed able enough to help.

She bound the guard's feet and released the straps of his wings. I pulled his wingset off, and without it, the bound guard froze, fearful of rolling off the plinth in his struggle.

"Throwing him to the clouds would be faster," Ciel spoke, but she hesitated, unwilling to do it. After seeing Dix throw fledges down, and after falling so far myself—twice now—I knew that would never be my way.

"Ciel, how long do they leave you to sleep?" We had little time to figure out how to escape.

We had rope and nets, two pairs of wings—mine and the guard's—both too big for any of the fledges. And we had a prisoner.

"Ciel, we need to go up. Fast." I shook her gently.

Tears glossed Ciel's eyes. "I figured no one was looking for us. A bunch of Singer fledges."

"How long, Ciel?" The fledge had been through so much. How much could she help in this state? But she straightened and looked up.

"When it gets brighter, they'll be back. We put the buckets on the pulleys then." She pointed to the pulley ropes. "And they go up full, then come back down empty for us to fill again. In the morning, blackwing guards bring food down here, then take bigger sacks away from the gate up there. Those float."

"They float. Like rot gas?"

Ciel nodded and pointed. Above us, the silver outlines of four skymouth husks, filled and floating held the platform aloft. "Like that."

Connections began to light in my mind like oil lamps in the towers. Mining heartbone; sending it higher; gas being removed from an alcove; the Spire dying. Someone was preparing for battle, making rot gas, using the excess for lift. At the moment, who didn't matter, although I knew Dix was involved. "I think I have a way to get us out of here."

I'd thought the fledges were running away. That once the Singers were cut from our culture, the city would be safer. My father's message chip swung from my wrist, its careful carvings deepened with moonlight in the Spire's shadow. He'd seen the truth of things, where I'd leapt to conclusions. I regretted my assumptions and wished Naton could see what I saw now, and help me understand it.

Liras had said we were on *the verge of a new age. New discoveries.* Whatever this gas was, it was new too. And it might be more treasonous and terrible than the old ways. But it was going to get us out of here.

I eyed the tethers that attached the skymouth husks to the platform. Without them, the platform would collapse, the heartbone and the fledges would spill into the clouds. But the metal pulleys that allowed the platform to circuit the Spire without pulling away? Those were a different story.

Ciel saw where I looked. "We tried to loose the platform, but we couldn't get the knots undone."

The only way we were going anywhere was on this platform. If we untethered it from the Spire, it would rise. But we had to rise fast. "Dump everything over the sides you can. The booms, most of the nets." I led the way. The booms struck the side of the Spire and bounced into the darkness. I was about to toss the windbeaters' wings down too, when Ciel touched my arm.

"Wait. We can use those, I think." She rowed the air beside us with one and the platform jerked against its bindings.

"Tether Moc well," I told her while I threw all but one of the buckets over. "All the fledges are too woozy to help." She bound one other fledge to the plinth, and grabbed another set of wind-beaters' wings, handing them to a third fledge who came to help. The two positioned themselves at the back of the plinth as I stepped close to the Spire wall and began untying the cams.

With one tether loose, the platform lifted precariously.

I waved for help. "Hurry, get the other side!"

Ciel dropped her foils fast as the platform lurched and skewed. She and I both tugged at the rope and metal until it snapped away. The platform began to drift up the Spire's side, an edge dragging noisily towards the gate above, and the bone and wire construction beyond.

I should have thought more about how to steer the platform before I cut the tethers. But Ciel already had an idea.

"Help me now!" Ciel held windbeaters' wing battens against the Spire, trying to fend us off the wall. She was too small to make much difference. I grabbed another large wingfoil and pushed too.

We rose, the skymouth husks bobbing overhead. It was still dark. We still had a chance to get away before the black-winged guards came with the fledges' breakfast. When we'd climbed three tiers, we passed the alcove. It was an old Gyre tunnel, the gate stuck open, crusted with bone growth.

Inside, metal gleamed in firelight. A row of pots bubbled over low fires, and above those, gas collected in upended bladders. A young man stumbled to the gate entrance. He moved towards the bone horn hung by the gate, but I leaned far out from the plinth and plucked the horn from its hook. Threw it into the clouds.

Then I grabbed at his robe. My fingers struck a hard surface beneath. Bone armor? He took two steps back and stared at me, at the platform, as we slowly moved past him. His mouth hung open, but he made no sound. His eyes looked like Moc's. Stunned. Drugged.

"That's the artifex," Ciel said, "who takes the heartbone from us and makes the floats."

Above, the bone outcropping loomed. We were going to run right into it. We needed to move. But we had too much drag to push ourselves sideways with only the windbeaters' foils.

"Quick, the guard." Ciel convinced another fledge wobbling in a half-drugged haze to help her shove the bound guard from the plinth down to the tier. He landed with a thump at the artifex's feet.

We began to move faster. Now we had more maneuverability, but less time to get away from the outcropping. Ciel and I pushed hard on the wings until we rowed ourselves downwind of the hazard. Ciel sat back on the platform, relieved, but I felt the danger more now.

Floating this way, we moved higher without having to circle on the wind or rely on a gust. But morning was coming. Soon Dix or her guards would return and find us creeping up the Spire on her stolen platform. We needed horizontal momentum too.

I shook the nearest fledges, pointed. "Best if we could go straight across the gap between the towers, to Bissel." Across the open sky. "We have to row really hard. All together."

"I have a better idea," Ciel said. "But you're not going to like it." She handed me a rope that had been used to weave netting.

I held the spidersilk tether in my hands. So much stronger than the ropes Kirit and I had used in the Gyre a day before. Was it only a day? Two?

"You want me to pull the platform, on the wing?"

She smiled, relieved I understood, that I was taking her seriously. "Yes. And we'll all row." Behind her, Moc giggled, half drugged still. I was already tying the tether around my waist.

"It's going to be unsteady." In the best of all worlds, that was all it would be. Worst possibility, the platform would drag too much, I would lose my glide, fall, and pull a section of the plinth down with me, dumping the drugged fledges into the air.

"If you don't, they'll catch us," she said. "Come on." She pushed two fledges towards the extra windbeaters' wings, then picked up her wing again. It was easily twice her size. Moc, seeing what she was doing, wrapped his hands around the frame too. He helped her lift the foils, still caught in the stupor of the heartbone-rendering Dix had given them to eat.

"Flap," Ciel said, her voice barely above a whisper. Then again. The fledges began to fan the air with the wings, in time with her voice. "Flap." The platform edged away from the Spire agonizingly slowly. It would be light soon.

Don't let me fall and kill us all, I whispered to the wind, to myself.

I tied myself to the forward husk, letting the tether line play out across the platform until it was twice my body-length long. Was that enough lead? It would have to be. Behind me, Moc watched, dully. "If I fall, you untie this line." I pointed to the knot I'd tied.

Moc nodded. He understood. I hoped he'd move fast enough.

"Hold on, everyone," I said, then ran the platform's length, the fabric sinking beneath my feet, and leapt into the air, aiming for Bissel.

A breeze caught my wings and filled them. I lifted and felt the tether play out, then, for a moment, pull taut. It worked! I towed the platform behind me for a moment, until it wallowed and tugged me back. My wings guttered. I was falling. I struggled to stay aloft.

Another gust filled my wings and I rose slightly. Looking below my wings, I saw the wide spans of the windbeater foils pulling hard at the air on each side of the plinth, in time with a whispered beat.

Slowly, our platform lurched across the sky.

8

BISSEL

We reached Bissel, barely.

By rowing the predawn air with the windbeaters' foils, Ciel and the other fledge managed to lessen the platform's drag. Meantime, I flew until I felt the rig rising to my glide level, then I turned and landed on the platform, careful not to tangle the tether. I ran and leapt again, launching myself back into the air. The platform pushed back with my launch, but the fledges rowed hard against it. Leap, drag, soar, return: we moved forward like that through the clouds until ledges appeared, wide enough for us to stand on. I aimed us towards them as best I could.

A strong breeze carried me close to the tower and a stronger gust pushed me high. My wings and head broke the cloudtop. For a few glorious moments, I could see the city in the dawn light. I wanted to stay there, to breathe the cold, drier air, but I scrambled to spill air from my wings. Shouts behind me: the platform was tilting with my sudden rise.

Close to the clouds, an oil lamp hung from the lowest tier. I let myself rise on the gust, slowly, and I aimed for it. A balcony appeared near the clouds. Barely habitable. But I landed there, rolling to a stop on my belly.

Once I furled my wings and could look behind me, I rubbed my eyes. The platform was nowhere to be seen, though the tether still tugged at my waist. I shivered, chilled.

The husks, which should have been well above the cloudline by now, were gone. I yanked hard and reeled in the line, feeling the resistance.

The line ended in the fabric plinth, and small hands grabbed mine.

I pulled and dragged until Moc was on the tier, then two more fledges. The bucket of heartbone. The windbeaters' foils. And finally, Ciel.

They turned and stared at where the platform should be. Ciel whispered, "Where did it go?"

We could see the platform's leading edge at eye level, but not the supporting skymouth husks. Like live skymouths, these disappeared in sunlight too.

"Quick, tie it down," I said, seeing before the others that the wind was pulling the platform away.

"It's rising," Ciel said.

"Let it go," Moc said. "Let it float away." He looked out over the sky. "It's bad."

It might be bad, but it was also evidence. I struggled to tie the line to the tier, but the usual bone cleats were worn away.

Above us, the tiers gradually looked deeper and less overgrown by bone core. We weren't far from the occupied tiers. A rope dangled nearby.

"Can you climb?" I asked the twins. Both indicated they could. I let them go first, then pulled myself and the platform, bobbing beyond the tier, up after them.

"Find any tier with people. Ask for shelter."

I hoped we'd find friendly hosts. Or at least no one hostile.

The platform dragged at my shoulder. I couldn't keep my grip on the rope. The plinth was too big; it was pulling away from the tower and would take me with it.

It was more important to get help for Kirit, find the fledges a place to shelter, and inform the council.

Reluctantly, I cut the line around my waist and let the plat-form float free. Soon I could no longer see it in the clouds.

We had much to tell the council, but little proof, besides the bucket and the word of four fledges. We needed allies. Doran? He'd had little interest in the Spire's state. Worse, he could know about Dix's project. Ezarit? Maybe. Although she did not control the council guards.

Both of them together, if Doran wasn't involved? That would be formidable. If I could finesse it.

Truth was, a newly elected junior councilor and apprentice getting two of the most powerful council leaders to agree on this issue was going to be as hard as flying into the wind. But I'd find a way. And then I could go home and tell my family what I'd seen.

The rope stopped shaking above me, and I hauled myself up the knotted fiber until I reached the tier where two fledges stood staring. The twins clung to a Lawsmarker-draped Singer, held tight in his Lawsmarker-bound arms.

We'd found the tier where Singers quartered. It was as low on the tower as the one Kirit stayed in on Grigrit, but not in the Spire's shadow. Sunlight crested the cloudtop and lent a soft glow to the mist still clinging to the tier's spare furnishings. The people inside.

I took in the length of the Singer at the balcony's edge. Stand-ing straight and tall beneath his cloak of Laws. More weight covered him than had the elder Singer on Grigrit, but he did not bend. Wik. He stared at Ciel and Moc with a worried look in his green eyes, the dark shadows below them purple in the brightening light. Behind him, a guard in a green cloak held a basket.

A weight gripped my left shoulder. Small talons. A beak at my earlobe. Maalik. Here?

Confused, I turned to take in the rest of the tier. Beliak

waited inside the balcony. He clapped my right shoulder tight. Held on, and clasped my left hand too. He smiled, his gap-toothed grin shy and relieved, but his deep brown eyes filled with concern.

"Maalik found us at Densira. I went to meet you at the council plinth. But you didn't arrive. You missed council. You never miss council! We sent birds to the towers you'd named, and this was the first place you were missing." Smart. Kirit had told Ezarit she planned to visit Wik. So Ezarit must know. Others too. "We've been searching. Were about to set out again, at first light."

"Ceetcee worried?"

"Won't be when she gets your message."

He handed me a blank bone chip on a blue silk cord, and I scratched the mark for "safe." Then added my sigil, and Beliak's. While I worked, a small figure rose from beside the cook fire. Tea-colored robes. A sparkle of glass beads at the hems, and in her dark braids. *Clouds.* Ezarit. Here.

"Where is my daughter?" she demanded. "What happened? What did you do?"

Beliak had not released my shoulder. "We thought you were cloudfood. You've been gone a whole day. We had to tell her."

"Kirit was entrusted to your care." Ezarit laid each word, distinct, heavy, on my head. I couldn't look away from her. Couldn't answer. Beliak took the message chip from my fingers, tied it to Maalik's leg, and whispered, "Home," to the whipperling. Released Maalik to the sky. But he didn't step between me and Ezarit.

"We were trapped in the clouds," I croaked, wishing for water. "We found—" All that we'd found piled into my dry mouth and stuck there. Between my fingers, my father's message chip snapped in two. *Entrusted to my care.*

We'd found much in the clouds: Treason, the fledges, why

the Spire was dying. I gripped the chip halves tightly, feeling their split edges press my palm. But what we'd lost—*No, don't think that. Nothing is truly lost until we let it go.* I cleared my throat. "We'll find Kirit. We'll recover what the city needs, rather than allowing it to disappear."

9

SKYTOUCHED

"Eat," Wik's guard said, pushing graincakes into the fledges' hands. "We'll find Kirit. We'll make a search plan." Although her name didn't come to mind just then, the guard's smile was familiar from Mondarath's post-wingfight celebrations; her brusque orders something I'd heard at wingtest and while fighting alongside her at Spirefall. Her guard-short haircut was new—softly curling dark hair pulled back in a cap—and her usually brassish-red skin was wind-chapped bright pink from many days patrolling the sky. She'd stuck a metal loop through her left earlobe.

Ezarit caught my quizzical look. "I asked Aliati to guard Wik, given everything that's been happening, and because he was kind to Kirit when she was ill. You should feel comfortable speaking before her." A senior councilor's prerogative, and a kindness, but Ezarit's words hinted that there was someone she didn't feel comfortable speaking around.

The fledges told Aliati and Ezarit, Beliak and Wik about the fall, the net. The Spire. They described falling from the sky with increasing panic, the shock of their experience wearing them thin.

Aliati handed me a graincake. "You'll all feel better once you've eaten. Then you can tell us everything."

"We are telling everything. Stop coddling me." Aliati might be Wik's guard on this tier, but she didn't know everything. I felt more agitated as Beliak's words struck home. *You missed council. You never miss council!* And *we were about to set out again, at first light.* They'd been looking for us.

That's what the city was supposed to do: take care of its people. Beliak helped me shrug from my wings. Took my damp cloak and wrapped me in his. I began to shake in the warmth.

At Wik's feet lay a silk game board, dyed like the one Doran had showed us. "They call that Justice at Grigrit," Moc said.

"Different names all over," Aliati said. "Same game. On Bissel, they call it Balance."

She pulled a handful of tower marks from her pocket and dropped them on the square. "I don't play, but the board is a useful map." The marks clicked softly as they landed and knocked together. "Ciel flew from Grigrit to see the council, right? You were headed to Bissel. The way the winds have been lately, your most likely routes were here and here." She placed two markers and used message cords to connect them to Grigrit.

She turned to each fledge in turn and asked them where they'd been going. Eked the information out of them, through their panic. Each time a child named a flight path, Aliati placed a piece of silk cord between tower markers. She let me help. I could work and gather my thoughts at the same time.

The area on the map between Bissel, Naza, Harut, and Grigrit in the southwest grew congested with markers and silk, the Spire at the center.

Aliati withdrew a metal tool from her robe, round at the top, straight at the bottom. I'd never seen anything like it before. With one finger on a ghost-thin mark in the metal, Aliati placed the straight edge by Bissel's marker. She stuck her tongue out, thinking, as she turned the metal on the silk square. "This is a guess, but I've been measuring my dive angles for wingfights lately. Found I can judge where I'll end up pretty well. You said you dropped twenty tiers?"

"Close to. Where did you get that metal?" Mondarath wouldn't have much like it, nor Bissel.

"Had it since I was young. Found it a couple of Allsuns before the wingtest, before I moved to Mondarath." She sounded as if she'd answered that question a lot. Then she refocused on the map. "We'd planned to search for you here." She touched the marker nearest Grigrit with her finger. "But we'll search closer to Bissel now for Kirit."

She stood, brushing dust from her robes. Lifted her wingstraps to her shoulders.

"Who will go with you?" Ezarit said.

"I'll go alone. I'll tether to Bissel. I won't get lost." The confidence with which she spoke implied she'd done so before. "We can send for more guards once the sun is up."

"Wait," I said. "There's more you need to know."

Secrets and horrors piled up, all trying to emerge first from my mouth. The windbeaters' foils and the reversed wind. The alcove with the fires and boiling heartbone. The drug that wasn't muzz. The voices in the clouds and the skymouth husks. I didn't want to sound skytouched. I wanted them to believe me. To act.

In council, Doran would appeal to what they understood first and build consensus, so I tried that. "Things are happening in the southwest. Unrest, anger. The wind disappearing." Beliak and Aliati exchanged worried looks. I pressed on. "Even little things. Grigrit has little food for its Singers. While here?" I gestured at a basket near the fledges.

Towers in the city varied in height and trappings according to many factors, but the lowest tiers in each tower were all similar in their poverties. The cold, narrow tiers were nearest the clouds' dangers and subject to all manner of abuse—intentional and not—from above. But this tier looked clean and dry. A cook fire was banked near the core and the sleeping partition blocked the worst of the winds.

Aliati followed my eyes. "It's not Mondarath, but Bissel has decent supplies, and is generous with them." She frowned. "Grigrit? Doran's already decided that the Singers must appease the city. Why bother feeding them?"

She was right. I'd wanted Doran's guidance to learn how to work with city council politics, but even I'd noticed he'd taken a course of action on the Singers well before the vote. I'd seen and chosen not to understand. Now I twisted the silk cord still on my wrist tight, angry with myself for being so obtuse.

I drank more water. Aliati let me have my fill, then handed me another graincake. I held on to it and wet my lips with my tongue. "Worse, Dix, possibly others, are using the wind—or lack of it—to pull fledges from the sky. To make them work in the clouds."

"Could that be a natural phenomenon?" Aliati frowned. "Some kind of wind shadow?"

"A fledge-dream. A bone-dust nightmare. You'd been sifting Spire rubble the day before." Beliak looked from the graincake to Aliati as if wanting her to say, "Eat," again.

"Not all of us at once." I was angry no one would take our word. Beliak was trying to look supportive, nodding when I spoke, but confusion shadowed his gaze, and worry too, as if he was wondering whether I'd gone skytouched, and what that meant for him and for Ceetcee.

If it was this hard to convince him, Aliati, and Ezarit, it would be impossible to convince the council.

"You could have hit your heads on something," Aliati said. "There's plenty down there that's dangerous."

"That doesn't explain why they fell, though," Beliak said. I swallowed a bite of graincake. As I chewed, I rolled what Aliati said over in my mind.

"You've been below the clouds?"

She nodded.

The connection lit up. The metal tool. Her ease with going alone beneath the clouds. *I'll tether to Bissel. I won't get lost,* she'd said.

"You're a scavenger?"

Aliati regarded me, unflinching. "Was. Yes. It was a way to stay alive, before I lived at Mondarath, before I became a guard here."

I couldn't abide scavengers. But I'd flown with Aliati. I'd cheered her team during wingfights. The council had made her a guard. I struggled to match this new information to what I knew about her. Decided I could tolerate it, for now, if she'd listen to me, believe me.

Ciel brought me the bucket from the platform. The smell proceeded her.

"What is that?" Beliak asked.

Wik stood, ashen-faced, his tattoos nearly pulsing at his temples. "Heartbone. Where did you get it?"

We told them. The more we described, the less they understood. But we had their attention now. Wik seemed to believe us. Ezarit too.

"Where is this platform now? You're sure it was supported by skymouth husks?" Ezarit paced, sounding concerned. When we told her we'd had to let it go in order to climb to the tier, she frowned. "Where was the tapping happening?"

"How far downtower are we?" I still didn't have my bearings, beyond knowing I was on Bissel.

"Lowest tier, sixteen down. Northwest," said Wik.

"The wind disappeared," Moc said slowly. "Not like a wind shadow. Worse. Like a downdraft in the Gyre. I fell twenty tiers. More." His voice was filled with disbelief—he was coming out of his stupor, but he hadn't been aware enough to remember the mechanism above the plinth.

His twin came to help him, chin high, ready to argue with

adults if she had to. "There's an artifex down there, at least one. They made a whirlwind." She spread her hands wide and spun them in the air.

Aliati shook her head. "That's not possible."

Wik agreed. "Downdrafts require windbeaters and height and windgates, like in the Spire. Nothing that can create one in the open sky."

Moc bristled. "It's true." He pointed at the wingfoils we'd managed to salvage from the platform. "It happened."

"Not even Singers could stop the wind," Wik continued. A dark cloud crossed his face. "But . . ." He tilted his head, tired. Worried. "It might be nothing. Before Spirefall, towers were beginning to seek ways to direct vents as Singers did. Looking to speed gliding between towers. They'd asked the Spire for help, for a windbeater or two, but hadn't received any."

Aliati stared at the map. "Channeling wind is easier than making it disappear."

"I saw what they used. I didn't understand how it worked, but I saw it. Like windbeaters' wings, but on a spindle. They made the fledges turn it."

Ciel backed me up. "This is what happened."

"Can you draw it?" Beliak held out a bone tablet and a piece of charcoal, but Ciel knelt in the dust instead. She drew the mechanism. "They used it to get more fledges. Pulled them right from the sky. Like they knew where we were."

Like they knew when they'd be flying past.

"Nat?" Ezarit stared at me like a hawk. I'd made a noise in surprise.

"Doran had asked Kirit when we'd be leaving Grigrit, and where we were headed. We were bringing the codex—"

I stopped. The codex. My hands went to the satchel I'd carried through the clouds. It was light. The flap was loose. No. Not like the arrows. I said a windprayer and opened the bag.

One bone page and several cracked pieces remained where once there were four hard-won codex pages.

My mouth tasted sour as I lifted the remaining page from the satchel. It weighed what a large gosling would, and was as awkward to hold. The left side was drilled for a binding. Marks scored both sides, carefully carved in Singer script.

Wik whispered, "Conclave." He peered into Kirit's satchel, searching for more. Tugged a brass plate loose from the lining. His finger tapped the metal but didn't pull it from Kirit's bag. "Where are the rest? Where did you find this?" He whispered so low I suspected that Aliati couldn't hear. But I could, and Moc. Ciel too.

"In the Spire."

He closed the satchel tightly. "Singer lore only hints about metal plates, brought up from below, stolen by thieves. Dangerous myths. Best not to show those to anyone right now." He meant before the vote.

More Singer secrets. This time, one I was carrying. "I don't like secrets, Wik."

He looked at me, green eyes set deep above his hawk nose. "Sometimes secrets are dangerous. Sometimes they keep people from harming one another."

Ezarit lifted the Conclave page from my hands and flipped it over. The other side held transactions with nearby towers. "I can't read much of this, but I see the time line."

She could trace back Conclaves. The two before Spirefall. Then a long stretch of peace with one Conclave. Before that, a large one, with many marks. Her finger rested there. Below her finger lay a mark for my father. Even now, so many years later, I felt fear, anger. This codex page would not be the balm Kirit had hoped for with the council. Instead, it would fuel Doran's drive for our own Conclave.

"We have to find another way to stop the vote," I said. Looking up, I realized Ezarit might or might not know I'd been involved, but she would soon. "The vote for appeasing the city."

She stared at me. "That vote happened yesterday. It passed."

You missed council. You never miss council!

"Birds went out this morning," Beliak said. "The towers are split. The city's been rumbling for days." He frowned. "This is what you were advocating for, not too long ago." He said it gently, though we hadn't talked about it ever at home. I'd obeyed Doran and kept my mouth shut. Not now, though.

"I was wrong." We were, all of us, wrong.

Beliak let out a deep breath. "Much of the northwest is protesting. Sending messages. Organizing." He looked about to say more, but stopped. Focused on Ciel's dust-drawing again.

"Why didn't you say something earlier?" I asked.

Beliak didn't look up from the drawing. "Why didn't you?"

I groaned. "I'll fix this." This was my doing, and Doran's. We'd convinced the south and the east to vote for Doran's proposal. "I'd hoped to tell the council what I'd learned from Kirit. To talk about how the Singers and fledges are faring now and how they've been punished enough, especially the ones who weren't Singer leaders. I should have listened more, earlier." How they were blamed for things they didn't do. Now what? Would a protest make a difference?

"You're not the only one, Nat," Ezarit agreed. "Good people were swayed. I'd hoped Kirit would—that the codex would . . ." Her words trailed off. "But it may be too late now."

It couldn't be too late. "The city has enormous problems, and a Conclave isn't going to solve most of them. Won't Doran, of all people, understand that?"

"You're Doran's apprentice, you know how determined he is," Ezarit began. "I couldn't take you on myself, and you needed a strong guide." Her words made sense, somewhat. The *couldn't* still burned.

"Couldn't or wouldn't?" The words left my lips before I'd thought through their impact.

Ezarit winced. "It was politics, taking on Hiroli. A favor to Doran for keeping Kirit's seat open. But I should have watched more carefully."

I nodded. That made some sense.

She continued, "Doran's vision for the future is powerful. But, Nat, you must understand, he can get caught up by his goals and lose sight of what's important. He's easily tripped up by his need for loyalty. I'd hoped you might help moderate him at some point, once you learned enough. Instead, we've been working at cross purposes for some time."

"Doran's good at maneuvering around dissent." And instead of moderating him, I'd helped him maneuver. "Why didn't you tell me?" But how could she have, without undermining a fellow councilor? Doran hadn't been entirely wrong that action was necessary. "Your patience, your compromises won't fix things quickly enough either. Not with the riots above the clouds; not with what is happening to the Spire below."

She tapped her lips with a finger, thinking about what I'd said. "Maybe not. But I wanted to try, to give the city a chance to heal. The whole city. Kirit taught me that."

Kirit. Her name kicked the wind from my chest. They were searching for her, I knew, but it didn't matter. I'd lost her. "On the net, after we fell, she fought her way free and was gone. I didn't go after her." Gone, into the clouds, with a bad leg and a torn wing. On my watch.

She wasn't dead. She couldn't be.

"She'd risk a fall in order to fight, yes." Ezarit stared out at the clouds, her face unreadable. The balcony was quieter now that the fledges had lain down to sleep. "You'll understand soon. There's nothing you won't do to protect your own." She spoke to me and to Beliak now. "At his best, Doran's that way too."

She chewed her words, thinking her ideas through before she spoke. "I regret what I said to you when you landed."

"I'm sorry for not telling you about the vote." A secret of my own. I'd kept things from Kirit too. I was not so much better than the Singers. And Ezarit—knowing now that she'd had plans for me, but had been waiting to tell me—that was the hardest secret of all. All for politics. Had it been worth it? What had we lost?

Ezarit frowned, speaking to everyone now. "It's the secrecy that causes so many problems. Lining up game pieces—and allies—to win a vote or a point. We can't move forward with a future bartered on secrets. And we cannot erase our past. We might as well ban singing."

"Doran considered that." The surprise on her face caught me off guard. "He decided it would be a ridiculous gesture," I added. "We need the songs. All of them—even the lost ones."

Wik, Aliati, and Beliak had stopped looking at the map to listen. Several fledges watched from the sleeping mats. Ezarit stepped back and included everyone in the tier when she spoke next.

"The Singers did many wrong things." She looked at Wik, who nodded once. "But they kept the towers safe. They knew we lived on the knife's edge here. Now we know it too. And there are different ideas for how to proceed. Different is not bad; it just takes longer."

Her words were conciliatory. Doran's had never been so. "I thought Doran a good mentor. A good leader. I wanted to do as he asked." I couldn't raise my eyes from my hands. I twisted the silk message cord into tighter knots.

"Councilor Densira," Ezarit said with so much grace in her voice my breath caught, listening, "you were doing your duty for the council. I understand that you did your best in extraordinary circumstances."

I looked at her then. My mother's best friend. My second mother, if I was honest with myself. They'd made a family out of pieces left by tragedy. I'd hero-worshipped her from infancy, even as I fought with Kirit. I'd been jealous that she hadn't chosen me to mentor. But she'd spoken words of understanding, while her daughter was missing and I wasn't. This was leadership too. Grace in times of great pain. Attempts at compromise, when I suspected anger and fear for her family rippled beneath her breast. I hadn't understood that you could feel both at the same time, not until recently.

Ezarit had always seemed as if she knew her path, and Kirit's, a long rise, straight up. That path hadn't seemed to include me, nor Elna, and I'd longed for that kind of direction. But families didn't always work the way they looked, and they were complicated. Ezarit was family too, and Kirit. I'd not forgotten, but I'd been blinded to it by the turmoil in the city. By what I'd wanted for myself.

My family now was a complex construct, a web of sinew and bone, bridges and chasms. The missing were as important as those who had always been there, and those whom I'd grown close to over the past few Allmoons. We might rise, but we could also fall. Same as any family. Someone threatened family of mine? I'd take them down as far as they could go.

Ezarit spoke again, this time to everyone still awake in the tier. "The council is souring. The towers are close to turning on one another. We cannot lead the city the way we need to. We need to stop leading out of fear and anger." She meant the vote. She meant me. "But we do need decisive action. On that point, Doran is correct, and I am prepared to act also."

Was she advocating for Conclave? I must have looked shocked.

"We can never undo a Conclave," Wik said, speaking my thoughts. The fledges watched Ezarit intently.

"I don't want a Conclave," she said. "I want the city to come together, and a Conclave provides only a false resolution. There are too many disturbances. The riots show there are many wounds left unhealed from Spirefall. We must address that directly."

"But first," Aliati said, "we need to stop the Conclave." She touched Ezarit's shoulder. "Get everyone looking for Kirit. Singers too. We'll find her."

Ezarit's shoulders sagged.

"The protest tomorrow at the council plinth," Beliak said. "I don't think it will stop the Conclave, but some are hoping to try." He looked guiltily at me, as if he'd kept a secret, or planned to join them. Then he said, "Ceetcee and Elna among them."

The thought of Doran shouting at my family for interfering brought me to my feet. "They can't. Elna's too ill. Ceetcee could get hurt."

"Elna's frail, and skyblind," Ezarit said. "But she wants to speak, and we should hear her. She's taught me much over the years, and she's stronger than you know. Ceetcee too."

She was right, and I knew it.

Ezarit pointed to the bucket of heartbone and the fledges. "If we combine strategies, Nat, and add your proof of what's happening beneath the clouds, we could stop this. We have to try."

❧ ❧ ❧

A kavik and a whipperling landed one after another on the balcony and chattered at us. Sunlight laid rainbows on the kavik's deep black wings and mottled the whipperling. The bone chips at their ankles dragged on the tier floor.

Aliati bent to release the yellow silk cord from the whipperling's claw. "Hiroli is bringing wings for the fledges," she said, nodding at Ezarit. "Your apprentice is resourceful." She lifted the next message chips from the kavik. The red cord dangled from her fingers as she groaned in alarm. "Guards are coming for the Singers. Soon."

"Already?" Ezarit's face fell. "They didn't want to wait and risk more dissent."

In the past, when Singers called for a Conclave, there had been little warning, and less resistance.

Beliak scratched a message on the chip's flat side. "I'll let Ceetcee and the protesters know." He began to tie the message to the kavik's leg.

"Use the whipperling," Ezarit said. "Kaviks have been unreliable lately." Her brow wrinkled. She was thinking hard. "I need to return to council. Let them know you have been found. Try—" She paused. Pressed her lips together. "When Hiroli brings the wings, you must hurry."

The fledges gathered around her, but didn't press. They watched her tighten her wingstraps. Within the furled silk, we could see the beak of the tea-dyed kestrel that marked her wings. Not a whipperling leader, after all.

She hugged Beliak and me. Pressed Wik's tattooed hand between hers, and then put her arm around Ciel. "It will be all right. You'll see."

Then she turned from us and unfurled her wings. Leapt from the balcony and swept a strong gust around Bissel, north and east towards the council plinth.

When she was gone, the tier seemed smaller. Emptier. Wik and Beliak spoke softly to the fledges and looked at the map.

Aliati nudged me. "Let me see the plate that Wik found in your satchel," Aliati said. "The one he doesn't want anyone to see."

"I thought you were going to look for Kirit."

"I am. As soon as Hiroli arrives with the fledges' wings and the guards come for Wik."

I hoped Hiroli would hurry. That the guards would be slow.

Opening the satchel, I pushed the codex page back to reveal the brass plate. Tilted it to the sunlight so that Aliati could see.

Across the tier, Wik rose from where he and Beliak studied the search map and started to protest. But then he quieted and knelt again, the Lawsmarkers rattling his shoulders. Beliak came over to us.

"I can't read these symbols," Aliati complained. "There are a few scavenger marks. This one says 'trade' but not what for."

"I can't read any of it," I said. "Wik said to keep it hidden."

Aliati frowned. "Do you think that's a good idea? Singer secrets. We could tell Ezarit, tomorrow."

I nodded. I couldn't imagine what tomorrow would be like, if Conclave happened. What had I done? A lifetime ago. I wished I could go back and fix it all. That Kirit were here. She could stop them.

But they had me instead. And four fledges. We would have to stop the Conclave with the truth. No more secrets.

Three guards landed first. Two wearing hunter blue wings, with a net. One blackwing. The blackwing pulled a small bladder of muzz from his belt. Carried it to Wik.

"*You* drink that," Wik said.

The blackwing held up his free hand, as if to strike the Singer.

"Leave it," the first hunter said. "His choice." They hauled Wik to his feet, scattering the map of flight paths.

"Let him go! Let him fly on his own!" Moc rushed the guards and tried to pry their fingers from his uncle's arms. His face was fierce, but his eyes swam with tears.

The second hunter lifted Moc off his feet. "You're that Singer fledge?" Moc's Lawsmarkers rattled at his wrists. "Danger to tower?"

"Bring him too," the blackwing said.

"No!" Beliak and I moved to pull Moc away, while Ciel and

Aliati yelled at the guards, calling them monsters, skytouched. Worse than Singers. Fledges dragged at guards' robes, their wings. Beliak landed a punch and was pushed to the ground.

"I'm a councilor!" I shouted. "Stop this." But the guards bound Moc's wrists and ankles with spidersilk. They tied Wik too. Made him climb into the net that all three guards dragged to the edge.

We shouted more, but the guards held us off. Even me. A councilor.

The blue-winged hunters leapt in tandem, pulling the net from the ledge behind them, and circling up, working the gusts hard until they flew level with the tier again. The blackwing attached Moc to a bone hook and strong-armed the struggling boy off the ledge with him.

Without another word, they were gone. Flying towards the council platform.

"I'll follow them," Beliak said. We raced to tighten his wing-straps. He met and held my eyes. "You're back. You'll stay? No more clouds?" He didn't look worried that I was skytouched any longer. Instead, he looked worried that I'd disappear.

"No more clouds," I said. Until I led the council to investigate Dix's Treason, I could keep that promise. He gripped my arm, tight, then turned to the sky.

Time slowed as Beliak unfurled his wings and leapt from the tier. By the time he'd found a strong gust, the guards and their burdens were already black specks on the far horizon, disappearing fast.

10

THE COUNCIL

By the time Hiroli arrived from the southeast with five pairs of fledge wings strapped to her chest, the six of us who remained at Bissel stood arrayed on the tier, staring out.

"Where's Ezarit?" Hiroli asked. "I have messages for her."

"Council plinth," Aliati said. "Urgent business." She'd been gathering the map and markers from the tier floor. Now she straightened and, with the air of someone who'd rarely done it but knew what was proper, bowed to the junior councilwoman. "You are welcome here, Risen."

Hiroli blushed, then untied the wingsets. She counted fledge heads. "I thought you said . . ."

Ciel stared at her, cheeks streaked with spent tears. "Give me a pair, quick."

With a confused laugh, Hiroli handed the girl a wingset. "We'll all go together," she cautioned, as Ciel fumbled with the straps. We quickly told Hiroli what had happened.

When she'd finished, Ciel took the remaining wingset and tied it to her chest. "For Moc." Her eyes defied anyone to challenge her.

Good for her. The girl seemed quiet, compared to her brother. But *only* compared to her brother.

I sealed the bucket of heartbone in a pannier and shouldered Kirit's satchel. The remaining codex page and the strange metal plate clacked together as they settled against my side.

Aliati lifted the windbeater wings from the balcony and laid them against the central core wall. Readying for a quick departure. Angrily.

Hiroli bowed to me. "Fly well, Councilor."

"On your wings, Councilor," I replied. How had she voted? She'd been a refusal in my count, but Councilor Vant had said he'd talk to her too. I hoped she'd voted against the Conclave, but I could not bear to ask.

If I manage to remain on the council, I promised the wind, *I'll seek more opinions than just my mentor's. I'll look beyond the council, to the towers as well.* A lesson hard learned. I hoped it had been in time.

All the fledges finally had their wings on. Aliati looped a long coil of spidersilk tether over her shoulder and doused the oil lamp. The sun was high above the clouds now, and it was time to go.

Aliati descended the rope with a wave. "Will let you know what I find." She ignored Hiroli's raised eyebrows. The codex pages were lost to the clouds, probably, but I hoped she'd find Kirit.

"I dropped something down below," I said. "When I found the fledges."

That was an understatement. And a truth.

"She doesn't want to help protest the vote?" Hiroli asked. Now I knew how she'd voted.

"She's needed elsewhere." I pulled the fledges to the tier edge, where Ciel waited, impatient and frowning.

Ciel and I leapt first, circling to wait for the fledges and Hiroli. When I saw Ciel preparing to glide off on her own, I whistled for a chevron formation. She joined us, flying with angry, jerky motions, but we flew together. Hiroli took point, I flew to the west, and the three fledges arrayed between us, with Ciel leading.

\ \ \

The council plinth hung suspended between Varu, Naza, and Narath towers. The woven fiber platform was decorated with tower sigils and oil-polished. Green and blue silk banners strung from the tethers curled and uncurled in the breeze. As if for a celebration. Or a wingfight.

Hiroli flew to the right of our formation, her wings bouncing the sunlight off the dark silk, each batten and seam taut enough to shine. As we neared the platform, Hiroli adjusted the curve of her wings and slowed. Let the fledges land before she did and scurry out of the way.

They gathered, pale wings, ragged, gray robes, in a knot as close to Wik and Moc as they could. Ten Singers and one fledge were assembled in the plinth's center, surrounded by blackwing guards. I spotted silver-streaked hair and knew they had Viridi, Rumul's second in command. She'd been one of the Singers who'd judged my wingtest, nearly three Allmoons ago. The white in her hair was more dominant now. Wik clasped her hand in his.

None of the assembled Singers wore wings. Not even Moc.

Beliak fought to keep the fledges from getting too close to the guards.

I curved my fingers around my wing grips, preparing to land. My wings responded beautifully, my descent slow and graceful. Like an established councilor, someone who should be heard. Except I knew the truth: I was such a fledge at politics, I'd only caused damage so far. What if I made things worse now?

By the time my feet touched the plinth, several councilors watched me with unfathomable expressions, including Ezarit. How would I fare, when facing my mentor? I furled my wings quickly.

Hiroli scanned the crowd as she approached us. "I don't see Doran yet. Nor any of his party."

Meantime, the entire city seemed to be assembling around the plinth. Citizens from all the towers mixed on balconies and tiers. Guards in hunter blue and others wearing many colors flew back and forth, preparing to repeat what was said on the plinth, even though the council had not officially convened.

Aside from the knot of Singer fledges staring at the impassive blackwing guards and the Singer leaders arrayed behind them, towers and plinth had a festival air, like Allmoons wing-fights, with people arrayed to watch, as if in sport. The horror of this made my limbs feel heavy. Ezarit's face was equally grim.

More senior council members landed, including those from Grigrit. From their groupings, I guessed at alliances. Macal, from Mondarath, with a councilor from Wirra; both greeted Ezarit warmly.

Doran Grigrit approached with Vant Densira, my senior tower-man, and a councilwoman wearing tower marks from Laria, one of the silkspinner towers in the southeast. They furled their wings and arranged their robes, looking between the groups. Looking for me.

I did not budge from my place beside Ezarit.

Hiroli Naza walked ahead of us, chin up, proud to be accompanying Ezarit in dissent. Tolerating me.

But the size of the group around Doran kept growing.

Ezarit cleared her throat, preparing to call the council to order. Doran lifted his right hand, and four blackwings sounded klaxon horns on each of the towers.

"What do you mean by this?" Ezarit asked. The other council leaders present swirled, cautious.

"My apologies, Councilor, I did not see you there," Doran said, bowing. "With such a large audience assembled, I thought it best to signal."

Ezarit inclined her head, an almost-bow. "A good idea." Then her jawline firmed, and she matched Doran's gaze. "Although I meant assembling Conclave so quickly, and without full lead council approval." No one missed the tenor of her words.

Doran bowed again, this time to me. "We had a majority. You were unavailable. Once the decision was made, it was felt that the faster we address this, the faster the city can begin to heal." His voice sounded sad, but strong. The guards in the air relayed his thoughts to the crowd.

"There are council members with new information," Ezarit challenged him, her voice even. "In the interest of fairness, we should give them a chance to speak."

Scattered applause came from the towers as her words were relayed, but more dissatisfied sounds—boos and shouts—drowned it out. Doran, preparing to speak again, gestured towards Naza, the loudest tower, and shrugged, as if to say *this is what the people want*.

I readied myself to step forward anyway, but even as I did, a crowd of fliers began to circle the plinth. Twenty in all, they carried nets between them. I recognized faces from nearby towers. Some guards. Artifexes. Sidra, Macal's partner and Vant's daughter. My own Ceetcee, carrying another below her. *No.*

"You must all sit at the towers," Vant shouted to the fliers.

"We will not," Ceetcee shouted, and landed, gently depositing the person she carried onto the plinth. Elna. "We are here to speak for the cloudbound, if no one else will."

The blackwings turned their focus on my mother, but did not move. I reached for my quiver by reflex. Found it still empty. Ceetcee stared at me, then shook her head. "And we will be heard."

She reached down and helped Elna stand. I heard my mother cough weakly and begin to speak. My anger slowly bled away, and pride took its place. They were speaking where I had not.

"Before you do this, take heart," Elna said, her words almost too soft for the guards to pick up. But Ceetcee repeated them loud enough. They were carried to the towers.

Oh, my heart. Doran had stepped forward, but Ceetcee and my mother faced them down. One young and tall, her long braids swinging like tassels over her furled wings; a third of my wingmark tied to one shoulder, Beliak's to the other. One bent and huddled in quilts, her eyes white and skyblind, her sparse hair white and blowing in the wind. I moved forward to help them. To share my evidence.

Ezarit's hand cuffed my upper arm in a vise, gentle but firm. "Let Elna speak. You will have your turn." She spoke to the towers, and to Doran also, as well as to me. Councilor Grigrit had opened his mouth to protest.

"My partner's life was forfeit to the clouds," Elna began. "My son's father. For twenty Allsuns, I've felt that loss, and the city felt it too. We needed Naton's wisdom. We need his knowledge of the city even today, but we will never retrieve it. Despite the fact that we know now his crimes were not crimes at all."

Agreement moved through the council, especially those gathered near Ezarit. As if in echo, the city rumbled softly beneath us. The guards relayed Elna's words, and someone shouted, "Get on with it!" loud enough to carry on the wind.

Elna continued. "You'll patch the problem, not solve it. You'll lose fine minds in the process. I am old; this does not matter to me as much as it does to the generations above me." She put her hand on Ceetcee's shoulder. Dared everyone to ignore the rise below Ceetcee's ribs, the new life begun there.

Ezarit released my arm. The wind snapped at the council flags, and I felt the eyes of the city on me as I took a place beside Elna and Ceetcee before Doran could begin speaking. I held up a hand. Felt the breeze on my fingers.

"I fell through the clouds and discovered," I said, raising the bucket of heartbone so that the smell caught the breeze, "that a tower in our city is being drained of its life on purpose. That it is dying, endangering those around it." Doran held his sleeve over his nose, and several more councilors followed suit.

"Worse," I continued, "the Singer fledges we'd thought run-aways? I found them, forced to do this work. There is Treason in the city, but it is not the Singers' doing. We must postpone this Conclave. The Singers are not the city's greatest threat." I prepared myself to name the traitor. Dix had many allies.

But Doran interjected. "How long would you postpone?" He dropped his sleeve, irritation turning to anger. "Until Kirit Skyshouter appears before this council? You were in favor of Conclave, but after one day with her, you've changed your mind. She's corrupted you."

"She showed me a different perspective," I said. The guards repeated my words and the city's gaze focused on me. Elna stood upright, her hand shaking on Ceetcee's arm, her eyes the color of the clouds, her chin up, head turned towards my voice, proud. "Then I saw more, below the clouds. The vote happened with-out enough information. I demand to speak in the Singers' and the city's defense."

As Doran's face reddened, Vant Densira grabbed my arm. "You cannot represent Densira in this way," he hissed.

"I represent the city, then." Before I'd spoken, the certainty that Doran had moved too fast buoyed me up. Now, as my own towerman shook me, angry, I worried. They played a bigger game; Doran had told me so. Now I'd jostled their board, tried to topple it. What would they do in return?

"You reside on my tower; you represent that tower," Vant said. "I apologize to the council for the junior representative."

Doran nodded. "I appreciate Densira's loyalty in this matter." He looked around the assembled council, preparing to address them again.

But the protesters, who had continued to circle the platform, began to chant, "Let Naton's son speak!" From the towers, shouts came fast and multivoiced, "Throw them down!" and "Speak!" both. Screams and sounds of fighting began.

The city had become a roar of my own making.

11

WINGFIGHT

In the tumult that followed, Doran dispersed guards to the tower tiers to quell the fighting and Ezarit raised one hand for silence, fingers sifting the air. The council platform quieted. Then the towers did as well. We'd narrowly escaped another riot. Ezarit chewed her lip. Doran glared at me.

When it grew quiet enough to hear her, Ezarit spoke.

"There are many issues the city must address. The Spire's condition and its new dangers. Rumors about stalled tower growth. Complaints from the southeast about certain southwestern dealings. The situation with the Spire. But we cannot now proceed until we resolve the Singers' situation," she said. I shifted, uncomfortable, and ready to acknowledge where I'd been wrong. "The Singers preserved our history. They saved our culture from the clouds. But they made grave mistakes, committed horrible crimes. What can be salvaged from this? What is required to heal?"

Angry muttering from the councilors. Angrier sounds still, when her words reached the towers, but the guards stood firm. There were no more fights.

Ezarit waited until the platform quieted a second time. "A vote was taken while I searched for my daughter, Kirit, while Councilor Nat Densira was missing. Not all voices were heard. We cannot continue to lead through fear. Nat will speak now."

Those on the nearest tower balconies leaned forward, some using scopes to see.

An angry rumble came from Varu. The Singers had punished that tower many times over, and their proximity to the Spire had meant a heavy toll when the Skymouths escaped.

Vant gestured to the towers. "The city does not want to wait."

Ezarit pointed to the protesters and their nets. "The city is a family. But even a family disagrees from time to time. There is dissent now, and that is valuable to hear."

Vant's face colored. He gestured to where the remaining Singer council waited: Wik, Viridi, the Grigrit Singer, and seven others I didn't know well. Plus Moc. They looked back at him, bone faced. "Consider too, that if these Singers do not face justice, the city will remain caught in arguments and riots. The very towers will—"

"Let us not go to extremes," Macal said from where he stood. "This is rhetoric, and I would like to hear Nat's proof."

"Proof," Vant spat. "Your brother is covered in Lawsmarkers. You should have no voice here." His tone indicated that if he had a choice, Macal would have no voice in the future.

Once, not that long ago, I would have been by their sides as they shouted down an opposing argument. Especially one made by a Singer. I'd seen Doran design a plan of decisive action. But now I recognized the strategy they'd worked out. Uniting a group not by fear, but by singling out a common enemy. A successful tactic, yes. But with a terrible toll.

A single Conclave wouldn't satisfy the towers for long.

Macal seethed. Though Wik was his brother, he'd left the Spire for the towers long ago, and renounced the Singers to stay on the council.

I spoke again, raising my voice to reach as many as I could. "Listen! What I saw yesterday when I fell below the clouds is a more immediate danger than what happened in the recent past."

"Distraction and lies!" Vant cried. Now another tower, Naza, began to chant again. "Throw them down." I was no longer clear on whether they meant the Singers, or me. Hiroli's face reddened. Her tower.

Doran stepped forward. "I understand a young councilman's desire to speak," he said, his tone suddenly conciliatory. "I've felt the same thing myself. But here, after the council has already voted? And inciting a near riot in the process?"

I met his gaze. Held it. "It was a rushed vote."

"You say this when you yourself helped organize the vote beforehand?" Doran looked around at the gathered council, at the guards relaying every word to the waiting tiers. To Beliak and Ceetcee, who stared at the plinth surface, eyes wide. Now they knew the depth of my mistake. Now Ezarit knew too.

My answer to him, and to them, was my feet firmly planted on the council plinth. My unwavering gaze. *I say this. I will fix this.*

"You ask for more time, and according to council tradition, we must consider this, despite the urgency. You've stirred ire in the towers, but offer no way to calm the dispute," Doran continued. His anger had cooled; he'd found a plan. Doran clapped his hands together, raised his voice in contrast to Ezarit's calm. Across the platform, silk robes rustled as councilors turned to listen to him. Two repeaters circled overhead, alternating their departures so they could relay his words to the rapt towers. "And you also now claim Singer traditions are important to understand. Their codex, their . . . 'heartbone.'" He gestured at the container I still held.

"You've made the same claims yourself." I nodded, despite Ezarit's fingers clamping down on my shoulder. Perhaps if I showed the towers I was willing to listen, Doran would have to listen to me also.

"Ah, but that was before I learned that Singers still plot against the city, even now."

"What does he mean by that?" Ceetcee said. Two councilors behind me whispered to each other, echoing Ceetcee. *What does he mean?* My heart pounded in my chest.

"You wish to delay the city's healing at the very moment when it is ready to move forward." He held his hands out to the towers, "When the slightest dissent brings fighting. The city can wait no longer; it is time for the guilty to be punished. Then we must move on, together." Doran turned from me with a sweeping gesture that included the whole city.

I drew a deep breath. Confronting Doran, halting a council? That had been terrifying, but now I had to do it again. But instead, Hiroli stepped in. She was speaking above her place, just as I had done, but she was Ezarit's apprentice, and she spoke as one who had lost everything after Spirefall. The council gave her their attention. "We *can* move on, but perhaps it will be most fair, and most unlike the Singer judgments, to allow further discussion from all sides." She gestured to me. "Even if we do not agree on every point." Doran glared at her, but other councilors nodded agreement.

The towers listened, quiet.

Doran thought for a moment. Ezarit held up a hand to interject, but Doran spoke over her. "Perhaps your newfound dedication to Singer traditions will win your request for you. Singers battled in the Spire for the right to speak, did they not?"

The world slowed around me. The flags flapped against the wind with hard beats. I heard an echo of Gyre winds and saw again my friend strike at me, and I at her, trying to wound, to kill. I had walked right into this trap and not seen it, though Ezarit had. "They did."

"It was called a challenge, and if you won, you gained the right to speak your truth to the city," Doran continued. "You attempted one yourself, and lost. Perhaps you see yourself now as a bridge between tower and Spire? As your friend Kirit

Skyshouter did?" He hesitated. "Or still does? Perhaps you can rescue those Singers so far fallen into crimes against the city, and restore them?" Doran gestured to the assembled Singer council.

"I do not pretend to forgive the Singers their crimes," I said. "But Elna is right. And we have greater problems right now. The council, the towers, must hear!"

Doran would not easily be dissuaded. He narrowed his eyes.

"Then you will need to fight to be heard over the council's decision."

Me. The fighter who'd already lost, Nat the game piece. *Justice. Balance. Gravity.* "If I must, in order to speak a truth to the city, I will fight. But how does adopting Singer rituals make us a better city?"

Doran was ready. "If it's a question of the city's safety, we do all that we must, without hesitation." He turned to the waiting council. "Who will fight this brave young man?"

Ezarit was by my side, whispering, "Don't do this."

"He can't tolerate dissent—but he wanted me to go to the Spire with Kirit. Why won't he listen to me now?" Had my mentor had used me?

She shook her head. "You cannot be sure. It is possible he meant well, but now, given the opportunity, he is using the situation in the way he knows best. To build advantage. To keep moving forward. He *is* a trader at heart."

That at least was true. "He won't find anyone to fight for him. This is too far. He'll have to concede."

But she pointed. Already, several blackwings had stepped forward.

Doran lifted his hands. I held my breath. Would he concede? The look on his face said no. "The councilor is right. A fight to the death is Singer ways. In the tower we will do it differently. More civilized. A wingfight. One on one. But will you fight for those who have plotted rebellion while they were nursed in the towers? Who have colluded with fledges to weaken us at our very heart?"

Did he mean Dix? Blackwings shifted and muttered around us. But no, Doran pointed at Moc, then at Wik. "These Singers have been conspiring to siphon the city's lifeblood from beneath us! I have proof." He pointed to the sky, to the southwest. We looked to the sky, saw a large flier approaching. The bulky outline resolved into black wings, carrying a burden.

Had one of Doran's guards discovered what was being done to the Spire on their own, or even found Kirit?

Beside me, Ezarit held her breath. But instead of Kirit, it was Dix who landed on the platform and dropped her burden: A larger container of heartbone. A pair of Singer wings.

Before Ezarit or Doran could speak, Dix held out her hands, towards both items. "The rebellious Singers have drained the life from the city!" she cried. "They are weakening the Spire to collapse it on the towers. They are why the city has been so unlucky!"

"Not true! You did these things! You were there!" Moc shouted before the blackwings silenced him.

Ceetcee lunged forward, but Beliak held her back.

"I saw her in the clouds, sabotaging the Spire! So did the fledges," I shouted. "She's the traitor. Bring me Lawsmarkers!"

No one moved to help me. Dix looked at us as if she pitied our ignorance. "I'm no traitor. I believe in the city and am willing to do what's needed to help rebuild its order, its strength. Unlike some. Where do you stand, Doran?"

Doran bristled at the question, and at the attention focused on him by Dix. For a moment, he seemed trapped by her words. He finally shook his head slowly. "I cannot believe one of my own blackwings is a traitor—not without more proof than the word of a councilor who couldn't even attend an important vote yesterday. What of you, Nat? Did you help Kirit Skyshouter escape before she could be called on to renounce the Singers?"

Dix coughed into her hand to hide a triumphant smile.

I shook my head. "We fell out of the wind!"

Around me, the towers laughed.

"Do you still demand your stay?" Doran said.

"I do! I will show the city what I found."

He shrugged. Turned to the towers. "As the challenged, I accept," Doran said. "Unfortunately, I cannot fight, due to a Spire-fall injury. But I will name a flier who must fight in my stead."

Not Macal, I thought. *Please do not test his loyalties.* Not Hiroli either. So many dangers here.

"I name Dix Laria, of the southern guard." Doran's voice rang out, and the repeaters carried his words to the balconies. A roar went up.

Dix. Didn't Doran know she lied? How could he not know what happened so near his own tower?

"You are a loyal guard in service to the council, are you not?" Doran asked her. Confusion jarred my confidence. Were his words for show? Or was Doran's bigger plan Dix?

"I am." She bowed, then straightened and tugged at her wing-straps. Already preparing.

"Then you will fight to protect it."

That look in her eye. She relished this. She knew now that I'd stolen her fledges, the heartbone, her platform. She would fight me, and it would be to the death, no matter what Doran said.

"Concede, Nat," Ezarit whispered. "That one has been dangerous since the Singers rejected her when we were fledges. She's so conflicted."

I remembered Dix's history with Ezarit, and how she'd disliked Kirit too, long ago. Remembered also her tone at the

Grigrit gaming table. But how could I concede? I couldn't give up and let this go. I'd win and make them listen. No. More than that. I would set right my mistake.

At an angle to the plinth, and slightly lower, Varu's guards took the nets from the protesters and tied them into wingfighting tethers on the towers.

Dix and I met on the side of the council plinth and bowed to each other as challengers, and my heart began to beat in time with my memories of the Gyre.

I did not want to do this. And there was no other way.

Kaviks took to the air to share the news of a wingfight. I watched the frenzy, allowing my mind to focus on the birds, rather than what I was once again about to do. To fight a flight Magister for the right to speak to the city.

There were no windbeaters here, no one to throw rot gas in the wind to add to the challenge. There were no galleries or walls either. A wingfight was not intended to kill or maim. We were supposed to knock each other from the sky, not kill.

"The fight terms?" I asked. I doubted any terms would be obeyed, but I wanted the towers to hear them and judge Dix's actions accordingly. Perhaps she would help make my point if she did betray the terms, and I still won.

"Best out of three," Dix said, naming her terms as was her right, but grinning at me. I would have one chance, at best, to win decisively. Unlike the Gyre, a death during wingfight combat was rare, but that wouldn't keep Dix from making a "tragic mistake" in order to win.

"Agreed," I said. Doran half nodded. Dix and I walked together to the plinth's edge, then leapt from it to go to our places at opposite ends of the speedily rigged wingfighting nets. As we flew, more tower citizens scrambled to gain vantage points near the nets. Several headed to Naza, where the shocked residents quickly moved furnishings to the backs of their quarters to create more seating. Ceetcee and Elna joined Beliak by the fledges. Ezarit stood near them.

The last time I'd done this, I'd lost. My mentor knew this. That Doran could demand it of me was one thing. *How could I have agreed?* I realized I'd known what Ezarit warned about: that Doran's political skill and desire to win cut both ways. His ambition had once helped me, but I'd crossed him. If I lost now, Dix could continue her lies, and Doran could proceed with Conclave.

Circling above the wingfight nets, readying my knives, I made myself a vow. I would win this fight. I'd get more time for the Singers' defense and the search for Kirit. I'd pushed for the vote, without understanding the consequences. Then Kirit had shown me the truth. I had to make it right.

The protesters settled at Varu and Naza to watch the wing-fight. They cheered my name. Someone on Varu blew a horn, making a semblance of a wingfight call. The net was ready. Dix and I both saluted and turned to each other.

"Good luck, Brokenwings," she said, which was not tradition.

"I would wish you luck, Dix," I said in the traditional way. "And windblessings on the city."

"I'll make my own luck," she replied. With those words, I was made aware again that Dix had flown wingfights, and she was good. I'd seen her fight before last Allsuns, while Kirit still re-covered. A match between Mondarath and Grigrit. She'd bro-ken Aliati's knife before the fight, a dirty move.

Dix finished her salute and dove for the net's center, trying for the best position. I dove to meet her.

We clashed in the air. Dix's wingtip dipped below mine, and she executed a spin that turned me sideways in a heartbeat's time. A knife flashed and missed. Dizzied, I let air spill from my wings, and once again I could not right myself. I crashed to the net.

Varu's horn blew one point, in Dix's favor.

But I could still fly. My wings were whole. At the net's edge, I spotted a feather rising on a nearby draft and leapt for it, slowly circling to put myself back on the fighting level, while I regained my breath. I tried to pull my mind away from the feeling of the fall. Dix had already regrouped and was preparing to dive again, waiting only for me to signal my readiness.

I tried to strategize on the wing. Dix, the last time she dove, had done so with a slight veer to the left. That was how she'd lured me in and flipped me so fast. I decided to try a Singer trick I'd seen Kirit use once. I dove and she followed, meeting me, wings locked and arms ready to grapple me and throw me from the air. I curved my wings hard and shot up over her head, then began a tuck and roll, to arrive behind her.

But Dix reached up at the last minute. She sliced through my footsling with her knife. My glide plane—that flat plank the body took when flying, arms in the wingstraps, feet supported from the footsling—broke into right angles and I spilled from the air, missing the net.

I could not control my fall. I heard a cry, and a shadow circled, diving like a hawk. Tea-stained wings blocked the sky. Ezarit hooked me and lifted me back to the council plinth. Her eyes were angry suns.

The tower rumbled again, and the horn blew. Two points, the match lost, though the towers' cheers were muted. It seemed many disapproved of the outcome, both the cut footsling and my rescue.

Ezarit kept her grip hard on my shoulder once we landed. Dix, hearing the boos, flew away from the plinth, back towards the south. No matter. It had been my fight to win, and I had lost the fight. I had failed Kirit.

Ceetcee hurried to me, Elna at her side. With quick stitches, they repaired my footsling for safety's sake. Elna's skill as a seamstress had not been damaged by her blindness. She sewed by touch. Her breathing was labored. Angry.

I pulled Kirit's satchel back over my shoulder and reached out to them both. "I am sorry," I said.

"It won't hold long," Ceetcee said. "Clouds take Dix."

Elna kept sewing, not bothering to look where her eyes could not see. "You tried. You gave the towers a chance to see what Conclave could mean, to reconsider. To see that Doran is compromised. That is what you needed to do."

But a look around the council platform revealed what Elna could not see: councilors congratulating Doran. Stepping away from Ezarit. Siding with the winner. In the stretch of time it took to patch my footsling, Doran's power in council doubled.

He shook hands and patted shoulders, then turned with a swish of his embroidered robes and approached me, holding out a conciliatory hand. Every muscle in my body tensed against taking it, but Ceetcee poked me with her needle and whispered, "Nat."

Politics. Yes.

I shook his hand, expecting him to crush the bones of my fingers in his grip. Instead, he patted me on the back. "That was a tough lesson to learn, apprentice. But a more important one is coming. You wished to speak for the city, but can you be loyal to its decisions?"

I waited for Ceetcee's needle to strike my foot again, but it did not come. Instead, she and Elna kept sewing, directing rough jabs at the cloth. I was on my own.

"How can you make this decision, knowing what Dix does? She enslaves fledges, Doran. And is killing the Spire. Did you know?" I met his eyes and held them. I could tell by now when Doran embellished in order to win someone to his side.

He met my gaze. "I will look into your claims. I promise." His eyes were troubled, but he was not lying. He hadn't known. "But you know what we must do now."

Ceetcee bowed her head. I nodded, swallowing back the bitter taste in my mouth.

"The Conclave will proceed," Doran shouted. The guards in the air repeated his words while the guards on the plinth turned to the Singers, checking their bindings, offering them muzz. All refused. Even Moc.

This time, none on the towers cheered.

12

SUNFALL

The sun rose higher above the council platform, and the city rumbled again. Doran stood near the Singers, waiting for the towers to calm. He paced and gestured to the guards to prepare to fly. "There is little time for this."

Ezarit strode across the platform towards him. Her fierce gestures gave no doubt Doran and now Vant were being buffeted by her words. Hiroli trailed her. As soon as my footsling was repaired, I followed. By the time I caught up, Ezarit was fuming.

"Ezarit, please. This is a guard's duty," Doran was saying.

"To fly Conclave? No. This is a council duty. Council voted it. We will not let someone else carry that burden." I heard echoes of Kirit's words atop the Spire. *You have no idea what you do. How horrible it is. These are people, Nat.*

Vant threw up his hands. "A trick! A distraction."

"If we order it, we must carry it out," Ezarit said, calm and deliberately. "You too."

Doran held up a hand before Vant, now gray faced, could argue. "The councilor is right. Each of us will carry a Singer, and the guards will help if they are needed. We'll draw markers." Hiroli picked Moc. Doran and a guard, Wik. Ezarit, the elder Singer. I had Viridi. Others moved to their charges as well. Macal, his jaw drawn tight, stood behind another Singer councilor.

The wind snapped at our robes, our still-furled wings. My stomach curdled. I thought of my father, his Treason Lawsmarkers dragging him down, falling through the clouds so long ago. Someone had carried him to the city's edge. Someone had let him go. Today I would be that someone. How could I go through with it? My fists balled, and I pressed them to my temples, trying to think of a way out of this.

Wik leaned forward and whispered, "Now you understand."

"Quiet!" a guard shouted.

I searched the crowd until I found Beliak. "Take the fledges somewhere out of harm's way." Beliak and Ceetcee, with Elna between them, herded the fledges to the plinth's edge, trying to move them away before the Conclave began.

"Councilor," Viridi whispered to me and Wik, "you do your duty." She wore a white robe decked with Lawsmarkers. This close, I could see the tattoos on her face and arms: knives, bows, several I couldn't make out.

Those five words choked me. "This is wrong."

"It is tradition," Viridi said, and no more.

Motion on the platform: the fledges leaping for Varu, the nearest tower, with my family readying to follow.

Elna turned and shouted at Doran and Ezarit. At me. "This cannot be undone."

Ceetcee kept her back to the councilors and Singers, her shoulders heaving. She didn't look at me.

Beliak raised his hand to me, then looked at it strangely as a shadow passed across his fingertips. He turned his face to the sky, and his frown darkened.

My gaze tracked his. A shadow now eclipsed all of us, but all I could see overhead was blue sky.

Ezarit looked up as well, confused. Wary. "Skymouth?" She reached for a knife. I, for my missing arrows.

The elder Singer from Grigrit laughed. "Would serve you all right." A guard silenced him as more people began to point, both on the platform and in the towers.

Ezarit gazed up as more of the plinth fell under full shadow. The glass beads in her hair dimmed.

A foul smell hit me. Rot gas. And something else. Another smell, fainter.

"Move! Doran shouted. "Everyone, get in the air!"

I unfurled my wings and saw Hiroli doing the same. Beliak took Elna in his arms and leapt from the tower. Ceetcee followed.

Instead of leaping to safety, many councilors stared at the sky.

Small suns began to fall onto the platform, catching the oil-proofed surface and setting it alight.

Smoke rose, curling around and defining the edges of a small shape above us. A curve of blue-silver shimmered in the air.

A floating plinth, suspended from skymouth husks. Maybe the very one we'd allowed to get away from us that morning at Bissel.

"Run!" I shouted to anyone who would listen. "Fly!" I grabbed for Moc, but Hiroli had him. Pushed a guard towards Wik. "Grab him and fly!"

In the smoke, the small plinth passing above us appeared to be lined in skymouth hides. Invisible, except when silhouetted against sky and smoke. Above it, the outlines of four inflated skymouth husks bobbed.

From the safety of the invisible plinth, gray-winged figures hurled flaming balls of rot gas down on the council. *Gray wings. Blue robes.*

"Singers!" Vant yelled. The guards on the council plinth, wings blue and green and black, took to the air to fight them. The councilor from Wirra shouted, "How many are there?" A southeastern junior councilor yelled, "They're trying to free the others!"

Singers?

Doran roared above the tumult, "Who has been hiding them?"

One attacker leaned to throw the rot gas clear of the plinth. He stared at me for a moment—dark eyes, face free of silver marks—then dropped his bone-chip-weighted ball of flame.

The rot gas hovered in the air over the council, trapped by the wind until the plinth began to burn in earnest. Flames licked sky. Strips of silk and tendon began to fall away. The rot gas itself caught fire. Screams and coughing cut through building walls of smoke.

Then the shadow passed beyond the smoke and disappeared. I felt full sunlight on my face, while a different heat pulsed around me.

"Move!" I heard Wik shout again. He was grappling with a guard, and the guard was winning, pinning him down.

The plinth burned and crumbled around us as the sun shone down, uncaring. More councilors began to reach the plinth's edges and to jump. Many tangled and fell: wings and arms and kicking feet.

A silk-wrapped foot hit my arm. A hand clawed the air above my head. I'd leapt without realizing it.

A roar of flames beating against silk and fiber nearly deafened me. The elder Singer who had laughed at Kirit fell past, his fingers reaching, grabbing. He touched the edge of my robe, then gravity pulled him free.

I fought the heated wind, trying to stay aloft. Too close and my wings would catch. Too far and I wouldn't be able to help. I searched for a way to assist, remembering Ezarit's dive for me.

In the distance, the fledges and my family landed on Varu's towertop. They were safe.

I dove into the smoke.

In the choking, screaming air of the platform, Wik tried to help people fly away, instead of throwing them down. Even as he, himself, remained wingless and exposed.

I tried to reach him. The platform tether to Naza began to burn.

A hot gust blew me sideways, towards Varu. I could not find Doran. Nor Vant.

More blackwings appeared, flying to the nearby towers and onto the plinth. Two lifted Wik and flew away. More followed, carrying their own burdens.

One came at me, arms reaching, but Ezarit shot between us, knocking the wind from the black foils and sending her tumbling. "Fly, Nat!" She dove then, her own wings locked, a gray-winged attacker behind her. A knife gleamed in her hand.

The plinth ripped into three flaming pieces and spilled its contents to the sky. I flew through the smoke as the city council's plinth fell into the space between the towers and tumbled, a flaming sun, towards the clouds.

I dove after it, and the people who were falling with it, my arms out, reaching.

PART TWO

STOLEN

Black kaviks, dodging heated air, flew a wide circuit around thick columns of smoke. They rasped at the shadows below, the struggling shapes fading from gray to white, but could not aid the fallen or the lost. The messengers landed on ash-streaked towers that bore the living through the air.

∽ FORTIFY ∽

Tower by tower, secure yourselves,
Except in city's dire need.

13

ASH AND MIST

Gray smoke tendrils wove through white clouds. Thick mist parted before me as I dove through hot air; ash tangled my hair, pushed into my lungs, darkened my tucked wings. I descended, resolving that those I could reach would not fall, searching for a place where the air cleared and I could breathe. Around me, shreds of silk and fiber drifted feather-light and fire-bright.

The smoke left traces on my skin like dark tears.

Below me spun a councilor from Haim, half-winged and flailing. He called for help. Shouts filled the wind, my ears.

Reaching, my hands caught his, and I arched my back, heading for the strongest draft swirling the smoke. The councilor kicked the air, trying to climb, dragging me down. I fought for wind and lift, but met only smoke and weight. To continue meant falling from the sky, from my family. I had to let go.

I peeled my fingers from his arm and slowly his grip tore from my wrist, breaking skin in his desperation. His screams wrapped around me, tore at my ears until I heard nothing else, long after the councilor had disappeared from view.

A hole in the mist slowly sealed, his passage erased, save for a ragged headache that would not disappear so easily. Circling up, my eyes burned, red from smoke.

The sky above cleared of attackers.

I dove again, deeper. Shadows spun below; the falling had passed me. They merged with the dark forms of towers, and I altered course, trying to avoid a sudden stop at the junction of wind and bone.

On a bone spur off my left wing, a figure gestured as if trying to brush the air away. I turned, built up speed, and passed above the spur. Grabbed a handful of robe, an arm. I kicked hard against the wind and caught a better draft. The person I held moaned, but did not struggle. I circled higher, shouting with relief.

I had a terrible grip on them, all angles and pain, and I couldn't see their face, covered as it was by part of their gray robe. Dark stains dappled the fabric. Blood. A Lawsmarker swung from their shoulder, near holes where others had torn free. A Singer, plucked from the smoke-filled mist while the council fell. A person, who'd fallen when the platform was attacked.

I fought my way up, aiming for Varu and searching for each strong gust that would carry me into the light, away from the sifting ash. Skyblessed luck let my wings remain unscorched and whole.

Doubled shadows passed above me, other rescuers, with those they could save.

An updraft carried me above the heated air, the wind strong around Varu—its profile lower than the towers around it a result of previous failed rebellion against the Singers. My arms and shoulders ached from grappling the Singer.

Only when I landed on Varu's slim tenth-tier balcony did I turn to look out at the space between Narath and Naza, where the city council's flags had played the breeze.

The attackers and their skymouth-floated, sky-cloaked platform had disappeared. Once again, the blue horizon held no gray wings, no Singer cloaks. Only blackwings circled the nearer towers. Several clustered around Varu.

A faint pall hung in the empty air where the council had

stood moments before. The wind dispersed the smoke, bled it bright-edged into the clouds.

❧ ❧ ❧

On the crowded Varu balcony, bone pots held struggling stone fruit trees. A dazed part of my mind wondered at this: the tier was too low and faced the wrong direction for stone fruit. The rest of me scrambled to save a life.

An empty whipperling cage sat on a low table. I pushed both aside and laid the Singer gently on the balcony floor. Blood-matted hair, mottling Amrath tower marks wound through amber and silver-streaked braids. The Singer had been trying to fit in with their host tower.

I bent and put two fingers against the ash-dark skin of their wrist. Felt a jumpy pulse. Watched their eyelids flutter. Open to pain-clouded eyes.

"Nat," the Singer whispered. They knew me. Viridi. Her tattoos highlighted the pallor of her skin, etched in silver.

"Help!" I shouted to the tier. "Someone help!" The wind swirled my words.

Her robes were burned in several places. When she rolled on her right side to vomit, I could see leathery, blistered skin through the holes in her robes. A gash over her ear. The burns smelled of rot gas.

"Shhh," I said, trying to comfort her. Swallowing hard to avoid throwing up myself. "Shhh. Someone will come." I tore a piece of her robe and pressed it as gently as I could to the wound on her head.

She was shivering. She wouldn't last long in the cold air.

"Councilor," she whispered when she finished retching. She stretched a hand towards my satchel.

"I have no water, Viridi. I wish I did." Blood oozed through the fabric of her robe onto my fingers, dark and sticky.

She pushed at my arm. "The codex page, Conclave? Wik said you found it. Do you have it still?" Each word cost her.

I couldn't lie to someone who might die. "I do."

"Break it. Now." She closed her eyes. Her fingers waved at my satchel.

Break it? After the trouble Kirit and I went through to get it? No—she was right: Doran would use the page to support another Conclave with the surviving Singers, if he could. Viridi was right.

I took her hand and put it over the cut on the side of her head. "Keep pressure, here." Then, remembering Kirit sorting through the Spire rubble, I pulled the thick bone page from the bag and readied to throw it over the tier's edge.

"No." Viridi groaned, trying to get my attention. "Someone could find it. Might use the Conclave count against us. Smash it."

Her injuries had rendered her incoherent. No help had arrived, and the tier was silent. She stared at me, her eyes demanding I act. So I stepped back and slammed the tablet into the tier, as far from her as possible. Maybe the noise would get us attention from the tower.

The Conclave page cracked into one large piece and several smaller ones. Between the bone pieces, brass gleamed, looking nearly new. I glimpsed etching, like the other plate in my bag. More detailed than my father's drawings had ever been. "What is that?"

"I don't know," Viridi whispered. Her pupils had dilated, she no longer focused on me. "A ghost. A story."

A clatter of wing battens made me jump and scoop up the bone shards and what they contained. I shoved all of it in my satchel as Hiroli landed close beside me, carrying Moc tight against her chest. Hiroli's wings were seared in places, but still held. Moc's were torn. Nearly gone.

I touched the boy's shoulder gently. "Ciel is above, on the towertop. I saw her. Safe." I held his gaze and repeated myself. "Safe with my family."

Moc took a deep breath and stared at me, then slowly blinked. Nodded that he understood. Then he saw Viridi. He pulled from my grip and went to her.

"Ezarit? Doran? The other Singers?" I asked Hiroli. Speaking made me cough, and once I started, I couldn't stop.

"You need water," Hiroli said. She turned and shouted, "Varu, help!"

No answer on the empty balcony. Varu had been under the Spire's interdictions so often, any sign of Singers probably terrified them. Especially the lowtower.

"I'm all right." I sounded like I'd been chewing bone. Worse than Kirit's voice ever had. I really wasn't all right. My chest hurt, and I didn't want to take too deep a breath for fear of coughing again. But I wouldn't look weak in front of Hiroli.

"We need aid!" she shouted again.

The balcony remained silent. Beyond the stone fruit pots, the tier was shuttered. I'd been so focused on Viridi, I hadn't seen it. They'd barricaded as if for a skymouth migration.

Hiroli beat on the shutters, but no one answered.

"Cowards," she said.

"Tower by tower, secure yourselves," I whisper-sang. Each word carved pain on my seared lungs. I'd once hid behind shutters myself. When skymouths attacked, warnings arrived by kavik that made all the tiers close themselves away for safety. Varu was remarkably quiet; as if the fighting had scared them inside.

I looked back towards the sky, seeking help. Panic and fear mixed with anger. I tasted smoke, spit ash. Cowards indeed.

Hiroli pulled me from the exposed balcony, behind a tangle of garden vines. "Look," she pointed. Blackwings circled through the towers, spreading out through the city like dark birds. Their wings matched the pair Hiroli wore. "The guards are helping."

Not very likely blackwing guards would help Singers, even ones we'd pulled from the clouds.

"I hope so," I said lightly, but I moved to guard Viridi as best I could. She was a Singer, and Hiroli wore black wings. Could I protect Moc at the same time? "What do you intend?"

Hiroli held up both hands. "I'm a councilor. I am Ezarit's apprentice. My tower makes the black dye, that's all. I mean these two no harm. They didn't attack us." She held her hand palm up, as if to cup the clearing sky, "But there were Singers in the sky!"

At Viridi's side, Moc pressed the sodden cloth to her wound. I heard a few snatches of song and whispers. *Don't die, Viridi.* "Where did they come from? Not many Singers—at least not the leaders—are left." The fledges, yes, and several older acolytes. They'd been spared from this morning's Conclave and were still at their quarters, hopefully.

Hiroli rubbed her forehead and spoke in a low tone, as if hoping Moc couldn't hear her. "There seemed to be enough to commit war and Treason, both."

"I'm not certain—" I began. "I saw one of the attackers' faces. No tattoos."

She shook her head. "They could have been covered up. Besides, not all Singers have marks. Macal doesn't." She was certain.

"But council confiscated all the gray wings a moon ago. Where did they get the wings?"

Hiroli narrowed her eyes, as if trying to remember what she'd seen. "If a tower is using Singer clothing and Singer weapons to wage war? Everyone must know so they can protect themselves."

Dix had access to the gas they'd used as weapons, as well as the floating platform. I didn't know where the wings were stored, but if it was at Grigrit, she had access to those too. Ezarit's words: *That one has been dangerous since the Singers rejected her when we were fledges. She's so conflicted.*

Who'd attacked us was not yet clear, but one thing was: The Rise warned of war. We were closer to it than ever.

City of my father and mother, ancient ever-rising city of towers and sky. City I'd flown to defend. Now wounded. Now broken.

A fresh gust of wind blew smoke and stench towards us, shouts and whistles too. A fresh crew of guards and volunteers were searching the towers for the fallen. These searchers didn't risk the clouds, but they scoured the lowtowers right to the cloudtop for survivors.

"The protesters," I said. "The councilors?" I'd seen my family safely landing on the Varu towertop, but who else survived? Who hadn't?

Hiroli shook her head. She knew no more than I did.

My headache grew.

Moc began keening as Viridi struggled and gasped for air. "She was good. She tried to help." He wept as he stroked her hair, hand as gentle as a breeze on a bird's wing.

"Varu, aid!" I shouted once more. Where were they?

Over the balcony edge, a guard spiraled lower, looking to pass nearby. The longer we remained on this balcony, the more exposed Viridi was. I banged once more on the shutters. Heard movement behind. Something being dragged to brace the shutter. I began to yell in frustration, borderless words that died in my throat.

I needed assistance, but could not afford to attract the roving blackwings' attention. "We need to go up," I said. "A tier with water. And medicine." Closer to the blackwings, perhaps, but on the towertop, we would find people who were not afraid.

My family was at the top of Varu. Could we make it there? Could Viridi?

A blackwing flew near Varu, just above us. I pushed Moc among the planters and pots and tried to hide Viridi in my shadow. Through the shutters at my back, I heard whispering.

A kavik landed on the balcony and opened its beak to caw. Hiroli reached into her robe and found a piece of graincake. Fed the dark-winged bird until it allowed her to brush ash from its head. Then she gently lifted the chips tied to the bird's foot before it could signal to the tier's residents that there was a message.

"The towers must remain Fortified for safety," Hiroli read. "Blackwings hunt traitors who have twice tried to destroy the city, once with skymouths and now with fire." She looked from Moc and Viridi to me.

"The Council, or what's left of it, is hunting Singers." The words chilled me, though I'd expected it. Kirit was still out there, somewhere. They had Wik. And I'd left Ciel with my family atop Varu.

Give this tier enough time, I realized, *and they'll trade Viridi and Moc to the blackwings in order to gain favor for themselves.* "We have to leave." I no longer cared where.

Had the attackers been Singers? Not a chance.

Hiroli shook her head. She lifted the skein in her hands. "And"—she pointed to familiar sigils on the chips—"they seek anyone who supported the Singers as well. Ezarit, Kirit, the protesters. Us."

Even as the smoke cleared and guards searched for survivors, the city had begun hunting its own.

14

REMEMBRANCE

Heartbeats counted loud time on the quiet tier. I grabbed for the kavik to see the message for myself. The bird was large, and when it opened its wings in panic at my approaching hands, it seemed for a moment to block the sky. A rude bird. But it didn't take flight. It snapped its beak at me, a stranger with no food. Tilted its head. Cackled.

So different than Maalik. Who was safe, I hoped. Beliak had sent him to the protesters. To Ceetcee, I knew now. Maalik knew her by sight. And Ceetcee was safe.

But I wondered at this kavik. "It doesn't know me." Kaviks of the same quadrant knew almost everyone. Like whipperlings, kaviks remembered faces. They seemed to share information among themselves as well: who carried food, who threw bone chips at them. There were no strangers. We were in the northwest, barely. "I've flown this quadrant since I was a fledge. Why does this kavik not know me?"

Hiroli shook her head. She didn't know. She'd woven a few glass beads into her dark hair, like Ezarit. They sparkled cheerfully in the light, but her face was smudged and scraped. "Sent from the south, maybe?" She bundled up the message skein so Moc could not see that he was named, and flapped her hand at the bird until it flew away. "The messages blame the Singers for Spirefall and for this attack, both. They sound sure of it. But I think the surviving council needs to know what you saw."

Hiroli was already tightening her wingstraps. "We'll go up to Ezarit's tier, uptower. She'll stop this."

Ezarit hasn't been able to stop anything, not for a long time. Not even a vote within her own council.

Viridi groaned; the side where she'd been snared by the bone spur oozed dark blood.

"I don't think she'll fly well," I said.

"Then you have to leave her." Hiroli didn't flinch at the thought. She was accustomed to obeying Fortify: towers must secure themselves, and people too.

But the Law didn't end there. *Except in city's dire need.* This certainly qualified.

"I won't leave her. This tier would turn her in or let her die alone. She doesn't deserve that." As Moc watched with wide eyes, I bent to whisper to the Singer, knowing these might be the last words she heard. "Risen, we must move again. You're injured. If you choose to go with us, I regret any suffering this causes you."

"I am tired, Councilor," she slurred, her eyes still closed. So soft was her speech, I wondered if I imagined her words.

"We'll go up," I decided. To the towertop. Eight tiers, maybe. There might be medicine up there. Water.

I lifted her again in my arms. She felt lighter now, her face still, frozen in a mask of pain. She'd died rather than fly again. I closed my eyes and lowered the body to the tier floor, unable to look at Moc.

"Aunt Viridi?" Moc whispered.

I barely kept myself from falling to my knees on the lowtower balcony. I'd wanted to take her to safety. Instead, I'd carried a Singer to her death.

Stifling my grief made my headache worse. I envied Moc's barefaced sorrow. He'd sung to her. He'd watched her die. His family. He looked suddenly very young, his face a mask of snot and tears.

I understood the feeling, even if I kept my emotions barricaded now. If anything had happened to my family . . . Though I knew they were safe, or had been, my heart raced at the thought.

My family. I had to get to them, but couldn't move as Moc sobbed. The whispers behind the shutters increased.

Moc turned from Viridi's body and rushed at the doors, his fists balled as if intent on breaking them down.

Hiroli grabbed him and tried to calm the boy, but he sobbed louder. How could I calm him? Wrestling him into the sky wouldn't do that, no matter how badly we needed to leave.

What would Elna do? She'd feed Moc. Get him water. We had none. She'd sing. That took time. Meantime, my heart pounded questions: Who survived? Is my family safe?

I knelt by the fledge and put my hand on his head. "We'll sing Remembrances for her." It would have to be quick.

Moc sniffled. "Singers don't have Remembrances."

"What do you have?" Hiroli asked. *Did you have,* I silently corrected her.

Moc bowed his head. "Their passage was marked in the codex. Their body fed the clouds, like everyone." He stopped crying, but his face was mottled with red splotches.

Tobiat had told me once that the Singers kept our culture intact when we rose through the clouds. "The Singers trained in every tower song and Remembrance tradition, for the towers."

Moc shivered. Wiped his nose with the back of his hand. His eyes, blue like his sister's, were ringed bright pink. "Ciel was studying those, before."

Very gently and still trying to think how Elna would talk to the fledge, but feeling every moment pass, I asked, "What's a favorite ritual, from any tower?"

He shook his head, so mired in grief, he couldn't help us help him.

We were so close to the clouds here. So close to death ourselves. I sang Remembrance softly, under my breath, the way Densira and its neighbors did these things. I tried not to rush it. Hiroli joined me.

> Return on the wind, friend.
> The city marks your passage.

We let silence hang in the air when we finished singing, and we all looked up to say good-bye. The sun was still high above us. We didn't look down, not at the clouds, nor at the smoke still lingering, patchy, in the sky.

I heard Moc gasping beside me, trying to stop crying. I bit my cheek hard.

"That was good," he finally said.

"I can let her go into the clouds, all right? You fly with Hiroli to Bissel's lowtower. Hide there. Aliati should be back from her search for Kirit soon. She'll need to know about the attack."

Moc nodded again. Hiroli stared at me. I took her aside.

"You have to guard him. They'll take him. He had nothing to do with this." She wore black wings. I was betting she could fend off the searchers. I couldn't take the fledge where I needed to go next.

She pressed her lips together. "We'll wait for you there." She lifted Moc and flew him away, closer to the clouds.

I used a tether to lower the Singer from the tower. Viridi's body disappeared into the clouds, carving a hole in the mist that slowly closed up as the air forgot her name.

15

HEARTBONE

As I pulled myself up through shifting gusts towards the top of Varu, my shoulders ached like I, too, was once more draped with Lawsmarkers. Smoke and sorrow pressed painfully against my temples.

I circled until I found a clear draft to Ezarit's tier, where she'd likely be protected by guards. If blackwings searched for me, they would find me there. I'd make the hunt easy for them.

The sky had emptied of fliers. Towertops and tiers nearest the missing council platform, once crowded with colorful robes and wings, now stood stark and nearly deserted. This portion of the city had obeyed the order to Fortify.

A small clutch of people remained on the balcony of Varu's topmost tier. Ezarit's quarters. As I coasted closer, I spotted Ceetcee's yellow wings wedged tight between two sets of black.

Blackwings hunt traitors. The tier was not being protected. It was being guarded.

Blackwing guards circled wary above Varu. I set aside my exhaustion, determined to take the hawk's path. Silent and dangerous. Sharp and sudden.

They wouldn't see the junior councilor; they'd see a hero of Spirefall.

The nearest guard met me in the air. Though I approached alone, she whistled to her fellows to warn them. I rolled, letting her streak past as I slashed out with my knife hand. My blade nicked a black silk wing, and I heard a satisfying rip.

I didn't look to see where she tumbled.

Fighting to regain my flight angle, I almost overshot the tower. Instead of circling again, I tucked my wings and spilled air, dropping fast. Only at the last minute did I extend the spans to slow my fall, landing hard on the balcony.

I shook off the impact and moved faster, not bothering to furl my wings. Silk seams fluttered in the wind as I strode towards the little group. They stood before a seated man wearing torn, embroidered robes. I pushed the next guard who rushed at me with the blunt handle of my blade. I didn't want to hurt them. They were watching for attacking Singers. Not a lone councilor, with a singular goal.

They will let Ceetcee go, or they will take me in her place. I rounded on the group and saw Elna seated on a stool, bracing her back against my partner's legs. *Elna also.* The two women shivered in the cooling air, Ciel kneeling between them.

Could I convince the guards to let them go? Beliak sat on the tier floor, wrists bound, eye swelling, as if he'd already tried to free them, and lost. *And Beliak.* All of them.

Could I convince Ezarit and the council to free them?

While the guards in the air had been patrolling the sky, the guards on the tier were caught between watching their charges— Ceetcee, Elna, Beliak, and Ciel—and coming after me.

Ezarit was nowhere to be seen. Her tier was wide open, unfortified. Furnishings from inside her quarters—several cushions from Amrath, two bone stools, had been repositioned so that Doran sat beneath the towertop's shelter, while Elna and the others remained outside. I heard the notes of Ezarit's scavenged metal wind chime from somewhere deep inside the tier.

Doran had arranged the seats so that he could speak eye-to-eye with Elna. It was considerate, and put him at a disadvantage.

I was beside him in three strides. As he turned, I sheathed my knife. Still, the guard to Ceetcee's right immediately lifted a blade to her shoulder. The blackwings in the sky circled closer. Another guard shifted their knife grip, preparing to throw, if necessary.

Doran held a hand up wearily. "The councilor isn't our enemy." He turned his ash-smudged face to me. "Are you?"

He'd named me a councilor still. Confusing, given the message chips. Given everything that had happened today.

"Where is Kirit, Nat? Did you help her escape? My own apprentice?" Doran rarely asked so many questions. He preferred to know answers *before* a discussion. His clothing, too, was in disarray.

"I didn't collude with anyone. I'm loyal to this city. As is everyone here, and Kirit too. I don't know where she is, but I know she wouldn't attack the council, or her family."

At least, the Kirit I'd grown up with wouldn't do that.

"And you, Doran? Are you loyal to the city?" I inclined my head towards the guards, forcing calm I didn't possess. Dix was nowhere in sight, but even so, asking was a risk. Still, I had to know.

A heartbeat passed. Another. Doran bowed his head and waved "stand down," to the guards. Then he stood, shakily, lifted a water sack, and sipped at it. He held the sack out, offering it to me. I drank my fill, and the pain in my head began to release.

He bowed, formally, and I could see the pain it caused him. "This is a day of great tragedy. You are welcome here, Councilor Densira. You flew well today, in the city's name. I am loyal to the city, same as you. And yet I may have trusted in

the loyalty of others too much." From Doran, it was a powerful apology.

It was also a strange greeting for a guest from another tower.
"Where is Ezarit?" She should have greeted me, not Doran.

"We haven't found her yet. She disappeared chasing a Singer."
He spoke truth. I'd seen the same. "Macal leads the search for
her. Meantime, I've quartered here by necessity, to be close to
the scene of the attack and await her return." His words were
quiet and tinged with despair. But as the drink cleared my mind,
doubt began to nag again. Had Doran been surprised by the attack, or was he pretending?

He sounded truly concerned for Ezarit's safety, though he'd
tried to outmaneuver her.

Beyond Doran, Ceetcee met my gaze, her clear brown eyes
set and determined. She'd spoken her conscience today. I knew
that look. She would take their censure and plan to speak her
conscience again, no matter how many Lawsmarkers they gave
her. But as long as I was still a councilor, there'd be no such punishment. She'd had a right to speak, as every citizen did since
Spirefall. As they had, at least, until the council attack.

The two guards I'd pushed through to get to the tier landed,
one carrying the other. They glared at me. Beyond Doran, Elna
looked exhausted, but she was unharmed. Beliak's left eye was
now swollen shut. No one spoke. Ceetcee's lips shaped silent
words: "We are fine."

That calmed me a little, as she'd meant it to do.

"And the fledges?" I didn't see the children I'd rescued from
the Spire.

"Taken to Mondarath, so Macal's people can watch over
them." Doran shifted in his seat. At his shoulder, a wound blos-
somed beneath a bandage. "Nat, I thought we'd prepared for
Conclave; we took the Singers' wings away, sequestered them.

That we could not be attacked like this." He was right. We had done all those things. "How could this happen?"

"How, indeed?" Kirit hadn't trusted him, and I hardly could either now, but I needed his help. I tested him. "With respect, you seem shocked by the day's events, Councilor."

"Weren't you? This is a terrible day."

Dawning possibilities. Doran had played Ezarit into a corner with the horns and Conclave. But the attack had foiled his plans to assume full leadership. Perhaps he *was* as surprised as the rest of us.

"I made many mistakes today," he said. He *had* been caught off guard: Doran didn't admit mistakes. But he continued, "I should have hunted down every single Singer and kept them from colluding. Their secrets and lies endangered us all for too long. Now I have endangered my council. My city." His words outraged me, but his grief didn't seem to be an act.

I weighed what I knew of him—that he loved the challenge of council leadership, the give and take of debate, that he had a vision for the city that demanded compliance and loyalty. Ezarit had spoken about him bargaining for advantage, and Kirit had warned that Doran did not like to be opposed in his own tower.

Elna had opposed him with her speech, and Ceetcee, by rousing the protestors, but they hadn't scuttled his wind entirely. Conclave would have proceeded, until the attack. This hadn't been his doing.

"So many are missing." Doran's shoulders bowed. Someone had nearly pulled the wings from his back. He put his elbows on his knees, his head on his hands. "I thought we knew where every Singer was. I thought you were tracing the runaways."

He suspected the fledges now? "Those were adults on the plinth. Singers had nothing to do with the attack." What I'd seen—and hadn't—was proof. "The attackers' faces? I saw no tattoos." I pointed at the guards. "They might as well have been these blackwings. And where are all the confiscated gray wings stored? How would anyone get hold of more?"

Doran looked up at me. Made as if to rise, but sat back down heavily. "Kirit goes missing and then there's an attack. The towers can see that *she* wears gray wings. They want a simple answer, so they can move on."

The smoking remains of the council platform had no simple answers. I doubted there was a simple enemy.

The nearest guard cleared his throat. "I didn't see tattoos either." Doran frowned at him, then nodded, considering his statement.

Pitching my voice so everyone assembled on the tier could hear me, I made my proposal. "Someone wants the city to blame the Singers for this. If you're not behind the attack, Doran, you're playing right into their hands."

The nearest guard drew her knife again. She closed her fingers around the grip. "Don't speak that way, Densira."

"Let him speak." Doran's order weakened to a smoke-filled cough at the end.

Keeping my eyes on Doran to better see his reaction, I made a plain shot, right at the matter's heart. "I believe Dix is behind this." No preamble. "Your fighter. How are you not involved?"

He frowned. "Dix is many things, apparently. But how could she launch an attack when she was been busy battling you in a wingfight?"

The guards looked at me, impassive. Ceetcee's mouth was a sharp line of distaste. She'd never seen Doran in a council debate until today. He might be weakened by surprise, but he wouldn't miss an opportunity to throw an opponent off balance, just like on the council platform. By reminding everyone that I'd lost, again, he'd tried to discredit me once more. But I didn't relax my focus. "Dix left right after the fight. There was enough time, barely, to fly south. To signal or send a bird." I waited a beat to let that sink in. "And she's been weakening the Spire below the clouds. Making a gas that would float a platform like that one." *Just* like that platform. Doran knew.

A long pause. Overhead, a kavik screeched at us, then flew towards the northwest. "I know of Dix's operation," Doran acknowledged. He tried to keep his voice low, but everyone heard.

Silence barricaded the wide-open tier, like shutters sealed the tiers below; the guards' faces were expressionless.

My friends looked between us in confusion.

"You knew?" Beliak rose, as if to move towards us. A guard grabbed his arm.

Doran shifted, uncomfortable on the stool now that he was under scrutiny. "It was for the future. At some point, towers will stop growing as we need them to. The city's too crowded to sustain that. The Singers knew we were close. They saw the towers slowing, their tiers getting more crowded, more brittle. We need the gases from the heartbone—"

I raised both hands in frustration, then lowered them slowly, calming Beliak. Kirit had been right not to trust Doran. "You knew of it. Who's to say you didn't know of the attack in advance too? You were pleased to see the Spire in danger, called it advantageous. Why not escalate?"

"I don't agree with Dix's methods, some of which I've only recently learned. But the heartbone was a necessity. And, Nat, I would never. An attack on the council is an attack on myself." He put his head back in his hands, then scrubbed at his hair with his fingernails. "So many of our people hurt."

He sounded truly unsettled, matching my own feelings. I remembered now that in the confusion, Doran had been among the first to shout, "Fly!" the first to sound the alarm. He'd seen the danger and thought of the people's safety. And was as sure now that the Singers were behind this.

Was I still certain they weren't?

Yes, he was manipulative and angry enough to pit me against Dix in order to fight to speak, but seeing him in disarray underscored the possibility he hadn't planned for this. Was it an act? Kirit would say *maybe*. I wavered. His wording still felt wrong: "necessity."

He saw my indecision and gripped my forearm. "I've made mistakes and trusted the wrong people. Now there is no time to waste, Nat. There are few enough guards, and fewer councilors who can keep the city from falling into chaos. There are calls for Macal to step down, and I need his vote. I need your help."

My family, assembled between the guards, watched us. "You have an odd way of showing it."

"Nat, your family aren't prisoners!" He looked shocked that I thought so. "I kept them here for their protection. The towers are raging, Nat, at what's happened to their councilors, their friends and relatives." He reached to pat Elna's hand. Elna gently pulled her fingers away from his touch.

"Spurred on by the kavik messages." I gestured for the message chips. Held them up on their yellow silk cord.

Doran looked at the chips, brow wrinkling. "Those aren't from me. Show me the bird?" He hadn't sent the message.

"Hiroli sent it back." The bird hadn't recognized me, and I hadn't recognized the bird. Curious.

"I'll look into it," Doran said. "Angry towerfolk—including from Densira, where Vant is missing—have already tried to attack the protesters in the air. They might have forged message chips as well. Your mother and Ceetcee were in danger, so I kept them here. I did that for you, Nat."

Doran's heavy brows arched over his dark eyes. Worry for the city and confusion about what was happening etched his face. The attack. The message birds. Someone had gotten the drop on him. Were they Spire or Tower?

He continued, "We are holding the surviving Singers. We'll find the rest soon. And then we will have a true Conclave. End this once and for all."

A Conclave, still. "You are making a mistake," I said. "That won't end it. You have a traitor in your midst. Even after a Conclave, the traitor will remain."

"But who? Dix? Where is the proof? She's done important work for the city, and has her own following in council. No one should accuse her without credible proof. Besides, she's sent a bird already. During the attack, her most talented artifex was kidnapped." He shook me lightly. "Don't you see? Perhaps there is a traitor, but it can't be Dix. She is loyal to me." I tensed so I would not shake him back. I was more sure than ever that it was Dix.

Whether his intent was good didn't matter right now. Doran had created a culture where power needed an enemy to work against. Now it seemed to be working against him. For a moment, I'd thought he'd heard me. But then he shook his head.

"You're reacting out of shock, Nat. The towers will demand justice, as soon as possible. And, if you are loyal to the city, I need you here. You are a hero. You showed compassion today, but now you need to help lead us out of this."

He needed me still. Was that a ripple of worry beneath his bravado? I pressed my case. "What if attacks continue after the Singers are thrown down? Who falls under suspicion next?" The fledges? The protesters? Macal? I couldn't allow that.

Doran pressed two fingers to the bridge of his nose. Worry building, I continued. "I see other possibilities. As head of council, you can give me time to investigate. To bring back proof that the Singers didn't do this. That someone else plots against the council, and against you."

He leaned back, intertwined his fingers into a towertop. "Your point about attacks continuing is a real risk. And perhaps showing myself to be fair during difficult times cannot hurt me. I'll give you until Allmoons to make sure I'm right."

Allmoons was only two days away. I had to figure out where to begin and how to keep my family safe. Doran looked at where the council plinth once hung, then down over the tower's edge. "Although I am afraid what you seek is lost in the clouds."

Memory of falling through mist and smoke. Of being pulled down and fighting free. I took a deep breath. "Then I will go into the clouds."

For a moment, the tier was so silent, we could hear the family below lighting their cook fire and preparing dinner behind their barricade.

"You can't be serious," Doran said.

I'd survived the clouds twice already, even if I hadn't gone very deep. And that was where the fallen council plinth would be. That was where I'd find answers. "I'm very serious. I'll start from the remains of the attack, if I can find it, and work backwards to prove that it wasn't the Singers. That it was Dix."

"And I'll go with him," Beliak said. He shook his guard free and came to stand beside me. Maalik wriggled from Beliak's pocket and flapped to my shoulder.

Beyond the balcony, the sky turned pink at the clouds' edges. These were shorter days as we approached Allmoons. Any survivors unfound by now would be stranded in the clouds' dark chill.

Below us, the city rumbled.

Doran stood, shakily. "Until you prove otherwise, I must hold the Singers responsible for attacking the council. They will be hunted in the city and punished on Allmoons. I cannot go against the city's will any longer than that. But I will give you until then." He waved at a guard, who gently raised Elna to her feet, then pulled Ceetcee forward.

Every muscle in my body tensed. "Leave them out of this."

"On the contrary, Elna put herself into it, with her rousing speech," Doran said. "She must be protected. She'll wait with me, and will be well cared for while you search for your proof that the Singers aren't behind this attack." A marker held as a guarantee against us escaping? Perhaps. But he would not harm her. I believed that. "And you, Ceetcee Densira. What will we do with you?"

Beliak tensed beside me. I twisted the silk cord at my wrist until my pulse throbbed against it. They could not keep her, but I wanted her safe.

"I will go with them," Ceetcee said. Not a drop of fear in her voice. "And we'll take Ciel. She can echo, and in case the towers turn on the Singer fledges, she'll be safer with us." She took the fledge's hand and walked to stand with us without waiting for permission. Her fingertips brushed the heel of my hand.

Doran bowed his head. "Very well. You have two days until Allmoons. You will go beneath the clouds immediately. No lingering, or I'll worry that you are in danger, or colluding. Send me a message by whipperling if you do find answers, or come here. And I will do one thing more, because I want you to know how important you are to me. I'll give you supplies: tethers, food, grappling claws. The clouds are dangerous, and few return. You may find answers there, or you may find something sharper of tooth. I'd like to see you come back to the city and help it grow past this tragedy."

Worry blew through the tier like an eastern wind. Cold and ruthless. I'd convinced him to hear me, but at what cost?

Ceetcee stood to my left, her long braids glittering, her clear brown eyes and long eyelashes the things I loved to see first each day. Beliak's rope-strong arms rippled beneath his robes too. His cropped hair and gap-tooth grin made him look younger than his twenty Allmoons.

Below the city, the clouds had swallowed Kirit Skyshouter,

my wing-sister, the council, and all those on the platform who had not escaped.

Now the city held my mother hostage while two I loved most in the world were headed with me below the city, into the all-devouring clouds.

16

LIGHTER-THAN-AIR

Doran and his people helped us prepare to descend into the clouds. One guard found me a new footsling and swapped out my patched one. Another, the guard I'd pushed aside earlier, reached for my satchel to fill it with supplies, and not gently. I grabbed for the strap, remembering the metal plates I carried there.

A singed spot on the strap tore with our pulling, and the woven bag upended on the balcony. The bag's flap fell open and the metal plates I'd carried for Kirit struck each other with a clang.

"What is this?" Doran moved very swiftly for an injured man. The light hit the plates and illuminated the careful, unreadable notations. The plates were more beautiful than anything I'd seen retrieved from below.

Doran lifted both plates and ran his fingertips over the engraved marks.

Dangerous myths. Wik's words. *Best not to show those to anyone right now.*

Too late. Doran grasped the plates with the kind of reverence that one would have for any metal salvaged from downtower. More reverently, in fact.

"Do you know what these are?" he asked me. "They're our birthright. Dix found one of these at Spirefall, hidden in Rumul's effects. She sold it to me. It took artifexes moons to realize it was a method of distilling gas, different than what we'd known. Nat, the Singers hid these from us. They kept the old knowledge of our people from us, what was lost when we rose through the clouds. Imagine the secrets in this one plate!" He let the plate etched with lines and circles tilt so that it reflected the sunlight.

"I don't understand," I finally said. "The plate had been inside one of the codex tablets for a long time. Little oxidation on the metal. No wear. Kirit didn't know they were inside. No one knew."

Doran held the plate reverently, as if it was more proof against the Singers. "They hid knowledge from us."

I rocked back on my heels. Doran hadn't only wanted Kirit to find the codex, he'd wanted her to find out if the codex might conceal more of the plates.

"Nat. Nat—" Doran protested. "The city needs these secrets. As many as we can find. We need the knowledge to rise higher, like we need the gas—the lighter-than-air. Imagine how we could evolve?"

I imagined, against my will, flying platforms, hang-sack sleeping nets transformed into living quarters. Explorations of what lay beyond the city's edge. Discovery. I couldn't ignore the attraction. Perhaps that same feeling had led Doran to ignore signs of Dix's treachery.

"Why would the Singers hide the plates inside the codex, then?" My curiosity was won. I would know this before I faced the clouds.

"Perhaps the right word isn't 'hide.' Perhaps it's 'protect.'" Doran held out one hand after the other. Then he wrapped his left hand around his right. "Perhaps they were preserving the plates, as they did everything. Maybe in a time of war. Maybe they hid them so well, they forgot where they'd put them."

"They left us a hint in our Laws," Elna whispered. "*Delequerriat*—to hide in plain sight, for the good of the city."

She was right. Maybe Singers put a clue in the Laws for us, to tell us to look. But once it was safe to bring them out again, we'd forgotten they existed, except for our myths.

"Why do we need the plates?" Beliak asked. "We have a traitor attacking us. We could be at war. We need weapons, not instructions for our ancestors' tools."

Ceetcee looked at him from where she and Ciel were rolling up quilted robes for sleeping in. "Wouldn't being able to fly higher than your enemies be an excellent weapon in war?" She was an artifex first and foremost.

Doran nodded agreement. "Nat, I will tell you a truth that few know, as a way to show my regard for you, despite your doubts of my intent. Yes, I can see it written plainly on your face." He patted my shoulder. "It's not only that tower growth is slowing. We need the gas because the towers cannot rise forever: they'll stop growing entirely. We've been looking for solutions for some time. And this gas—lighter-than-air—Dix understood that."

"Why not tell the city?" Ciel asked.

"Can you imagine what people would do if they knew the towers wouldn't keep rising?" Doran paced before me. "The city wasn't ready for it when Naton fell. They weren't ready when the Spire broke. And now, thanks to this attack, they may never be. They'll see the gas as a weapon. This attack ruined my plans. If you succeed below, when the council re-forms, I'll need you there. Now that you know. Together, we'll leverage the towers' unity. We'll show them the good we can do with this new tool. You're a unifying figure. A hero. You helped save the city once. They'll listen to you on this. I need you to help save it again."

Ciel charged forward, looking to fight him, me—it didn't matter. "*You* go into the clouds, then!" but Beliak caught her and drew her back before the guards bound her too.

"You show your needs in interesting ways, Doran. Enslaving fledges?"

"Dix said she'd take care of getting the heartbone we needed, and I trusted her. Perhaps too far. We couldn't tap the occupied towers. The Spire was . . . an opportunity." Doran stood now. We were the same height. He'd always seemed taller, before. "We need you too, Nat. Your heart is in the right place."

He offered me power, but it was tainted. What would my father have done? I found Naton's broken message chips in my pocket and flipped them over, thinking. He would have drilled holes in this plan.

Elna lifted her head. Her clouded eyes reflected the sky over Doran's head. "Did you put this to the council?"

Doran coughed. Once, a simple negation, backed with smoke. "Council wouldn't understand, not immediately. We were going to *show* them proof. To float them in the sky. We were going to rise again, beyond the towers this time—free for a moment from the city's rumbling, its crowding . . ."

He held out his hand, palm out, fingers opening. Expansion. Exploration. I saw his plan for the city.

"Instead, they saw your proof when it attacked them. Who did know of this?" Aside from me, perhaps Kirit, and the Singer fledges.

He scratched his head with the same fingers. "Inaro, one of my wives. Rya, my daughter. I prepared them for changes that would occur because of shifts in the city's economics. Ezarit."

Elna's shock echoed the word. "Ezarit knew?"

Doran smiled at her. "She knew. She endorsed it. I'd had arti- fexes working on the gas for years—trying different kinds. The Singers were little help. And then we came across the plates: older downtower experiments, notes from older artifexes."

"Ezarit knew?" Elna was louder now. "How could she know and do nothing?"

"She didn't know how the gas—we call it lighter-than-air—" Doran frowned. "She didn't know how that was procured. She knew only that it existed. That it could be, eventually, traded and sold. Of course she endorsed it."

Ezarit wasn't here to defend herself, either. What would he say about us, if we failed to return? He'd said he wanted us to succeed, but if we were lost in the clouds, we, and our arguments, would be safely out of the way.

We were going into the clouds with Ceetcee pregnant, Beliak's eye swollen shut. Ciel. "Ceetcee cannot go," I said. "Let her stay with Elna."

"Clouds take you, I'm going," she answered. "No child of mine will grow up under a lie. I am healthy and can fly for several moons more."

I knew the look on her fierce face well. There was no arguing. Beliak nodded. Ciel watched as a guard prepared a pack for her. Pointed to one of the knives in the guard's sheath. The guard shook his head, no. He did consent to share from his quiver of arrows with me, for which I was grateful.

Doran turned to me. "You want to know the city's secrets, Nat. I know you do. I've shared what I know with you. Now you must find more answers, and help the city by doing so, I hope. On your wings, Councilor."

He addressed Ceetcee. "You're a bridge artifex. You know the problems Dix is addressing. If not Dix, we need someone skilled to guide this project. You might be one of those people. Come back safely, Risen."

Ceetcee narrowed her eyes. She liked the idea a little, I could see, but she didn't like Doran. "The weakened Spire is still a risk. Your project puts towers in danger, and people. Now the lighter-than-air you've made is a weapon. How can we live this way?"

Doran squeezed her shoulder. "We'll fix the Spire's danger with the lighter-than-air, Ceetcee. More lighter-than-air means we can float families to other towers quickly if we need to. We have enough stored to do that." Before the council platform's ruins, Doran's vision expanded.

But we'd heard enough. We had no lighter-than-air here, and it would do us no good below the clouds. Doran clasped our hands, murmuring, "On your wings," until he got to Ciel, who demurred, eyes down, as if she was shy, but I saw her teeth clench.

I kissed Elna's thinning hair and whispered, "I'll be back for you."

"I know you will," she said. "Mercy on your wings."

Then Doran's guards launched off the hightower balcony and circled, waiting. There was no more time. Ciel leapt from the tower and wobbled on her fledge wings, followed by the three of us. The guards whistled a chevron formation, allowing Ciel to draft behind them.

\ \ \

A clean, westerly breeze filled my wings, buoyed me up, and brushed my cheeks cold.

Wind always forgets the harm done to it. It bears no grudges, no scars. Not like us.

Off my windward pinion, the sun dipped into the cloudtop, tinting the bases of towers brass and rose as we passed them. We flew as an arrow-point through the evening, not towards the city's edge, but to its center.

When we came to Bissel, we passed the tier where Hiroli said she'd meet us. Found it empty. The blackwings searching for

Singers must have gotten to them first. Ciel looked towards me, worried.

"We'll find them," I said, not sure at all that we would. Worse, we would have to protect Ciel, more than ever. Until we found the traitor, all Singers would be hunted. Even fledges.

The guards took us to the edge of the mist. Left us on a ledge three tiers below the cloudtop and slipped back above, into the setting sun.

Atop the ledge, I shivered. We were here, now, because I'd wanted to be on council, to lead. To never be downtower again. To uncover the city's secrets. For a few moments, I let myself think miserably about what my ambition had brought to my city, my friends, to my family. Then Ciel nudged me, her face far more serious than I would have thought possible for her age, until I remembered what she'd been through. "We'll find the traitor," she said.

"We will," I promised her. "We'll make things better for you, and for everyone."

"Do you think Doran's telling the truth?" Ceetcee asked. "About the plates? Dix? Do you think he believes the Singers did this?"

"I think he's telling the truth as he sees it," Beliak said. "I think he's telling the only truth the city has right now."

We would have to sift through layers of truth in order to find the answers we needed. We had to find a new truth below the city so that we could tell it above.

PART THREE

FOUND

On the wing, the new flock of black kaviks attacked smaller whipperlings as they discovered them. Circling, they watched the brown bodies drop to the clouds, before continuing to the next tower, and then another.

⌒ **TREASON** (revised) ⌒
The city betrayed, whether Council or quadrant,
Removes danger with unceasing might.
None are exempt, none immune.
To preserve the city,
all excise blight.
⌒ **WAR** ⌒
No tower will sabotage or war
With neighbors near or far.
We rise together or fall apart
With clouds below, our judge.

17

GHOST TOWER

Our world divided now between below and above. Missing and not. Proof and rumor.

City children learned early the clouds were dangerous. For us, now? Safety wasn't guaranteed above the clouds, and below, we were on our own.

We had until Allmoons to prove the Singers weren't at fault. To find out who'd attacked the council, who'd stolen the artifex, and why.

Two days.

We peered into the mist, unsure of where to begin.

Across the cloudscape, evening light slanted through thick air to reveal more towers' forms. They loomed gray and green in the distance, some rising right through the clouds, others ending before they breached the surface. Larger shadows moved the depths below.

"What's that?" Ceetcee said. Her resolve wavered now that we were downtower.

"Could be gryphons." I tried to keep my voice light. Skymouths? Bone eaters? Worse? "Let's find shelter." Before anything could rise to investigate our presence.

The winds were more turbulent within the clouds, as we'd learned before. But they were still rideable. The guards had oiled our wings against the damp, had provided us warm quilts, and food. Some weapons, for most of us.

Something moved beneath my foot. A tether, tied to a piton and a weathered grip. One of the shadows began to creep up the side of Bissel, moving closer to us. I unsheathed my knife. Beliak drew his too. Then I grabbed the tether and gave it a snap. "Stop where you are."

"Nat?" Aliati's voice, muffled by the clouds.

Beliak reached down and hauled her to the ledge. "Greetings, Risen," he said, with a sad grin.

She stood, brushing damp threads of moss from her robes. "What happened? I've been searching the undercloud all day. I saw the Conclave. They didn't fly the Singers to the city's edge?"

Conclave? Realization dawned. "*No,*" I said, trying to put words to the disaster. Reeling at what she'd seen from beneath the clouds.

She frowned, confused. "If that wasn't a Conclave, what was it?"

"That was the council. They fell." I gripped her arm so tight she tried to pull away. "You saw an attack on the platform." More than that, she'd seen them fall. "Did you see where they landed? Will you take me there?"

"I can, in the morning—it'll be easier." She looked up at her dry quarters, and readied to climb.

But we couldn't wait. We had to find shelter below the clouds, to hide Ciel, and Ceetcee too, from the angry towers. I showed her the message chips. "We have to go below. You've done this, when you scavenged. Tell us how?"

She frowned, slowly turning her head to look at the cloud-top. "I've never spent a night in the clouds. Don't know many who have."

Many, not *any.* That meant some. "Please, we need your help. We must go now," Ciel said, her voice edged with fear.

Aliati thought hard. Then made a decision. "There are caves

where scavengers leave supplies, in case someone gets caught out, or hurt."

"Scavengers look out for each other?" Hard to believe.

She caught my look of doubt. "We work alone, keep what we find, each to ourselves. But we leave caches for others in need, in case we need one someday."

Scavengers had more kindness in them than some citizens in the towers.

"What we must do is not get lost," Aliati said. "First rule of working in the clouds."

She knelt on the ledge and pulled the small Gravity game from her robe. In the dim cloudlight, we could barely see the tower sigils on the silk. Bending close caused my shoulders and leg to throb, from landing on Varu.

Using a bone chip to mark the tower where we stood now, Aliati said, "There's a broken tower, just there." She pointed to a space in the clouds. "It's what scavengers call a ghost tower. It stands between Bissel and Naza, but far lower, hidden by the clouds. That's why those towers are so far apart in the city, when other towers are close."

She pulled out her tools. Laid the straight edge against the game sheet. "I don't know exact distances, but it usually takes me about two verses of The Rise to get there." She began to coil the tether, then half-hitched it to her shoulder strap.

"Are you proposing we go now?" Beliak said.

"Unless you want to stay on this ledge all night? My echoing's getting good, but I'd rather not risk getting separated."

She wasn't merely proposing we go to the ghost tower. She was proposing to come with us. "I'll show you where the council fell tomorrow, if you want to employ me. Other scavengers have been searching, paid by the towers, but I'm the only one who knows where the council is. So far."

Ah. She wasn't doing this out of the goodness of her heart. "I'll pay you," I said. I would get Doran to give me tower marks. "And as for not getting lost, we can pick windsigns," I said. "Keep track of each other like hunters do." I whistled one as an example: "defend." Two long notes, one short.

Ceetcee considered for a moment, then whistled "bridge," a long note with a curl at the end.

Aliati chose "retrieve." Three long, piercing whistles.

Beliak chose the call for a circle formation. One long note with two short notes following.

Ciel couldn't decide. So we gave her the windsign for "home." She liked that.

"We'll find Moc," I promised her.

"I believe you," she whispered back.

One more thing. "Keep an eye out for survivors." For Ezarit. For Kirit. For others.

"If we find too many survivors, they will slow us down," Aliati said.

"If we find any," I said firmly, "we'll help them. We are not cowards. We won't turn away someone in need."

ᒃ ᒃ ᒃ

Aliati searched for the strongest vent she could find, asking Ciel to echo with her in order to help her see the wind's shape. I scanned the darkening clouds for invisible menaces. The sun began to set as we flew for the ghost tower, tinting the clouds around us orange and gold, then rose and blood.

She took us lower than I'd flown near the Spire. Lower than the net where I'd lost Kirit. Everything above disappeared. Then what were once layers of mist shot through with beams of light, now turned opaque. The tower shadows we'd been using to orient ourselves faded. We could still hear just fine, but we couldn't see very far at all until our eyes once again grew used to the dim light. I focused on Aliati's wings, the sound of her whistle: the three long notes. *Retrieve.*

"Stay together," I whispered. My jaw ached. I'd been grinding my teeth. My fingers wrapped my wing grips tighter. Then Beliak whistled, and I whistled back. One long and two short notes for him, two long with one short flourish for me. *Defend.* Ciel whistled next, one long note. *Home.* A pause. Then Aliati again. We whistled in rotation, spilling air if anyone sounded too far behind. We must have gone twenty rounds or more, we flew so long.

We flew straight until Aliati said, "Should be here."

Below us and to the left and right of our wingtips, we saw shadows, but we couldn't see the ghost tower. I circled lower and lower until my feet grazed sturdy bone. I whistled and the others landed in the midst of a heavy cloud that had blocked much of the moonlight and faded to gray. We gathered close together, barely able to see each other's faces.

"We'll need to wait here until the moon rises high enough to cast more light into the clouds," Aliati said. She held her voice calm, which made me more nervous. "If we move in the thick clouds, we could get lost." We sat, knees and elbows touching. Fingers intertwined, hands holding on to what was left of everything we knew.

I expected Ciel to cry. Everything she'd known, gone twice over. She surprised me by humming a song instead. Not The Rise. Something I'd heard last when Tobiat was alive. I felt warmer, as Ciel began to put words to "Corwin and the Nest of Thieves," an old Singer ballad.

> *Corwin dove down and down again,*
> *Through the clouds, fought the deep and the dark.*
> *He returned to the city, once more risen.*

Beliak and Ceetcee laughed to hear it, remembering our sessions with Tobiat. Corwin was a rogue—like Tobiat had been—and the song had a rowdy turn. But he'd won in the end.

Aliati didn't say a word when the first verse was done. The thieves, I remembered too late, were scavengers. "She doesn't mean any hurt," I whispered, hoping to broker a peace. "She's been through a lot. Her brother's missing."

"I know," Aliati said. "Doesn't mean she can hurt someone else to ease her own pain."

She had a point.

"Ciel, we're not Corwin," I said, finally. She'd been nearing the song's end.

"I know," she said. "Maybe we're the thieves. I'm changing things." She sang on.

> *But what Corwin missed was a tear in his robe*
> *As the thief struck from behind, quiet and bold,*
> *And what Corwin thought was the treasure cold*
> *Against his skin, was the wind on his backside, and the*
>   *light leaking in.*

The new verse had even Aliati laughing and clapping along quietly.

Not bad, for a Singer fledge. I dug into my satchel and handed Ciel an extra-large piece of fruit, then passed the rest around. We ate in companionable quiet, occasionally singing more.

The city had songs for Remembrance, and adventure. But there were no songs for the living cloudbound, the missing. Once the city sang Remembrances at Allmoons, it let the lost and the dead go.

We would make our own songs.

The moon finally shot pale shafts of light through the cloudtop, marking some paths, obscuring others. "Do you want to try now or wait for morning?" Aliati asked.

The thought of spending a whole night on the towertop was not a pleasant one. I stood up. "I'll go. We'll come get you soon." The others gathered closer, preparing to wait.

Aliati and I set grip hooks in the tower, dislodging chunks of gray bone that rattled down the towerside until they disappeared. She tugged at the grips to be sure they were secure. Then we each tied tethers to them, using looping knots Aliati taught me. We tucked the other tethers' ends through our footslings. If we needed to, we could reel ourselves back to the top of the ghost tower.

"As long as you don't get hung up on something." I tried to make it sound like a joke.

"If I do get tangled, I'll cut the rope and shout until you find me." Aliati wasn't joking. We weren't playing at thieves, and this wasn't a song. She was as serious as I'd been while trying to drag the fledges away from the Spire a few days before. Neither one of us was willing to pull down those we cared for.

I appreciated that about her. That and her abilities beneath the clouds. "I'll do the same."

We needed to find the scavengers' emergency shelter. I hoped it was safe and dry and out of sight.

Aliati and I let ourselves down the tethers simultaneously. I spared a look up. Silhouetted in the moonlight, Beliak, Ceetcee, and Ciel knelt on the ghost towertop watching us search, their faces hidden in the shadows, but each of them for a moment outlined in silver moonlight. Then the clouds closed again.

When we were out of earshot, I asked, "Any sign of Kirit?"

"I didn't find her," she said. "Many good reasons for that. Some not so good."

A heavy weight settled over me, and I held the rope tightly.

"But?" Her words had an empty space at the end, as if she wanted me to ask.

"I found signs of her. A bit of blood spilled on a Spire grotto, as if someone wounded had bedded down there."

"Show me. Tomorrow. After we find the council."

Aliati leaned against the tier, her toes jutting out over the ledge. "What if Kirit's alive and doesn't want to be found?"

I couldn't think about that. "The city doesn't need another ghost, Aliati. She's alive until we know otherwise." All of the fallen were.

In the city, anything fallen into the clouds was forfeit. That was tradition. But I'd fallen in and lived. We were here, now. Inside the clouds, there was hope until there wasn't.

"I don't think she'd hide on purpose without saying something. Without making sure at least the fledges were safe," Aliati said.

"The artifex who was working for Dix is missing too," I said. Aliati might have passed his cave in her travels.

Aliati looked up at the clouds and brushed hair back from her eyes. "Strange." She sighed. "We should be looking for the cave, not talking so much."

"What about that there?" I pointed at a shadow on the tower. A section of core wall not altogether grown out? The shadow was small, though. And then it moved.

Aliati chuckled. "Not the cave. Probably a wild bird. Or a bat."

Probably.

Unsettled, we went lower. "It's close," she said. She pointed to a mark carved in the ghost tower. "Scavenger marks." But the only things nearby were a ledge and a divot in the tower, not anything deep.

In the distance, the moonlight outlined another thick cloud. "We should head back," I said. "There's nothing here."

"Listen, Nat," Aliati said. "In the clouds you have to be patient and look closely. You can't decide you don't like something because it's below the clouds and you don't want to be below the clouds."

She was right. We used pitons and grips to work ourselves closer to the divot. As we approached, we saw the cave was bigger than it had appeared through the clouds. But a cairn sat outside the cave entrance: a pile of jagged, hollowed bones, emptied of marrow.

A bone eater's cairn? I wanted to leap from the tower and rise, to warn my friends. Aliati put a hand on my arm, stopping me. "Wait. They're dry. Not new."

But my eyes scanned the tower, searching for danger. "Don't move," I said, pointing. "Look."

Not too far above us, near where Naza might be hidden in the clouds, shadows tangled and flew apart. When they separated, wings blurred the air, scattering whorls of mist. The moonlight edged a sharp beak. An enormous bone eater, bigger than the one Kirit and I'd seen in the Spire, flew there.

And the second shadow that chased the first? That outline was the unmistakable form I'd fought to never see again.

"Birdcrap," Aliati said. She pressed herself into the shadows.

Though their skin gave them near perfect camouflage in the city above, in the clouds, skymouths blocked the dim light, and this one's outline shimmered darkly. The shadow-monster's tentacles curved out from its bulbous frame. Even without being close to its mouth, we could see that it, too, was enormous. Skymouths in the wild, deep clouds. Amazing. Seeing it, I hoped the skymouths' smaller cousins, the littlemouths that clung to the towers, lived this far downtower as well.

Many tiers over our heads, the skymouth grappled a bone eater. Aliati and I hid in the mouth of the scavenger's cave as glossy, black feathers fell against the towers around us, making a sound like rain.

"The others," I said. "We have to get back there."

She gripped my arm, tighter this time. "If they're smart, they'll lie down on the towertop and won't move. Like we're not going to move, got it?"

I got it.

We hunkered below the overhang of the cave, keeping our eyes on the clouds above us. The bone eater screamed, though the clouds muted the sound, and dug its shadow-beak into the skymouth's shadow-side.

"That big thing lives here in this tiny cave?" I couldn't imagine a bone eater squeezing inside the opening.

"No. Too big," Aliati said. "Scavengers put cairns like that out to keep bone eaters like that away. Let's take a look?"

She sounded more certain than I felt, but we needed shelter—a safe one—so we ducked inside the cave mouth. Despite Aliati's assurances, I drew my knife and held it ready while Aliati echoed all the way to the back of the cave. "You're good at that."

The echoes stopped. "Been studying. Useful trick those Singers had." She picked up echoing again.

It was dark, and all I heard were the clicks she made and the sounds of my own footsteps bouncing back to me from bone walls. If I closed my eyes, the clicks seemed to make a pattern, but I couldn't quite understand what it meant. I banged into a wall, reached a hand out to brace myself and touched a cool surface. Nearly cut myself on a sharp edge that was cool like metal. Something Scavengers had put here? Whatever it was, it had become embedded in the cave wall long ago. In old towers, like Lith, I'd seen metal spikes used to split growing bone into sections, so that tunnels appeared, or could be cut more easily later, after the core wall grew past. Tower residents didn't do it often, because it weakened the tower, but a scavenger could, using a larger piece of metal than we could afford up above. A metal piece could have caused the gap in the bone that eventually formed this cave.

Besides the spike, the cave was nearly empty. Aliati found two small caches. She clicked her tongue to her teeth, a thoughtful sound, this time. "Food, we don't need. Oil lamp, we do." She lit one and hung it from a hook in the cave ceiling. The space was tiny, but crowding five of us inside would be better than hanging nets from a tower in the mist below a skymouth fight, which had begun to look like our other option.

While I worked my way around the cave once more, making sure no bone eaters hid in its walls, Aliati went back to the cave mouth. Moonlight outlined her profile, looking up. I joined her. The two creatures had descended close enough that we could see the bone eater clearly now, and the skymouth hardly at all, except for silver glints of refracted cloudlight. The bone eater's body bent at an odd angle, its beak opened and shut without making a sound. Its feathers were pressed close to its body, and as we watched, they began to bend and stick out at odd angles. We heard the cracking sound of ribs breaking and the enormous bird gave a strangled squawk. The skymouth had wrapped invisible tentacles around the bone eater and was squeezing the life from it. Dark silver skymouth gore dripped across the bone eater's face. We heard the hiss of it on feathers. The bird's still scrambling claws must have punctured the skymouth's ink sacs.

A small win, too late. The feathered body, nearly half the size of Kirit's tier on Grigrit, sagged. Its head flopped, its long gray tongue dangled in the air, as its body slowly began to rise.

A skymouth in the blue sky over the city was terrifying enough. A red tear would open from nowhere and the last thing anyone saw was the gaping mouth and rows of glass teeth. But we were in a new habitat now. The dark red maw opened in the gray clouds, and we could see the impact of its enormous flowing tentacles, the size of its body. Giant bones snapped as the skymouth began to tear its prey apart.

The wild skymouths weren't all gone. Once I overcame my shock, the awe I felt at the sight of them surprised me. In the clouds, the monstrous was magnificent.

When the last of the bone eater had disappeared into the monster's jaws, the mouth closed and the skymouth disappeared, save for a few silver glints that traced a curve of tentacle. Then we saw the shadow in the clouds below us, growing smaller.

"Never thought I'd see something like that," Aliati said.

"Nor me." We'd lost so much of what we knew from the city above already. No sky but the swirling clouds; no stars, no sun, nor moon, but the beams the clouds let through. Seeing the skymouth fight drove all I'd been taught to fear about the clouds from me like mist. We were here, in our new element, not dead, not lost. We would survive this. We had to survive this.

To do so, we'd need to do one thing that few besides scavengers had done before: to come back alive from deep within the clouds. "We can't go back until we can convince the city that the Singers weren't at fault," I said. In the morning, we'd try to do that, when we found where the council fell.

"I think the city will figure that out eventually," she said. "City needs its enemies right now. But it will be too late. It's not like you can convene a vote from here."

"Ouch." She'd kept her eye on city politics.

"Scavengers trade in metal and gossip, Nat."

The air was clear of giants now. Aliati and I marked the cave with pitons and another oil lantern, then scaled the ghost tower. Led the others down the tower's side to the cave before the next fog rolled in.

"Someone will stand watch," I said. "Always." We would all look out for each other. Like scavengers did.

They agreed, each in turn. I chose first watch. Then we un-rolled the robes Doran's guards had offered us from Ezarit's tier—patterns of sepia tones, flecked here and there with small glass beads. Ezarit's favorite. Our small nest of thieves huddled close and finally slept. Outside the ghost cave, wind whistled and howled around the tower trunks.

18

COUNCIL FALL

In the morning, we flew east from the ghost cave in a dove formation, taking the Spire's moss-covered wall close on our right wingtips as a guide. Overnight, the clouds had thickened around us, blocking much of the sunlight.

"The plain isn't directly beneath the council tier," Aliati had explained before we left, while tendrils of mist curled into the scavenger's cave, lapping over our feet, and her game board. She'd laid her tools and string over the Gravity map to show us the arc of how the council fell. "The wind was strong, pushing everything towards Haim, but not that far. It's about three verses of The Rise from where we leave the Spire, then a fast drop after two of the towers grow together."

Thicker clouds gathered, casting all that we passed into shades of tea and moss against the white. Water beaded on our oil-proofed wings. Occasional wind licks tried to toss us, but we managed to keep fairly straight.

Ciel whistled "home," from the formation's center. I answered her, then heard Beliak whistle behind us, and Aliati in front. Last, Ceetcee, distantly, on the formation's far wing.

The drop caught me nearly unawares. Just before, a broken tower's center core had merged with the core of another tower. At first, it seemed their only link was a bridge between covered in sparing bone growth and hanging moss, but below that, the towers had thickened and grown close enough together that they formed a small ridge.

It was beautiful: the bridge, the ridge below it. I flew over the connected towers, and if Aliati hadn't whistled "attention," followed by "descend," I would have kept flying and missed the valley entirely.

Instead we curved our wings, following Aliati's shadowy form, and dove five tiers so fast my ears popped. I whistled to make sure everyone was still together. When I heard Ceetcee, then Beliak whistle back, though I couldn't yet see them in the mist, I let out a breath I hadn't known I was holding.

Above us, the tower trunks rose, never-ending shadows, into the white, the blue sky a distant memory. Below, a series of ridges and towertops had connected, forming a valley. Scraps of silk fluttered in the higher reaches like Allmoons flags. As we passed close by one tower, circling for a place to land, I could see how the winds had brought most of the council platform's fallen to rest here.

The silk scraps had been torn from wings by the jutting bone outcrops as they fell from the sky.

"We're lower than even the ghost tower," Aliati said to Ciel after we landed. "Go much lower than this and you can start feeling sick, so be careful."

"Sick?" I asked, concerned.

"Especially if you descend fast. It's a giddy kind of sick. There are stories about scavengers laughing themselves to death, if you believe it." Aliati landed and signaled it was safe.

"Why isn't the breeze completely shadowed?" Ceetcee asked once Aliati had showed us where to land. Her voice rang loud in the valley's confines, and she dropped to a whisper at the end.

Aliati pointed to moss-draped vents, where the vegetation lifted in curls and arabesques as the breeze toyed with it. "Watch where you step. There's abyss below, and not everything is solid."

Ceetcee felt her way with her bone hook, sounding the ground before us. "This valley's like a net strung between towers, almost," she said as she walked. "Or a bridge, completely overgrown. Probably temporary too, if it never becomes bone encrusted." Even in the dim light, she peered at the valley, fascinated by the possibilities.

My footwraps grew damp, and mist curled up our legs as we picked our way across the shadowed field, searching for answers. For survivors.

Beliak found another bone hook, fallen unbroken, and used it to help test the ground for safe passage. A stench deeper than the dank moss began to make my eyes water. It was nothing like anything I'd smelled in the towers.

"What is that?" Beliak said, keeping an eye on Ceetcee, who had turned pale.

"It's going to get worse," Aliati said. She tore a strip of silk from a bone spur and wrapped it around her nose and mouth.

On a nearby ridge, a gray-robed Singer hung, their Lawsmarkers-draped shoulders snagged on a bone spur. Before us, the valley's dark surface bore the arcs and angles in shades that did not belong: blues and greens, yellows and a few darker hues. I jumped as Ciel's small fingers wrapped around my hand for comfort. Squeezed. I squeezed back. Another Singer's wing-less form lay nearby.

"Not an attacker," I said.

Ciel heard me. Answered, "No wings, only Lawsmarkers. And those make bad wings."

Someone she held dear? I raised my eyebrows, and she shook her head. "The angry Singer from Grigrit, I think." The one who'd laughed at us. She touched her eyelid and pointed up, remembering him.

Before us, there were so many more to remember.

Beliak waved, waited until we slogged our way across the soggy surface. At his feet, a blue robe, crumpled at odd angles. One broken gray wing, its mate torn off and dangling nearby. Hair matted with blood and dirt. "Wait here," I told Ciel, and approached the body.

This time, the smell drove me back, gagging. While the valley's winds had dissipated much of the odor of decay, it was still very strong.

Someone retched behind me. "I'm taking Ceetcee up higher," Beliak called. He looked pretty green himself. "Where the air's clearer."

They began to ascend the ridge on foot, bent and miserable. Not for the first time, I wished they'd stayed safe, above.

I'd never smelled the dead up close, nor had any of us. No, I realized, that was a wrong assumption. Aliati seemed unfazed by the smell, and she'd known to put something over her nose and mouth. The scavenger moved through the field, peering at a form here, lifting a wing there.

Aliati had wrapped a scrap of her robe over the original silk scrap. Tearing two strips from my robe, I gave the first to Ciel and then covered my own face. The robe didn't block the smell entirely, but it did reduce it a little. Even so, my eyes watered.

Aliati knelt and pulled at yellow silk, bright in the gloom. She found a pocket in the robe she held, removed a laden purse.

"What are you doing?" A councilor's purse?

Aliati put the sack, heavy with marks, into her satchel. "She won't need it." She pulled a knife sheath from a green-shaded arm.

"Stop that!" I shouted. There was a respectful way to treat a body, and this wasn't it. In the city, the dead—if they weren't lost to the clouds—were wrapped in their robes and flown to the city's edge before they were released. They weren't left to be picked over and robbed.

Ciel tugged at my hand. "A body doesn't need tower marks, Nat."

Aliati handed the corpse's knife to Ciel. The girl mumbled thanks through her mask and slipped the haft into her belt. Then the scavenger looked at me. "We need weapons. Spare, undamaged wings. Anything we can find. Doesn't matter who had it before the clouds took it."

I'd thought scavengers mostly looked for their treasures on abandoned lowtowers, not among the fallen. *Now we'd become scavengers and worse: monsters who picked clean the bones of the dead.*

Aliati narrowed her eyes, as if she could read my expression above my mask. "You've gotten your hands dirty, some," she said. "But you still don't understand the clouds. We take what we need to survive here."

She held up a second knife gleaned from the councilor's form. I accepted it, sliding the glass blade into an empty space on my sheath. She moved nearer to the valley wall, and a bone spur there, where a body hung, wings still whole. Gently, Aliati unstrapped the wings from the body and lowered it to the ground.

I took a deep breath and walked through the smell until I could kneel by the gray wings, the crumpled robe. Carefully, I gripped where I thought shoulders should be and turned the form over. The face was a mess of green and blue, smashed bones and dried blood. But the skin bore no tattoos.

Another gray-winged body had come to rest nearby. I checked that one too: Skin was mottled by death and gravity. But neither the tattooist's brush nor a skymouth's ink had marked it.

"No tattoos anywhere," I muttered. The body was big enough

to be an adult. Graying hair. Not a fledge either. This was proof. Was it enough?

On the ridge, Ceetcee shouted and pointed. I followed the angle of her arm down and across the valley. Two bone eater chicks had dropped onto the moss. They ignored us, focusing instead on something lying in the ground.

A gryphon circled, waiting.

The birds were huge and black, but still small enough that we could chase them away. I knelt to grab arrows from a quiver, saw tower marks woven through hair, and recognized an acquaintance—a guard from Varu. I brushed her face with my hand, trying to close her eyes, quickly, but the lids wouldn't budge. She stared at me, eyes cloudy, filled with ghosts.

"Forgive us," I said, then turned my attention to the bone eaters. Their heads bobbed like needles, plucking and tearing. They grabbed something between them and pulled. Then one lifted, carrying a silk-draped object. Flew it high, past the gryphon, and dropped it with a crack against the bone ridge.

"They break the bones to get the marrow," Aliati said, returning to my side. Ceetcee and Beliak were far enough away to be safe, and the second bone eater was still pulling at the form on the ground, when we heard shouting coming from that end of the valley. A wild-haired figure limped towards the bone eater, waving a spear and screaming, trying to drive the birds away.

I'd know that scream anywhere. "Kirit," I whispered.

She had survived; we'd found her. Relief flooded me. I could tell Ezarit, when we found her, that Kirit was safe. I wanted to go to her, to put my arms around her, but she looked like she would strike down anything that touched her.

᠍ ᠍ ᠍

"Kirit!" Ciel yelled and lunged.

I grabbed Ciel's robe and pulled her back. "Stay here!" The

girl struggled and fought me until Beliak descended from the ridgeline and carried her away.

Aliati and I covered the distance to the bone eater chicks in long strides. Kirit didn't turn. She waved her spear. Stumbled. Threw it at the nearest bone eater.

She missed, and the young bird opened its wings and flew away, bearing its find with it.

Kirit howled wordlessly at the departing bone eater. Then she turned on us.

She lived. Clouds. Kirit was alive, but her robes were splotched and greasy, and she stank. Her eyes were wide, too much white around the edges. From a distance, she'd looked like the Kirit I knew. Close up, I barely recognized her.

She stared at us. Turned her head when Ciel yelled, "Kirit!" from high above.

"Are you dead?" She finally spoke.

"No." I held a hand out, palm up. "Not dead. Nor are you."

She waved my hand away and turned back to the ground around her, muttering. One wing was askew, the other ripped. Gray silk fluttered from the batten, trailing her movements.

"We will help you, Skyshouter." Aliati took Kirit's left side, while I flanked her on the right. On this side, the bodies were fewer, but I saw a hand in the moss, pale and still. Farther off, two different colored robes tangled together, two fliers tumbled like lovers in a deathfall.

"What do you seek here?" My last dregs of hope for survivors faded with each new find. No one had survived here. The landing was too hard, and bodies and wingsets both bore scorch marks and burns. "How long have you been down here, Kirit?" I asked gently.

She kept her eyes on the ground, searching, but waved her hand and her fingers twitched. One, two. "They chased me from the bridge. Lost me in the ridgeline. I fell. I was trying to

202 · FRAN WILDE ·

climb out when I heard a noise, something hit the valley. Then more."

Her breath came in stitches. She stopped walking and put her hands on her knees. Waited for balance. "They fell all around me, Nat. They fell."

I tried to touch her arm, to lift the horror from her, but she knocked my hand away. "Don't!"

Slowly, she got to her feet again. Went back to searching, poking at the ground with her recovered spear. We joined her, walking the valley quietly with her. She never looked at me, but she sped up her pace to match ours.

Kirit's eyes widened as she saw something in the shadows, near the valley wall. She limped faster, reaching the crumpled wings even as Aliati and I saw their pattern. Tea stained. A kestrel pattern.

"Ezarit," Aliati whispered.

No.

꙳ ꙳ ꙳

We reached Kirit's side as she lifted the crumpled wing, still locked for fighting. Beneath the silk, Ezarit's body lay curled like she was sleeping.

Kirit collapsed to her knees.

"Mama."

The word, a wail. She lifted one wrist and held it to her cheek. Rocked back and forth.

Ezarit.

All the valley fell away around me, the sound of rushing clouds, the void, the fall, enveloped me. The world was ended. We were in the clouds; we were like the dead. We were ended. Ezarit was gone.

Aliati knelt by the quilted robe. Lifted an edge.

I yelled, "Not Ezarit!" and grabbed at Aliati's shoulder. She would not steal from Ezarit. Never.

Through my tears, I saw Kirit look up, face streaked and pale. She stared at me, then Aliati. Kirit's fingers wrapped around a knife hilt in the belt of her robe, and she drew it slowly out. "Get away from her."

She meant both of us.

"Kirit."

"Get away!" She rose to one knee, tried to stand. Collapsed again, her blade on the ground beside her, her face buried in her mother's robe, sobbing.

I wheeled on Aliati. But the scavenger, the wingfighter, the woman who had led us into the clouds had reached for Ezarit's robes again.

"Look," she said.

A knife hilt stuck from Ezarit's back. Blood caked the tea-colored robe around the wound.

"She didn't fall. Someone killed her." Aliati grabbed for the blade, but Kirit slapped her hand away.

"We will find out who did this," Kirit whispered. "I promise."

The skies had darkened over the valley, and I couldn't see Beliak and Ceetcee anymore. We'd been down here too long. We'd found proof the attackers hadn't been Singers; we'd found a survivor, and a murdered councilor, but it wasn't enough. Now we needed to find our way out of the valley.

Kirit began keening. A horrible sound, her rough voice tore the air with her pain.

"Shhhh," I tried to calm her.

"Let her," Aliati said. "Let her say good-bye."

Loss echoed through the valley. I closed my eyes against it, but it seeped through my ears, my skin. I echoed Kirit's promise in my mind. *We'll find who did this.*

I meant the knife. I meant the council platform. I meant the broken city.

"Nat," Aliati whispered, "open your eyes. Hurry."

I opened them a crack. Wiping tears away on my sleeve, I spotted a soft glow over my robe cuff. Another, at the edge of my vision. At my feet, Kirit raised her face from her mother's robe. Her mourning quieted, but did not stop.

A soft light pulsed the cloudscape. On the nearest ridge, two orbs glowed a diffuse blue. Kirit's voice stilled in her throat, surprised. The lights faded.

"Don't stop," Aliati said. Kirit looked up at her, angry. But Aliati gasped. "Your face. Your skin is on fire. Blue fire."

It wasn't fire. Kirit's tattoos and scars shimmered, like the skymouth had against the clouds. Not a lot, but enough to scare Aliati.

She raised her hands. The mark traced in skymouth ink on her hand, and those more organic scars left by the veins and seams of the skymouth skin she'd draped over herself had a bluish glow to them.

"Sing, if you can, Kirit?" Aliati said.

Kirit looked at Aliati with dead eyes. "How can I sing now? Ever?"

The blue glow faded around us. Her tattoos faded too. I remembered the few blue pulses I'd seen in the clouds, thinking I'd imagined them. I'd never seen their like in the city above. This was something the clouds kept for themselves.

Footsteps quietly approached, and the sound of footslings dragging on the moss. Ciel and Ceetcee, with Beliak behind them. Ciel put her hand on Kirit's shoulder. After a moment, Kirit touched Ciel's fingers with her own.

Ciel began to sing Remembrance. Kirit, after a moment, joined her.

They sang through the verses once, then again. A third time.

Kirit's tattoos pulsed, and the valley filled with soft blue lights along the ridge walls and in the moss.

One was close enough for me to reach out and touch. My hand brushed slick skin, a curved tentacle that grabbed for my finger.

Littlemouths. The glow was coming from cloud-born little-mouths.

Across the valley nearest where Kirit sang, they clustered, numerous. A few pulsed farther from her. Kirit and Ciel finished the song. Aliati drew Ezarit's robe over her head, while removing the knife from her back. All bathed in a blue glow.

In the silence that followed, the lights slowly faded, and the ridgeline shadows grew longer, as darkness took the valley for its own.

19

THE ARTIFEX

We left the valley's shadows and climbed the ridgeline to get high enough to fly.

Kirit walked in silence, leaning hard on Ciel. She'd agreed to let Ceetcee remove her gray wings and fouled robes down to the undersilks. She hadn't protested when Ceetcee wrapped her in a spare overlayer—my hunter's cloak—and slid a pair of green silk wings that Aliati had found over her shoulders.

Now we walked from the valley at her side, thinking our own thoughts, occasionally whispering, but Kirit's silence felt like a void where no sound could enter or leave. We wove our presence around her like a net.

The resolve I'd carried with me from Doran's to find the traitors only strengthened as we climbed the ridgeline above the valley where the council had come to rest. We would honor Ezarit's life, her sacrifice. We would honor them all.

We had a single day until Allmoons now. When we'd climbed high enough on the ridgeline to fly, I could send Doran a message about what we'd found. I hoped he would listen, and that he could get the city to listen.

Over my shoulder, I asked Ciel to pass back a request: "Beliak, ready Maalik to fly."

The ridgeline turned, obscuring our sight of the valley. We angled up, away from one tower's expanse, towards another. The mists parted in front of us, layers of fine curtains. Occasionally, we saw littlemouths in the distance, pulsing once, twice, then disappearing.

Walking next to Aliati, I searched the ridgeline for signs we were clear of the valley's wind shadow. In the mist behind us, Ciel held tight to Kirit's hand. Kirit had pulled my cloak's hood over her head, closing herself off from us. Ceetcee and Beliak brought up the tail end of our group. He raised a hand in acknowledgment and broke a graincake into pieces for Maalik. The bird bobbed and snapped at the food from Beliak's shoulder.

Kirit walked slower with each step, as if an invisible tether kept her tied to the valley. Ciel towed her along, and Beliak whispered encouragements from behind. *Keep moving.*

Overhead, a shadow passed, still high enough in the clouds to have indistinct shape. Another. Birdcrap, we couldn't let Maalik go up if he was going to be snapped from the sky by a predator.

But the way Aliati watched the shadows made me wonder. "Scavengers?"

She tilted her head. Looked again. "No. Scavengers work the towers mostly. They don't stray too far from a way back up, rarely come this low. Those are gryphons, maybe. Or blackwings. They've been searching the clouds around the Spire since you, Moc, and Kirit fell from the sky. But most can't echo so it's taking them a long time."

"Think they're still looking for Kirit?"

"Maybe. Maybe something else." She bit down on the last word, as if she regretted saying it.

I considered what Doran had said the day before. "Or they're looking for the artifex who went missing."

"I didn't say that." Aliati turned on me, sharply.

I knew only what Doran had told me, that Dix had sent a message about the missing artifex. When I'd mentioned it the day before, Aliati hadn't reacted like this. Now, I was concerned. "What do you know, Aliati? Scavengers seem to have connections everywhere. If you know something that could help us, you should say so."

She shook her head, no. Trudged on. I followed her closely. Changed the subject. "Where's the knife you took off Ezarit's body?"

She'd seen me watch her do it. She wouldn't keep that knife as a scavenged trophy. Not while I was leading this group.

She reached into her satchel and pulled it out, wrapped in a strip of Ezarit's robe. "I want to show it to someone."

I took the wrapped knife from her. "Sell it, you mean. No." Turned the bone handle over in my palm. This looked like the knife of a wingfighter. Not many glass-tooth knives left these days. No skymouths being caught, no glass teeth for knives. But I'd seen one with a similar handle at Grigrit, when Doran showed us the game, Justice. "There was a similar knife at Grigrit; Kirit and I both saw it." Aliati and I turned to look back at the young woman trudging up the ridge.

On hearing her name, Kirit slowed. Looked up at us. She didn't speak, but she listened. Ciel wrapped her hand more tightly around Kirit's fingers. Kirit leaned on the girl's shoulder.

"I've seen the knife before too. Over a game of Gravity." Aliati had said at Bissel that she didn't play. Now she did. What was the truth? The latter, probably. She had her own game board. "No, I would not sell this knife." Her voice said, *Don't be skytouched.* Her eyes spoke more sharply.

The more I learned about Aliati, the more I wondered what we'd gotten ourselves into, trusting her. She'd accompanied us below the clouds on little more than a whim and the offer of payment.

"Who do you want to show the knife to?" The fewer people who knew about our task, the better. Especially when it came to people who played strategy games with Dix's confederates. Anyone who warned Dix or the knife's owner would put us in jeopardy.

"A friend." We'd crested the ridgeline. Above us, the bone-encrusted bridge ran from one tower to the next. Above that, shadows and clouds. A bird-shadow circled over us. Aliati chewed her lip. "You need to talk to him too."

"Who?" I'd twisted my finger in the silk cord that once held my father's message chip. Secrets. I hated them, what they did to my friends. "Aliati, tell me."

For the first time since I'd known her, Aliati sounded frightened. "The artifex. The missing one. You need to talk to him." But she didn't slow her pace, she pressed on towards the bridge.

I stopped so suddenly, Kirit walked right into my back.

I grabbed Aliati's arm, stopping her, making her look me in the eye. "How do you know where the artifex is?"

Yes, she was afraid, though I couldn't tell if it was for herself, or for someone else.

She opened her mouth, then closed it. Pressed her lips tight enough to turn white. Then, finally, spoke. "Because I took him. I took the artifex from the Spire and put him someplace safe."

❧ ❧ ❧

With a single sentence, Aliati became immediately more useful in the undercloud, and far less reliable.

"You took the artifex?"

Doran and Dix each sought the artifex. We needed him. And Aliati had both stolen him and forgotten to mention it at Bissel.

"You took him where? And when were you going to tell us?" Beliak joined us at the front of the walk. He'd tied a yellow silk tether to Maalik's claw.

Aliati scratched her ear. "I didn't want him in danger. He's a friend I've known a long time." Simple words, and so devastating.

Kirit spoke, her voice hoarse. "We aren't friends, then."

"You're wrong, Kirit." Aliati turned. "I wouldn't be down here if we weren't. I don't let my friends go into danger. But if they're there, I try to help. Djonn—the artifex—was in danger, and neither of us had realized how much. When I couldn't find you, I saved Djonn."

Kirit stared at her. Aliati pulled on the hoop in her ear and looked away first. I stepped between them, eyes on Aliati. The scavenger wouldn't meet my gaze either.

A friend. Her friend, whose work required kidnapped fledges. But also, an artifex who knew more about Dix's operation than anyone.

If Dix was involved with the council attack, Aliati's friend might tell us. But why hadn't Aliati told us? Scavengers lived by their own codes, certainly, but she'd known what we were looking for. And had wanted to protect the artifex from the blackwings, from the city. From us too, probably.

Unbidden, the tune for "Corwin and the Nest of Thieves" echoed in my mind. Ciel had sung it when we first came below the clouds. Corwin had retrieved something for the Singers. Something metal. We'd come here to retrieve answers. Aliati had descended into the clouds to look for Kirit, but had stolen the artifex instead, the man who had figured out enough of the cryptic marks on the metal plates to make lighter-than-air.

> Corwin found a gleam of hope
> He lifted himself by wing and rope
> And returned the city to treasures old . . .

The Singers had maintained Corwin's song through generations. When Tobiat taught it to Beliak, Ceetcee, and me, it had

seemed like a bawdy, archaic myth. But not one of the songs
the Singers kept as part of their legacy was purely for fun. They'd
sung to remind themselves and others what happened to rebels
and thieves. The towers had no such legends. When we made
it back above the clouds, we could change that.

I made a fast decision. Moving away from Aliati, I knelt on
the ridgeline and cut a message chip: *Meet between the Spire
and Naza, at dawn. We'll find you.* Then I took Maalik from
Beliak's shoulder and tied the chip to the yellow silk cord. "Varu.
Doran." Maalik had flown to Varu many times and recognized
Doran. If he made it out of the clouds, he'd deliver our message.

We would bring proof to Doran: no tattoos among the
fallen attackers, a very particular knife, and the artifex and his
thief.

I tossed the whipperling into the sky and watched him
circle up until he disappeared into the clouds.

Aliati watched me, pale. "I'm not the enemy, Nat."

We needed her help, to show us where the artifex hid, to talk
to Doran. I was wary of her, certainly, but could not make her
a captive, couldn't drive her away. When Doran needed to keep
ties to a dubious ally, he spoke of need and trust. He sometimes
shared a secret with them. With me, up in the tower, he'd shared
the secret of the brass plates. Ezarit had done things differently.
She'd listened to both sides, tried to understand.

We had no time for either. The woman who'd flown at our
side during Spirefall, who'd guarded Wik but refused black
wings, who'd hidden a friend away to keep him safe—and who
had endangered us all.

"Take us to the artifex. Now."

She gestured to the ridgeline's peak, where another bone pile,
this one much older and overgrown, stood before a small cave
entrance. "We're already here."

ʹ ʹ ʹ

"We can't all go in," Aliati said. "Nat and me, maybe Kirit if she wants to. Djonn needed someplace safe where he could recover. Dix was drugging him too, for much longer than the fledges." Emotions played across her face: anger, concern.

Another shadow rippled the clouds overhead. We plastered ourselves to the entrance wall, feeling the slick bone cool through the silk panels of our wings. Another shadow followed, this one distinctly wing-shaped, and dark.

Blackwings. "We're all going in. None of us stays exposed."

A metal grate had been set into the bone, a few steps inside the cave entrance. It was latched.

With swift fingers, Aliati pulled a latch pin. The grate swung with a low squeal, and we stepped inside the artifex's hideout.

The space, lit golden by a single oil lamp, was cluttered with gear. Large bone and metal tanks toppled together, a silk cord binding a stack of skymouth hides, invisible except as defined by the boundary. Two small, filled husks were tied down at the back of the cave, still large enough to float a person each.

"What do you do there, Aliati?" A young man slowly stood up from his place by the fire. The deep circles beneath his eyes, and the grease and stubble on his face made him seem much older than when I'd seen him last, when I'd passed him on the Spire.

On the floor, by a small cook fire that coughed acrid smoke, lay a brass plate like the ones Doran had taken from us. Over the cook fire, a small pot with a goose bladder above it slowly filled with gas.

The artifex took something from his robe and began to chew on an edge of it. It was the color of heartbone, and smelled worse. When he swallowed, he closed his eyes.

Aliati snatched the rest away. "I thought you'd done with that," Aliati whispered. "We need you to focus."

All of us crowded into the small cave made the space warm and uncomfortable. Ceetcee shivered, despite the heat. She hated tight, walled spaces, more than most tower-born. I looped my pinky finger through hers. Beliak took her arm on her other side. She squeezed back and seemed to relax, enough to ask the artifex, "How long have you been below the clouds?" Worried notes in her question. She always thought of the person before the job.

The artifex—Djonn—coughed. "Since before Spirefall."

He looked away, but Aliati poked him with a finger. "Tell them!"

Reluctantly, Djonn began again. "Doran had us working on experiments, and wanted us to keep quiet. Undercloud was the best place for keeping things quiet. Dix moved me from Grigrit's lowtower to the Spire after Spirefall. So . . ." He counted on his fingers. "Since before last Allsuns, at least."

I shuddered, chilled by the thought of staying down here for a few days, much less that many moons. I pointed at the small pot on the stove, at the plate on the floor. "Do you know what you were making the gas for? What the plates are?"

The artifex scratched his head. Flicked his finger against his chest. Tap tap tap. A hard sound. He looked at the plate. "Dix found that after Spirefall, and Doran asked us if we could sort out how it worked. I was the one who figured it out."

"That doesn't answer my question," I said, frustrated.

Aliati put a hand on my wrist. "Give him time. He's been through a lot."

That doesn't make it right.

Djonn met his friend's eyes and smiled softly. "We worked on the gas for moons, always below the clouds, using different supplies. Some mixtures we tried made poison. Some exploded. The gas took so many of us. Then I managed to distill enough gas from the heartbone to fill a small bladder. It floated. It worked."

He was dodging, I was sure of it. "We know Doran ordered the lighter-than-air for the city. Who ordered it for the attack?"

"What attack?" Djonn said. He looked at our clothing and soot-stained wings. His eyes grew wide. "No, no. The gas helps people fly. Even if they're hurt. You can't attack with it."

He knelt awkwardly by to the cookstove, and I could see he wore a brace of some sort beneath his robe. He clipped the small bladder above the pot between his finger and thumb and slid it off a coiled metal tube. Knotted the bag closed and tied it with a string. Aliati saw the metal coil and smiled. "That was a good find."

Djonn attached another bladder to the tube and left it hanging limp. He took a container and poured more heartbone into the pot below the bag. The whole operation took moments.

Then the artifex attached to the first sack a wind-up toy. The kind parents gave to children in the tiers, attached to a tether. He wound the small wings at the toy's feet. When he let the toy go, it flew, bumping into the cave walls with a clicking noise.

"How did Dix pay you?"

He looked down. Hit his chest with his hand. It made a hard sound, of flesh meeting bone. "I am in some pain. The distillation process made a residue that lessened it. They let me keep that."

Aliati shook her head and looked at the piece of residue in her hand with disgust. "They played on your pain." Then she turned to me. "His spine's twisting. He can no longer fly. It's very painful now and could kill him later. That's why I couldn't leave him in the Spire, not when the blackwings were chasing Kirit. He'd have been at their mercy."

"What did you see, Djonn?" Beliak asked. "Did anyone come talk to you?"

"Only the blackwings who took the gas away. Once, Dix."

"Where did they take it?"

"I went up once, to where they stored it. In a spinner tower. Laria in the southeast. I saw them there."

Time to see if Djonn's story matched Aliati's. "What's your connection to Aliati, here?"

Djonn smiled. "She's my friend. She brings me metal and things she finds sometimes."

"Did she take you to the blackwings, ask you to help them?" Aliati stiffened by my side at the question.

But Djonn shook his head. "No. I worked with the Singers, before the Spire fell. I didn't know what else to do after, so I kept working. Then Dix found the plate. I work with the Singers now too."

The cave went deeply quiet.

"No. You don't work with Singers," said Aliati sharply.

Djonn shook his head. "No, I don't."

Strange indeed. Aliati turned and tried to push us from the cave. "This was a mistake," she said. "He's mad with the drug. He'll say anything." But she looked truly afraid for Djonn. For herself.

I edged around her. Knelt next to Djonn at the cook fire. "There are no more Singers," I said. "Not since last Allsuns. Only citizens. You are mistaken."

How long had he been working in the clouds? Had he gone skytouched?

Djonn smiled, his eyes more relaxed now. "Dix let me meet the Singer, after Spirefall. He was very ill and couldn't talk, but she said he needed to move around and couldn't use the bridges, couldn't fly. Said he needed me to try to perfect the gas for him. Said I had to work in secret, like before. They gave me the brass page." Djonn smiled. "And I did it. Better than anyone has."

My throat closed in dismay. A Singer. If Singers were involved, Doran would continue with his punishment. The protesters would be in jeopardy too.

"Describe this Singer," Kirit said. Her voice cracked.

"Gray wings," Djonn said. I shook my head. Anyone could wear a pair of gray wings. We knew that now. "Tattoos, like some of yours." His fingers traced shapes on his face. A knife. A spiral.

"A spiral. Like this?" Kirit held up her hand. Djonn bobbed his head. *Yes.*

A low growl rumbled from Kirit's throat. "Only one person had marks like that. A very dead Singer."

"What were his injuries?" I wasn't following Kirit's line of questioning. I knew some of the tattoos, but not specific ones. "What did this Singer look like?"

"He'd broken his back. His legs were dead. His arms too. He couldn't talk. Dix said he whispered to her. She could understand him. And she carried him, which was easier because he was very thin. Worse than me." Djonn put a hand over his scalp, thinking. "He was bald, so I could see he had a big scar on his head, too."

Realization bloomed on Kirit's face before I fully understood. She bolted for the door, knife drawn, but Beliak and Ciel caught her. Meanwhile, in the span of two breaths, I held Djonn by the robe. The cook fire guttered. I pushed Djonn backwards until his back was against the cave, bone brace against bone wall.

Aliati's own knife glinted as she held it up in the lamplight, near me. "Everyone, stop. Djonn has done nothing but tell us what he knows."

Beliak moved behind Aliati, ready to stop her from striking anyone.

"Rumul," Kirit said, coming to stand closer to Djonn, dragging Ciel with her. Ciel whimpered and pulled her fingers from Kirit's grip. Shook them in the air.

I held out my hand for Aliati's knife. Only when she'd given it to me did I release Djonn.

"When did you last see the Singer?" Ceetcee asked Djonn. Her voice was gentle.

"Before Aliati took me from the Spire. Dix came, carrying the Singer. Dix wanted the gas, my tools." Djonn put a foot possessively on top of a metal case. "She couldn't take them. She grew so angry, she said she'd kill me one day, when I was no longer useful. Then she told me why Rumul still lived."

Djonn looked outside, eyes searching the clouds for hunters, then back at us.

"What did she say?" Kirit asked, her voice tight.

He swallowed hard. "Dix said she kept him because—for better or for worse—he'd been the city's last true leader. That he was still useful. She said that the city was unlucky now because it lacked strong leaders. That it couldn't rise without them. With Rumul under her control, Dix said she'd become the leader the city needed."

❧ ❧ ❧

The circling hunters tightened their path, drawing close around us. They hadn't discovered the valley or the cave yet, thanks to the cloud cover, but each time their wing shadows appeared near the ridge wall, I knew they were closer.

As the sun set below the clouds, it tinted the towers and ridges around us red and orange.

Kirit hugged the entrance arch, leaning against the grate. "We need to talk to Dix." The way she said it, it didn't sound like she planned to talk much at all.

"We will," I said to her. I put my hand on her shoulder, but she flinched it away. "But we have to leave here first," I said. "And we're taking Djonn with us."

Aliati protested. "How can I know we'll be safe with you now?"

"You're not any safer here," I said. "As for us, I could tell you secrets to gain your trust, or lies. But I won't. You'll be safe with me as long as you are honest with me."

She nodded, thinking. "As good as you get with scavengers. Take the equipment you can carry. Take the tools."

Outside, silk rustled in the wind. A pair of black wings dipped past the cave. Another pair followed.

I looked to Ceetcee and Beliak, Ciel and Kirit. "Move away from the entrance." Mentally counting arrows, I wondered if the two blackwings had friends.

If not, we seven stood a chance.

But Aliati pushed aside the jumble of equipment, revealing a low tunnel through the bone. "There's another way out. Follow me." She reached out a hand to Djonn and pulled him through the tunnel. They moved down the path, and the rest of us followed, until the tunnel opened out into a larger passage. Djonn straightened painfully and balanced his lopsided weight on Aliati's shoulder. They kept moving.

This wasn't a cave on the ridgeline. This was a tangle of passages. As we ran along the path, metal gleamed at intersections. The bone ridge's interior had been purposefully shaped into a shelter long ago. The spikes, and even a few rectangular plates were weather- and age-worn and looked very old. Ceetcee balked at the entrance, then took a deep breath and put her hand on Beliak's shoulder. She followed us in.

"You know your hiding places in the clouds well," I said to our scavenger.

Aliati frowned but kept moving, her breath coming fast from the effort of helping Djonn. "People used to live down here. Remember? We're close to where several towers stopped growing. I'd heard rumors about this one, but no one ever comes here. Took a chance when I needed a place to hide Djonn. Found where the council fell when I came back to bring his supplies."

A small hand dragged on my sleeve. "How much farther?" Ceetcee whispered, her voice tight. We seemed to be ascending deeper into the ridge, not out of it.

Aliati answered. "We're going back to the ghost tower, if we can make it to the other side of the ridge. Otherwise, there's one other hideaway that I've heard of. But it's far and dangerously low. Scavengers say it's—" She turned to look at me. "I want the city to know we helped you. That we aren't part of the attacks."

"They'll know," I promised. The path brightened and pools of cloud ran along the floor. A breeze brushed my cheeks. Aliati's strong arms lifted Djonn to her chest and crossed her wingstraps over his shoulders too. He tucked his legs around the backs of her knees, light as a child.

"Try to keep up," she said. And then she dove into the darkness.

I lifted Ciel and flew her the same way; both of us on my wings was still faster than her fledge wings.

Kirit and Ciel both echoed, although Kirit stopped now and then and had to be snapped aware with a brusque "Kirit!" from Ceetcee. We moved quickly through the moonlit clouds, away from the ridgeline now below us.

Once, looking back, a glimmer of skymouth appeared outlined against the darkness. Once, I glimpsed black wings passing in the distance. I whistled to Aliati, and we sank lower in the clouds. No blackwings pursued us farther on our flight from the ridge.

We stopped once to get our bearings, at a low outcrop near

the Spire's trunk. After Aliati confirmed we were going the right way, she and Ceetcee flew a circuit of the area to make sure we could approach our cave without being observed.

Several blue luminescent pulses at varying distances in the haze kept us company while we waited, until it became too light to see them. Now that we knew that they were littlemouths signaling, their presence comforted.

"What do you think they're saying to each other?" Ciel wondered.

Beliak watched them thoughtfully. "Maybe they're telling each other that they're not alone."

That seemed to satisfy the girl, who leaned against Kirit and closed her eyes, whispering, "You're not alone."

Before Aliati and Ceetcee returned, the sky darkened, then brightened again, sunrise replacing moonlight. We took off in early morning light, singing The Rise softly.

By the time we reached the ghost tower, we were exhausted. We circled up to the towertop, where Doran waited with his scope, scanning the clouds for signs of us.

20

PROOF

Kirit made a mad landing, furling her wings while still in the air. She dropped beside Doran. The fall jarred her injuries, and she yelped, then shouted at the councilor from Grigrit, "You dare come here?"

I rushed my own landing, just as Kirit tried to grasp Doran's throat.

"Easy," I said as gently as I could, pulling her back. "He's not your enemy." I tried to see where Doran had placed his guards, but could not spot any nearby.

Kirit turned on me, eyes wild, scars livid. "He's close enough! Dix fought when he asked. Dix knows the man whose knife—" She bit back her last words and spun towards Doran again, who looked astonished to see her. "Where is Dix?"

Doran addressed me, not her, his voice loud in the mist. "I wasn't followed. You gave good directions." Now Kirit looked like she wanted to throttle me instead. Doran continued, "But what do you mean by bringing this Singer unbound to threaten me. Is she your proof?" He had one hand tucked inside his robe, and he'd swapped out his fancy Liras Viit wings for those of a Varu guard.

Kirit struggled against my grip on her robes. "You are not innocent!"

"She's not my proof," I said, hanging on to my friend. "Ezarit is gone." Kirit did not bend, she did not weep when I said it. She turned hard and silent as bone.

Doran's demeanor collapsed into shock. Sorrow clouded his eyes. "I feared this, but hoped she would be found."

"You aren't allowed to hope anything," Kirit said to him. To me.

"I'm trying to help," I said. Kirit had to understand.

The others landed, and Ceetcee tried to pull Kirit away. Only when Ciel clasped her hand did Kirit take a step back. Aliati landed a few steps away carrying Djonn, with Beliak close behind. He nudged the scavenger towards me.

"My proof," I said looking Doran in the eye, "is the artifex, here."

Aliati cried out. "You said we would be safe!" She put a hand to her knife hilt.

With everyone furious at me, I continued, "The artifex is under my protection, as is his guard and friend. If you don't agree, we will disappear into the clouds again, and you will be lost. Listen to what they have to say."

We made Djonn tell Doran his story again. When he said "Rumul," Doran interrupted. "Singers! I knew it. Clouds take them all."

"Don't you see?" I said. "It's not Singers. Dix has Rumul, but he can't speak, can't walk. She's helping him, or controlling him."

My proof laid out, I waited for Doran to react. Had I been wrong to give him another chance? Would he tell the council, and end the Conclave? Then we could come back above the clouds, and Ceetcee and Elna would be safe. Ciel would be safe. And Kirit could find the man who owned that knife.

But Doran's face reddened and his fists clenched at his sides. "She's doing more than that. In the short time you've been under the clouds, Dix has roused the city against me for putting off the Conclave." He looked at me as if this was partly my fault. His voice thickened with anger, but he didn't shout. "If we hadn't waited for you, she wouldn't have been able to do this."

"If you hadn't waited," Aliati said, "she would have found other means. You fell for a show of loyalty. Now she's making her move."

"To what end? What does she want?" Ceetcee asked.

I shook my head. "Power." What I'd thought I wanted, once.

Doran shook his head. "Her kaviks have spread messages across the towers enjoining citizens to return to protecting the city. Some say the city is unlucky now but that she can fix it." He held up a skein of chips and showed us. "Her kaviks attack birds they don't know. They almost killed Maalik."

The councilor withdrew his other hand, heavily bandaged, from his robe. He held my whipperling out to me. Maalik's feathers were mussed, and blood speckled his wing and breast. "I fought the kaviks off with my bare hand. I'll shoot them from the sky next time."

I took Maalik and held him gently. He settled in my hands, cooing. His heart pulsed, rapid but steady against my fingers. "Thank you." *Dix will pay for all of this.* "Where are your guards?" *Why didn't they help you?*

Doran reddened again. This time, the words came slower. "My blackwings, most of them, have left. Dix promised them a revelation after Conclave: a way to move forward, while harnessing the strength of the past. She's promising to fix the towers, to rise again, but to do so, she must throw down Wik, Moc, and the protesters from the Spire at Allmoons. She is demanding you, Nat, and your party as part of the appeasement."

The ghost tower bristled: all our knives, bows, and sharp edges appeared before he finished speaking. Ceetcee cried, "Betrayal," as I scanned the clouds for guards, expecting to have to defend my friends from my mentor. Kirit held her knife ready to throw it at the clouds. But Doran shook his head. "I've changed winds, Nat. Whether or not Dix was involved, the council attack made a hole in the city's leadership, and she has stepped in to fill it. She's fanning people's superstitions, their twined love and fear of the city."

Doran lowered himself to sit on the towertop, mist swirling around him. He looked tired, and much older than I'd ever seen him look. I didn't stow my weapons. "I refused to support her methods when I learned what they were—especially not the fledges. I won't condone her actions now." He paused and met my gaze. "Don't worry. Elna is safe on Varu, with loyal friends. With my family."

"Where is Dix?" Kirit asked again, staring into the mist.

"She's taken control of the lighter-than-air storage on Laria. Says she won't help any towers that do not tithe to her. She's allied herself with the poorest towers, and is encouraging them all to rise up against the city. That blasted game—Justice—is in every tower. And each time it appears, market riots follow. Plus, her kaviks are everywhere; few messages get through any longer, except for hers. With the exception of the northwest and Macal, few city councilors are willing to oppose her. In those that do, their towers are turning on themselves."

Beliak shook his head. "The towers are smart. They must know she's behind the riots and the fighting."

"The towers are afraid," I said. "And superstitious."

Doran blinked. He'd tried to use fear as political leverage. Now he'd been deposed by it. "Dix says she's found a way to bring the city luck again. Those who wish to live within it must tithe to her, and must allow the Conclave."

"She is cloudtouched," Ceetcee said. "She's got nothing to offer."

"On the contrary," Doran sighed. "She's got the south. Bissel and Laria." He sighed heavily. "And Grigrit."

"Worse than that," I realized, "she's got captives to throw down."

ↆ   ↆ   ↆ

Shaking off Ciel's grip, Kirit said, "I'll stop her. I'll end this."

"You will do nothing of the sort," Doran said. "We need Dix alive."

"We?" She looked at Doran, then at me, and laughed. A hollow sound. "You two made a bargain, not me."

I couldn't argue. But Kirit had turned back to Doran. "Why do we need her alive?" Her look of anger and sorrow spoke more evocatively than her words. *Why does Dix get to live while Ezarit does not?*

Doran pressed his lips together and massaged his injured hand, stalling. "Dix has manipulated the city better than anyone: her kaviks spread conflicting messages. People don't know what to believe, except that the city is unlucky. They can see as much in the cracked Spire, in all the Remembrance banners. The Justice game reminds them of tower war. Dix has the city so riled up that one wrong move, one bad death, could set off just that war. Unless she swoops in to fix everything."

He was right. We needed Dix alive, and Rumul too. We needed to argue a case before the city, with proof. They might not give willing testimony, but it was easier to see the faults of the living than the dead.

One look at Kirit told me she disagreed. She seethed as she leaned on Ciel's shoulder. Would she listen?

Ciel tightened her grip on Kirit's hand. "We'll make it all right again," she said.

"Maybe," Beliak said. Ceetcee knelt, tired, on the towertop, back against his legs. He turned on Doran. "We are seven. I have no love for Dix, nor Rumul. Nor much for you either, after everything that's happened. Will you put yourself at risk to stop Dix's Conclave?" He looked at me, then away. "So far, you've been happy letting others do your dirty work."

A sharp pain at my wrist. I'd twisted the blue silk cord so hard, it left a purpling dent. I wanted to reach out to Beliak, to say I was sorry. That I'd made mistakes and was trying to fix them. But I couldn't here, not in front of Doran. I gave the cord another twist and stayed silent.

Doran frowned and bowed his head, but his was face red and angry. He looked like he had at Grigrit, when Kirit questioned him. I braced, prepared to fight him if I had to. Beliak did as well.

But Doran sighed. "I understand. My mistakes have been terrible, and my accomplishments are no trade for them."

Ceetcee rose and stepped forward until she was toe-to-toe with the councilor. She was smaller than him, and exhausted, but she held his gaze unflinchingly. "You will not lead us, Doran. But you may join us in the clouds." Her voice was as light as silk wing, and as strong as the battens shaping that wing.

For a moment, Doran's face fell, his eyes softened. Then his cheeks reddened again. "I am still a councilor."

Kirit watched him carefully.

"What's your reasoning?" I asked Ceetcee.

She looked at us all. "We need Doran's connections, the guards who are still loyal to him, if we want to rescue Wik, Moc, and Hiroli, and end Dix's pursuit of us. I don't doubt Doran wants to regain power." She didn't embellish. "But I think in the end he intends well for the city. I don't think the same of Dix. I think she intends only to do well for herself." She'd made a bridge between our two goals, and when she was finished, she sat down to rest again.

We watched the two halves of Doran's emotions struggle like

the skymouth and bone eater had in the clouds. I willed the calmer side out, but knew now that the real Doran, the one with fears and anger, the one who needed loyalty, was the one who could betray us. It was the source of the fault in his politics that allowed Dix to sneak in and subvert his work.

Doran finally nodded. He clasped Ceetcee's hand.

Beliak knelt with Djonn and Aliati on the ghost towertop. They sketched several ways to capture Dix and reveal what she hid from the city, then discarded them. Plotted rescue attempts using decoys, long climbs up the towers. Most plans, worked through to their logical end, led us from the clouds, to Laria, and capture.

No one was happy, least of all with me.

They stared at the silk square with the tower map on it. "What if—" I broke the tense silence. "We tell the people on Laria and nearby towers *how* they're being manipulated. We tell them about the fledges, the kaviks. Show them how they could be next. Some will rise against her. Then we visit Dix at Laria before the Conclave, before she gains more power—"

"Why not fight now, and get it over with?" Kirit interrupted.

Ceetcee answered, "I think most towers just want to survive, so many will turn away from fights unless they're sure they can win, because they want to be safe. There's been too much loss already. If we can avoid more violence, we stand a better chance of swaying the city away from Dix."

"That means fewer people to fight, if it comes to that," Beliak countered.

"I'll alert the guards I have left at Varu, and the strongest fighters from Densira and Mondarath," Doran said.

"I wish we had lighter-than-air, and more weapons, in case it does come to a fight," I said.

"That," said Aliati, "Djonn and I can help you with."

21

TREASON

Aliati and I dressed in hunter blue cloaks from the scavengers' ghost tower cache. Mold flecked the hoods, but not too obviously. I secured my knife on my arm, my bow across my chest. Aliati mimicked my preparations, and I showed her how to slide her quiver of arrows beneath her wingset, out of the way, but ready.

We'd look like hunters heading to market. I didn't want to think about why scavengers would need hunters' cloaks.

"Are you sure you want to choose sides?" I asked her. "Even if it risks your safety, and Djonn's?" *Even if it means the city knows you to be a scavenger and a thief?*

Aliati tilted her head at Kirit, sitting at the cave mouth, sharpening her bone knife over and over again. "She's chosen a side, and it's neither Tower nor Spire. She's chosen the city," Aliati whispered. "I choose the same." She looked long and hard at me. "You didn't give me a choice before."

"There aren't any easy choices left." No one was right; no one was a hero. Not anymore.

"Hearing you say that eases my mind," she said. "Maybe I'll choose your side too."

Somewhat comforting, that, even from Aliati.

We left the others in the ghost tower cave, with Ciel watching over Maalik's recovery. Ceetcee and Beliak carved message chips to alert the towers about Dix. Djonn began making something he said would help us deliver the messages.

A mist-filled wind buoyed our wings, and we slowly spiraled up the morning gusts until we rose close to the cloudtop. By flying to the south from the ghost tower, we reached the core wall of Ginth and drove in our grips. The tower to the left was Harut. The tower to the right, Laria.

"We're going to need a reason for being there," Aliati said. "And a distraction. I'll do that part. You find where the lighter-than-air is." She handed me a series of long tethers, tied together, then looped into a coil so it could be carried over a shoulder.

I stared at the tether. "Wait. I'm the thief?"

She grinned and nodded. "You can't get caught if something happens in the market. Dix would throw you down. I'm invisible. If it works, I'll come help you." We thought the tethers, together, might reach all the way to an old handgrip on Laria, hidden just below the clouds. We hoped to tie up the sacks filled with lighter-than-air, wait for dark outside the tower, then pull the sacks through the webs and down to us. As long as the tethers held and no one spotted us sneaking into the storage area. Or caught us pulling them out. "We'll just be faster," Aliati said when I questioned that part of the plan.

"What kind of distraction are you thinking?" I'd always gone at problems head-on. Aliati had different tactics, ones I wasn't at all comfortable with, even now. Especially now.

She shrugged. "Let's wait until we know what the market's like. Then we'll know better how to work our way into the silk-spinners' storage."

Many in the city kept a small hatch of family silk spiders for household needs from patches and netting to bandages, or for silkweb and thread sale at market. They preferred not knowing too much about silk production for wings, robes, screens, and banners. The silkspinner towers weren't pleasant places to visit.

I'd been no different. We'd bought our silk from traders like Ezarit.

A larger hatch, the kind needed to make silk production viable, required a tower working together to ensure the spiders were well fed, gently harvested, and continued to breed. And the mess. Even a few silk spiders could speckle the floor beneath their webs with the acid they used to digest their dinners.

Dix had chosen to stage her revolution from Laria. I shuddered. I hated the very idea of wandering the silkspinner towers. Aliati looked as uncomfortable as I felt. I wondered if she'd made me thief and risked the greater danger of getting caught in order to stay out of the webs.

She pointed at the dirgeon nest perched precariously on one of Ginth's lowtower tiers. "See if there are any eggs." She pointed, and I climbed up to the balcony. The nest contained eggshells and hatchlings.

Aliati stuffed the wriggling baby dirgeons into her satchel. "Excellent. We'll be hunters with something to trade."

A flier passed between the towers, moving quickly towards Laria. We followed them, staying back enough to avoid being spotted, we hoped. Gliding several tiers above the clouds, moving from one set of tower shadows to another, the flier wore dark wings and robes patterned with dark dyes on lighter silks. They doubled back twice, causing Aliati and me to dip into the clouds when we saw her wings curving for a turn. Once, they shifted gusts so abruptly, I wondered if they'd spotted us.

They made their second circuit of Harut, then spun on a draft, searching the sky for someone, and continued more directly on their way.

Aliati and I followed, still below and behind them, tracing shadows across the cloudtop. The flier disappeared into the same tower we were heading for: Laria. On the market tier.

"Wait a few moments," I said. "So we won't be challenged for following them."

Aliati shook her head. "Even if we are, few will recognize us as being from a different quadrant, especially as dirty and weather-worn as we are." The moldy cloaks were useful for that. "Don't talk too much. If someone asks, remember we have hatchlings to trade."

But when we landed at Laria, we were relieved to find the black-winged flier was nowhere to be seen. The market area of the tier was clear of webs. The stalls looked sparsely supplied, but there was still food to buy. A family passed us, the children carrying a basket of stone fruit and tiny apples. A small bird carcass hung upside-down from their mother's fist.

Though the stalls were sparse, several nearby tables were filled with Justice players, and more crowded around, watching. Another noisy group surrounded a small birdfighting ring. Several blackwings stood near a line of hanging webs, blocking access to the more-interior spaces. Aliati nudged me. "The storage space is behind those."

"How do we get back there?" I asked. We needed something that would give me enough time to slip past the guards and get to the storage space.

"The easiest thing would be to shout 'fire,'" Aliati said. "Silkspinner towers hate fire."

I thought of the stampede that might ensue. "What about flipping a stall?" I eyed one selling raw-silk dolls.

She frowned. "Not enough of a stir."

"We don't want a riot," I said. I'd only seen a wisp of one, before the Grigrit guards stopped it, but it had been enough. I'd lost friends on Viit.

"Then we'll trade first," Aliati countered, and she led me into the crowd.

↖ ↖ ↖

Aliati showed the dirgeon hatchlings to a silk spider stall closest to the back of the market. "We're hoping to trade. These are pretty fat." The birds were crawling with lice and had shat all over the inside of her satchel.

"We've no tower marks yet," the young girl behind the tower said. "Let me fetch one of my uncles." She put a boy of five or six Allmoons in charge of the stall. Then she ran, her brown knees showing through tears in her robes and leggings, past the guards and through a hole in the webs.

Aliati and I waited, hearts pounding. We could see her move through the silkwebs into the back of the tier. I noted how carefully she parted them with a child's bone knife. She passed into a living space of sorts, where shadowy bone supports braced tunnels and covered nests for sleeping kept out the worst of the yellow webs. Creeping out into the market, the ceiling rippled with hand-span-sized spiders, their striped legs and weavers' claws making soft taps and drags as they skittered across each other, drawing out new trails of silkthread as they passed.

A hatch of young silk spiders was walled off near the market, the silkthread there grayer and less strong. The family was smart to keep hatchlings separate. Silk spiders ate their own young.

The girl burst back through the webs near the residence and handed us two Laria markers each. "Uncle says if you know where more dirgeon nests are, you should come backtier for tea to discuss returning." She pointed at the way she'd come be-fore resuming her place at the stall.

Aliati inclined her head in thanks. "I have business elsewhere, but my friend would be grateful." Then she turned her attention to the marketplace.

I walked towards where the girl had indicated, every muscle tense. Aliati walked farther into the market.

As I came to the webline, I heard Aliati shout, "Spirebreaker! I saw her!" *Oh no.*

People rushed to where she pointed, including the children from the stall. I turned to look, like everyone else, but Aliati was already gone, ducking away through the stalls. Two black-wings hurried towards the gathering group.

With a clatter, a stall fell over near the market entrance. More people moved, some jostling each other. Someone yelled, "Spire-breaker!" again, farther away.

Doran was right; the city was so tense anything could light it up. The families in the market scrambled to the shadows, herding their children to safety. A fight broke out by the gam-ing tables. When the shouting reached a peak, the tower's guards—all blackwings—rumbled past us, towards the ex-panding melee.

I kept moving, and soon Aliati joined me. I frowned at her and she shrugged. "It worked, didn't it?"

Beyond the market, Laria's silkweb draped everywhere. Al-ready this morning, lowtower women and children stood just inside their balconies, harvesting great hand spans of silkthread that had collected around them in the night by looping the silk from palm to elbow. They seemed undisturbed by the noise from the market.

Down the thickened tunnels of this tier, close to the central core, I heard voices. One familiar one. Aliati echoed softly.

"There's a larger room that way." Away from the voices. "That's where the air sacks are."

"You go," I said, handing her the tethers. She could be the thief now. I'd be a spy. "I heard something. I want to see who's in there." If my ears hadn't misled me, Dix was here. For the rest of our plan to work, we needed to know where she was, and how many guards she had. We heard loud conversation break out near the tower core.

I turned, drawn by the voices and walked right into a web.

The sticky net shook and split raggedly. Nearby silk spiders dropped on their threads and began to vibrate. Their movement woke others until at least a hundred hatches quivered on threads all around me. Even to my non-Singer-trained ears, it sounded like tiny fingernails dragged across bone. Aliati winced and we held our breath, not daring to move until they'd stopped. Then I slid away as quickly as I could, farther into the shadows. Aliati went the other direction.

Barely in time. Two hooded guards with furled black wings rounded a curve in the webbing. One carried an oil lantern, throwing the walls into high relief. They pushed through the overgrown web tunnels. "Can't see what got them going, but I can feel it in the threads," the first said.

"Supposed to be good alerts, spiders," the other grumbled. "But what they are is busybodies, jumpy at every odd thing. Like as not, it was the wind that set them off again. Or a tasty bird."

The guards turned back the way they came. After a few breathless moments, I followed.

ʕ ʕ ʕ

The two blackwings disappeared around another curve in the web tunnels. I kept my hood up and my hands tucked into my sleeves. Tried breathing through my mouth. The smell increased the farther into the tier I walked.

Elsewhere in the tier, as the riot grew louder, Aliati tethered the sacks together and lowered the line that bound them into the clouds. If everything proceeded as planned, she'd slip away and we'd pull the air sacks from the tower while Laria slept.

Ahead, lanterns illuminated the silk, showing golden depths amid hatchworks of dark and light: threads crisscrossed hundreds of layers thick. This tier didn't look like it had been harvested, except to hold open this single space up against the tower's central core. A tower like Laria traded silk to feed its citizens because it gave most of its tiers over to silk growing. That they'd left a tier untouched was astounding. I crouched low, trying to get as close as possible without casting a dark shadow among the reflective webs.

While seeing was hard, I heard voices without difficulty through the webs. Dix's strong consonants bounced off the silk-webs.

"How can you not know in which tower they are hiding?" she asked. Then, "You are lying. Where are the pages that Kirit took from the Spire? Where is the Spirebreaker? Where are her friends?"

At the thud of a bone hook striking bare skin, followed by a pained gasp, I tensed. Every muscle in my body readied for a run through the webs into the room.

I couldn't tell who Dix's victim was, but I wanted to make her stop hurting them. I forced my muscles to relax. Going in now would destroy the rest of the plan, and the others were counting on me. We acted as a group or not at all. I stayed crouched on the sticky floor.

"They've stolen our work, our artifex. They're destroying the city." Another thud. "Tomorrow, you will help us begin to repair the city."

A cough shook the webs. Someone inhaled deeply. Dix paused, said, "Yes. I understand."

One of the guards spoke. "What did he say?"

"He told me we need to double our efforts to heal the city before more bad luck can come to it." She sounded so certain. "When we do, we'll return to a time of peace and growth, with the heart of the city's wisdom, supporting tower, not Spire. He said he trusts me to do this."

A crackling step on the floor stopped me from moving away from the tier. "What is it, Moc?" said Dix. She sounded fond of the fledge.

"I can help," Moc said. His voice was oddly soft. Like he'd been drugged again. "I can send a bird. Get my friends to come." He laughed at this.

He *was* drugged, I could hear the same tone in his voice as on the floating platform.

Dix chuckled. "You certainly can, young one. You and Hiroli." I could imagine the greasy tail of her words wrapping Moc's arms, Hiroli's neck, pulling them in. The sound of Moc, relaxed and even laughing along with his captors, made the hair rise on my arms.

"We'll let you have a bird for that, certainly. Tomorrow," Dix said. "They're very good birds, much better than your old kaviks. You'll like them. And your new pair of wings too," Dix said. "I've ordered them from Viit already. The kind that an heir of Rumul deserves. Here, have a seat and something to eat."

Two captives. I wanted to cut through the webs and grab the fledge. Where was Hiroli? I listened, waited. I heard Moc say, meekly, "Thank you."

"Tell us again what the codex pieces that Kirit and Nat found looked like." Dix paced a circuit around the interior space, her voice coming closer to where I was standing, then moving farther away.

Moc stayed in one place while he described the pages, bet-

ter than even I could have. He'd been sneaking around my
satchel before we flew from Grigrit so long ago. I'd known then
he was troublesome. "There were thick pieces, broken. They
looked hollowed out too. And two whole brass plates with markings on them that I couldn't read," he continued, describing
each page, including the Conclave page and the plates I'd later
given to Doran. Dix listened intently.

The fledge was trouble, sure, and nosy too. Still, I'd trade our
brass plates to the blackwings to get him back. For Ciel, and
for me too. I couldn't give him, or anyone, up for lost again. Not
Moc, nor Wik, nor Hiroli.

Dix had told the city that two would be thrown down at tomorrow's Conclave. Meantime, she was drugging at least one
captive into compliance, and beating another. While pretending to talk to a nearly dead Singer. She was skytouched, for certain. She had to be. The alternative was much worse: that she
believed she was doing what was best for the city and was
using everyone she could towards that end.

We had to rescue our friends before they were no longer useful to Dix.

I crouched among shadows and spiderwebs, weighing needs.
If I moved now, Aliati's efforts to free the lighter-than-air
would be for nothing. And if Dix escaped, or I failed, no one
could warn the city about the new kaviks Dix was spreading.
We had to tell Doran as well. He'd need another way to signal Doran's still-loyal guards. I would return quickly, with
friends.

I started to crawl away, slowly. Damp silk pressed my bare
cheek, and I pulled back, wiping the creeping feeling away. A
thick web blocked my path. I shuddered again. Surely this was
the way I'd come?

Silk spiders had made quick work of the gap. I sliced impa-
tiently with my knife, and a small section opened with a soft

ripping sound. The nearby threads began to quiver. Soon more were shaking as the spiders vibrated an alarm.

I got up and ran for my life, coating myself with webs and spiders as I passed through and dove, wings still furled, for the nearest balcony and the clouds.

22

WAR

Once I was in the air, I tried to snap my wings open. I pushed my hands into the grips and tried to extend my arms, fast. But where the wingset should have unfurled, silk and battens held my arms to my sides. I fought back panic and tried again. A look over my shoulder with the wind whistling through my ears told me why: spiderwebs snarled the wings at key points, binding them. Another jerk of my arms, stronger this time, stretched the webs, but the cams and gears still jammed.

I had little time, I knew it. But pulling too hard risked breaking the wings. I would drop like garbage. I opened and closed the mechanisms gently, extending a little farther with each effort. I tried to breathe in time with my motions. Meanwhile, my fall accelerated, the white cloudtop grew closer.

Tower children learned falling was the worst thing that could happen to a person. The clouds were full of danger, darkness, and storms. Up high was the safest place to be. To the towers, "fallen" meant grief. And "cloudbound" meant dead.

What I knew now was different. The wind beat at me as I spun, but below the cloudtop were more chances to right myself, if I could stay calm. I continued to stretch my arms, to move my bound wings in ways that would loosen the webs. It was working. Slowly.

I broke the clouds still half furled, spinning. The warmer, damp air came as a shock after the cold dryness above. Below me, the hidden towers' ridges and shadows were barely visible, but I fell ever closer.

I had a slim hope that Aliati would return at the same time. Had she seen me dive? Could she catch me? I even, for a moment, wished my pursuers would net me and haul me from the clouds. Though I no longer feared falling as much as I had, I dreaded impact against a hidden wall. I grew dizzy as I spun into the clouds.

Come on, Nat. Keep working.

The damp air weakened a strand of webs, and these gave way. My left wing spread wide. Before I could spin too far on the single foil, I flexed the right wing harder. The wind screamed in my ears now. Shadows grew deeper. Something loomed far below.

The last of the silkthread stretched far enough to part. Falling headlong towards the ghost tower's dark shadow, my wings finally snapped open most of the way.

My heart caught in my throat as the wind filled my wings. I'd fallen but I had not died. I flew below the clouds, alive, though I wobbled and fought for control. My footsling brushed against an outcropping near the ghost tower.

As I recovered enough to fight my way higher, my breath rasped in the moist air. I shook with relief, then struggled to keep my wings balanced in the breeze.

ʕ ʕ ʕ

Finally, I righted myself and caught a good gust towards the ghost tower.

"Nat!" Aliati cried, waiting atop the tower. "I waited for you until I couldn't. What did you see?"

"Did you tether the lighter-than-air?"

"Better than." She grinned and pointed to the ghost tower, where a spidersilk line anchored to a grip hook. The line rose *up,* swaying in the wind. Aliati had done much more than tether the air sacks. "There was such a mess in the market, I was able to pull the lighter-than-air they were storing in skymouth husks down with me. No one saw."

I wanted to shake her. "You don't think someone will notice it's missing? Like the artifex?" Unauthorized scavenging risked undermining our plan.

But her smile broadened. "I left enough in the storage area to make it seem like it's all there. Now we don't have to wait."

There was nothing to be done now. Hoping she was right, I told Aliati about the kaviks, about Dix. About the near-worship of Rumul—or at least what was left of him. "I'll go update Kirit and Doran," she said. "This changes our plans."

Inside the cave, Djonn had set his and Doran's two brass plates out on the bone floor. Beside them, he'd placed what looked like tiny, twisted wings next to small bags of lighter-than-air. He'd decoded an engraving of wings from one of the plates. In Ciel's lap lay bands of stretchy birdgut and small wing-mockups.

Ciel's fingers, now covered with scratches from working with Djonn's tools, wove together the rounded wings. "Small fingers," Djonn said, "make excellent work."

I frowned, thinking about where I'd heard that before, but Ciel laughed and kept working. Her design looked like the windbeaters' foils Dix had used to create the hole in the wind, in miniature. She set those down beside Djonn until he was ready for them.

Meantime, Djonn put one tiny wingset on a base carved from the same piece of bone Beliak and Ceetcee were using for message chips. He wrapped the birdgut around it and twisted until the gut was tightly wrapped in a spiral around the bone. Then he let the contraption go.

The small craft whirred across the cave.

"You spent all that time making a toy?" The two of them. We were risking everything, and they were fiddling.

"Not a toy." Djonn held one up. "A delivery system for messages. Or for fire, if we need weapons. They fly on their own until the band uncoils. I call them firebugs."

I sat down beside Djonn, taking a moment to look closer rather than rushing through. A good leader would know the talents of his crew, and it seemed Djonn had talents. He could make anything: from firebugs to lighter-than-air. Naton would have loved watching him work. Elna too.

Djonn picked up a firebug and wound it. His knotted hands worked fast. Another of the bugs sat beside the first, ready for its own twist of birdgut.

Ciel knelt beside us. "Can I help more?"

Djonn smiled. "Yes. With this, and with the bigger things. You remember how the blades worked on the tower-tapping plinth?" Djonn asked her without a note of condescension, so different from the way Dix talked to children, to Moc.

Ciel wrinkled her nose. "Yes."

"We can use broken wings for something smaller, but similar. It could be useful in an emergency. Would you like to help?" Ciel nodded. "Do we have any nets in the cave?"

There was a medium net holding the cache of food off the cave floor. I dumped the food out and brought the net over. Knelt next to Djonn. "You helped repurpose the windbeaters' wings from the Spire into the blades that pulled the wind from the sky, didn't you?" I pointed at the tiny wings on the firebugs. "When you worked above the kidnapped fledges."

Djonn frowned. "I knew there were fledges down there. Dix told me they were working for tower marks."

"She drugged them, like you were drugged. She's doing it still." His face turned ashen at my words.

Djonn finished the last firebug. "She'll pay for that, someday."

He was clear of the heartbone drug now, and sounded angry to have been so used. I hoped Moc would be the same.

Allmoons was tomorrow. The year's shortest day, when the city gathered to light banners of Remembrance. So many banners clustered around the towers this year. The city looked very unlucky.

To restore the city's luck, Dix wanted to throw our friends into the clouds without wings.

"She'll pay for it tonight. We have the message chips, the delivery system, the lighter-than-air. We can go now." Only we had no way to signal our allies in the towers.

❧ ❧ ❧

Ceetcee found me pacing, trying to work that one out. She hugged me tight.

"Where's Kirit?" I asked.

"She, Doran, and Beliak went to try something with the undercloud littlemouths after they heard about the birds. They think Doran's guards might see their lights from the towers, especially if they can get littlemouths to signal to one another up the towers."

"We're guessing that the littlemouths use light—and maybe echoes too—to communicate in the clouds," Djonn said. "They have to communicate somehow or else they'd lose each other. Just like us."

Ceetcee chuckled, nervous. "If it works, Kirit thinks she can send messages that way. Doran's people have spread through the city, talking to people about Dix. They need a way to know when we're going up." She looked at her hands before I had a chance to say anything. "We came up with most of the plan while you were at Laria. Your news about the birds confirms what Doran suspected."

"It's a good plan." It didn't matter to me who came up with

which elements. We were pieces of an artifex's mechanism, working together to stop Dix. We were nearly ready.

I hoped Doran was telling the truth about how much support he still had in the city.

"Surprise is our best weapon," Djonn said, putting his firebugs into a sack and giving them to Ciel. He was right. But surprise belonged to our enemies, too.

〰 〰 〰

We carefully rigged the air sacks Aliati had stolen with the extra wingstraps we'd taken from the council field. Each flier who would be tied below them—myself, Ciel, Ceetcee, Beliak, Aliati, Doran, and Kirit—held enough ballast that we would rise slowly, until we were ready to enter Laria.

"We won't attack if we don't have to," I reminded them. "We want to talk and to remove Dix from the tower alive. Rumul too. Meantime, Beliak and Ceetcee will get Moc, Wik, and Hiroli."

"And the man whose knife this is?" Kirit lifted the blade that had killed Ezarit.

The guard playing Justice with Dix at Gigrit. "Him too, if he's there. Taken alive. We need to show the city who they are and what they've been doing. The city needs answers."

Aliati nodded, grimly. "We'll try."

Atop the ghost tower, Djonn waited beside the net he'd set up, and the whirlwind he'd rigged beside it. The spare wings raked the air in a circle when he twisted the improvised haft he'd made from tools in the smugglers' cache. "It's modified to spin twice as fast."

He handed Ciel and me pieces of flint from his toolbox. "If the first person to fall through the clouds could be Kirit, or Ciel, that would be useful," he said. "They could help me."

Kirit laughed a little. "No promises," she said.

I thought about it. Kirit and Ciel could sing the littlemouths into signaling, once Djonn's net was ready for us. "Do you want Ciel to stay?"

Ciel, already strapped into an air sack rig, made an affronted noise. "I'm going! My brother's up there. And Kirit's going."

Djonn agreed. "You need her to float highest above Laria. She's the only one light enough."

No one asked if Kirit wanted to stay below.

Ciel promised she would come down as soon as her part of the job was done, and we ascended to the cloudtop and prepared to let the first air sack rise as dusk darkened the city.

The air, colder than I remembered, and very dry, smelled of home: oil lamps and cook fires. The towers rising high above us blocked out the stars.

Attached to a skymouth husk that was also attached to Laria, Ciel drifted almost invisible in the sky.

After the sun set, during the darkest moment of the city's year, Kirit began to keen. I held my breath, hoping it would work.

She flew in a circle around Laria, mourning Ezarit, the lost councilors, the Singers. As she passed, the littlemouths clinging to the tower began to luminesce.

This was the signal to Doran's guards to begin making a distraction on nearby towers, to summon Dix's blackwings away from Laria.

The lights faded as Kirit completed her circuit. In the closest tower, Ginth, we heard yelling from far uptower, a fight breaking out. Had the guard seen the signal? I hoped so.

Kirit returned to the ledge in time for us to strap her into the lighter-than-air sacks. We slowly let ourselves rise unseen up the spider tower's side, the updrafts buffeting us, but not knocking us off course.

In the dark, we were invisible. Above, Dix's guards bristled at the top of Laria, peering at the ruckus on Ginth. Meanwhile, towertops in the distance began to light up with Remembrance fires.

Far above us and to the west, a riot horn sounded from Bissel. Another from Naza. A group of blackwings leapt from the top of Laria and raced towards the towers, flying to protect the city, as Dix had promised she would.

You cannot lead through fear. Ezarit's words. I would honor their truth. I wished I could hear them again, from her own mouth, but that would never be. Instead, I vowed not to let fear keep me from acting, either.

My thoughts churned as we rose silent in the crisp air. Ceetcee and Beliak released a sack of ballast, bones from the bone eater cairn. I did the same.

We heard horns in the east, and southeast too, as Doran's people started fights on more towertops during the city's most solemn ceremony.

Doran had kept his promise to accompany us. He looked as ready to fight as we were.

Kirit dropped the most ballast and slipped past me. She and Aliati raced to Laria's market tier. Then Ciel's signal came. A single firebug, lit like a shooting star, moved across the sky before it burned out.

More of Laria's guards took off from the towertop like bats, chasing the flare. Ciel pulled closer to the skymouth husk, camouflaging herself in the dark night air. The blackwings shot past her and chased where they thought the firebug would be.

We found the updrafts then. Unfurled our wings, which we'd rubbed as dark as we could with blacking from Djonn's supplies. All of us, night-colored, like blackwings, and the Singer nightwings before them. Kirit had tied a tea-colored ribbon from Ezarit's robe at her shoulder. I had done the same. Aliati, too. *Not exactly like the blackwings. Nothing like, if we could help it.*

When we cut ourselves loose from the skymouth husks,

letting them float away, the wind caught our wings, and we shot into the market tier, past the guards. We furled our wings fast and rolled into the silken maze. Aliati whistled, loud and fierce, a tower alarm.

The silkwebs picked up the sound and reverberated. Kirit, followed by Aliati, disappeared into the webs. I heard the sound of running feet pounding the tier above us.

Bone horns sounded from Laria's towertop. That was Ciel's signal. She began dropping the bone chips we'd carved: *Rumul hides within your tower, a Singer. The blackwings are helping him.* The chips urged the tower residents to attack the tower's market tier.

From the lowtower, people began to emerge. A few carried sharp blades, lanterns. Some climbed the ladders. Some took to the wind. Others peered out from their balconies, still reading the messages.

At first, the guards must have thought the citizens had roused to help them find the flare's source. They let them come. But when the first blackwing fell from Laria into the clouds, they began to fight.

And Laria rose up against Dix.

23

RUMUL

We ran the tower's webbed passages, spreading out across the tier. The light of Allmoons streamed silver across the floor, turning the walls opaque until we split them apart.

Doran, Ceetcee, Beliak, and I sliced the silk walls with our knives and stepped through the openings. When we reached the innermost wall, we stopped, still hidden, and peered through the webbing.

Inside, Dix and her inner circle gathered around plans for Conclave. Blackwings and tower councilors stood beside her. On a low sling chair, Rumul huddled beneath quilts piled high, his bald head dented and shrunken, silver tattoos pulled into strange patterns by several scars.

Behind us: shouts, then fighting, as Dix's guards alit on the lowtower and Laria's people confronted them, asking questions. We had the tower nearly surrounded already, without a single arrow loosed.

I couldn't count my successes yet. Too many uncertainties still remained: if Ceetcee and Beliak could find Moc, Wik, and Hiroli quickly; if we could capture both Dix and Rumul; if Dix's guards would give way to the tower's people; if we could escape without harm.

All we could do now was wait until we had enough of Laria at our back, then confront Dix.

From the corner of my eye, movement. Kirit began cutting

her way through the last of the webs early. Draped in stray spidersilk threads, her tattoos stark against her skin, she looked like a ghost. Her eyes were narrowed to slits, and she moved silently, trying to get within a knife's throw of Dix.

Aliati and I moved to grab her, too late. Before we could catch her, Kirit charged through the webs at Dix, knife drawn. Three of Dix's guards and one councilor overpowered and tackled her.

Once, before the fever, she might have fought her way free. But Kirit was still weak. She struggled as they bound her arms and dragged her before Dix.

Clouds take her, this is not what we planned.

"Kirit," Dix said. "You saved us the trouble of hunting you down." Beside Dix, Rumul's waxy face remained impassive, his eyes stared at some invisible middle ground.

As the guards stepped into the corridors to investigate, I slipped between the webs' shadows and saw Aliati and Doran doing the same. Beliak and Ceetcee had already gone in search of the captives. There was no way to warn them.

With our surprise blown, we would have to fight.

Everything went still, save for the scuff of footwraps over bone floors. I could hear the rasp of Rumul's breathing. My heart beat a tattoo: his name, then Kirit's.

"What do you bring us, Spirebreaker?" Dix said.

Kirit's voice shook the webs. "I bring truth. When the city discovers who you shelter here, they will not forgive you. Nor will I. The city needs this truth."

Dix laughed. "The city needs to be told what to see in order to discover anything, Kirit. Without strong leaders, it has only bad luck left to it. You offer neither leadership nor luck. But when I searched the Spire after you cracked it, I uncovered both. Rumul was the Spire's heart; he sacrificed to lead. And now he's skyblessed. He shares his insights with me. That is what the city needs: the past's wisdom and strength to do what's right for the future." Dix put a gentle hand on Rumul's unmoving head.

As we listened, growing increasingly alarmed, Doran gestured that he would try to distract Dix. That I should get Kirit and drag her off the tier. Then he stepped out from among the webs. Said to all who would listen, "You don't know what leadership means, Dix. You never understood." A few Laria citizens crowded behind him, straining to hear over the sounds of fighting on other tiers. "You wanted power, and you use that husk of a man as a signifier. That isn't leadership." He held a hand out and walked closer. "You can stop this now."

He nodded to the assembled councilors. Several bobbed their heads in reply.

I'd been edging around behind Dix, getting closer to Kirit. But before I could grab her, a guard, one of the men who'd played Justice with her at Grigrit, shouted, "Enough, Doran!"

When Doran didn't stop speaking, the man drew another glass-tooth knife from his belt and threw it.

The point edged Doran's robe at the hip and fell away. The councilor wavered but remained standing. He spoke again. "You play with towers, you set people against each other. How will you lead when you have no more people, only game pieces?"

I moved fast then. With a piece of Djonn's flint, I lit an oil-soaked rag we'd tied around an arrow. Shot it through the webs. It left a widening hole from its passage before it struck Doran's attacker deep in the gut and brought him to his knees.

More shouts came from beyond the web-encircled room. The outer-tier crowd drew closer, as web walls split and dropped.

Ceetcee and Beliak appeared as one wall fell. They had Wik and Hiroli with them. Wik's Lawsmarkers lay heavy on his shoulders, blood oozed through his robes, and he looked dazed. Hiroli appeared little better, her head lolling as Ceetcee half dragged her. Moc wasn't with them.

"You won't stall the Conclave again," Dix yelled when she caught sight of Ceetcee. "You'll be part of it." The muscles in her arms and neck tensed. "Rumul says there must be a Conclave."

A man in the growing crowd behind us whispered, "Sky-touched."

But Dix clutched the edge of Rumul's sling chair, and drew back the quilt that covered the broken Singer. Blood beat hard in my ears. Moc lay in Rumul's lap.

Dix began dragging the two of them towards the tier's edge, her guard pulling Kirit along behind. Another guardsman started towards Ceetcee.

"In fact, he says I could have Conclave right here." Dix motioned as if she would throw Moc from the tower immediately.

"No!" Aliati shouted. We burst through the webs, tripping on thick skeins. I landed hard on my hands and knees, then got to my feet and raced for Moc. Was he alive? I thought his chest moved, but I couldn't be certain. A high-pitched voice behind me screamed, "Murderer!" Ciel.

Aliati turned on Dix while Ceetcee ran for Moc. She lifted him away from Rumul, then leapt from the tower. The two flew away through the illuminated night as Remembrance fires bloomed on towertops high above us.

A charging blackwing tried to wrap his arm around my neck and drag me from the tower. I ducked and twisted, and he fell free, without me.

Inside the tier, all was confusion. More of Laria's citizens emerged and shouted at Dix's guards, and at us. The peace of Allmoons was shattered. In the melee of blackwings and silk-spinner tower fighters, few noticed a Singer fledge approaching the chair where Rumul lay. I saw her and tried to fight my way closer. Each time I knocked a guard aside, another charged me. Finally, I got clear, just as Ciel snuck close enough.

She screamed again at Dix, tears streaming. "Murderer! My brother!" A knife gleamed orange in flamelight; a small hand dropped hard to an old man's chest. Ciel stared at the result, hands retreating from the knife hilt, eyes wide.

A towerman stumbled into me, bleeding. Then rose and ran for shelter. Meantime, Dix howled as if she'd been struck herself. "Traitors have killed the city!" She pulled a knife from the sheath on her leg and lunged at Ciel.

Aliati reached Ciel before Dix or I could. The scavenger grabbed the girl and swung her away, into the sky.

In the sling chair, Rumul stared unblinking at the burning Remembrance flags. His wheezing breath went silent. Dix threw her knife at me instead, and I ducked, readying another arrow. The blade spun through the air, struck a target. Beliak staggered, clutching his leg. He dropped to the floor.

The world slowed then, as I tried to get to Beliak. I dragged through webs, past blackwings, screams and shouts. None of that reached my ears as loudly as the spider bodies being crushed and ground to paste beneath my feet. Doran lifted Beliak and dragged him from the tower. "I've got him," he yelled. "Get Dix!"

In the outer tier, Kirit helped Wik from his Lawsmarkers and into a wingset torn from a guard. Hiroli slowly pulled on another wingset. The tier was filling with smoke.

Through the smoke, Dix shouted, "They've kidnapped Councilor Doran Grigrit! Kirit Spirebreaker, Nat Brokenwings, and their thieves—they've killed . . . they've doomed the city!"

I found her then, standing beside Rumul's chair. When she spotted me through the smoke, her lips pressed to a pale, thin line. Dix pointed at me as I approached. "There! There's the traitor!" Nearby Laria citizens slowed, confused about whom to listen to, and who spoke the truth. A silkspinner lunged for me while Dix ran for the balcony, preparing to jump away from her attackers and the fighting. I dodged his outstretched fingers and leapt over a guard's body, pursuing Dix. But the older woman moved faster towards the balcony than I did, towing Rumul's chair behind her.

In the moonlight, a telltale silver gleam outlined small lighter-than-air sacks bobbing above Rumul's head. Dix maneuvered these well clear of the flame-licked webs.

No. She would not get away like this. I drew my knife and closed the distance between us, too late.

With a great shove, Dix tipped Rumul's seat over the balcony edge. She leapt after it, snapping her wings open. The sacks of lighter-than-air buoyed both her and the sling. She began a slow, burdened glide towards Grigrit.

I leapt into a fast gust and caught her footsling in the air. Jerked the fabric backwards. Dix flipped, and we clawed air and silk, trying to tangle each other in the tethers that held Rumul in the sky.

Grasping Rumul's sling, I rolled hard, tearing Dix's hands from its frame. A tether snapped, and Rumul's body slid, hung suspended for a moment, then fell. I grabbed for it, snagged his robe, tore it. Silk in my hand, the sling rising lighter, while the body continued to fall, striking tower outcrops until it disappeared into the clouds.

I turned towards Laria again, blinking grit from my eyes. Dix circled lower, keening. My fingers gripped the sling, the silk robe.

Rumul, who had been close to death for a long time, was gone. He'd been a game piece. A remnant to be knocked over. Dix had made him a rallying cry for her cause. Something that Kirit had always refused to be.

A blackwing soared towards me. The world and the small battle within it had not stopped. But he flew past; the tethered skymouth husks hid me from view.

On Laria, the remaining web walls were on fire. Smoke choked me. Kirit huddled with Wik and Hiroli.

Below, a small circle of blue lights appeared dimly in the cloudscape, then faded. "There!" I shouted. Dix's guards had regrouped and were headed for them. My friends leapt from the tier, wings tightly tucked. They plummeted to the glow in the clouds and disappeared.

Above me, more fliers began escaping from the tower, the blackwings coming from Grigrit now, fresh for battle and well armed. They chased us, but could not fall as fast, because they feared the clouds. That would not stop them for long, but it was enough for now.

I cut two air sacks from Rumul's chair and sank through the night, my wings heavy with spidersilk. The plan had gone all wrong. The towers were in disarray, and we had no proof of anything to show the city except the empty robe of a dead man.

Far below the clouds, Djonn had spread the net beside the ghost tower and anchored it to the last of our skymouth husks. He double-cranked his whirlwind wings in reverse, faster now, sending gusts of air up towards the tower. Only when we were in the clouds did we extend our wings. The updraft slowed our fall.

Aliati circled, bow ready. Ceetcee landed, carrying Moc. Doran and Beliak fell into the net, then Kirit and Wik, then Hiroli, and the rest of us guided them to the tower.

When the net was clear, I helped Djonn crank the whirlwind faster, sending gusts of wind towards the tower, trying to blow our enemies back. Ceetcee bandaged Beliak's leg as best she could on the towertop.

They kept coming, circling in the high cloud, trying to see us in the dark. Our eyes had grown used to the dim light. Nearby a littlemouth pulsed on the tower over Ciel's shoulder, where she sat sobbing, holding her brother. The boy moaned. I was glad to hear the sound.

Djonn groaned and stood upright, the blisters on his hands seeping. I could see sweat across his robes where they'd tucked under the lip of his brace. The whirlwind slowed, then stopped. He stared at the cloudtop: "We can't keep them at bay."

We'd been fools to think we could.

"You should have let me kill her, Nat. Saved yourselves more trouble." Kirit's voice, angry and despairing.

"No," I said. "We tried to save everyone." *We tried.* That was my pulse, saying that. *We tried and lost.* Dix had escaped. Her guards had a new enemy to turn the city against: us. We had no answers anymore, except Djonn. We were cloudbound. My friends were hurt. It hadn't been enough.

On the ghost tower, we stood together as morning dawned.

The moment light pricked the mist, ten blackwings broke the clouds open. They dove for the ghost tower and the caves, looking for us.

PART FOUR

HIDDEN

Dark messengers flocked at Laria, awaiting orders. Black-winged guards tied chips to each kavik claw and sent them aloft. One by one, dark wings parted the breeze and pushed it away. They churned the air between towers. In Amrath's shadows, a hush, then the twang of a bow. A messenger fell, but more of the kaviks flew undaunted, then returned home to roost.

⌒ CLOUDTOP (new) ⌒
None but blackwings fly the clouds.
For safety's sake, avoid
The lowtowers and the white-spun shrouds.
⌒ COUNCIL (new) ⌒
When council speaks,
All attend; when Laws
Make, all obey.
⌒ SINTER (new) ⌒
To break a bridge,
A moment's pause, for city's sake.
Two towers middle-meet, unarmed
A last resort, for both to take.

24

BLACKWINGS

Aliati grabbed Ciel and scrambled to the ghost tower's edge. They launched themselves deeper into the clouds. Beliak and Ceetcee followed, holding on to the sling chair with Djonn inside. Blood had already seeped through Beliak's bandages.

Wik lifted Moc while Doran dragged Kirit to the tower edge. Together, they prepared to fly into the void below.

"Spirebreaker! Brokenwings!" a circling blackwing shouted. "You attacked a tower. Broke Laws. Kidnapped a councilor. You'll be held accountable."

"What of Rumul, the betrayer of the city? Was he held accountable?" Kirit shouted back. "What of Dix? She'll turn on you next."

An arrow flew past me, too close. The blackwings surged lower. They were trying to find the tower by our voices.

"Stop arguing and fly!" I yelled. I leapt from the towertop and began a fast dive, locking my wings. As the figures above receded into dim, moonlit shadows, I readied my bow. We could still hear them calling.

A strong gust curled mist skyward, and I rode it up to meet them.

The blackwings saw me coming up from the shadows and tried to turn away. My first arrow flew low, but a second pierced a guard's wing. He fought to stay aloft long enough to reach the safety of a tower ledge, his wing sliced open and flapping.

Our pursuit reduced by one, and more cautious now, I turned and flew after my retreating friends.

Aliati, with Ciel, zigzagged ahead. "Follow," she whistled, as I came close enough to hear. Our group coalesced around her, and she flew into the depths, echoing. The wind rushed in my ears and the towers grew close around us. We flew lower than we ever had. Above us, blackwings' shadows flickered past, then disappeared, only to reappear dark and distant on our tail.

We dove again, desperate to get away. Any moment, I expected to strike a ridge of bone or a dim tower trunk, but Aliati continued to whistle "follow," and we did, in a close formation that was more like falling than flying.

Soon the towers grew together to form tunnels and gaps, crannies and valleys. The wind grew trickier, with more shadows and fewer gusts. As a group, we wobbled and fell, then fought for balance again as we swept through gathering ridges. The light was tinted soft green. It played tricks on our eyes. I thought I saw joined towers. Walls. We passed beneath an old bridge that had calcified. From its spans, small towers dripped down, leaving arches and finials that would have been beautiful if they weren't dangerous.

Moc did his best to help Wik fly straight by staying as still as possible, but Wik's injuries made holding the boy difficult. Ceetcee and Beliak struggled with Djonn's seat, until the two closest fliers, Kirit and Doran, took over for them and eventually cut another gas-filled bag loose. Aliati spilled wind from her wings and narrowly avoided an outcropping crusted with moss. She shouted a warning, and we scuttled out of the way. Kirit, Doran, and Djonn shot up, over the ridge, while the rest of us passed below it.

Behind us, three blackwings came out of the mist, screaming at each other. They looked disoriented and afraid. Judging by their panicked shouts, their eyes had not adjusted. Mist coated their unsealed wings, dragging at them. They didn't see us as we hurtled away.

Aliati flew ahead of us, echoing, trying to scout the best wind. Beliak weakened behind her, the cut on his leg bleeding through his robe.

I could not see our other three fliers.

A shadow passed over us, moving faster than we had dared. A cry of fear broke the air, pierced at the end with agony. I spared a look up. A blackwing had struck the bone spur we'd barely missed. Now his wingset seemed paused midflight, stilled in time. Aloft, air-filled, and unmoving.

The other blackwings slowed, more careful now, then ended their pursuit and rose back up to the light.

I shouted to my friends to wait, to find the missing three, but Aliati continued to dive, drawing out the distance between where we'd last seen Dix's blackwings and us. Between us and where Kirit, Doran, and Djonn had disappeared, too.

She descended lower than anyone had ever dared, taking us with her, though I whistled "stop" until my lips ran dry.

❦ ❦ ❦

Past an overgrown bridge, we saw a wide cave. Split bones littered the ledge below its mouth.

Aliati whistled "danger," too tired to say more. I ached to land there or anywhere. To ease the tension in my shoulders, the tremors of my arms. To look for our friends. But she was right, it was too dangerous. We slowed, lacking pursuit for the moment, hoping that Kirit and Doran could catch up. We whistled but couldn't find them.

"We should go back," Wik said, concerned.

Mist curled around our wingtips as we flew, searching. A breeze brushed my cheek. Scanning the clouds for a sign of my friends, I began to chuckle. We'd done it, attacked the tower.

We'd lost everything. And everyone. The others laughed back, including Wik.

We flew lower, our laughter increasing.

Aliati flew among us, worried. "Stop. We have to go back up."

Wik laughed. "I don't see the others. The guards. Where's Kirit? We should go lower." He laughed harder, the sound of it high-pitched and echoing.

His laughter should have worried me, but instead, my mouth curved hard in an unstoppable smile. Ciel began laughing too, and that was even funnier. I chuckled, then joined in the laughter. Soon I was trying to catch my breath, and I couldn't comprehend why. Next to Ciel, Ceetcee wiped away a tear and smiled. Beliak and Hiroli giggled.

Aliati shouted, "We have to go back up. Now." She whistled "follow" again.

This made us laugh harder. She sounded so serious. My sides began to hurt. "What's happening?" Tears streamed from my eyes. "Why can't we find Kirit and the others?"

Ceetcee gagged and knelt on the ledge. "Why am I laughing?" Her question was a wheeze.

"We descended too fast; the depths and the air are making you ill," Aliati said. "You must follow me." She grabbed Ceetcee, then prodded Wik with a bone hook. "Help me."

Wik and Beliak grinned at each other, but did what she asked. I followed gamely, feeling lighter and happier than I had in many months, despite an undercurrent of worry for the others.

"Aren't you afraid of the blackwings?" I shouted to Aliati. She hushed me, but nodded. Then she yelled at Ceetcee, and they both rose, driving Wik, Moc, and Beliak before them. I made Ciel go ahead of me, and bumbled on a turbulent gust of wind behind them until we'd reached a ledge a half dozen tiers from where we'd last seen the blackwings.

Near where we'd last seen the others.

This ledge was deep and well-shadowed, though not as protected by overgrowth as the bridge below. Wind whistled over the bone spur that rose little higher than Wik's head.

As my head cleared, nothing seemed so funny anymore.

"What happened?" I demanded as soon as we'd settled.

Aliati looked at me, ashen. Then at Beliak, who was still smiling happily, and Ciel, who giggled with a hand over her mouth. Moc was the only one of them not laughing. "We might have to go up again even higher, if they don't recover."

As we stood on the ledge, a drizzle began to fall. More moisture than we'd ever seen at one time. Ciel giggled harder and opened her mouth to drink it. Choked and coughed. Ceetcee drew deep breaths, her color returning.

Somewhere nearby, I heard water running. A cloudbound waterfall.

Ciel's giggles slowed. She looked at Wik, then at Aliati. "What's happening?"

Aliati leaned against the ledge wall. "Scavengers have another verse of 'Corwin and the Nest of Thieves.'"

She hummed the tune, then sang it awkwardly.

> *Five descend beyond the nest, far, far below.*
> *They find metal fine carved and bright of shine,*
> *but to it cannot hold.*
> *Drop it down, chase it down, ever farther down.*
> *Two return, with laughter burn, from far, far below.*

"And then Corwin comes and takes the rest of the metal from them," she finished, waving her hand.

I'd begun to feel more like myself, and I shuddered at the scavenger's ghost story. *Two return, with laughter burn.* I remembered Aliati's scowl when Ciel first sang the song. "Is there something in the clouds that makes us ill? A plant? A poison?" *No one comes back from the clouds.*

"I don't know," she said. "But in the song, they'd descended fast, and the ones who turned back survived." Just as we had.

If the Singers knew that verse to the song, Tobiat hadn't shared it with us. Without Aliati, we might have disappeared, laughing, without a trace.

"You saved us." The sound of more water splashing nearby, but with a different level of intensity, stopped me from saying more. Around the bone spur that shaded us, and a short leap away, was an unprotected ledge. Three blackwings sat there, legs dangling over the edge. The mist between them and us had eddied until it was thin enough to see through.

They leaned on each other, sides heaving with hilarity. One toyed at the air with his bow while another stood urinating off the edge. The waterfall sound.

"Aliati," I whispered. Pointed. "They're sick too, and they're not as far down." And what about the others? Kirit and Doran and Djonn?

Aliati pressed her fingers against the bridge of her nose. "They've spent their entire lives in the towers. We've been below for a few days." Her brow was furrowed.

Ciel squinted. "Some of us fledges couldn't stop giggling on the tower-tapping platform. But most of us got better."

We watched the blackwings. They didn't look like they were getting any better. They looked as if they could barely breathe from laughing.

"Leave them there," Aliati said. "Let nature and gravity do what's right."

Ciel stared, waiting. She sniffled a little and looked at her hands, perhaps remembering the fight at Laria. Meanwhile,

Aliati sat on the ledge and turned her attention to her wings, checking the seams.

We were many tiers below where the council had fallen. I pictured a blackwing deadfall down here, realizing I wouldn't wish that fate on anyone. "We need to make them go. To try at least. We can't leave them here to die."

"They'd leave us." Wik turned, frowning.

I'm not them. I would never be. I couldn't throw the rest of the bone markers in my satchel. That would only draw the blackwings farther downtower, making them more ill. I walked the ledge to where Ciel sat. "Do you have any firebugs left?"

She unclasped her satchel and looked inside. "A few, but no fuses. No gas."

"Give me one anyway." I took it in my hand and wound it. Pulled a piece of Ezarit's robe from my pocket and tied a stretch of tea-colored silk to the firebug. Threw it back the way I thought we'd come, letting the catch go on the wound wings.

The little firebug whirred away, dragging behind it the swath of silk. The fabric caught the few rays of sun that slanted through the clouds and shone bright.

A blackwing shouted. One who'd been standing tumbled off the edge, but found enough of a gust to right himself. The others followed suit, and soon all were on the chase.

My companions got to their feet and watched the piece of silk disappear.

"What were you thinking?" Wik said. His robes had turned dark with sweat and damp. A scrape on his cheek crossed an earlier scar. "We have no advantages down here. That's three more blackwings we may have to fight again."

I knew what I'd done, and why. Wik did too, he just didn't like it. "That would be a terrible way to die." I looked away from him, to Beliak and Ceetcee. To Ciel, who sat in a miserable huddle on the ledge.

The girl's face was white. "You showed mercy," she whispered. "I didn't."

Wik leaned down and touched her shoulder. Pointed to where Moc lay, breathing, still drugged. "You saved your brother."

"Not fast enough." Ciel climbed over our feet to curl up with Moc.

Beliak reached out to touch my shoulder. "You did right." Then, "I was angry with you, earlier. For signaling. For keeping council secrets from us."

"I know. It's all right to be angry. It's good to talk about it too." And it was, somehow, all right that I hadn't been the perfect leader, the perfect me, and that he still stood by me. And I by him. For a moment, I felt warmth, despite the clouds. My stomach growled. Beliak's did too.

"We'll find food once we find a cave," Aliati said, hearing us. "If we find one." She looked at me, eyes troubled. Another *if*. This one life and death. The cold caught me again.

"If the weather ever clears," Wik countered, ignoring Ciel's crestfallen look. Hiroli shook herself more awake. She'd kept up with our dives remarkably well.

A clatter of wings and a groan made us all jump.

Doran and Kirit landed on the ledge, towing Djonn. They'd come from the tower's opposite side, away from the blackwings. "Saw your signal from above," Kirit said. She looked ill and tired, but it was she who supported Doran as he hopped towards us. His footwrap was a bloody mess.

"Blackwing arrow. Almost missed me," he said.

Aliati and I both bent to look at the councilor's ankle. He'd flown true, not run straight for the blackwings and safety.

"Just a nick." Aliati sat back after inspecting.

I was less calm. "You could have been killed." *You might have killed each other.* But they hadn't.

"No chance," Kirit said. She reached a hand out to me. "I was looking for you. Echoing. You shouldn't have stopped to signal, not until the blackwings were gone."

"I didn't—" I started, but Doran interrupted. His bandaged hand had also begun bleeding again. "Kirit, you flew true. You could have left me. Instead, you guided us back. Thank you."

Was Doran playing both sides still, looking for advantage, even below the clouds? Kirit looked away, as uncertain as I, but proud she'd found us. For now, that would have to be enough too.

Aliati peered at the clouds, shaking her head. What I'd done with the firebug and the silk had nothing to do with survival, with getting away. It could have backfired and endangered her, us.

I'd questioned her loyalty when she chose to rescue her friend. Now I watched her think about the impact of my actions on the group's safety. I saw the broader horizon: how she looked at Ciel, Kirit, and even me. She'd saved us not once but several times. Her knowledge kept us from greater danger.

"You didn't have to stay with us, you know," I said. "You weren't being hunted."

She cut her eyes at me. "You haven't paid me yet," she muttered, and kept thinking. Finally, she breathed deep and turned to me, then dipped her head to the right. "We go on from here," she said.

To where? Visions of tower guards patrolling above the cloud-top chilled me. So too, the blackwings' shouts about us making war on the towers.

"Down," said Aliati. "Now that you're acclimated, it should be safer. We'll find a cave and regroup. We can't go up yet, and there's only one place I can think of trying to reach, from a very old song. I hope I can find it. I hope it exists."

We were caught in the towers' deadly shadows, the sky forbidden to us.

On every side, traitorous clouds cloaked our path. To survive, we had to put our trust in songs and myths. Words once nearly lost to the city would now be our only guides.

25

NEST OF THIEVES

From our ledge, we could see through the mist a short glide in several directions. Gray and green shadows gathered everywhere, except upwind. There, a dark cloud brewed, seeming to grow larger, then recede. Aliati watched it warily, so I began to do the same.

The wind carried few sounds to us, save an occasional dark rumble from the cloud.

"I'll search first. Rest." Aliati tied a tether to the bone spur so she could find us again and leapt from the ledge.

Wik shared pieces of dried bird his captors had given to him. He'd saved what he could, biding his time. Preparing to escape, even when addled by Dix's drugs and cruelty. He hadn't given up. I took a tiny strip of dirgeon. Kirit and Beliak did the same. We chewed it until it lost all taste and went stringy in our mouths. Ceetcee tried but spit hers out.

Beliak reached into his sleeve, to the pocket he'd had sewn there. He withdrew my whipperling, gray and shivering, but unharmed. "He's been tearing up my arm, and my head's pounding. Take him?"

"Maalik!" I was glad to see he was safe. But who would we send a message to down here? I let Maalik roost in my satchel. He settled down next to the brass plates, cooing at his faint reflection.

Ceetcee, Beliak, and I tethered ourselves to the ledge wall

behind an outcropping in order to rest. Ciel curled up next to us. Soon she snored softly. Doran wrapped himself in his cloak and glared out at the mist, and Djonn leaned against the wall next to him, blowing on his blistered palms. The ledge grew quiet, each of us wrapped in our own aches.

Upwind, Kirit whispered to Wik, "What happened at Laria? Did you hear their conversations?"

Wik whispered back, "I didn't hear much." His voice faded, then returned: ". . . kept me secluded, but the webs carried sound if you knew how to listen."

"Is Dix skytouched?" Kirit asked.

I listened hard for Wik's answer.

Wik shifted, the silk of his robes rubbing against the wall. "I don't know. She believes she knows how to save the city. Rumul believed the same thing. People are willing to follow belief." He paused and took a deep breath. "But even Rumul had doubts and fears. Dix is so certain." Wik's voice quieted after each phrase. Then he coughed. "I am sorry about Ezarit."

On the ledge, Kirit drew a shuddering breath. Wik hummed to her, at first tunelessly, then finding the notes for The Rise.

"Shhhh," Kirit said sadly. "Blackwings might hear."

I closed my eyes and let them mourn in silence. When I slept, I dreamt fitfully: Moc in Rumul's lap, laughing at me. Doran demanding answers about a vote. Dix shouting and pacing, carrying a dead man on her shoulders.

I woke up stabbing at the air with my hands. Ceetcee whispered, "It's all right," in my ear. Around us, the others slept. Aliati had not returned.

"How do we go from here?" I leaned my head against Ceetcee's shoulder. "We can't return to the city. Not while Dix has control." Our botched attack had delivered the city to her.

She squeezed my hand. "We'll return. We're part of the city too."

When I looked up, she had set her eyes on the clouds. "I thought by protesting Conclave, I could end it," she said. "That we could escape that debt to the cloudbound we all carry." Her grip on my hand tightened. "We can't undo what's been done in the city's name, but I could try to keep it from happening again." Ceetcee frowned, then leaned towards me, nearly nose to nose in the darkness. "Shifting the way people think isn't simple. The Singers and Ezarit knew that. Even Doran knows it. I think Kirit was trying, with her refusals. With the firebugs and the blackwings? You helped people think about what was happening. What I attempted with the protest? You achieved."

"And I've dragged us here." My voice wavered. "Stranded us. Stranded you."

Ceetcee stood on her tiptoes and pressed her lips to my forehead. "Others in the city will begin to question because we've questioned. They may not follow Dix so easily. Sometimes it just takes one action to change things."

Curls of cloud began to lick at the ledge and at our dirty footwraps, trying to disappear our legs beneath the mist. Ceetcee swung her foot until she could see her footwrap again, and I mimicked her motion. We kicked at clouds until they swirled away from the ledge, distracted for the moment from our griefs.

To be still in the clouds was to risk disappearing. I refused to disappear.

❧ ❧ ❧

A shadow appeared in the cloudbank. Wik tensed, alert. I reached for my bow.

Through the mist came a familiar windsign—"retrieve." Aliati dropped to the ledge, shaking her head. She'd had no luck.

"We need to search lower, more of us," she said. Her hair was slicked to her head, and her wings, though they still repelled the rain, dripped water onto the ledge. The spidersilk spans were soaked, despite their oil-proofing. "Storm's coming." She gestured to the growing dark clouds. A buffeting crosswind was building. "We need a real shelter."

"I'll help," I said. As I spoke, the wind increased. Our wings began to flutter, caught between the ledge wall and the swirling wind. Something struck my cheek, sharp and cold. I brushed it away, and my hand touched ice. Another piece hit me above my eye.

Ciel shouted, "Ow!" as more ice fell. Moc struggled to his feet, looking for an enemy.

The dark clouds nearest our ledge had grown nearer still and doubled in size. We'd experienced wind squalls in the towers, with rain, we'd watched lightning and thunder battle in the clouds. But a storm of this intensity was new to all of us.

What I had thought was darkness now seemed light by comparison to that cloud. We tethered as many as we could to the tower trunk, bodies huddled together behind the windward outcropping. Then the wind swirled and shifted, driving rain at us from the opposite direction.

Ciel squirmed, shocked. "It came on so fast." Her face was suddenly illuminated: cheekbones, wide eyes. Then the ledge and sky turned white, the air smelled sharp, burnt. Hiroli nearly tumbled from the ledge with fear. "What is it?" she said. "Why is it happening?"

"Lightning," Aliati said.

Beliak groaned. We tried to shelter him from the rain with our bodies, but he shivered with cold. Aliati knelt to press on his bleeding leg with a section of her robe. She looked up at me, water streaming off her face and braids. "We have to get him a place to lie down soon, out of the weather."

She was right, but we couldn't move the group in this storm. The winds would toss any but the most skilled flier into a tower or the abyss. But one flier could risk it. How far did the squall stretch? I began to untie myself from the tether.

Djonn grabbed my arm. "Storms that come quick go quick. Stay fast."

I hoped he was right. We huddled miserably in the battering wind and rain, waiting.

When the thunder quieted, I caught snatches of Ciel singing The Rise to Moc. She'd added a verse. I heard the word "Skyshouter" woven into the song, then "Brokenwings."

"I had no idea," I said, "that storms were this strong."

"They pass," Aliati whispered in the darkness, agreeing with Djonn. "But they come in groups. Usually a couple at least."

"How big are they?" Even as I asked, the rain slowed. Would the winds reach as high as the ghost cave? Could we go up again? "How much time between bands?"

Aliati shook her head. "No idea."

I climbed from behind the outcropping and peered across the ridge, but saw only gray shadows, gray rain. Djonn, sitting nearest, said, "You should take shelter again."

He tugged on my arm, then pulled me gently back as the humidity increased around us. I'd never felt so heavy, my skin sticky as spidersilk. An enormous boom made everything and everyone on the ledge jump again, but the tethers held us tight. Maalik, resting in my satchel, cooed fretfully. Moc began to shiver, and Doran and Ciel whispered to comfort him.

I readied myself to fly as soon as the weather passed, checking wingstraps, the contents of my satchel. Then light flashed and the crackling smell came again. My vision swam and my ears rang.

Hiroli jumped again at the noise. Ciel calmed her, trying to explain. She made a hand motion that Elna had used once. A sign for war. The clouds went to war sometimes, and made those sounds, those lights. When we were children, Elna had told

Kirit and me that story, often. They must have told it in the
Spire too.

I missed Elna searingly. Remembered watching a nighttime
storm from the towers as a child. How the cloudtop lit up, then
went dark. How red sparks sometimes danced for a few seconds
atop the clouds. Elna had said the ghosts of our ancestors were
fighting again. She'd said to never go looking for them in the
clouds, that I would be lost.

"It's letting up. I'm going to search." I untethered and stepped
from behind the outcropping before anyone could argue.

"And I," said Wik.

"I saw a tower on my last search, right at the end of my tether.
I'll show you," Aliati said.

Ceetcee and Doran agreed to remain with Beliak, Djonn,
Hiroli, and the twins. They huddled against the ledge wall,
trying to keep out of the spitting rain. Kirit hesitated, wanting
to accompany us, but knowing the others would need help if
the blackwings spotted them.

"I'll guard them," she promised. "I will stay."

❧ ❧ ❧

"The tower I saw was farther down, and to the left," Aliati said.
"There were bones out front, but they looked very old." She
didn't say whether that could be a scavenger cache or not.

We had few tethers with us now; most were anchoring our
remaining friends to the ledge. We relied on the single tether,
and worked to stay together, flying close enough that we might
not lose one another. Aliati began to echo, and Wik joined her,
hoping to sound out any towers hiding in the shadows.

They echoed to their offsides as we flew, and all of us kept
our ears open for blackwings or bone eaters. If we found a
cave, we'd be much safer from them. And drier, and eventually
warm.

Each time lightning pulsed, mist shimmered like glass beads on our wings. My legs ached from long stretches of flying and the footsling's pull. Aliati had said storms could make old wounds ache too, and I was starting to believe her. I didn't like it.

The clouds thickened and we began to whistle in order to stay together. "Retrieve," for Aliati. "Defend" for me. Wik caught on and whistled four short notes. "Protect." The clouds swelled and darkened ahead of us.

"Cloudburst," shouted Aliati, breaking our small chevron formation. "We have to go up or down."

"Down," I said. The wind began to swirl. We dove as fast as we could, trying to get beneath the squall.

As we descended, rain and ice pelted us, sharp as spears. I could barely see Wik off my right wingtip. Weather rumbled around us, and white-hot light arced between thick clouds to our left.

"In there!" Aliati shouted and turned hard against the battering wind. Wik struggled for control and I, trying to make the turn in the turbulence of their wings, was blown up and nearly away. I tucked my wings tight, making as small a foil as possible, and fell. When I was low enough, I fought them open again and followed Wik and Aliati below the storm, into the shadow of a stunted tower trunk.

The tower's bone overgrowth reached out to its neighbors, forming a wall. Thick knobs of bone slabs and bulges obscured what could still, in some places, be seen as tier divisions. Gaps along the outgrowth might allow us shelter, but we saw few places to land away from the hail and lightning.

Finally, Aliati pointed, "There! Two caves! One above, one below." I could barely hear her voice over the wind's roar now, but I followed her tack. In our rush to descend, we'd been blown off course. We'd overflown the cave and worked our way back around to it. We were nearly at the end of the tether's length when we landed.

We clawed our way down the overgrowth, hands finding purchase in the soft green moss and lichen that grew on the tower trunk.

The higher cave was tiny and narrow. We climbed past it. The one below looked better for our needs.

ϟ ϟ ϟ

As Aliati had said, the old bone pile in front of the lower cave was undisturbed. No fresh feathers. No bone eater stench.

The overhang provided more shelter than the ledge we'd left the others on, and the cave stretched back into the darkness. Light flashed behind us and something glittered within.

"I'll guard the cave mouth if you want to scout," Aliati said. She anchored the tether—our only connection to the ledge through the mist—with a looping hitch around the largest bone in the cairn.

Scouting was dry. I stepped farther inside, into darkness. Behind me, the opening framed the cloudscape, dim except in comparison to the cave.

My skin prickled. "No chance you have a lantern and a flint?" Djonn had both with him, but he was on the ledge. We'd lost much from the ghost tower's caches, and we hadn't much to lose to start with.

Aliati laughed. "No flint. Better you than me."

We could use any light. Even luminescence. Kirit had been able to wake the littlemouths. So had Ciel. Something in their voices, in their Singer training. Wik had been trained to hunt skymouths and control them. Could it work on littlemouths?

"Hum something?" I asked him. If there were any littlemouths on the tower trunk, we might get some light. I hoped the storm hadn't driven them into hiding. Wik looked at me strangely, but obliged. He began humming The Rise.

The area outside the cave stayed dark. *Birdcrap.* I stared into the rain, not looking forward to exploring the cave by bone hook.

"Look!" Aliati pointed, but not towards the outer tower. She gestured into the cave, where a single littlemouth glowed softly blue-green against the cave wall.

For a moment, all Wik could do was stare. "I didn't know they could do that."

The small creature didn't generate a lot of light, but even a little was comforting. I felt my way forward until I stood next to the cave's back wall. My fingers touched its dry hide. A loop of tentacle wrapped my wrist. Then it pulled away and the light faded. Wik had stopped humming.

"They like your voice. And Kirit's too," I said, hoping he would hum again without me needing to ask.

Aliati, silhouetted in the cave mouth, spoke through the dark. "Djonn thinks they luminesce so they can find each other in the clouds."

I nodded, remembering the conversation, "Like our wind-signs." Wik had grasped those easily.

Wik tried again, louder. Slowly, in waves moving away from me, the cave glowed. Wik's skymouth-ink tattoos reflected the light in response.

"That's amazing," Aliati said. The luminescence revealed a medium cave, with three alcoves. I gasped when I saw what had glittered in the lightning. Metal poles ringed in the walls, the alcoves. I walked to the nearest one, letting the littlemouths light the way. The tower core split around each pole, creating gaps that eventually joined to form the cave. Like the ridge wall near the council fall, this cave had been shaped deliberately, but with much more skill.

Metal was so scarce in the city, so valuable. Poles this size would be wealth beyond belief in the city—an upper tier's worth, maybe, if we could pry them loose. Or ever go back home.

More metal glinted on the alcove walls.

"All right in there?" Aliati called. Behind me, Wik had already turned back, prepared to get the others. I ached to explore, but that could wait until everyone was safe. This cave was a much better stopping place than the ledge above.

We'd seen no evidence of recent bone eaters, but as I left the middle alcove, my foot brushed something that rustled dryly. Glass sparkled in the littlemouths' glow. I bent closer and touched teeth nestled in an ancient skymouth hide. The whole husk was rimed with dust. A young skymouth must have once stumbled in here; the hide and teeth were all that remained.

Cupping my hand, I scooped the teeth into my satchel. They clattered against brass. Maalik squawked at me, awakened. "Sorry, friend." The littlemouths on the walls slowly faded.

"Nat, there's another squall coming," Aliati shouted over the building wind. I hurried to the cave mouth, one hand tracing the wall. The bone was warm. Still alive down here. Alive, and trained long ago to shelter people within the expanding bone, rather than forcing them to climb higher, like our city.

A stretch of lightning reached across the clouds and lit up the cave.

"Look how long the boom takes after the light." Aliati stared into the gray. Wik counted silently until a muffled boom sounded upwind of us.

"We might only have time for one run."

More lightning flashed. Illuminated, the cave looked smaller, but we could see now that nothing lurked in its walls. There were no scavenger caches, but it felt safe enough. We could

recover here and try to hunt for food. As long as we all survived the storm.

"Here's where we'll stay." I reached in my bag and handed
Aliati and Wik a glass tooth each. Aliati's was the length of her
hand, Wik's slightly smaller. "Some good luck for our journey."
And for our survival. Those teeth would make good knives,
eventually. My companions stowed them away.

"Can you carry Djonn, Nat?" Aliati asked. "I need to manage the tether."

Djonn was lighter than Beliak, but his brace made him awkward to carry. I thought for a moment, then remembered the
sling. Could I fly him solo? "I think so."

"We'll have to fight our way back to the ledge against that
headwind," she said. "Wind's shifting."

The clouds spun slowly in a great circle, the distant thunder
much closer now.

ᒼ ᒼ ᒼ

To rise as high as we could before leaping into the wind, we
climbed the tower trunk above the cave mouth and used the
moss along its ridges as handholds, sinking our grips only when
we needed to. We worked up and around the tower, reeling in
the tether, until we were closer to the direction of the ledge.
The plants were spongy and slick between our fingers. Some
looked like old men's beards, but clung to the tower side with
the strength of spidersilk. Every surface cupped water from the
storm, and our hands, knees, and feet grew wet. I shivered. I
slipped, then regained my footing as I cursed the clouds.

Faster.

The clouds hung gossamer thin between our tower and the
ledge, though nearby, darker bands of cloud gathered. I hoped
we were high enough. Wik leapt first, and we followed.

When we launched, battered by the headwinds, Wik flew

zigs and zags to reach the ledge. First we swept towards the ghost tower, far in the distance. Then we made switchback turns, flying synchronized, like Nightwings of old in the dark city skies. Aliati echoed now and then to help Wik, and the littlemouth began to luminesce on my shoulder.

"They can hear you too!" I laughed. She sounded delighted, but focused on coiling the tether as it grew slack. The ledge came into view as we hit the rain line.

On the ledge, Wik and I helped Ceetcee into her wings. She looked green, nauseated. "It's normal," she said, a hand on her belly. "Just harder than usual down here. I can still fly." She winked at me while I tightened Ciel's wingstraps, but I caught her looking nervously over the cloudscape. She knelt by Beliak, and I joined her at his side as she whispered, "Everything will be all right."

"It will." I touched her cheek. I hoped she was right. "Fly safe." She pressed my hand close to her skin, warming it.

When they were ready, Ciel and Ceetcee jumped from the ledge and circled in the dark gray sky, waiting for us. Wik hooked Beliak, I lifted Djonn in the sling, and Doran followed with Moc.

Aliati and Kirit flew behind us with Hiroli.

We crossed between the towers on a storm gust, the most direct, most dangerous way. It was rough going, but with the wind behind us, we neared the cave quickly. At the very end, a spill of wind hit Ceetcee and she spun wildly and fought to right herself. I dove behind her, trying to help her and carry Djonn at the same time, until she evened out on her own.

The edge of rain began to splat the cave as we landed. Lichen and fern fronds clinging to the incline below the cave dipped and rebounded as each drop struck. The wide tower trunk's overgrowths shuffled the wind into new patterns around the cave mouth. I set Djonn down as Ceetcee landed, then banked away until they moved inside the shelter, making room for me to land.

From the cave mouth, Ceetcee watched the sky, shivering. By the time the others came into sight, the rain fell in sheets and thunder had begun to boom again. Kirit and Aliati trailed behind, and Hiroli struggled.

I yelled out to them and at the gusts that bore them. "Hurry!" I leaned into the storm, reaching, trying to pull them closer with my voice. We were few enough, and too far lost already.

26

CLOUDBOUND

Aliati and Kirit shepherded Hiroli towards the cave while storm winds surged.

The junior councilor's eyes grew wider with each bolt of lightning. Storm-panicked, she flew erratically, paying little attention to the changing wind currents. Only with the others' whistled encouragement did she make it to the cave.

When Hiroli landed in a shivering sprawl on the ledge, we pulled her inside. Ciel helped her out of her wings. The other two spiraled close again, but the wind blew them off course at dangerous angles. On her next approach, Aliati crashed into the tower wall above us, then slid down its side. She dangled feet-first over the cave edge, wings dripping.

We caught her and helped lower her into the cave.

"That must have hurt," Wik whispered.

Shards of light broke around us, and thunder crashed repeatedly, drowning out Aliati's curses to the tower, Hiroli, and the wind.

Meantime, Kirit fought hard to avoid getting blown away from the tower. Finally, she tucked her wings and crashed deliberately below the cave. She landed with a thump in the undergrowth, her wings snagging on the clinging nettles there.

In the city, "cloudbound" meant to disappear. No songs marked the lost, no Remembrances.

In our storm-struck cave, "cloudbound" meant that the city

had disappeared. No one would help us. We were all we had left.

Doran anchored a spidersilk tether for me, and I handed him my satchel with Maalik safe inside before descending the tower's overgrown wall to reach Kirit.

"All right?" I shouted in the lashing rain. I laced my fingers into broadleaf ferns growing on the towerside to avoid skidding down the slope. Kirit did the same as she crept towards me, grimacing. Her replacement wings dragged behind her, the yellow silk streaked with dirt and leaves.

"I'll live," she said, shivering hard enough to make her teeth chatter.

Her footwraps torn and filthy, Kirit began to climb. Rain soaked her gray robe, the hem dragging damp against the tower. Finally, she pulled herself over the ledge and disappeared into the cave.

Lightning cracked, filling my nose with burnt air. Unwilling to be singed next, I scaled the tether quickly. Kirit and Wik reached over the edge and caught my arms.

When they dragged me back into the cave, I stripped my soaked wings from my shoulders, then peeled off my outer robe. I wrung that out by the cave mouth. Four useless tower marks spilled from a pocket. I leaned my wings on the wall, next to the others' frames.

We'd led our group of Lawsbreakers to safety without losing anyone, but safety felt wet, dark, and tremendously cold.

I paced, trying to warm up. Ceetcee beckoned me over to where she huddled with Beliak, Ciel, and Moc, but I didn't want to drain their warmth. Besides, I couldn't sit still.

My pale under-robe wrapped damp around my shoulders, a mildew taint strong in my nose. There was no getting warm here, no being dry.

Aliati, her palms and the left side of her face scraped raw,

watched Hiroli jump at each new roll of thunder and shook her
head. Then she helped Djonn settle, exhausted, against a wall
and began searching through their satchels for anything dry.

"We left so much in the ghost tower that we'll need down
here. Flint, lanterns, oil. Food."

"I have flint," Djonn said. "I lost only my toolbox, not the important things." He reached his hand to a pocket and fished
out a chunk of ancient flint and a striking stone.

Aliati pulled a dry robe from her satchel and gave it to
Hiroli. She took the flint from Djonn. "Now all we need here is
dry fuel." She laughed hollowly. "And to figure out where we
are."

Where was here? My eyes met Aliati's, and I didn't have to
speak the question aloud. Bigger than the ghost tower cave,
this one was also colder and darker. After being buffeted by
the storm, I wasn't really sure where we were, either.

Aliati finally said, "No scavengers have ever come this far.
We're running on rumors and myth." "The Horror of the
Clouds." "The Bone Forest." Those were the myths. They got
us here. But there aren't any songs about how to survive here.

I'd gone into the clouds seeking answers, hoping to undo the
damage I'd helped create on the council. Now I'd stranded us
farther from the city than even scavengers were willing to go.

"We'll make do," Ceetcee said from where she sat. She huddled, wrapping her arms around herself and the twins. She
began to hum The Rise, then thought better of it, switching to
"Corwin and the Nest of Thieves." Very slowly, Ciel joined her,
weaving the new verse in. The littlemouth clinging a nearby
wall glowed softly when the girl sang.

As the two began to make up more verses and rename songs,
Kirit joined them, and even Doran, once he picked up on the
words. The cave echoed with Ciel's and Ceetcee's high notes,
Kirit's rough ones, and Doran's, cautious and deep.

We waited for the rain to stop, singing, and even laughing. The others sat, but I could not stay still, instead I paced a damp circuit of the cave.

Kirit watched me from where she sat huddled miserably in Wik's robe. "We need to go back. To finish this."

"Maybe," Doran said teasingly, "if we'd waited to confront Dix together, we'd be above the city right now." The words hung in the air; though they'd sounded playful, he hadn't been teasing at all.

"That's enough," I said, though I, too, wished she'd waited, or that I'd moved faster to stop her. Doran shrugged and got up to search for fuel.

"We're hungry, cold, and out of sorts," Aliati said, glaring at all of us. "No need to make it worse."

Wik shifted uncomfortably, unable to lean against the wall thanks to the lashes on his back. Djonn watched pain cross his face. "Dix didn't give you anything for the pain?" he asked, a tinge of jealousy in his voice.

Wik grimaced. "You're the artifex Dix was looking for. Where were you?" He sounded like a Singer of old, demanding answers.

Djonn waved his hand and reached into his satchel. Hummed Ciel's verse from "The Nest of Thieves." "Into the clouds. And I took Dix's precious lighter-than-air plans with me." He held it up so that it reflected the next lightning strike, shining light around the cave.

The wind filled our silence with hollow sounds as we took in Djonn's theft—both the brazenness of it and the danger.

Hiroli roused from where she'd been half asleep near Doran. "She's going to want that back."

"I think you're right," Djonn said, nodding. "Though she can't read it. No one knows how to but me."

Doran watched Djonn wave the plate in the cool air. "We should put that someplace safe."

Without another word, Djonn tucked the plate back in his robe. "Done." The two stared at each other for a long moment. The cave suddenly felt much smaller and more uncomfortable.

The rain kept falling, and cold gusts whistled through the cave. I knelt by Ceetcee and Beliak. He'd closed his eyes, and his skin was hot to the touch. I pulled a half-empty water sack from my satchel and set it near him. Clinging to the damp side of the sack were the broken pieces of my father's message chip. I pressed them between my fingers, wishing Naton could help us now.

In the quiet, Wik asked Moc about Laria. The boy shook his head, refusing to answer. Wik turned to Hiroli next. "They didn't hurt you?"

Hiroli looked at the bone floor near Djonn's feet. "They couldn't. I'm council, and they knew I didn't know where Nat had gone, or anything about the plates. They kept me in a foul alcove anyway, filled with webs. Dix didn't want me telling anyone that she had Moc." She swallowed. "When they fed me just before Allmoons and I got woozy, I started to worry." She turned to us and smiled. "But then you found me."

Wik frowned, as if he could still taste the drug. "People can share a Law or a song easily. But Dix wants to possess those brass plates, or at least what they represent. They're trouble." He looked about to say more, but winced instead and tried to find a more comfortable place to sit.

The temperature in the cave dropped again. "You could say that about any metal," I said.

Aliati nodded agreement.

"Perhaps." Wik shrugged as if he didn't really think so.

Now that I was dry, I wrapped my arms around Ceetcee and Beliak, trying to shield them from the cold air. But my thoughts were far away, in the towers above the clouds, and Laria in particular. Even if we were safer now, not everyone was. We'd told the silkspinners about Rumul, and they'd confronted Dix. Friends from the northwest quadrant had sounded alarms and distracted her blackwings. Doran's guards had started fights to draw them away into the night. We'd rescued our friends. But then we'd left those above defenseless against the retribution of Dix and her blackwings. And we'd left others we loved up there too. Macal, guiding the northwest. Those who had spoken against the Conclave.

"Who's with Elna?" Was she alone, after Doran had promised protection?

"My daughter and her mother," Doran replied. "Both good fighters, if it comes to it."

That didn't ease my mind. Doran looked troubled too. "They'll hold their own," he said. "And Elna's stronger than you give her credit for."

It wasn't his right to tell me about my mother, but I held my tongue.

The cave air grew thick with lost opportunities and broken chances. If Kirit had gone along with the plan. If Hiroli hadn't been captured. Ciel. If Doran had been able to keep hold of the city while we'd been searching for answers. If I'd been faster.

If Dix hadn't found the brass plate among Rumul's effects. I began to pace again.

"Hiroli and Moc, you were at Laria for days," Doran said. "You must know something more." I remembered Dix leaning over Rumul's body, interpreting his whispers, and shuddered.

Moc looked bleak. "They promised me wings. I offered to help find Nat in trade for new wings, I think." He put his head on his knees.

"That was the drug, Moc," Djonn said. "It makes you helpful. Compliant." He looked down. "I know—it did the same to me."

Hiroli blinked. "I heard Dix talking, a couple times." She

smiled grimly. "They thought I was sleeping. She told visitors Kirit was colluding with rogue Singers now, that she'd infiltrated the Spire on purpose years ago."

I growled and began to pace the cave. "That's ridiculous. Kirit was taken by the Spire. Used by them." As my father had been. Between my fingers, the broken pieces of Naton's drawings clicked together, useless, but comforting.

Hiroli massaged the bridge of her nose, trying to remember. "Dix said the northwestern quadrant had planned insurrection a generation ago. That Ezarit had schemed with an artifex to gain power. Kirit had seen the plan through."

That could be only one artifex: She meant Naton and the holes he'd drilled in the Spire. "She's saying Ezarit set that up, then sacrificed her daughter to the Spire? She's cloudtouched."

Hiroli waved a hand back and forth as if pushing the idea away. "She's convinced the southwest towers and some in the east. Everything that's happened since? It's proof Ezarit didn't deserve to lead the city."

"Don't speak that way of the dead, even if you're just repeating," Aliati said before the rest of us could. Hiroli bowed her head.

Kirit kicked Wik's robe away and stood, fist curled around a knife handle, looking ready to head back to Laria and fight again. "Dix is the one killing the Spire. She's bringing on a collapse."

Wik growled. "Doran, you heard these rumors too." He tugged at Kirit's hand, trying to get her to sit back down.

Doran shrugged, but began to walk the cave as well, limping on his injured foot. There was little space for the two of us. "I heard, but didn't believe them."

Beliak began coughing and shivering harder. Ceetcee lifted the bandage. The wound had darkened and puckered. "Bone dust," she whispered. "This is bad."

"Kirit survived an infection. Beliak will too." He had to. But even Kirit blanched at the threat of a bone dust infection. She'd been sick for months, with all the medicine the city could provide. Down here, there was no medicine. But Ceetcee nodded, her eyes hopeful.

Would others succumb to the fever as well? So far none had, but without food or warmth, we'd all sicken. The scratches I'd received at Laria throbbed, but my old wounds from Spirefall were painful too. The dust and deep clouds were affecting all of us. Kirit was right. We needed to go back.

A loud boom rolled through the air, nearly overhead.

Bright light illuminated the cave, throwing enormous shadows behind us. Our wings, propped fully spread against the cave walls to dry, glowed and rippled. Hiroli jumped again. "We need to find a safer place," I finally said. Home. The city.

Aliati looked at me and shook her head slowly. "We're safer here than anywhere else. So few suspect this cave exists, and it's too deep in the clouds to scavenge. I didn't think about looking for it until Ciel's song."

It struck me then. "This is the nest of thieves?"

"I think so," Aliati said. "Though it's pretty small."

Doran snorted. "Dix's guards won't stop until they find us. We have her brass plates, her artifex . . . Kirit. And now Ciel too."

"Don't," Wik began. Ciel nestled closer to Ceetcee.

"I'm not saying anything that we're not all thinking." Doran ignored Wik. "Ciel took something from Dix. So did Djonn. Dix will be looking to—"

"Enough!" Wik shouted, reaching for a blade that didn't exist. He grabbed a fistful of robe instead.

I stepped between them, blocking Wik's view of Doran. "No more of that. Not right now." If this kept up, we wouldn't make it through a single night without becoming our own enemies.

Aliati made a calming gesture with her hands, smoothing the air. "I think they can try looking for us, but it will be like finding a skymouth in the open air." Ciel nodded and relaxed. Doran toed the dust on the cave floor. But Wik looked out into the storm, as if blackwings might appear there any time.

Kirit regarded Aliati. "Are you planning on living down here the rest of your life? Don't you want to go back to the city? To help people fight? Dix could drain the city of heartbone to make more lighter-than-air. She could kill towers, enslave more fledges."

"You don't know that," Hiroli countered. "Besides, before, Dix was just doing what she'd been asked." Hiroli jerked a thumb at Doran. "Following orders."

She wasn't helping the situation. I frowned at her, but she didn't notice.

Doran sat down slowly. "Dix isn't following my orders now," he muttered. "She lied to me too. My needs momentarily matched hers. Then she wanted more power."

Momentarily. "Do you really think that she's done with you? She'll keep using you to gain favor in the city. She'll try to rescue you, to save the council leader from the Lawsbreakers. Will you go along with that to survive?"

I wanted to shake my former mentor until his teeth rattled. He'd taken advantage of the council's situation to build his position—whether it was purely to speed the city's healing or to speed his rise to power didn't matter. He'd used Dix to build more advantage, and she'd played on his weaknesses, pretending to be loyal to him. She'd outplayed him. Now he was acting wounded. "You built a fire, and the wind changed. You got burned. Will you return to try again?"

Doran looked at the floor. "I know. I shouldn't have trusted her. I learned to trade by building nets of people. In politics, that's like getting consensus before a vote. But building consensus means you rely on loyalty when the vote comes around. Dix used that. Used me. Can I tell you how awful that feels?" He looked at me. "Nat, you of all people should understand."

The Singers had used me once, and Elna and Naton. I did understand.

Ceetcee looked up from where she tended Beliak, then looked away, shaking her head. But Kirit spoke. "You're singed, but you're still playing the game, or hoping to."

It wasn't a question, but Doran nodded anyway. Kirit spun her blade on the bone floor, thinking.

Not for the first time, I worried Doran's manipulations would eventually burn us too.

᛭ ᛭ ᛭

Stomachs growled. Our group shivered in silence. The cave wasn't a large space, and each time elbows or knees connected or rainwater dripped in the wrong place, soaking a drying robe, tension bloomed. Like the clouds outside, the mood in the cave grew darker. When Aliati began picking the lichen from her robe and staring at the mess of ferns and moss left on the cave floor from our ascent, I prepared myself for more grumbling. Instead, she knelt by Djonn, propped against the wall, his eyes closed tight. She nudged his arm. "Does skymouth hide burn?" She stared at the sole sack of lighter-than-air we had remaining, suspended above Djonn's sling chair.

"Try this instead." I hurried to find the dried hide at the back of the cave.

She made a frame of bones from the cairn and placed the carcass on top. The flint sparked, and slowly the hide caught and smoked, but the fire was close enough to the cave mouth that it didn't smother us.

I peered outside, eyeing the smaller cave. With the rain easing, I could search it for more fuel, as well as food.

Aliati's small fire didn't do much to warm the space, but it did cheer us. Ceetcee helped strip leaves from the lichen stems. It sounded like tiny wing rips, seam by seam, leaf by leaf. Aliati took Ceetcee's water sack and held it outside in the slowing storm to fill, then put the stripped lichens inside and swung the sack over the fire on a bone batten from the wing.

She caught me staring at her. "Thieving isn't a scavenger's only skill." Her face broke into a grim smile as she swung the water sack, warming it above the fire. "We also start fires. Bring me your robe."

I hesitated, picturing my robe aflame, but when I obliged, she pulled more broken fern stems and green lichen from the hem, where they'd caught, damp. She added these to the sack with the lichen Kirit had pulled from her robe. We busied ourselves picking through the sparse vegetation we'd dragged in from outside.

"Why not these?" Wik asked, pointing to the pile of yellow-colored lichen Aliati had set aside on the floor.

She shook her head, dropping the greens in the sack. "Yellow's poison. Good to know it's out there, though."

Wik raised his eyebrows. "Indeed."

Outside, lightning flashed again, but farther away, while Aliati cooked. I remembered the same feeling of anticipation watching Elna bake apples or graincakes as a child. Finally, Aliati pulled the sack of rainwater and greens away from the fire to let it cool. My mouth watered, even at the bitter smell that came from inside. The others edged closer as well.

She picked a bone shard from the pile by the cave mouth, rinsed it clean in the rain, and lifted green shoots from the water so they steamed in the air. After a few moments letting them cool, she held the trailing greens out to me.

I took a piece eagerly and chewed. Coughed into my hand so no one would see the expression on my face as I kept chewing.

"Good!" I finally said around the mouthful of greens. They were bitter to taste and tough, but all we had. They might have been good with goose, possibly. Or even something smaller, like dirgeon. They could have been good with anything. If we had anything, which we didn't. My stomach growled.

"We'll get more food from outside soon, but this will help," Aliati said, smiling at me. "I'm not a great cook. I don't know many cooking songs."

Ceetcee eyed the greens cautiously, then nodded once. "We'll have to make our own songs."

27

LITTLEMOUTHS

When the storm rolled away and only cold drizzle remained, Ciel took Moc and skidded down the slope outside the cave to hunt more greens for Aliati. We heard them squabbling down below, but couldn't make out the words.

I stepped outside and climbed the rough outcroppings to the smaller cave above, searching for more fuel, and maybe a dirgeon.

The small cave was bigger than it looked from below, but so squat I had to crawl into it and couldn't straighten up once inside. It reeked of guano, and I didn't like the idea of getting a face full of the stuff. I reached forward with my bone hook. Felt dry weeds rustle. Tapped a hard shell.

Eggs. I whooped loud enough to send small rodents scrambling and something larger flapping outside.

Carefully, I drew the nest filled with three eggs into the dim cloudlight. Too small to belong to a bone eater, the eggs were still each as large as my hand, colored a speckled gray.

"What did you find?" Moc shouted, looking up from below.

"Food," I grinned. I tucked the eggs in my robe and threw the empty nest down to the ledge.

By the time I'd scrambled down the tower, the twins had climbed back up to the cave. Their gray robes were streaked with moss and sap, and they clutched fistfuls of lichen. They eyed the egg-shaped bulges in my robes with great interest as the bitter, beardy plants dangled through their fingers.

Once they passed the lichen to Aliati, I gave them two of the eggs to shake, and demonstrated how to prepare them with the third.

Kirit fed the nest to the fire. "What kind of bird lays giant gray eggs? A gryphon?" she asked, joking.

"You always think it's a gryphon," I replied.

Using three battens from Kirit's wing, Djonn and Ceetcee built a tripod over the fire and suspended a small bone trivet beneath. I placed the eggs in the trivet, and we waited hungrily.

When they were roasted, we cracked the eggs open and shared out the white and gold insides among everyone.

"Delicious," Ceetcee whispered.

They even tasted good with the greens.

Our bellies finally full, we curled up on the cave floor and against the walls, and slept.

ᘓ ᘓ ᘓ

The cawing woke me first, before the gryphon's beak descended. I rolled away, barely awake, and the night-colored raptor speared only my robe. Ceetcee shrieked and batted at the wings.

"Someone's unhappy about the missing eggs," Aliati said as she ducked into one of the alcoves with Moc and Ciel. The angry gryphon's wingspan filled the cave with dark feathers, toppling the tripod over the now-cold fire with a clatter. Maalik woke from his roost by Beliak and flew at the gryphon, but was driven back. The larger bird screeched and chased me deeper into the cave.

At the other side of the cave, Hiroli cowered, while Doran tried to shield Beliak. When the gryphon's hooked beak started to jab at my arms, drawing blood, Ceetcee swung at it with a bone hook. The bird dodged it easily. Wik grabbed a batten and poked overhead, but that only enraged the gryphon. It chased me farther into the back of the cave, claws extended.

Finally, Aliati managed to swat it with her satchel, stunning it. She and Wik pushed the gryphon out of the cave and over the edge.

"Dinner." Kirit was the first over the cave ledge, knife drawn. Aliati stopped just long enough to put her newly dry wings on and followed her.

"Mighty hunter," Ceetcee chuckled, holding out a hand to help me up.

I laid my finger against her lips. "Shhh."

Wik, close behind us, peered at the cave wall.

"Something's here." Wik pressed his fingers into a crack beside the metal pole. With a shuddering creak of bone moving across bone, part of the wall turned slowly on an invisible hinge.

The alcove became a slim opening, revealing a narrow, dusty tunnel beyond. The space was so dark we couldn't see the end of it, but I felt a cool breeze brush my cheek.

"Be careful," Ceetcee said. I squeezed her hand, wanting her not to be nervous about the tight space, but she batted at my arm. "I'm not just saying that for me. Voids can weaken a tower, like on Lith. That one doesn't look too bad, but you don't want an old tunnel falling in on you because someone got ambitious."

I looked from her to the tunnel, then back. Wanting to see what was back there, but not wanting to leave her with more worries. She shook her head. "I'll stay with Beliak. You go. Just be careful."

Both Wik and I could see metal lining the roof of the tunnel and a graceful curve of bone. It looked like a good bet that the central core was intact. "Keep the others out of here, at least until we know more?"

My heart still pounded from being woken so suddenly, and perhaps a little at the thought of going through that narrow passage after Ceetcee's warning. But we needed to make sure the passage was clear of threats. And, I admit, I wanted to explore, too.

While I hesitated, Moc and Ciel ignored Ceetcee's muted "wait" and squeezed between me and the crack in the alcove, their heads bumping my scraped elbows.

I looked behind me. "No one else yet, all right?" Ceetcee nodded.

I felt along the outer wall until I found the littlemouth from the day before and lifted it gently to my hand, where it clung. Wik hummed, and it lit up, illuminating the tunnel for a short distance.

"A real thieves' cave," Moc said. "I can't see anything."

"Try humming," Ciel whispered to Moc.

Moc still looked pale and drawn, but with his twin urging him on, he hummed in the dark passage. A soft glow appeared down the tunnel, then went out.

"Do like me," his sister said again, then she hummed louder. The end of the cave brightened as several littlemouths responded. The tunnel glowed blue, and we could see it wrapped around a corner. A few steps farther, metal sparkled in the dim light. Beyond that, the glow kept getting brighter. Ciel watched her brother, holding her breath to see if what he saw pleased him. "They can hear us, Moc."

"Fine, Ciel," Moc whispered, annoyed that she could do it better than he. His sister's face fell. She stopped humming.

The light in the tunnel dimmed, then grew bright again as Wik hummed, a low baritone.

The littlemouth I held pulsed with a flitter of undercurrent. A message, but not for us. For whom, then?

Ahead of us, Moc cursed, surprised. "Clouds, Wik, your face."

Wik turned for a moment, and his muted laugh made me grin. His Singers' tattoos were glowing softly. Like Kirit's scars had, in the meadow where we'd found the council.

Although the tension of the day before had eased, the world we'd entered was much stranger than the one we'd fallen from. From the far back of the cave, more light showed dimly, though Wik had stopped humming.

The glow increased around the first branch of tunnels, and we watched it build. For the first time since Laria, Moc began to look awake and interested.

"Want a job?" I asked him. He nodded, hesitant. "I name you chief explorers." They both grinned.

"But Wik and I should go first," I said. "No telling what's down there." The former Singer seemed much more comfortable in narrow spaces than I felt, but I'd brought them here. I should move into the lead.

Ciel made a face and kept walking. "We'll be careful."

Behind us, on the other side of the alcove, Ceetcee tended Beliak in a cold cave. And above us, Elna sheltered in a stranger's tier.

"If I'd been more careful, my family would still be safe at Densira."

"If you'd been more careful," Wik replied, "the fledges would still be in the undercloud, mining the Spire. You didn't cause this, Nat. Dix has been manipulating the city since Spirefall."

And the city had fallen for it. Easier to have an enemy the towers could call unlucky, or worse, than to learn who we were now, and who we wanted to be. Even I'd fallen for Dix's manipulations early on. Deciding the fledges were lost, the Singers were to blame for the riots and everything else. How many had helped her do what she did? Doran, even if unintentionally. Were there others? Something Ezarit had said about not knowing who to trust nagged at me.

Ciel pulled at my sleeve. "If you're going to lead, *lead*."

I laughed. "We might as well know where we are."

Slowly, the boy's face brightened. "I could help."

Ciel smiled at me. "I bet there's no gryphons back here." She squeezed her brother's hand and giggled as I grimaced.

Now Wik hesitated. Before Spirefall, a Singer like him would have led the way into the passage. Now I remembered his temperament during the time he helped care for me at Lith—after I fell to Kirit in the Gyre. He'd have struck out against Dix too. She went against his sense of order. But now? After Laria and especially after Spirefall, he was all caution. He tested his knife. "We should find more weapons to take with us."

I touched my arm sheath. Two knives, though another had gone missing in the gryphon attack. It was enough. I was beginning to feel as eager as the twins to see what was down the tunnel.

"Maybe there are weapons back there," Ciel said, leaning in the direction she wanted to go: towards the tunnels. "Maybe a whole cave full."

That idea seemed to draw Wik's attention. He coaxed a littlemouth onto his shoulder and stepped into the tunnel.

The walls sparkled here and there along our path, pricked to light by the littlemouths' glow. I stepped closer and saw more metal shards. Brass and other metals too. My fingertips brushed time-dulled edges, crusts of bone growth over other shapes, barely distinct now. The objects were so old, some were merely ghosts of themselves.

Many were unreadable, at least by me. They could have been records of trades or gambling debts, awful jokes, or important formulas. It was impossible to tell. No matter what, the walls held what Doran had wanted most for the city: knowledge that the past had failed to share with the future.

Ciel ran a finger down the markings. Puffs of dust rose.

"What does it say?" She looked around the turn as if expecting to see an ancient artifex, or the thieves from her song.

Wik leaned close, trying to see in the blue light. "It looks familiar. But only just."

Who were the people who grew this cave and the hidden tunnels here?

Bone overgrowths made the tunnel hard to navigate, especially in places where a plate had fallen to the floor. Still, we moved carefully through the tunnel's turns. It felt as though we walked the tower's perimeter, at the very least, sheltered within tunnels of bone. Ceetcee had no need to worry about tunnel collapses.

Ciel disappeared around a bend, taking Moc and much of the light with her. Wik still hummed quietly behind me.

The twists and turns continued to remind me of Lith, the broken tower barely visible above the city, where the lawless had for generations carved passages and hiding places through the bone. The feverish days I'd spent there, nursed by Elna and Tobiat with Wik's help, were seared into my memory.

"I never said thank you," I said over my shoulder. "I should have."

Wik looked at me from under heavy brows. I remembered his strength, fighting at my side during Spirefall. His Lawsmarker-draped shoulders at Bissel. Conclave. We'd been on opposite sides only when Doran's politics demanded it.

No, that wasn't true. When I'd allowed Doran's politics to change me.

Wik walked closer, still behind me. "After the market riots, when the city turned against us, I felt unworthy of the city. I let your council pile Laws on me and tell me I'd wronged the towers. Meantime, you saved Moc and Ciel."

"But I wouldn't have, if Kirit hadn't led the way."

He walked slower. "When they carried me to Laria, when I

saw"—his breath caught, then rushed from his nose—"Rumul. Barely alive." He drew another breath. "When I guessed Dix used the riots to destabilize the council and turned the towers against themselves, I lost hope again. And then, there you were. We fought together again, after all this time."

I squirmed, uncomfortable. "We're stronger when we fight together."

"You could have left us there with Dix, at Laria, but you didn't," Wik said.

"You could have told Dix about what we'd found in the clouds, but you didn't."

He held out a tattooed, callused hand, and I clasped it for a moment, feeling tension ease, but not dissipate. How did battle wounds heal? Did the wind forgive the towers for striking it, or did it just keep going?

Somehow we needed to figure that out, even Doran, or we'd die in this cave.

Ciel and Moc began arguing ahead, and we sped to catch up, passing old carvings on the walls: A shoulder and head, a pair of wings. A crowd running. A bone eater.

By the time we reached the twins, the glow had intensified. Littlemouths speckled the tunnel walls and clung thick around the mouth of another alcove.

After days in the dim clouds, the brightness made us squint.

"It hurts my eyes," Moc said.

"Can you calm them?" I whispered to Ciel.

She shrugged. "How? Any rhythm I make, they copy. Even when I talk. Watch." She hummed a pattern, and the walls pulsed with light. She thought for a moment. "Viridi sometimes calmed the skymouths." She made a shushing sound. Like a mother to her child.

The littlemouths dimmed, but didn't go out. We could see

easier in the half-light. Around the cave, littlemouths clustered along the ceiling and down the walls like bright bats. In a corner, a clutch of eggs glowed softly, tiny dots on the wall.

"Oh," said Moc. "That's where they come from."

When we stepped inside the room, we could no longer hear echoes down the tunnelways. Ciel's soft shushing overtook us. The high ceiling and the littlemouths clustered across it reminded me of a night sky, close to Allmoons. Ciel and Moc tiptoed around the space, eyes on the ceiling. None of us wanted to break the quiet spell the room cast.

The littlemouths had been so bright, I almost missed the carvings and panels embedded in the walls. As the blue faded, Wik pointed to them, his jaw slack with surprise.

"Moc, would you get Djonn? The others too," I asked. "Tell Ceetcee it opens up back here." My fingers brushed brass engravings, felt detailed carvings beneath my touch. So many panels. Many codexes' worth. More than anyone could carry.

I trailed my hand lightly over the wall, careful not to disturb any littlemouths. Five more plates. Images of tools with uses I couldn't fathom. Left behind here, as if the occupants had more than they needed.

"Nat," Ciel whispered. The light dimmed around us. "This is important, isn't it?" She squeezed my hand and began shushing again. The glow returned to the cave.

I felt the sound course through me, through all of us. *Shhhh.* The world slowed in the cave. It would be all right. Relief and something more washed over me. Hope. We would go on, somehow. "This is important. This is the true heart of the city."

Footsteps echoed down the tunnel. Djonn arrived slightly breathless, Aliati at his side. When he saw what the walls contained, he froze. "So many." He, too, reached out to touch.

"What tools do you have?" I asked Djonn, my voice steadier

than I felt. I hoped he kept more tools on his person than flint. I wanted to take each plate back to the city and make sure it was safe for the next generation. I understood now, how Doran might have felt when Dix brought him that first plate after Spirefall.

Djonn passed me an awl, then walked in a circle, staring.

With Djonn's metal tool, I began chipping at the bone, trying to pry a plate loose.

"Don't," Ciel said. She stopped my hand.

"We need it." These were our history, and, if Doran was right, our future. They would be our proof to the city above that there was lost knowledge down here. That the Singers hadn't been wrong, but they hadn't been right either. They might help us topple Dix and let us return to the city.

My fingers itched to see what was on each plate's other side. To search for a key. A way to translate them.

More footsteps and then Doran's hand on my shoulder. He pulled me aside, then pried at a plate with his fingers. "We must recover these."

"You can't," Ciel said again, putting her hand over Doran's. "The plates are keeping the room from filling in. Look at the tunnel if you don't believe me. It's just like the poles used to sculpt the cave. This place isn't ours anymore." She pointed at the littlemouths, at the eggs on the wall. "If you move the plates, they'll have nowhere to go."

She was right. Without the carvings placed as they were, the living bone core would eventually fill this space. The tunnels too. We couldn't remove them without damaging the cave, and the littlemouths that lived and bred here.

I put the awl in my pocket, but Doran kept prying.

Finally, Wik reached out and stayed his hand.

"These plates belong to the city," Doran said. "We can take them back above the clouds. Regain the towers' support."

"Everyone in the city should see these, and benefit from them," I agreed, stealing Doran's wind. "But not at the little-mouths' expense. Everyone will know of it. We'll make sure they do."

I hoped Doran would listen. Would not demand agreement with his plan. He'd seen the downfall of his demands for loyalty. Had he changed enough?

Doran frowned, then shrugged agreement. He let the plates be.

❧ ❧ ❧

Five of us—Doran, Djonn, Aliati, Wik, and I—looked long and hard at the plates while Moc and Ciel explored. When we'd circuited the room, I touched the last brass square on the wall. It felt rougher than the others, the diagrams less careful. The drawings were of weapons, I realized, much like the weapons we used in the city now: a bow, a spear. Jagged cuts marked the outlines of skymouths and bone eaters.

The skillful hand that had etched the glorious tools on the plates Djonn and Doran carried was long lost by the time this plate was carved. Fear radiated from its surface. Especially rough was the etched winged figure, flying, lifting someone without wings up and away, so much like carvings of Singers in the Spire. Looking closer, I saw a shadowed indentation, like an etching had been made, then polished away.

More figures had once stood behind the pair. Gone now.

Hiroli's and Ceetcee's voices echoed down the passage from the alcove, growing louder and more agitated. The littlemouths' slow pulse began to dull and wink out. Wik hummed, and the littlemouth on his shoulder glowed, tentatively, but none of the others. We worked our way back to the alcove, and found another alcove panel open, on the left-hand side. Ceetcee wasn't in the main cave. Her shouts came from beyond the next alcove.

306   · FRAN WILDE ·

I stepped through the small opening and followed it around another curve, my hand brushing the rough bone wall. Wik followed me, with the others close behind. We found Ceetcee glaring at Hiroli before another, smaller room.

Ceetcee held a small marrow-sucked bone like a weapon. She lowered it when she saw us. "She has a bird—a kavik! I found her back here, feeding it."

Hiroli clutched the small black bird. She tucked a handful of graincake in her robe. She'd had food with her the entire time.

"Where did you get it?" I meant the bird. I knew whipperlings would go to sleep tucked in a robe or a pocket. That kavik looked like it wanted to chew its way out of her hands.

"I stole it from Laria. Fed it some of my dinner." She'd given it Dix's drug. That made sense.

"She wants to send a message to the city," Ceetcee said.

Hiroli glared at her, then waved her worry away. "I didn't say I wanted to talk to the city. I said we need medicine we can't get down here. We need food and supplies."

"That's as good as telling Dix's guards where we are," Ceetcee said. "We don't need the city. We can use what's down here: ferns and lichens heal wounds. Aliati knows how."

At mention of medicine, my worries returned, the magic of discovery fading. Illness, dampness. Would a mythical Corwin come for us too?

"If we wait here for the blackwings to find us, surviving on leaves, we'll be easy to defeat," Hiroli said. "The air isn't good for you, Ceetcee. Nor the food. It's not good for anyone."

"We have the gryphon, and we'll find more food," I said, although I saw Hiroli's point. She hadn't told anyone about the kavik. Why not?

"There's no time. We aren't staying here," Hiroli countered. "You're looking at carvings and etchings you can't read, from people long gone. They mean nothing, and Dix wants them. Let's offer her some to get help for our friends."

Now she spoke cloud Treason. "Councilor, you're out of order. You've not seen what we've been," I said. "You were—"

"Trapped at Laria, by Dix," she finished. "Yes, I remember clearly." She narrowed her eyes. "I'd been waiting for you to return, as ordered! Did you think I went there by choice?"

Doran touched her shoulder. "Nat doesn't think that. No one does."

But Hiroli's words struck a chord, and the note was sour. I'd left her at risk on Bissel while we argued with Doran on Varu. Now she was right. I was worried about Ceetcee and Beliak. I wanted to get back to the city more than I could say. Hiroli hadn't been through what we'd been through. But she'd had her own trials. "Dix would destroy this place to get her hands on the plates. And she'd want more than the plates—she'd want the artifex too."

"She can get another artifex," Doran said, patting Djonn's shoulder. "This one is ours."

Djonn stepped away from Doran's hand rather than answer. I didn't like Doran's possessiveness either.

"You've been back here, exploring, when we should be planning. But you missed a whole alcove," Hiroli said. "You'll understand better once you see it."

Hiroli had been exploring too, without us.

"What is it?" I said. I had to duck low to get into the alcove Hiroli had found; the entrance was tiny. When I made it through, I could see shadows clustered along the back wall.

My eyes adjusted to the dim light and I moved closer. The piles were bones, left where they'd fallen. Not normal undercloud fare, either. These were human bones.

I recoiled, and Hiroli whispered, "Shocking, isn't it. So many bodies." She was right. We didn't keep our dead in the city. In the past days, I'd seen more bodies than I should have in a lifetime. But I returned to the room, curious.

Each pile's skull had a hole in it, or broken ribs, as from an arrow or a knife blade. People had fought and died here. Judging by the dust, a very long time ago.

Around the room, rough overgrowth marked places where brass plates and rods had been pulled from the walls. I saw outlines of four plates. Touched the plate in my satchel. Djonn had one also. Doran two. Four had fallen into the clouds. Had all of these and more been pried from this room long ago?

Without the metal to restrict growth, the room was slowly growing together, pushing on the bone piles and absorbing them in the process.

Wik waited outside, peering in; he was too broad-shouldered to enter. "This is what I meant by dangerous. The plates—they can be stolen or taken by force. Songs and Laws get memorized and passed up. No one kills for them," he said.

Only Hiroli's small footprints and my larger ones marred the dusty floor. But Wik was right. In this cave—the nest of thieves—the builders hadn't left their metal behind. They hadn't abandoned the littlemouth chamber when they'd risen up the towers.

They'd died in its defense.

28

THE TOWERS

"Who were they?" I asked the cave.

Aliati came up behind us. "They weren't scavengers." Wik, who'd been staring at the skeletons dissolving into the city, jumped, startled by her voice.

Some bones were grown into the floor, the city taking them back in a slow process. *What had happened to them?* "How do you know they weren't scavengers?" I asked her.

Aliati said, "They died here. They made a home and they died in it. That's not what scavengers do." There was a note of admiration in her voice.

"But why didn't these piles attract a bone eater?" Wik wondered. "Why did they leave the other plates?"

"Maybe it did attract a bone eater, or worse." I thought of the skymouth husk in the other room. The teeth we'd reclaimed, that Kirit was turning into knives. Perhaps it had chased the attackers away.

Ceetcee still fumed at Hiroli. "Take her kavik before you start mulling history. She shouldn't send a message until we all agree to do it. Even knowing what we do now."

Hiroli looked meaningfully at the bones, frowning. She held the kavik tightly.

"Ceetcee's right," I said, and held out my hand.

Slowly, Hiroli passed the bird to me. I gave it to Ceetcee, who tucked the wriggling thing under her arm with a glare.

We had no cloth to cover the bones with, and we couldn't lower them into the clouds. They were part of the city now. Looking up to the clouds for Remembrances seemed wrong here.

"How do you mourn the past?" I wondered.

Wik knelt at the entrance to the space. "By remembering it." He drew a pattern in the dust. The sign for Allmoons. "Mercy on your wings, citizens."

We backed away from the room. I planned on never returning. Leaving those particular ghosts at peace.

Walking up to us, Kirit coughed. "Beliak is finally asleep," she said. She stared at the bones and reached out to Wik, unable to tear her gaze away. "Mercy on their wings."

I'd turned to lead her and all of us back into the main cave, but Aliati whistled "follow." She'd ducked through an opening, and beyond it, the passage broadened and grew light enough to see by without the littlemouths' help. As we traced her path, the light grew brighter still. We stood at another cave mouth, one that opened onto a sky meadow.

Oh. Green with vegetation and flooded with mist, the meadow filled in the space between the tower, the ridge walls beside it, and two more towers in the distance. Outcroppings stretched between them, joining into walls. It was beautiful. Behind me, the others crowded the cave mouth, exclaiming.

The storm had passed for now, and the meadow's greens sparkled with moisture.

Moc lowered himself down the tower's side.

"Don't—" I said, thinking of another valley, where the vegetation had been thin in places, and easy to fall through. Too late. Moc's feet crushed the plants growing above the moss near the tower; he waded through a mass of nettles, yelping now and then while gathering more stems for food on the way. The meadow remained firm beneath his feet. He focused on a stand of tall branches that curled into spirals: Ferns. Giant ones.

Moc stopped and looked back at us. Pulled a bone hook from his belt. "I'll be careful, I promise. Ciel, come down here. I can see the whole meadow, and the towers."

He sounded like the old Moc again, like he'd shaken loose the last webs from Laria.

Drawing out my last tether, I knotted the line to a wing grip on the wall. The tower gate had once been carved with murals, but age and weather had worn those away. I climbed down the wall and landed close to Moc. My feet crunched fern leaves. The uneven surface rolled and compressed like the guano and loam mix Beliak used in balcony planters uptower, though richer and lumpier. I stumbled more than once.

Nettles scraped my legs where my robes were torn, burning my skin. The pain barely registered. I was walking between towers. Not flying, not crossing a bridge—I could turn in any direction and keep walking. It was like flying for the first time. Moc's face showed similar glee. "We don't even have to use wings!" He'd been without a wingset for so long. Now he didn't need any.

At least for now. We would have to return soon and decide what to do. How to confront the city.

Beside me, Aliati, Doran, and Ceetcee climbed down into the meadow to pick the ferns and lichen. Ceetcee held out corners of her robe to make a bowl. The wet tearing of roots sounded like fabric ripping. "You sure this is solid?"

Aliati held up a batten, caked with at least a hand span of dirt. "We won't hurt it picking a few leaves. Just watch where you step."

From the corner of my eye, I caught movement by the cave entrance. Kirit had fallen to her knees.

For me, for Moc, this meadow held wonder. For Kirit, it must contain echoes of another valley, the memory of councilors falling from the clouds. Her mother. For a moment, I smelled the awful scent of the fallen again. She'd lost almost everyone. I still had family, even here. For now.

I started towards Kirit. She'd been lost beneath the clouds, and the council had fallen to the ground where she'd stood. We were no longer rivals in the Gyre, and we weren't wing-siblings either. We'd both changed and made mistakes and survived.

But I'd want her fighting by my side, or at my wingtip, no matter what. As I would fight at hers.

Though I moved fast, Wik got to her first and waved me away. Wordlessly, he helped Kirit back inside the cave.

Moc, meanwhile, had moved forward, towards the far towers. Chief explorer. Ciel followed, but yelped when she snagged on a nettle. It didn't stop her for long. Careful where she put her feet, she spun in a slow circle, taking in the dirt beneath her feet, the towers around her, rising dark and gray up into the clouds.

\ \ \

"Three towers, together!" Moc pointed. "Which ones are they, do you think?"

"We shouldn't take too long here," I said. "See if there are more plates, more weapons, then head back."

The boy made a face. "Djonn's gone to sit with Beliak so Wik could stay with Kirit. Everyone's fine," Moc said. "Please?" Ciel echoed him. They sounded like children again.

I couldn't say no.

But when we reached the base of the next nearest tower, we faced a wall of solid bone. The core had grown out and over the tiers. "Nothing," I said, preparing to turn around.

Moc clambered up a bonefall and prepared to leap to another pile of bone closer to the next tower's edge. I was about to argue him back down when footsteps crunched the ferns nearby. Ceetcee approached.

"Moc! Careful. We can't patch you up as easily down here." She turned to me. "Aliati's making poultices for Beliak. She hopes it will help him, as well as Doran and the others who are injured." With Ceetcee distracted by talking to me, Ciel had joined her brother on the bonefall. Ceetcee frowned but didn't scold again. "Doran's trying to talk her into scavenging the metal in the cave, but she's resolute. Says this is a scavenger sanctum. She won't touch it."

"That's good news." We needed someone else to keep an eye on Doran—someone who wasn't Wik—who could understand Doran's interest in salvaging while still disagreeing with him. "How are you feeling?" I watched Aliati and Doran climb the wall back to the cave mouth, pulling themselves hand over hand by the tether.

"Better," she said. And she looked it. "Food helped."

"We'd had food with us the whole time, in Hiroli's pockets." We just hadn't known it. "Hiroli knew."

"She did. And she's scared. I'm trying to forgive her for the bird. She wants to go back up as much as the rest of us. Which is why Aliati and I've been thinking about where we are, in relation to the city—Careful!" The last was shouted as Moc climbed closer to the next tower and Ciel followed him. Bones clattered as they scrambled and leapt between piles.

"We're undercloud," I said, turning in a circle. It seemed all there was left to us. The twins had reached a safe spot on the bonefall.

But Ceetcee pulled a silk square from her pocket. "I borrowed this from Aliati." The Justice game. She walked towards the tower and spread the game board on a broad block of fallen bone.

With the city above spread once more before us, Ceetcee put her finger next to Bissel. "The ghost tower is here. We flew south and west from Laria to the ledge. Then turned this way, I think," her finger traced a pattern. "So that tower"—she pointed behind me, back towards the littlemouth cave—"is probably Varu, unless it stops before it reaches the clouds. The next one, where Moc and Ciel are, might be Naza. Or something close by. Those are good, stable towers." Bridge artifexes knew the towers nearest where they worked, but were fascinated by all of them. And Ceetcee was a good bridge artifex. "If we need to shelter down here for a long time, this is a good place to do it."

She glanced back towards the cave, then returned her attention to the map. I could guess her thoughts: *If Beliak recovers.*

During the cold, quiet night, each of us had probably thought about staying below. I certainly had. It wasn't a pleasant idea. When could we return to the city? The question was more pressing for Ceetcee. Every day below the clouds meant she drew closer to the days she'd be too gravid to fly. I hadn't thought past staying alive each moment and keeping everyone else alive too. But she had. Returning meant risk. Staying, too.

Chagrin shook me that I hadn't thought it through. "So once we know where we are, we can try to fly close to a friendly tower, like Densira or Mondarath, and send Maalik up?"

She nodded, glad I'd seen where she was going. "He could take a message to the northwest towers." It was a good idea. Practical, no-nonsense. That was Ceetcee, even in the clouds.

At the third tower's wall, Moc studied a mottled indentation carefully. He gestured to Ciel, and she pressed her fingers along the marks.

"If the towers are Naza and Varu, we've traveled far vertically, but barely moved across the city." Maalik would have a long way to climb, and then fly.

At the tower wall, Ciel let out a surprised cry. Water spilled down bone somewhere nearby. Rain again? I didn't see any dark clouds on the horizon. Then came the sound of bone grinding against bone.

"A windgate!" Ciel said.

A panel in the tower wall slid open as a hidden cache of water released. The tower rumbled and shook like the whole thing was about to come down. "Get back!" I shouted, forgetting the map. I ran to pull the twins from the bonefall and wound up holding Moc by the armpits. Only one tower in the city above had windgates still, and it was cracked and dying. Was this the Spire?

"Let me go!" Moc squirmed, all elbows and knees, ignoring the risk, and I dropped him on the lichen. "We were only looking! See! It's shaped like the entrance to our cave, but much deeper."

Ciel pointed and I looked back at the entrance to our own shelter. Even from here, I could see mottling around the opening. Carvings I'd thought were decorative. "But our gate must have been stuck open for a long time," she said.

The opening gate before us revealed a cave similar to that of our own shelter as well. I relaxed a little. The twins climbed back up on the bonefall.

"What do you see?" Ceetcee called, catching up with us. Her breath came heavy. "It's so overgrown here. So green."

My hunter blues stuck out against the shades of green, gray, and ocher, but the bottom of Ceetcee's fern-stained yellow robes had begun to blend in with the towers. All around us, the bone was draped with green patina, rimes of moss and lichen layered over generations. Moss darkened ridges where bone core overgrowth had folded itself into lumps and bulges. The air was thick with green here too, and we could breathe so much easier. But the rich smells were overwhelming. Ceetcee held her nose, but kept going.

We climbed the bonefall as the twins crawled into the cave. "I see wingsets," Ciel said. "And weapons. All along the tunnel." Her voice receded as she followed Moc. I scrambled after them.

"I'll get the others," Ceetcee said. Then she paused, one foot on the bonefall. "Unless you don't want everyone to know?"

"Maybe for now." Secrets tended to break groups apart. We'd learned that from the Singers, from the council. But Hiroli had been keeping secrets too. Ceetcee remained by the windgate.

This tunnel was longer than our entire cave, and filled with spiderwebs. As Moc had said, several shallow alcoves lined the path. Moc stood in one, examining a stash of bone arrows and spears.

"Good find," I whispered, beckoning him back.

"Look!" Ciel pulled us to another alcove and pointed at a broken double slab of bone held tight by a large bone screw atop it. "What's this?"

I shook my head. No idea. "That's a loom, though." The bone loom, bigger than any we had in the city, was cracked and pushed on its side up against the wall. "These were made here," I said. "Too big to carry up." But with what tools?

The wingsets Ciel found were in decent shape. The silk had rotted away, but the wingframes were intact, and very basic. No controls. No fine-tuned batten structure. Only simple geometries. Ciel pulled one away and peered behind it. Coughed. "More bones." She backed from the alcove, pushing me into Moc, who'd come running from behind, trying to catch up.

"Nat, a codex!" he held a rectangle made of something soft and thick, not bone. It crumbled in his hands. Not silk either. The rotting rectangle was folded into the basic shape of a codex, but held nothing inside. "There are lots of them," Moc added. He'd found more bone piles in the tunnel as well. But these bones hid nothing but dust. No injuries. No hints about who they'd been or why they'd died.

I shook my head. "It makes no sense. They were living down here. Making things. And then they were gone, and everything's piled in this tunnel." I toyed with the screw on the double slab of bone, the break in the slabs too straight to be accidental. Ciel pried the slabs apart to reveal a bit of brass plate pressed into thick dust.

She stared at it, understanding dawning. "Djonn figured out the lighter-than-air process by doing the reverse of the plate drawings," she said. Her eyes lit up. "He thought it was a code." She grew more excited. "He wasn't backwards. The plate was. Watch. He'll love this."

Everyone in the tunnel looked up from what they were exploring. The littlemouths' light wavered at the sound of Moc's voice. "Why does that matter?"

Instead of explaining, Ciel took a small bone jar of blacking from her satchel and smeared the plate with it. She scooped the piece of brass from the slab, wiped most of the blacking off, and flipped one side of her robe upside down so that the paler, cleaner side showed. Mashing the plate onto her robe, she pressed down hard. When she lifted the plate, all I saw was a mess on Ceetcee's robe. Then I noticed that the small imprint looked almost readable. At least the symbols were flipped a familiar direction.

Moc understood first. "They could share guides for building things without memorizing songs or lugging carvings around. Sometimes the best way to fight is to teach."

"Maybe once that was true, but something happened." I gestured to the broken slab. In the dim tunnel, the walls seemed to crawl with shadows.

"Ugh, spiders," Moc said.

It was damp in the tunnel, but spiders should have scattered when we opened the gate.

Ciel hummed until the littlemouth on my shoulder glowed again. There weren't any bugs. The walls of this tunnel were also covered with carvings. Angles, like Aliati had made on the map to trace the fledges' flight paths. A picture of a scope. A perfect circle.

"People might have lived here for generations," I said, looking at the interplay of carvings, but thinking of what Ciel said. Most of the symbols were unreadable, but a few, if reversed, almost looked familiar. One resembled the tower sigil for "tradition," upside down.

"It's like someone tried to start a city below," Ciel whispered. "I like it here."

"Was Corwin's Thieves before or after The Rise?" I asked, still studying the carvings: men and women weaving, holding up sheets with more symbols on them. Though she was still young, Ciel had learned Singer ballads for many years, while all I'd had was a few moons' study with Tobiat.

"Much later, I think."

"So maybe," I mused, sensing Moc's impatience, "some people didn't rise with the Singers. Maybe some stayed here and didn't fight tower against tower. Maybe they kept artifexing. . . ."

Moc picked up my train of thought. "Maybe there were differences over how to live." He put aside several arrows and pushed a bow away from the wall. His finger traced the carvings to the cave mouth, ending at a place where several figures were dug out with deep hatch marks.

I drew a calming breath. We'd seen similar in the littlemouth cave. The reversed symbols. The interwoven marks. The erasures. Perhaps once there had been a difference in how to live. Perhaps not everyone had agreed. Tower versus tower war, in this perfect cloudbound meadow? I hoped not.

But one thing was clear. *We were one people once, not Spire and Tower. We understood many things. Then we came apart.*

"Let's keep going," Ciel said. "Coming, Ceetcee?" she shouted down the tunnel.

Ceetcee hesitated at the windgate. "You go ahead if you must. If there's a collapse, someone will need to go for help." She kept her voice light, but I knew she was uncomfortable.

Her caution gave me pause, but the twins were already running ahead.

"Slow down. There could be bone eaters or worse." *If they got hurt on my watch, I couldn't forgive myself.* Ciel paused, eyes wide. The littlemouth's glow stayed with us as Moc moved farther away. "Moc!" Darkness closed around him, and silence.

That fledge never listened. Ciel and I chased after him.

The tunnel ended in a black gap that echoed empty and wide. I smelled old bone, dust, and dampness now. We'd walked deeper into this tower than we had in the previous one, and the gap would have alarmed Ceetcee.

But when we emerged from the tunnel, I knew a bone void wasn't the danger. This tower *was* dying, without a doubt, but it wasn't from natural causes.

I had a better guess where we were now. And it was neither Naza, nor Varu.

Ciel and I stepped into the dim light; Moc stared up in gape-jawed amazement.

We stood on a narrow ledge that ran nearly the tower's full circumference. After the ledge, there was nothing but dust-filled air, lit by the littlemouths on our shoulders. Above us, for as far as we could see, black-shadowed galleries rose until they disappeared.

"Ciel," Moc said, turning to see that she too stared up, stunned.

His voice startled the walls. A flight of bats peeled away and went screeching and wheeling up the tower's center.

I'd fallen deep into that void once—although nowhere near this deep.

I'd climbed into its ruins and tried to steal its secrets. Now

Ciel turned a slow circle, taking in the carvings, the empty void, but not understanding.

Moc whispered again. "Ciel, we're home."

We'd found the Gyre's edge, deep in the Spire's depths.

And from back down the tunnel, we could hear Ceetcee calling our names.

The bats disappeared into the tower's upper reaches. Ciel moved slowly, reaching out a hand to touch the carved walls. Bone had spread into deep cuts and erased lighter marks, but outlines were still visible. Her hand came away white with bone dust, reversed, blurred imprints of the same symbols and marks from the littlemouth cave, interspersed, higher up, with a few marks much more familiar.

I saw, too, carvings of people working in our meadow. They bent over strange mechanisms; unfurled familiar—if simpler— wings. They wove a plinth between the towers, just as I'd imagined. But the carvings stopped well before the symbols.

By the time Singer script appeared on the walls, the carvings were entirely gone.

Ciel touched each one, whispering their names for me, "Knife. Wing. Challenge. Arrow."

"You see how they once all worked together?" I said, pointing at the meadow, the carvings. "And how it ceased?"

Behind us, cold air expanded, and the dim light from above disappeared entirely. Ciel's littlemouth pulsed, alarmed.

A crash echoed down the Gyre. I searched the darkness for bone eaters. Instead, an enormous piece of rotten netting drifted down, followed by shards of bone from above.

Ceetcee had been right to worry, even if she'd been wrong about the tower's name. "The Spire's too unstable. We have to go."

I pulled Ciel away from the wall and pushed her towards the tunnel. Dragged Moc with us as more bone continued to fall.

We scrambled back through the tunnel, Ceetcee's shadow growing visible as we drew closer. She was sheltering within the tight space of the windgate. Outside the gate, rain fell again, big drops by the sound of it, landing on the meadow. A chill blew through the open gate. "This isn't Naza," I said, thinking how she and Aliati would have to change their maps, wondering what else we might find in the towers.

Ceetcee ignored my news, turning from the gate and pointing at the sky. "Nat! Look!"

Though the sky had darkened and a cold wind blew across the meadow, the sounds weren't from rain at all. High above, winged shadows passed overhead.

Message chips dropped to the meadow floor, bound in ones and twos.

29

PROMISE

"They've found us." I skidded down the bonefall, causing a small collapse. "They're coming!" We'd need arrows and spears. Those were in the cave I'd just left. I scrambled back up.

Ceetcee tugged at my sleeve, drawing me back from the cave entrance. "Wait. They could be strewing the chips everywhere near where we disappeared. They don't know how far down we are or where, exactly, any more than we do." That was true. She'd made her best guess with the map, but I knew she'd guessed wrong.

Moc climbed the ridge wall and peered over the side, into the depths. "They're falling out there too. Ceetcee's right. They don't know where we are yet." Ciel trailed him, picking up chips and throwing them, furious.

I fished a message strand from the branch of a fern. The three white bone chips strung from a blue silk cord hung small and vivid against the dusky green and deep brown branch. The marks on them read REWARD FOR TRAITORS, for those who might seek us, and YOUR CRIMES WON'T BE WEIGHED WITH THEIRS, to those among the cloudbound who might return to the city without prejudice—Doran, Hiroli, Aliati, and Djonn. Both groups might turn us over to the blackwings. SURRENDER was aimed at the rest of us.

Across the meadow, chips gleamed white from where they'd

fallen in the vegetation, looking like skyblind eyes. Most were Lawsmarkers with the sigils for Treason and War.

Even if we hadn't been discovered yet, the blackwings were too close. We would be found. Did we need to flee again or to make a stand? I didn't know yet.

Kirit would want to fight. Wik and the twins too. Hiroli would flee. With my family here, I wanted to do both: run and fight.

We sped back across the meadow, ignoring the nettle stings. At the other side, Aliati, Doran, and Hiroli stood looking up.

Hiroli held several chips in her hands. She absently ran her thumb over one.

"Come on," I said as we passed them. "We've got to go."

Aliati took Ceetcee's arm and helped her up to the ledge. She'd tucked one of the markers behind her wingstrap. None of the rest of us even had our wings on yet. She was preparing too.

"Run or fight?" she asked me. The metal hoop in her ear swung back and forth.

Doran half blocked her way into the cave. "Or deal," he said. He raised his eyebrows, asking the question, *would you?*

"Deal? Do you expect Dix to keep a promise?" Aliati shook her head, laughing. "Maybe to you, but not to Kirit or Nat. Probably not to you either, actually."

We edged our way past him. Farther along the tunnel, Kirit yelled, angry and fierce. "You can't make that decision for all of us!"

We rounded a curve to find Kirit and Wik standing close, Hiroli just beyond them. They were past the small alcove with the bones. Beside them, Djonn leaned against a wall.

"Kirit," Hiroli said warmly, her hands crossed on her chest, "I'm not making decisions for you. I'm making my own decision. It's clear we can't stay here to starve in peace." She looked at me darkly. "It's only a matter of time before they really find us."

"You don't know that!" Ceetcee said. "They want us to panic. We're doing a great job of it."

"We should have a vote on what we should do," Doran said.

A *vote*. He would start that again here? "There's no council in the clouds."

Doran frowned and tilted his head like a gryphon. "I think that's been obvious for some time. You've been making too many decisions on the wing, Nat, from the failed attack at Laria onwards. When you should be preparing, you've been exploring. You've got wounded, children. Ceetcee. Djonn. Things could go downtower so fast."

"Don't undercut him," Wik said. "He's doing fine." I was grateful.

Ceetcee seethed. "We can take care of ourselves." While Moc muttered from behind me, "We won't give up."

"I agree," Doran began, his palms out, pleading. "I want consensus."

"You can fight," Hiroli interrupted. "But for how long? You have no wings, Moc. And how long can you keep running?" She looked at Ceetcee. With each question, she took a step backwards. "I'd rather live." Then she turned and ran for the cave, for the fire where Beliak slept. Where Ceetcee had tied up the kavik.

We chased her, squeezing through the bottleneck and out the alcove, into the cave. We were fast, but she was faster.

Knotting a message skein around the bird's claw with one hand and her teeth, she swung out to the ledge and started climbing the tower's overgrown ledges.

"Hiroli!" Doran shouted. "Stop!" He grabbed his wings from the stack where they'd been drying. Struggled to get them on. I did the same, while the others ran to the cave mouth.

Only Aliati, who'd donned her wings the minute they were dry, could take a running leap from the cave and get in the air before Hiroli let the kavik go. I drew my bow on the ledge and tried to sight the bird, but it was already too high, and flapping hard. Aliati couldn't find a gust strong enough, nor one going in the right direction. She circled back around and plucked Hiroli from the tower wall instead.

"What did you do?" she said, shaking the young woman over the ledge. "You had a message already written. What did it say?"

Hiroli refused to speak, even after Aliati dropped her on the cave floor. She sprawled there, staring at us, panting from the climb.

Wik knelt beside her, gripping her upper arm. "Why did you do it?"

She smiled, slowly. "I want to sleep on a dry tier, and eat real food. I doubt I'm the only one. But I'm the one Dix will reward."

Suddenly everyone was shouting all at once, but no one shouted louder than I. "You were Ezarit's apprentice. You know how she died. Would you hand us all over to her murderer?"

Hiroli's smile faded. "If it got me out of this cave and back into the city? Yes."

My breath caught. "We saved you at Laria." And she betrayed us beneath the clouds. "What did you write?"

Hiroli had the grace to look me in the eye when she said, "I told them where we were. I told them we had the artifex, and the lighter-than-air plate. And that there were many more plates here besides."

❦ ❦ ❦

We bound Hiroli's hands behind her and took her to the small cave with the bones, though she cried to be let out. Wik tied her ankles together and slipped the tether through the eye sockets of a skull. "One move," he said, "and I'll drop you into the clouds."

I'd been thinking the same thing, without the "one move" part. A look at Doran told me he felt the same.

"Isn't dropping people what you're good at, Singer Wik?" Hiroli shouted, so loud we could hear her in the main cave. "You all are cloudfood when the blackwings get here, but Dix will take me home. How do you like that?"

Ciel and Moc huddled by the alcove, looking down the tunnel to where Wik stood. Ciel leaned her head on her brother's shoulder.

Doran paced the cave, while I knelt by Djonn. The artifex was pale, his hands shook. "She told them where to find me," he said. "She told them that I took the plates."

The cave grew so quiet, we could hear more Lawsmarkers land on the slope. They sounded like slaps now.

Aliati held out a hand to the artifex. Her face was drawn up tight as a bowstring. "You're not going back. I promise. That kavik might not even make it out of the clouds."

"But what if it does?" Doran asked. "What if it makes it all the way back to Dix? What then?"

"Nobody needs to hear that right now," Kirit said. She sat on the floor, against the cave wall, sharpening her new glass-tooth knife.

"I respectfully disagree," Doran said. "We need to say the words. We need to plan, to get ahead of this if we can. We need to send another bird, with an offer for a truce. We need to appeal to what Dix wants most."

He barely had time to finish before Aliati gripped his robes and shook him. I pulled her away. Doran hadn't sent the bird. He was trying to help. But he was wrong.

"Respectfully," I said, "we don't need to send another bird. We need to run."

Doran looked to where Beliak sweated, half awake, his

head in Ceetcee's lap. She stroked his temples, trying to soothe him. "With Beliak that ill?" he said, "And two wingless among us, against blackwings? We have to deal. We cannot fight."

My fists clenched to keep them from shaking with anger. "She'll throw the rest down, first chance she gets." And Elna too.

Once more, I imagined I stood on the council platform, with the wingless Singer I'd been ordered to carry to the city's edge. Once more, I held Viridi while she died in my arms. We couldn't let another Conclave happen.

Doran spread his hands. "Given enough time to talk to other towers, we can stop Dix from doing that. Your attack let me begin that process, Nat. There are others aware of the danger now. People pay attention to good leaders. More will figure out that Dix isn't one. But to do that, to get there, we need to reach out to her before she reaches down to us with a flight of blackwings."

Wik had come to the alcove entrance, not far from where Hiroli was bound, but close enough to speak. "He's not wrong. But what can you offer Dix, if it isn't the artifex? Or the Singers?"

Now Doran smiled. "We'll offer her the towers. Tell her she needs to see for herself what we found."

Stunned silence. Ceetcee stared, slack-jawed. Kirit put down the knife. It was a brilliant trade, a terrible trade.

But Aliati said, "This can't belong to her. This place belongs to the city, to everyone. It's a scavengers' sanctum." And it was, because she named it so.

"What do you want most, Aliati?" Doran said. He touched Djonn's shoulder. "For your friend to be able to work, to be safe and free from pain?" She nodded, though she looked like she didn't want to. "And Kirit wants to kill Dix."

Kirit stared at him. "Yes."

"What if I could make those things happen? What if we could get medicine for Beliak, and Ceetcee could give birth in Densira's hightower, as she'd planned?" Doran's voice cracked. He was working very hard to control his emotions, but I knew that voice. He'd already decided this was the action he wanted to take.

"In return for our cooperation? For letting you negotiate with Dix?" Slowly I stretched the muscles in one hand, then the other. They ached from clenching them.

Doran bowed his head and clasped his hands. "For trusting me, yes. For giving me Maalik and letting me buy us a truce, to gain us more time." He wove a net of promises around us and drew the neck of it tight. In the dim cave, every eye was on him. And Doran relished it.

I banged my winghook on the ground, loudly, trying to cast off his promises. "What if Dix brings a flight of blackwings with her? How do you keep her from doing that?"

"That part is simple," Doran said. "We tell her we'll destroy the plates and kill the artifex if she brings more than two."

This time, I didn't pull Aliati away from him. This time, she hit him hard.

30

SURRENDER

Doran reeled, rubbing his cheek.

Surprisingly, Djonn was the one who reached for Aliati's robe and gently pulled her back. "Listen," he said. "It's what will get her attention."

The artifex sat by the hastily built guano fire. Smoke blew around the cave, making our eyes water. "It's too damp down here, too much pressure." He chewed a fingernail. "I need to go back to the city."

Aliati squeezed Djonn's left hand. "We can find another way." She glared at Doran, his face red where she'd slapped him.

Doran put his hand on Djonn's shoulder. "He's in tremendous pain. He'd been holding himself together for days by the time he helped you attack Laria, and then we got chased farther down here. His muscles are seizing up. He's barely slept. The damp and his own twisting spine conspire to torture him. If we can get him back above the clouds, we can find him medicine that will at least ease the pain."

"Even if that means working for Dix and hurting your friends?" Aliati kept her eyes on Djonn, ignoring Doran.

"I don't want to work for her," Djonn said. "But it might be the key to us—to some of us—getting back into the city. To sabotaging her. Like Doran wants." He looked at Aliati. "You came to rescue me. I can rescue you too."

She pressed her palms to her eyes, groaning. "I don't want you to rescue me." Then she turned to the group. Took a deep breath and opened her eyes. "*If* we decide to make Dix think we're willing to do this, I will be the one in charge of the knife," she said. "The one Doran intends to hold against Djonn's throat. No one else."

"Absolutely," Doran agreed. "I'd planned that you would."

Aliati remained standing, staring at him, while Doran turned to Kirit next. She barely lifted her head when she nodded.

I couldn't keep quiet. "How will you make good on your promises, Doran? Hiroli, tied up, has more power in the city than you do right now."

Doran knelt on the floor and spread the Justice map out. He reached in his pocket and drew out a handful of tower markers, including several Spires. "Because Aliati and I will meet Dix in the meadow. We'll hold back the things she wants most: Djonn, the lighter-than-air." He raised his eyebrows, looking around the cave.

Doran put a marker down between Varu and Naza and looked at me. "You, Wik, and Kirit will be stationed on the bridge and nearby towers, ready if Dix pulls any tricks. Kirit will have a clear shot if something goes wrong."

"And if it goes right?" This was the first time Ceetcee had spoken.

"If it goes right, then we go back to the city. To the northwest, where we'll be protected, among friends." Doran smiled. "Macal, Wik's brother, is the towerman at Mondarath."

"For how long?" I asked.

"We'll have to move fast once we're up there," Doran admitted. "But getting up there is half the battle." He frowned. "We've spoken too long. We must act. Is everyone agreed?"

Djonn nodded. Aliati whispered, "Agreed."

Kirit touched her knife tip to the bone floor. "Yes."

"Agreed," Ceetcee whispered, looking at me sadly, then at Beliak. "He'll get better, faster, in the city."

Clouds. "You can't possibly trust Dix to keep her word," I said. "If she agrees to this at all."

Doran frowned, but took a deep breath and clasped my shoulder. "Nat, I want us all to be in agreement. I don't trust Dix now, any more than you. We'll hold back those things she wants most until she makes good on our treaty. And I'll make one more request, for proof that Elna is safe."

Good news and bad: I wanted that proof desperately, but I didn't want to need proof. "I want her taken to Mondarath. Put under Macal's protection."

Doran nodded, tightening his grip on my shoulder. "We'll do that."

Finally, I gave in. Doran was determined, and even Ceetcee wanted to try negotiating. So I knelt by Beliak's side and watched Maalik nestle in his roost in the crook of Beliak's arm.

Sweat beaded Beliak's brow.

While I fed the bird a few remaining crumbs of Hiroli's graincake, Ceetcee and I took Beliak's hands in ours. "We won't let you—" I couldn't say the word. My jaw moved, but no sound came out. Ceetcee squeezed our hands harder.

He opened his eyes for a moment and looked at us, confused and feverish. Closed them again. My heart broke in three pieces. How could I not try to help?

When I lifted Maalik from the warm roost, the bird puffed feathers and cackled softly. I tied a pale silk cord to his leg, taken off one of the meadow messages. Given a task to do, he calmed.

I knelt by Ceetcee once more. "Say the word and we'll run instead."

She brushed a dirty braid behind her ear. Smoothed Maalik's

feathers with gentle fingers. Finally, she looked at Beliak, then at me. "No more running. Send the message."

Beyond the cave ledge where Doran waited, the city's message chips still dropped in ones and twos, fewer now, but still falling. The half-light of the clouds was calm and storm-free. Overhead, shadows dappled the white sky. I rose and stepped outside.

Doran's hand clasped my shoulder. "This is a tough thing you do," he said.

I ground my teeth, but I let him say it.

"In time you'll understand. This might not be what you want, but it's what's safest, and best. Dix will meet us in the meadow and then we'll go back up to the city."

Did he really think that? "How long do you think it will take to remove Dix's influence from the city?"

He smoothed his hair. "That's a tough question to answer until I get a good read on city politics. But this is a good first step." He tied the message skein to the silk around Maalik's ankle while I stared at him.

He'd made his plan up on the fly. "You convinced everyone you could."

"I know we can get her attention. What we do next is up to us," Doran countered. "I'm not perfect—she fooled me for a long time, but I've learned a lot from watching her these past weeks. I've drawn the same conclusions from her behavior at Laria that you have. And I've noticed the citizens' reaction to her. If she's too intractable, we have one thing that will help."

Moc peeked around the corner of the cave. "We have Rumul." He'd been eavesdropping. "Or at least Rumul's cloak." The boy held up the span of silk. He'd been going through my satchel again.

"Moc! Put that back." I watched him do it. I'd sleep with the bag beneath my head tonight.

Though my skin crawled at the memory of Dix interpreting

Rumul's whispers, I realized that in this, Doran could be right. The cloak was spattered with blood. "She'll want the last relic." It could work. But never again would I trust that Doran had everything planned well in advance.

Doran tried to brush Maalik's head with a finger, but the whipperling snapped at the air. He sighed. "Send him to Mondarath. Macal will deliver the message for us. Let's hope he flies true."

Maalik always flew true in the city, straight like an arrow.

When he flew today, the undercloud winds buffeted him until he disappeared into the white expanse.

\ \ \

While we ate the last of the gryphon down to the marrow, careful not to break the wings—an old city superstition, the message chips and Lawsmarkers finally stopped falling into the meadow.

"Hiroli's kavik arrived," Doran said. "They'll be preparing." He sounded so sure. Now I knew better. It wasn't a bad theory, but it was a guess.

Still, the others followed his lead.

Kirit swept the gryphon carcass outside. The bird's wings were all that distinguished it from the rest of the bone pile by the entrance. We no longer cared that fresh bones might attract animals. Our time here was short, one way or another.

"How will we know when Maalik delivers our message?" I asked.

"I suspect we'll know very quickly," Doran said. "I said we needed an answer or we'd assume she was attacking and take the necessary steps."

Kirit sharpened her blades loudly.

"I suggest we sleep in shifts while we wait for a response," Doran said. "Aliati and I will map which angles Dix might approach from, given the wind. Where best we can meet her in the meadow."

"What about the depth?" I remembered how sick we'd gotten. "Dix and her guards will be disoriented from the descent. That could work to our advantage." That had promising ramifications. Even so, I still didn't like this plan.

"Dix needs to show the city she's strong. She needs a decisive success," Aliati said. "If Maalik doesn't deliver our message, she'll attack."

Kirit and Wik walked outside to plan the tower and bridge defense. I flew Djonn and Ceetcee to survey the meadow and look for ways we could take advantage.

The two short towers and one full-grown one were good defense points, as Wik had already figured out, but the meadow that connected them? Ceetcee shouted and pointed at the bone growth supporting the meadow. It looked like a bone-sturdied plinth, woven with broad straps. Below it, moss hung down and blew in turbulent winds. When we flew close to the three tower trunks below the meadow, we saw bone-overgrown outlines of many bridge wrappings.

I imagined artifexes training the towers to grow ridge walls and tunnels crisscrossing the air between towers to weave a plinth between them. The towers' closeness in the clouds made it easier. Over time, bone and moss had covered the plinth, or had been trained to grow there. As I stared at the meadow, I could almost see our ancestors walking across it for the first time.

If my vision was close to truth, it was an incredible feat.

To work on the meadow, Ceetcee tucked her feet into the ancient webbing of the underbridge and tethered herself to the platform. She cut out a hand-sized piece of the woven platform away and wove bone battens into the structure as a replacement, in a complex pattern. She did this repeatedly, the patch growing bigger, until it was wing-sized. The meadow did not give one creak of complaint. Djonn hung from the sling-chair and made adjustments to Ceetcee's meadow supports.

It was a long drop from there to the next tower, the shadows of the abyss below shifted hungrily. Aliati arrived and we hovered around the undergrowth like fledge parents on first-flight day, ready to catch the bridge builder and the artifex. When they asked, I brought them more old bone wingsets from the Spire's tunnel. The process took most of a day.

"What are you making?" Aliati finally said.

"A last-gasp option," Ceetcee answered, though the wind played at her words. "In case we need it."

The wingset spans and battens supported a section of the meadow where the woven platform had been cut away. Djonn rigged a bone hook to a particular point in the middle of the pattern's intersections and pushed that through the undergrowth. Above, the bone hook was barely noticeable, sticking through the foliage. We climbed exhausted to the meadow and slept there, too tired to go all the way back to the cave.

When the clouds grew light again, I woke to see Kirit and Wik walking the other edge of the meadow. They leaned on each other, arms wrapped around waists, gray robes swishing over the lichen, like two towers growing side by side. They made a half circuit of the meadow, pointing at the bridge, the towers. After a moment, they climbed back into the cave.

After a decent pause, we followed them. Aliati went to the littlemouths' cave, sitting against a wall. The littlemouths glowed softly in her presence, but didn't signal.

Djonn joined her, leaning against the same wall. I lingered too. "What would you be doing," he asked. "In the city today?"

"Exploring," Aliati said. "Finding things people didn't know they'd lost." She took a breath. "But I don't want to lose this place, Djonn. Dix will destroy it."

"She'll have to come through me, and Wik, and Kirit," I said, startling her. There was something I wanted to ask. "You said before that scavengers wouldn't be caught here. That scavengers didn't stay."

She shrugged. "It's true."

"Why are you still here? Why do you want to defend it? You could go back above the clouds at any time. You don't need me to pay you. You'd be rich with all you've found here."

The skin around her eyes crinkled. "I guess I became a terrible scavenger," she said. "Once I found something I wanted to keep."

↘ ↘ ↘

When we returned to the main cave, Aliati stirred a yellow mixture she'd been heating over the fire since after our meal. "I think it's ready," she said. "The poultice for Beliak."

After Maalik flew, Beliak had worsened. He thrashed, half awake, his eyes bloodshot, his skin dry as bone.

Aliati looked at me. "After this there's not much more I can do. If we don't help him, he might not survive the journey back up to the city."

Memories flooded in. Beliak playing the dolin while Tobiat and Ceetcee sang. His eyes when he laughed. The strong sinew of his arms, from twisting the rope that held the city together.

"He can't die," I whispered.

Ceetcee sat with her head bowed as Aliati placed the yellow lichen on Beliak's wounds and bound them up with strips of silk from her own robe. Beliak groaned again when the heat hit his skin. I lay down on one side of him, and Ceetcee took the other.

Sometime during the darkest part of our watch, I fell asleep on Beliak's shoulder. When I woke, he smiled at me; his eyes were clearer. He was groggy, but his fever had lessened. His wounds were less swollen.

Aliati clapped her hands, delighted and relieved.

Wik sat down beside us, heavily. "Hiroli's asleep."

Kirit followed. "Beliak looks better! I could have used you when I was ill," she said. Aliati glowed.

"I'll never forgive Hiroli," Ceetcee muttered. "We should give Dix her body." I'd never heard Ceetcee say anything like that. Kirit looked impressed.

"She says she only wanted to do what was right. That she was afraid. That she missed the city." Ceetcee snorted. "I don't buy it."

Tendrils of color threaded the clouds. I wasn't sure whether it was morning or night any longer. The light was odd down here: never completely dark except at night. Today, green shades played the mist, lightening and fading. Between evening and morning there were little more than different tints.

"I kind of understand how she feels. All I ever wanted was to do what was right."

"You're not like her," Kirit said. "You're family. You made mistakes, and you fixed them."

"I don't know that I'd call this fixed." A cold cave, clouds. Friends, alive.

Kirit snorted. She nudged me in the side with her elbow, sharp as a wing. "I have your back this time. I'll stick to the plan."

"It's not my plan," I said.

Wik began to hum, and three littlemouths on the tower walls nearby glowed softly. In response, Wik's tattoos glowed a soft silver against his olive skin and Kirit's scars shone dully against her cheeks and beneath her hair. The clouds encased us like a wall of bone touched with light.

But the light was strange. I wanted my nights back, my days restored.

Clouds. I missed the stars so much it hurt.

31

BALANCE

Before the sky grew dark again, Maalik returned, with Hiroli's kavik on his heels. Both had the same carvings on their message chips, the fronts marked with Dix's sigil and the sign for Sinter. The law admonishing two towers to meet before they severed a bridge between them was clear. I'd helped write it, hoping to hold the city together. Now Dix was using it, even after she'd dragged the towers further apart.

On the back of each chip, another message: She'd hear us out, personally. She would see the wonders Hiroli had written about. And she would collect Rumul's robe and the stolen plates, or Elna would pay the price.

Wik woke the fledges. "I want you to guard this tower with Ceetcee. Don't come out until you hear one of us whistle Ciel's windsign."

Ciel made a face. She reached up and grabbed Wik's little finger. "You don't mean guard, Uncle. You mean hide." She twisted his finger until he whimpered. "I know I'm young. But I can shoot. I flew the Gyre, a little. I'm allowed to try to make things better. Or make sure Dix stays below the clouds." Her fierce words brought a sad smile to Wik's face. "Since Moc has no wings, he'll guard the second tower."

"Ciel!" Moc protested. But he conceded.

"You should be soaring through the city. Learning. Not hiding in the clouds. But you'll get hurt in a fight."

"I am learning," Ciel said. She tightened the sling on a spear launcher Djonn had made her, based on one of the brass plates' images. Tested it so that the sling twanged the air.

Wik chuckled. "That makes me more afraid."

I pulled him away from the twins. "I'll wait on the bridge with Kirit."

"I'll cover you both from the third tower," Wik said. He stuffed bone spears in his satchel until they rattled like a bone eater. "There's a watergate about six tiers up. It's got good vantage points, no matter what tower it is, or once was. If there are tunnels inside leading down to the meadow gate, I'll try to sneak closer to where Dix will land." Wik checked his wings.

Kirit put her knives in their sheaths and slipped a bow over her shoulder.

By the fire, Djonn worked on a last-minute adjustment. "We weakened the meadow in the middle, a bit left of center. Used the wingset battens to make it look stronger than it is. If you need to break the platform beneath it, pull out the bone hook. Put weight on it and it collapses."

"That sounds like a good way to break off negotiations," Wik said. "Or cause an accident."

Djonn didn't seem bothered by the critique. He went back to his drawings. "Consider it a secondary option."

"If you see too many blackwings, guard here first. If they attack, we'll drop the meadow."

"Not until you're off of it," Wik said. "I'll have clear sight of the bridge from the tower." After a long pause, he said, "With Moc and Ciel."

At next light, we all sat with Beliak. His color had improved, his temperature too, but he was weak. I touched my forehead to his and looked in his eyes. "I'll return," I said. I stood and wrapped Ceetcee in my arms. She would guard him here. I reached into my satchel and pulled out the pieces of my father's message chips. "Hold these for me?" I swallowed hard.

A heartbeat, two. She bit her lip, but took the markers. "I won't cry." Her fist closed on the broken bone. "Bring news that Elna is safe, and that we're going home."

"I promise," I said. My throat closed up. *That, or I won't return.*

ᘐ ᘐ ᘐ

Long before there was any sign of the blackwings, the Singers took their positions in the towers and on the bridge. Doran and I rode the gusts above the meadow, searching the clouds for Dix.

Aliati and Djonn waited below.

Doran coughed. "I've been hard on you, but I admire your sense of honor, you know. It's why I selected you as apprentice."

"How is that?" Mist swirled at our wingtips. I was confused.

"You have principles. They get you in trouble, but people know where you stand."

The wind whistled around the towers and picked up speed over the meadow. Finally, I said, "I tried not to have them. Tried to gain advantage when I saw weakness." I weighed each word, wanting to tell him how his duplicity had harmed me. Harmed the city.

He surprised me by laughing loudly. "Nat, we all have principles. Some of us hide them better than others."

"Another lesson?" It felt like a lifetime since I'd been his apprentice.

"Ambition and leadership fly together. Sometimes you have to trade on your principles to lay groundwork for the future, for the greater good of the city. Often, you have to seem more confident than you are, to hide your doubts."

I kept silent. The groundwork he'd laid left the city vulnerable and wounded. But compromises weakened it as well. And all the losses from fighting. From not fighting. Allmoons had passed while Laria burned. Had Elna lit a banner in my name?

Around us, towers rose high in the air. A littlemouth pulsed and disappeared on a wall: Ciel, marking her position. Another, on the third tower. Wik. Then two, brighter, for Kirit on the bridge. We were surrounded and guarded by friends.

Aliati whistled "defend," and I followed the line of her arm to see a dark mark in the clouds, spiraling down. Behind the first flier, four more dots appeared in the clouds.

Five fliers. They held the heights, all the weapons. They didn't need an enormous force to threaten us.

Meantime, we ten Lawsbreakers had only one advantage: ourselves.

❦ ❦ ❦

All too soon, the dark smudges on the cloudscape resolved into Dix, diving hard in the swirling wind, followed by her black-wings, who bore a heavy net.

Descending to the bone bridge to take my place with Kirit, I took a breath and let it out slowly. My heart pounded; my stomach clenched.

Dix's wings tilted, and her fingers tightened on cams and pulleys, preparing for landing. The heavy net that her guards carried now looked too big to be medicine or food.

As the group slowed over the center of the meadow, Dix circled. The blackwings dropped the net with a thump and took to the air again.

The net wriggled.

"Clouds." Doran started running towards the net. "Don't move!" A stray move might kick the bone-hook trigger Ceetcee had planted in the foliage. Might drop the entire field.

"Where is Hiroli?" Dix shouted, still in the air. "I want to see her."

Moc led Hiroli from the cave on a tether and tied her to the bonefall. He scrambled back up to the cave lip. In the meadow, Doran opened the net and was untangling the figure within. He gently pulled the net from around the wingless woman. She stood with a hand raised, touching the air. White hair. Her cheek was bruised. Her eyes the color of clouds.

Proof of life. Dix had brought Elna here.

Elna's confused laughter echoed all the way to the bridge.

Overhead, Kirit shot from her hiding place on the towers, heading like an arrow towards the meadow. I leapt from the bridge as all Doran's plans fell away from me in shards. The reinforced meadow platform creaked in the wind.

Even if she didn't fall through, Elna couldn't last long this far down in the clouds. Not after a lifetime in the towers, not as frail as she was. "You have to take her back up!" I shouted. She'd become very ill down here if she stayed.

"Lawsbreakers!" Dix called, ignoring me. "I am here to meet with you under the rules of Sinter. You should know that any harm that befalls me will impact the city immediately. My blackwings will attack the northwest if I do not return by evening."

Doran straightened, holding Elna's hand in his, trying to help her to her feet. He looked at Dix, then at me flying towards him, anguished. Aliati adjusted her grip on the knife she held to Djonn's throat.

Dix and one guard landed three steps from Doran and Elna. I dropped to the ground behind them, already running. Dix barely bothered to furl her wings, leaving them half extended. The night-dark spans flapped in the breeze as she nodded to her nearest guard, who withdrew a bone knife from his robe, and closed the gap to Doran and Elna.

"Of course, you do not have the same kinds of safeguards as I do," Dix said, even as I screamed, "Knife!" and lunged for Elna. But the guard sank the blade in Doran's back, twisted hard, and yanked it free.

Dix turned to Aliati as Doran collapsed on the meadow.

Her knife glittered as she held it out. "Kill the artifex, I dare you. I'll watch."

Aliati tightened her fingers on her own knife, then lowered it away from Djonn's skin. She looked at him and shook her head. "No."

"This ends now!" Kirit shouted. She drew down on Dix, from the air. But she didn't fire. The blackwings had all taken aim at the net. At the blind woman standing within it. Their bolts aimed at her heart.

With one move, Dix had taken the towers.

Two steps more, and I stepped within the circle of arrows, ignoring them. I took Elna's hand, slick with blood. Doran's eyes closed. His hand opened, releasing the knife he'd used to cut the net. He fell unconscious.

"What is it?" Elna whispered. She turned her head wildly, trying to hear. Clicked her tongue, trying to echo. To make sense of the void. "Who is this?"

I held her hand tight. "I've got you. You're all right." Her fingers closed around mine. But she didn't stop echoing.

She wasn't all right. None of us were. Already Dix walked towards Djonn. I had to stop this.

"What do you want, Dix?" I shouted.

The woman smiled, glanced at Kirit, circling in the air, and looked over her shoulder at me. "I want everything. Don't you?"

I had. Once. I'd wanted the high tier, the council position. Everything. Now, I held my mother's hand. Elna's breathing was as loud in my ears as my own heartbeat. She wobbled as Kirit landed beside us and took her other hand.

Elna pulled us both towards her. Whispered, "Don't hesitate!"
And let my hand go.

The blackwing nudged Doran's body with his foot. Blood
rushed from the wound, and Doran, panting, moaned. At the
sound, Elna knelt to press her hand, her robe, to Doran's side,
brushing aside the guard's sodden foot. Kirit helped her. They
ignored the blackwing.

The other guards aimed their arrows at me now, and Kirit.

We were nine Lawsbreakers. When we'd stepped out on the
meadow, we'd already lost. Elna wavered and sat on the ground.
"What is happening?"

"We need to move her higher," Kirit shouted at the guards.
"She'll die."

The blackwings stared impassively, and the one who had
stabbed Doran wiped his knife on Kirit's shoulder. I'd seen this
guard thrice before, including gaming at Grigrit and being
chased by Ezarit after the council fell.

Kirit's fingers tightened around her knife. Her other hand
twitched at Elna's fingertips. Impasse. The blackwings bows
tightened. We could not move.

Dix untied Hiroli. A guard brought forward a new pair of
blackwings for the junior councilor and cloud-traitor.

"You were Ezarit's apprentice," I said. Every muscle in my
body tensed, wanting kill her. If Elna had not been there, held
in a cage of arrow points, I would have. We all would have.

Hiroli smiled, tightening her wingstraps. "Dix made a better
offer. Ezarit was a trader. I believe she'd understand."

I grabbed Kirit's arm in time. Her fingers dug into my skin
as well. Together, we each kept the other from striking Hiroli
down and putting everyone in danger. Hiroli stepped back farther from us, as Dix finally turned to me and to Kirit.

"We'll take Elna higher once I see the brass plates. Hiroli
says there's an alcove full of them. Then I'll take Rumul's robe

and his little killer. My men will take the Singers. For your help, the rest of you can remain in exile here."

She didn't know about the Spire base, or what hid within it, because Hiroli hadn't known. And she only knew about some of the brass plates. We might conceal the rest from her if we were careful.

She began to cross the meadow, the uneven surface giving her trouble. Hiroli walked by her side, steadying her. They pulled Aliati and Djonn with them. When Dix reached the cave entrance, she stood below it, looking up. "A fine shelter, for thieves."

Hiroli climbed the ridge wall and leapt into the air, circling the meadow, searching for the Singers she knew were missing.

Shadows moved in the cave mouth. Moc, then Ceetcee, blocked the entrance. They aimed bows at Dix. "You cannot come here," Moc said.

Dix gestured to Elna and laughed. "Even if it means she dies?"

"She would not want this," Ceetcee said, not looking at me.

"You didn't come here to make a truce," Aliati said. "Though you accepted Sinter. You could kill us all here. Tell me why we should not destroy this entrance? We have the means to do it."

She exaggerated, but the blackwings didn't know that. Dix laughed. "More brave words, but no action."

Kirit released my wrist. "Go," she whispered, her words tight with anger. I took another step away from my mother. "I'll stay with Elna." She knelt, putting her knife on the ground, not far from her hand. She cradled my mother's head and stroked her cheek, humming The Rise, surrounded by blackwings.

I walked across the meadow, towards Dix and the cave. She had us outmatched. We could not fight. We could not run. What could we do?

"You had no intention of honoring Sinter."

She turned and laughed. "Who'll know who broke what law if you're trapped down here?" Dix sounded as if she was explaining a flight lesson, not doling out a death sentence. "You'll be forgotten, another myth in the clouds."

Dix's trick had worked, just like at the wingfight. This time, she hadn't stopped at slashing a footsling; she'd done much worse to gain advantage.

Dix held out her hand. "A bird away, more blackwings wait. You have no such reinforcement. Bring me the robe and the brass plates and the girl. The one who was so good with the knife."

Moc's face went pale. "You won't have her." He aimed his bow, until Ceetcee stayed him.

In the meadow, a glow pulsed in time with Kirit's singing. Littlemouth. I prayed Dix didn't see it. "What will you do with the plates? No one in the city can read them. Not even you."

Dix didn't turn from Moc, but she answered. "Nonsense. You saw their power above the council plinth. That, from just one plate. You saw us rise without wings. No need to wait for a breeze. We'll use them to make the city better."

"Not without an artifex. A good one," I said. "None but Djonn had figured out lighter-than-air."

Dix colored. "We can train more artifexes. The Singers kept the plates safe for us!" she shouted. "To hide them away is a crime against the city."

"Singers' inventions?" Djonn held a plate up, let it catch the light. Dix's eyes narrowed. "These? Were not created by the Singers. The Singers stole them. Hid them."

Dix blinked. Her blackwings muttered. "The Singers knew everything," Dix said quickly, "before you destroyed them and broke the city. You have no right to touch those."

"Surely you don't believe that?" Aliati said. She pitched her voice so that everyone on the meadow heard her clearly. "Did

Rumul tell you that before Spirefall? Or after, when you were interpreting for him? The Singers destroyed themselves, much like the culture down here did. Just as you will if you continue to mine the towers and reinvent the past. We can prove it."

Dix looked around her, taking in the towers, the meadow. "What would you have me do? Tell the towers there is no future? That the tiers will stop growing and we'll live in ever-narrowing spaces until we're all pushed off?"

"To counter that in time, you'll need teachers," I said quietly. "People who understand the plates, the towers, and the myths around them."

More muttering among the guards.

"You need people who could teach the city how to mold bone again, without weakening the towers," Ceetcee said. "People who can understand the tools of the past, and pass them on." She caught my eye. *Sometimes the best way to fight is to teach.* "Let us return to the northwest quadrant. We'll teach the city from there."

Dix's smile grew. "Ah, the northwest, with their plots. They've already argued their support for your group in council."

Hiroli landed on the meadow, Ciel dangling from a winghook. "I found her!"

Ciel struggled, but once on the ground, Hiroli tightened her grip on the girl.

I spoke fast. "You need that quadrant. You need the artifex. You can't hold the city without them. We'll give you the plates." I pulled two from my satchel. "And we'll offer ourselves as teachers."

Djonn coughed and stepped forward. "You can take the plates, but they're meaningless without me. Let my friends go."

"No," Aliati whispered. "She's not taking you. Or the plates."

Dix laughed, watching Aliati's face. "You see how easily you turn on each other? That amused Hiroli. Your integrity." She spotted the satchel I carried. Out of reflex, I shifted it away from Dix as she said, "Think of how many inventions were nearly lost to myth. We will make Laws about the proper care of such things."

I knew then that she would take it all, every bit of history, and use it for her own goals, rather than the city's. Perhaps Doran was right, that the only way forward was to control what Dix saw.

And perhaps, with Dix distracted and Wik still hidden from the guards, Kirit could find a way to get Elna to safety.

Dix reached for the satchel. The brass squares inside knocked together sharply when I grabbed her arm and twisted fast, pinning it behind her, her back to my chest. Now she was between me and the blackwings. She struggled, outraged. "You will not survive this. There's no way out of here without me. There are Laws—"

"Laws are for the sky, Dix. We are of the clouds." But even as I spoke, two guards had closed on Kirit and Elna. I relaxed my grip enough to step backwards. "Let me show you now what you don't know." Before her blackwings could react, I dragged her inside the cave, past Ceetcee and a stunned Moc. Hiroli rushed to follow.

The blackwings aimed, but Dix held up a hand as she stumbled to keep up with me. "Let him try to show me something new, to prove he's useful. Otherwise, he's running out of time."

"No!" Aliati said. But Ceetcee stilled her.

Across the meadow, Elna lay with her head cradled in Kirit's lap. Littlemouths glowed softly in the grass beside them. Beside Doran's body too, now covered in Kirit's cloak. It took great effort to tear my gaze away from my mother. Would I see her again?

"Family is so very inconvenient, isn't it?" Dix whispered. I choked on my answer, and she chuckled. "If you show me what the plates mean, I'll have her taken higher. If she lives long enough. And if you prove to me you have something to teach, perhaps I'll take you higher too."

"A promise from you is just words made of wind," Ceetcee said behind us. I looked back at her. She caught my eye and pointed with her chin across the meadow to the tower where Wik hid. A littlemouth pulsed in the mist. "Defend."

Wik was prepared to act. Was Kirit? Ceetcee coughed to get her attention. Kirit nodded. She was ready if she got a chance. I spoke loudly to distract Dix and Hiroli. "There are secrets down here that can kill you. Others can help you gain knowledge, and increase your value to the city."

How could we hand the meadow and its treasures over to Dix? With each step farther into the cave, I recalled Ciel's shouts at Laria: *Murderer!* She was that, and more. I gritted my teeth. *We all have principles.* Doran's words. *Some of us hide them better than others.* All I needed was to lure a few of the blackwings into the cave with us, and Wik could take advantage as the others regrouped.

"Many secrets, then?" Dix asked.

I had her interest now. "Like the lighter-than-air. It could take years to understand just one."

Dix stopped walking. "Then the fewer who see this, the better." She shouted to the blackwings just coming to the cave entrance, "Stay there. If I do not return, kill the old one. No need for blackwings in here."

Clouds.

"Only us," she said. "Until we can determine who will use the secrets best."

Now that I was committed to this course and trapped within the cave, I had to keep going or risk Elna's life, and the others' too. Doran's need for control was beginning to make more sense: each decision was filled unseen risks.

Moc followed us at a safe distance, humming, causing the end of the tunnel to luminesce. Now or never. "Then I challenge you," I said, "to look past the inventions, and see the message from the past with clear eyes. See how your actions are repeating a path of destruction that kept this knowledge from us for generations. You believe the Singers were leaders. This is your weakness. You must learn the truth of them."

"I know all the songs," she said, tugging to free her arm. "I know the truth."

I refused to let go. "I'm sure you think you do."

Moc hummed louder from the door behind me. The littlemouths glowed, and Dix gasped. She turned a slow circle, her face illuminated.

"Living above this all our lives. We would have died without knowing." She reached for the plates on the walls. The awe in her voice gave me new hope. Perhaps Dix could still love something.

"This is what we are protecting, as our ancestors protected it. Would you fly against this? Would you drain the towers above when the city is so alive, here?"

Was I getting through to her? She scanned the room almost reverently.

"Now you need to see more." As before, I took her arm and pulled her to the last alcove in the tower, where Hiroli had spent the past days. *Quickly now, for Elna.* She followed me willingly this time. I showed her the marks on the walls, the bones. "They died defending the people of the city. Would you do the same?"

Dix's expression was unfathomable. Tears streamed down her cheeks. Her eyes reflected the littlemouths' glow. "I knew I was right. That Rumul was right. The plates are our inheritance. The city needs them. People are willing to die for them."

Through the mist, on the third tower, I saw a struggle. One

guard fell from the tower. Another called for support. Had Wik been captured?

More blackwings circled Kirit and Elna. Djonn and Aliati had been moved to join them. Elna's eyes were closed, and Kirit stared at the tower where Wik had been. Her hand went to her knife.

I whistled the windsign for "defend." Kirit repeated it. She shifted Elna in her arms so that if she had the chance, she could lift her and run. And while the guards yelled at her to be quiet, I saw a small littlemouth pulse in the mist, farther from the meadow: the old tower windsign for "justice." Wik was still out there. Balance. Justice. We would try to take the guards, at least for a moment. Long enough for Kirit to fly Elna away.

"Quiet!" Dix shook her head, staring at the lights. "This is all ours now."

I swallowed hard. Doran had accused me of planning too many things on the wing, even as he'd done the same. But we'd prepared, and we had no other options. That was the greatest risk of all.

32

GRAVITY

We emerged from the cave in time to see a blackwing pull Wik from behind the second tower.

Below us, in the meadow, blackwings surrounded my friends. Aliati shielded Elna with her body, while Kirit stood, preparing to fight. Our last plan had failed. When Dix discovered the Spire below, she would be even more resolved to silence us, as the Singers had done generations ago to those who lived in the meadow.

A roll of thunder in the distance. Soft raindrops splatted the lichen and made the ferns bob in the meadow. Water beaded on Dix's furled wings and on the shoulders and backs of the guards.

Beyond the ridge wall, darker clouds gathered. We needed to get inside before lightning struck. Unaware of the risk, the guards herded us all to the meadow's center.

"I'll take the satchel now, Nat," Dix said, ignoring the rain.

"We hoped to show you the true history of the city. Where we came from. Where we may be heading." A dim rumble of thunder echoed in the clouds.

I gripped the satchel's straps tight as she reached towards me.

"Thank you for this." She pulled a brass plate from my bag. Held it up to show the blackwings. "The former councilor from Densira is right. There is a vast library of knowledge in these towers, and we will search them all. Several of these

354 · FRAN WILDE ·

Lawsbreakers know how to translate it. We can't kill them yet, but we won't let them escape."

Dix waved a hand, and the guards drew back to encircle us. Hiroli knelt and rewrapped her foot.

Elna, in Aliati's arms, groaned and shivered in the rain. "At least let her shelter inside," Aliati said. "The artifex too. Otherwise, they'll become sicker. If they sicken, we won't help you."

Dix nodded and signaled three of the guards. "Take these three inside." The guards lifted Elna and, with Moc's help, escorted Djonn into our cave. They took Aliati too.

When Dix turned back to us, she spoke first to Hiroli. "The Singers shared with us only a little of their knowledge. Now that I know more, thanks to your friends, I can better decide what the city needs. How to use that knowledge. Who should know it. We'll have no more problems with the northwest soon. Meantime, this area must be controlled. None must know about it above the clouds."

Her blackwing guards shifted, the words sinking in.

Dix put her hand on Hiroli's shoulder. "You will remain here, as valley guardian."

"Guardian?" Hiroli paled, and laid one hand on her own throat. "No. It's not safe. You said you'd take me with you, that I'd manage the artifexes—"

"I know what I said, and think of it. All of this knowledge. You'll learn so much. The guards will help you. Djonn will remain here too. You'll need all the help you can get." She tied a tether around Ciel's waist and handed it to Hiroli. "And the brother, too." Hiroli shook her head in disbelief and shock.

"For those who can't, or won't share their knowledge?" Dix looked directly at me. She threw a kavik in the air, and it flapped off. "You have a short time to say your good-byes."

Everyone in the cave. Everyone on the meadow. My family, my friends. They were mine, not Dix's. I shouldered the satchel with the brass plates. Dix hadn't seen any reason to take it from me, because she thought everything in the meadow was hers now.

I knelt beside Doran's body and wrapped my hand around the bone hook Ceetcee had planted in the meadow.

We had one more thing to teach Dix.

Gravity.

❧ ❧ ❧

With pops and cracks, the hook slid from the ground. I stood atop the pattern Ceetcee and Djonn had woven out of ancient wingframes and tools and felt the bones shift.

Then I unfurled my wings. Seeing me do that, Kirit and Wik followed suit. Then Ciel. The ground slid, then began to pit visibly. The meadow shook.

Hiroli stared, then fumbled with her wings, tangling them in the tether that held Ciel. I lunged to cut the tether, Dix's voice in my ears: "What did you do?"

But it was too late, a wing-sized portion of the meadow collapsed, and then more of it where the guards stood, and all of us slid into the void amidst clumps of lichen and ferns.

The noise the meadow made as it collapsed sounded like the city rumbling. Like the world ending. The smell of fresh-turned dirt and crushed greenery filled the mist.

As I tumbled, I saw others above me falling too, scrambling for solid meadow turf. One blackwing already flew free below. Hiroli tried to grapple Ciel. Kirit and Wik, wings locked, turned in the air. Ready for battle. In the meadow's underpinnings, a gaping hole was still growing, though still more of the woven platform held fast.

A blackwing dangled from the plinth. Doran's body tumbled into the void below. I fell too, then righted myself. Wind caught my wings and the silk filled.

Dix clung to the meadow platform, feet kicking, her wings half furled. Four blackwings tumbled through the hole in the meadow and swooped below her to help their leader right herself.

Kirit flew a tight path around the shadow-towers, pursued by the guard who'd killed Ezarit and Doran. She held a glass-tooth knife in each hand. I joined the chase, locking my wings. Drew my bow and sighted, fighting the wind. The guard didn't know how to fly below the clouds. Kirit led him on a weaving path through the building storm. I finally saw my shot and let the bolt fly.

It struck him in the wing and passed through. Blood spattered on the silk as it shuddered and tore. The murderous guard curled. His wings folded and he fell, my arrow sticking from his side.

I circled once to make sure he wasn't coming back. Kirit flew beside me. There was no triumph in her expression. She looked worried.

"The northwest," she shouted. "We can't leave them unaware." We slowly banked around another tower, to the deep void beyond. We dove to build up speed and caught a gust that shot us towards the northwest, flying pinion to pinion. It was coming on evening. Dix's blackwings would have pulled her from the shadows by now. They would attack soon, either us or the northwest. Ahead, we saw Wik chasing Hiroli through the clouds, blocking her wind and making her fight to stay aloft, exhausting her as she pursued Ciel.

Blackwings raced behind us. An arrow swooped past, narrowly missing me.

Hiroli dove at Wik as thunder cracked overhead, then lightning. She drew a knife—my knife—and threw it. The blade tumbled between Wik and Ciel as lightning streamed the sky again. We smelled the bolt's acrid passage, but I'd closed my eyes against the light, not wanting to be blinded. The residual light made bone look creased, wingsilk pocked, and the clouds as solid as bone.

Hiroli shrieked and fell far behind, panicked. Perhaps unable to see. Two of the guards went after her, and the rest of us climbed away into the lighter clouds.

Wik managed to fly another guard tight against a tower. She scraped a wing and spun into the clouds. The remaining blackwings went after their fellow guard instead of pursuing us.

"Rise!" I whistled, and the other three flew with me. We circled to find a strong gust, and this time, we rose into the upper cloud as one. Even Ciel on her fledge wings. We were so used to the lower cloud darkness, everything felt brighter here, even in the storm.

Thunder rumbled and rain stung our skin as we flew northwest, towards Mondarath and Densira. Toward home.

We still had our bows. Our new glass-tooth knives. We couldn't deliver to Mondarath the brass plates as I'd planned: the blackwings were too near for us to climb the tower and fight.

But Kirit was right, we had to warn the northwest quadrant. To protect my home—and Ceetcee's and Beliak's, Elna's. We'd left Laria to fend for itself; we wouldn't leave Mondarath.

"If rumors of what happened at Laria have spread, word of the cloudlight might have spread too," I called to Kirit, who still flew close on my wing. I hoped that was the power of myth and rumor. "We could try to signal from the clouds."

"If no littlemouths are clinging to the tower sides, we'll have to risk the blackwings in force above the clouds," she shouted back. It was a big if.

"And then?" Wik yelled.

"And then when all the towers are warned, we fight," I said.

Soon we reached the topmost layer of the clouds, looking up at Mondarath's lights through the mist. We flew a single circle of the tower, with me as a lookout for blackwings.

A gray scrim of mist hid the tower's details, its gardens and flags. Would they see us? Would there be littlemouths here?

Wik, Kirit, and Ciel began to circle the tower. The former Singers began to hum. Ciel's littlemouth glowed. On the tower here and there, reaching up from the clouds, the few little-mouths clinging to the bone walls and tiers pulsed in reply. So too, the walls at Viit and Densira.

The clouds around Mondarath took on a soft glow, ebbing and flowing with the Singers' path. The littlemouths pulsed in windsign: a simplified warning. *Danger, attack, danger.* If a tower guard on lookout remembered Laria, they'd know a fight was coming. If they could translate windsigns from pulses, they might get the full messages. If not, tower citizens would at least know something strange was happening and would be on their guard.

A shout, "Spirebreaker! Brokenwings!" An arrow struck the tower above me and fell away into the cloud. Blackwings. Not caring whether they were the leading edge of Dix's attack, or our pursuers from the meadow, I dove, trying to draw them away from the towers, to double back on the main force. Above, the clouds were lit with littlemouths, like small stars. They faded as the Singers followed me back towards the center of the city to make our stand.

ᐟ ᐟ ᐟ

"Nat Brokenwings, you will be forgotten!" Dix's voice came from upwind, close by. She'd recovered from her fall while we'd flown away from the meadow. Now, dark shadows circled above me, searching for me.

"They'll sing of us," I shouted back, hoping to draw Dix down and towards me. "A fierce song of thieves and knowledge." Another lesson to the city not to forget. Then I dove again.

They broke through a thick cloud then, where they'd been hiding at the city's edge. Hiroli flew at Dix's side, a bow in her hands, an arrow nocked. When she released it, the bolt tore a corner of Ciel's wing, but the silk held. Ciel struggled to keep up with Kirit, her wing spilling air.

Kirit slowed for her.

Hiroli dove for Kirit and Ciel. I dove too, and blocked her angle of descent. Swept the wind right out from beneath her, and she went spinning again. She recovered faster this time and dove at me. We swooped lower in the darkening clouds.

My ears popped. We'd dropped again, dozens of tiers, past the ghost tower's elevation. I got my bearings and located my companions. Overhead, Wik circled a blackwing, a spear in his hand. Below, Kirit guarded Ciel, whose left wing bellied and puckered from the tear in the silk. Behind us, Dix shouted orders, gaining on us.

Hiroli dove again, knocking Kirit away from Ciel. Then she snared Ciel with her bone hook just as we passed into the rain line again. I shouted as Ciel was pulled away.

Dix chose that moment to hurtle towards me, wings locked, arms extended as if trying to grab me from the sky. I rolled away and she followed. Above, the blackwings scattered, chasing my friends. We were separated across the clouds. Dix dove at me again, and I forced my wings into a tight turn, right into the dark storm cloud. Riding wind gusts battering my wings, rain driving my hair into my eyes, I flew until I thought I'd risen high enough, then banked out of the cloud. Below, Dix's dark wings and robe blended with the storm, while her long hair, woven with tower marks, made her easier to see.

But I was out of arrows, with only one knife left.

She dove within the mist, trying to lose me in the clouds,

then get above me. I matched her turns, refusing to let her out of my sight until I could get a good shot. She could not rise with me above her, so she dove again.

For all their skill, the blackwings didn't know the clouds like we did. The depths disoriented them as we passed the meadow's elevation. Without oil-proofing, their dark wings grew damp as they flew lower, the silk wicking moisture from the clouds until they were heavier and slower than us.

Days ago, Doran's people had oiled our wings before we left the city. Now the moisture beaded and spilled when we turned, faster than the blackwings. They began to straggle. Wik and Kirit chased them down into the clouds as we closed low on the city's northeastern edge.

I heard Hiroli yelling at Ciel in the mist. "Sing, clouds take you. Make some of those pretties light up." They were lost in the clouds, and Ciel wasn't helping her. I heard a wing rip, and Hiroli shouted again. "You've killed us both, fledge!"

I dove for them, hoping to catch Ciel. Saw them tumbling through the clouds.

An arrow cut through my wing, then kept going. A small hole, not like a knife tear. I listened for the telltale sound of silk ripping, but the hole held. The proofing had more than one benefit.

A shout came across the wind. "Before I drop you, Brokenwings"—Dix dove at me—"you'll give me the satchel. The plates!" I'd taken them from the meadow, had hoped to leave them at Mondarath. She would not get them now.

Her next shot flew true, though. The bolt tore through the air, and into the muscles of my upper arm, my knife arm. I screamed with the pain and then again as the bolt jerked me from my glide path.

Dix had secured the bolt to a tether before firing it. Now she

reeled me in on the length of rope that spanned the gap between us.

I shifted my knife to my left hand, as Dix had done, a seeming lifetime ago, when the city was whole.

"You'll never have the plates, the city's knowledge." I let my
injured arm dangle as she pulled me. I became her kite, her
victory.

She gloated when we were close enough to see each other
clearly, the wind still pushing us forward. "You've lost. You and
Kirit. I know where the meadow is. Where your family is. Now
I have the plates. Soon I'll have the artifex too."

My breath jarred from me as she swung me towards a bone-
encrusted bridge that hung askew on the city's northeastern
edge. I landed with a clatter. The bridge smelled of rot and moss.
The slick rime beneath my knees soaked through my robes and
blood seeped from my arm to stain the bridge where I lay. Beside the bridge, Dix had set a bone grip and secured herself with
a tether. She swayed beside me, her feet braced on a small outcropping.

I didn't feel much pain, just a twinge when she tugged at the
bolt. The corners of my vision began to ripple. Blood dripped
slow from the bolt line, measuring out my life. But I did feel it
when she began sawing at a strap near my shoulder. Worried
about the littlemouth there, I batted her hand away. Grabbed
at the satchel as she took it from me.

"You don't know how to use them," I whispered.

She smiled back, almost close enough now. "It doesn't really
matter what they mean, Nat. Only what I tell the city they
mean. And they will worship me for that." She was close enough;
I felt her breath on my cheek. Her face moved in and out of
shadow beside me.

"The city will do no such thing," I whispered. I said a

windprayer for Aliati to take care of my family. Then with my last energy, I threw my shoulders back. I drove my body weight against the bolt in my arm and kicked out with my feet, hard enough to yank Dix off her handgrip and make her wobble on the outcropping.

Screaming through the sudden, searing pain, I flipped forward off the bridge and raked at her face with my knife. I tried to drive the point into her shoulder, her neck, but it fell from my hand. I grabbed Dix's silk robe hard enough that her grip tore free of the bone wall.

We slid together down the rough, moss-encrusted tower. The satchel flipped open, spilling brass plates in every direction.

Dix shouted outrage as we dropped. She grabbed the bolt haft and twisted. I howled, my vision fading to a pinprick that encompassed only her face and the clouds above.

"Now see what will come for you," she said. She tore the bolt from my arm.

"Us!" I shouted. "What will come for us!"

I wrapped my hand in her hair, her robe. Dragged her backwards with me, into the clouds.

PART FIVE

BOUND

Dark kaviks wheeled the pale clouds, fighting gravity. They scaled the gusts, their beaks piercing the homeward winds that would take them back to bone tower, to roost, and to flock. Thick clouds closed around them as they rose and disappeared.

⌣ WAR ⌣

No tower will sabotage or war
With neighbors near or far.
We rise together or fall apart
With clouds below, our judge.

33

BONE FOREST

Spinning, we fell until we struck an outcropping hard. Bone crunched beneath me, and Dix gagged and groaned. She'd broken my fall. When she rolled to her side, she spilled me over the edge and the bolt's tether came free. I slipped from the ledge, screaming.

I flipped and struggled to find a gust to lift me anew. Curving my wings to find enough wind was not enough; I strained at the cams. Failed. I could only pull hard on one cam, so I spun and flipped again. Dizzy and losing blood, for a moment I saw those above me—blackwings and friends both—blurred into a whorl of wings and weapons.

Then they too tore away on a slightly stronger wind, black specks on gray clouds. I flipped again, and my wings filled with a little air, enough to slow my descent but not enough to glide. Gravity drew me like a needle through the clouds. The updrafts disappeared. Silk fluttered noisily above. Then a blackwing plummeted past, his legs kicking, his wings empty.

The wind weakened until it could no longer bear us.

I was no longer as afraid of falling as I'd been once. But hitting something? That terrified me.

In my dizziness, I imagined towers becoming clouds, growing together, and swallowing me whole. The city's familiar gusts and the clouds' turbulent winds were gone. Nothing supported my weight.

And then the cloud disappeared. Light dazzled my eyes with unforgiving sun and a flash of blue sky.

I fell from the bottom of the cloud. The ground spun beneath me: huge stretches of dark green and gray. Beyond those, madder red surfaces swirled with dust. My eyes saw, but my mind couldn't understand that such wide expanses weren't sky or cloud. The weak wind whistled. My hands grasped air. The red dust hurtled through the spinning sky to meet me.

When I hit, impact pressed the breath right through me. My ears rang. I sank into the rough surface and fought to pull a breath in. Coughed and tried again. Opened my eyes to stars and light, swinging in wild circuits. I squeezed my eyes shut again.

Dead. I was dead this time, I was sure of it. Ceetcee, Beliak, and Elna were far above me, and alive. I hoped.

It was very hot to be dead.

I opened my eyes a crack. The stars didn't reappear. I saw clouds.

I groaned. I hated clouds.

Above me, the white and gray sky was dotted with wings. Shapes wheeled and spun, falling. A scream came fast and in the distance, a pair of black wings folded and fell from the sky, landing hard with a loud snap of bone.

I lay there, breathing, the sun hot on my face. Finally, I summoned the strength to roll to my stomach, on my good side. When that stopped hurting and I was able to breathe again, I dragged myself to my knees. The world flipped inside out, and my stomach with it.

After I stopped retching and the world stopped spinning around me, I looked at the surface beneath my hand. Pale dust covered a rough topography of gray and green crags. The terrain did not feel cool like bone, but warm. When I moved, the surface gave slightly beneath my knees and palms, like a thick skin might.

Fighting pain and dizziness, I turned my head slowly. A wall of bone rose to my right, the ground gathering around it tightly. The wall rose higher again in sideways tiers that disappeared into the distance and up into the clouds. Smaller bone ridges pricked shadows on the horizon, as far as I could see.

Settling to my knees, I tore a strip of silk from my robe and bound up my right arm. The bolt had gone clean through. When I secured the silk bandage, tucking in the edges, I screamed. Now I knew I wasn't dead. Death couldn't possibly hurt this much.

I crawled away from where I'd landed, bled, and been sick. If I could get to the bone wall, perhaps I could climb up. Now that I wasn't dead, I needed to figure out how to get home. Back to my family. Back into the clouds, and then the city.

A shadow loomed over me, blocking the sun. Foul gray robes, streaked with blood and dirt flapped before my eyes. Two hands, one holding a sharp glass-tooth knife, the other extended to me.

"On your wings, Nat," Kirit croaked. She knelt beside me, her eyes wild. "You didn't catch me when I fell."

"Mercy on your wings, Skyshouter." Blood matted her ear and traced her tattoos. I must have looked similar. "You didn't catch me either."

"Where are we? Where is the wind?" Her questions came fast.

I got to my knees and steadied myself by leaning on her shoulder. I had no answers for her.

For a time, the world narrowed to the sound of our breathing and coughing.

Above us, the clouds formed a dark, thick sky that devoured the bone wall. I could barely remember the white towers and blue sky of home. Beneath our feet, the thick gray-green surface was flat, but soon it became folds and valleys, then drops into darkness. Beyond it, I could see the red, dusty surface I'd spotted in my fall, a drop of ten tiers at least.

We stared at our surroundings until the sun rose above the clouds and the light grew tolerably dim again. Everywhere we looked, the terrain was the same, gray and green below us, bone wall to our right, red dust beyond: a landscape of ridges and creases, steep drops and rolling expanses.

A weak breeze ruffled my hair. I held my fingers up to test it. I could barely call it wind.

A few steps from us, my wings lay crumpled, a spar jammed into the ground. Ribbons of shredded blue and sepia silk hung from the frame. Kirit's wings had fared better, with only a few tears. But even if our wings had been whole, there was not enough breeze to lift us from the ground. No wind we could ride through the cloud and back up to the city.

We'd fallen from the cloud. We were trapped below it.

ᕃ ᕃ ᕃ

We got to our feet and walked, slipping on refuse and grime. Once, my foot sank deep into an oozing crust, to a dank pool below. The rancid smell made me ill. Kirit grabbed my wounded arm and dragged me out.

I screamed in pain.

"If it hurts, you are lucky." She was right.

But fear bubbled in my gut. We'd fallen. We weren't dead, but we were lost, and those above were lost to us. "Are there songs for this?"

Kirit shook her head. Kept walking. Now and then, she looked up at the clouds. Then out across the horizon, her lips pressed tight together as if to stifle a scream. She twisted a ribbon of wingsilk between her fingers. I caught myself flexing my uninjured hand—grasping air in empathy, but Kirit didn't notice. She limped and stumbled. She slowed, then knelt, coughing.

"We have to keep going." I pulled on her arm, trying to lift her one-handed, without wings, or a good breeze to fill them.

"Where do we go?" Her lips were cracked.

We would go to the bone wall. "Up. We'll go up. We'll find a place high enough to launch you from. You'll fly for help."

Even as I said the words, I wished I could go up instead of her. She had a working set of wings. I didn't. Still, the thought that we'd fly again? That was enough to keep us both moving. We saw a broken wingframe, and beneath it, one of Dix's guards. They'd landed so hard it was impossible to tell whether they were male or female, old or young.

We muttered Remembrances over them and pointed skywards. We kept walking. The sun descended below the cloud wall, and the world steamed around us. We dragged our feet. We didn't look at the horizon, not much, the sky not at all. We kept our eyes on the ground, so we wouldn't trip. Neither one of us asked if we'd seen anyone else. If I'd asked and Kirit had said yes, it would have broken me. If she'd said no, that would have meant we were alone with the dead.

The sun passed below the horizon, trailing orange and purple across the sky. The air cooled around us. The dim light felt like we were back in the undercloud again, except with solid ground beneath our feet. We could cover more distance now, before the sun came back.

If we stopped to watch the horizon, we'd never find a way high enough for her to try to launch.

The purple light faded. I dreaded stopping to sleep, though I knew we needed it. I didn't want to slow enough for understanding of what had happened to catch up to us. To overwhelm us. So we kept walking in the near dark.

Ahead, in the tip of the bone wall's shadow, a darker shadow: Black wings. Gray robes. Kirit gave a cry and ran. "Wik!"

The Singer cradled his arm. Deep scrapes crossed the tattoos on his face and hands. He stared at us, at the thick clouds above. "To fall so far," he whispered.

Kirit and I lifted him gently. With pieces of my wings, we splinted his arm. As we helped him, his daze cleared, and he looked at our surroundings, confused. "Where is the city?"

My eyes scanned the green ridges, the red dust beyond. I had no answer for him.

"We'll find it," Kirit said. "Can you walk?"

He tried to stand, and when he had his balance, we moved slowly on, towards the bone wall. Once, we might have glided that distance without a thought. Instead we walked until we couldn't any longer. We'd barely drawn closer to the wall when Kirit knelt on the ground. "Enough. Rest."

Somewhere above us, the northwest had been attacked. The fledges, our friends and family were still in the midcloud. Elna—I did not want to rest. But my body would not listen. My legs wobbled and failed me. I settled next to Kirit on the ground.

Wik groaned as he lowered himself beside us and hummed a song. It sounded familiar, like one Tobiat had taught us about long ago, but with a slightly different cadence. I remembered a few words. *Go up, away, rise, and live.*

"What's that from?"

"'The Bone Forest,'" he confirmed. "A very old song," Wik said. "Singer archivists had been trying to figure out the mystery for years. Go up from what? What did our ancestors have to rise away from?"

We looked at the bone walls rising as high as we could see, dark shadows of uneven ridges and spires on the end and side nearest us, thick towers grown together running its center and up into the cloud wall above. My eyes drifted closed, and I was powerless to stop exhaustion from pulling me down into sleep.

I jerked awake when, below us, the surface seemed to move in one long roll. Kirit whimpered, groggy, and then sprang fully awake. A sound louder than any city rumble made us clap our hands to our ears. When it stopped, Wik had risen to his feet, on alert. He held his spear in his uninjured hand, ready to throw. Kirit clutched her remaining knife. But no enemy came. The ground continued to rumble softly beneath our feet for a long time afterward.

"We might be about to find out what they had to fear," I said. Nothing I'd ever hunted made a sound like that. Not even a bone eater. "Stay alert."

Wik handed me a water sack, half full. I gulped a mouthful, then spat mud and blood on the ground. Tried again, swallowing this time. Passed the sack to Kirit. As she drank, I tore another blue strip from my broken, bundled wings and we changed the bandage on my arm. Wik helped us both to our feet, wincing as we tried not to jostle his arm. We aimed ourselves now for one of the lower edge spires, hoping there would be an easy way to climb it.

The landscape went on forever, and I felt certain that we'd walk the strange surface always. We'd finally come close to the edge of the bone wall, and we circled the thick ridge that surrounded it, looking for handholds, access.

In the dark, I did not see where the ground dipped low, then fell away until I nearly walked right into it.

"Careful." Wik caught my good arm and steadied me, pointing. We could not see the chasm's end. We stopped, not wanting to trip into another chasm, until sunrise pricked the horizon, then lit it orange and red. Warm air that promised another sweat-filled day replaced the cool night breeze.

Far out on the horizon, silhouetted by the sunlight, three dark shadows moved, enormous. Puffs of dust rose in their wake, glittering red.

"What are those?" I pointed.

Wik shook his head. "I can't tell from here. Too much dust."

I slid down a small incline on my backside, hoping to get closer to the chasm, so I might look over the edge.

Wik slid beside me, trying to slow his descent with his feet and hand. I'd not thought to do so. When the dusty surface slickened with moisture, I began moving too fast and couldn't stop myself. I slid farther and skidded off the edge. Despite Wik's efforts, he tumbled after me, spilling into a dark ravine with a surprised grunt followed by a pain-filled groan.

"Are you all right?" Kirit remained up above.

We'd landed side by side on a pile of bones that shifted beneath us and pricked at our robes and skin. Skulls piled on long leg bones sucked clean of marrow, ribs. A large beak stuck point first from layers of smaller bones, barely a hand span from my leg. "We're all right."

We picked our way carefully from the bonefall, back out into sunlight, and found our path blocked by another green ridge, thicker than any tower in the city.

Wik turned to look up at Kirit, and then out at the horizon, his back to the wall. His hand shaded his eyes as he looked across the landscape. Broad yellow expanses of cartilage stretched out beside me, layer upon layer, and curved like a bone eater's talons, their color much darker than tower bone. The edges and tips were chipped and peeling, ridged with mud. One moved, lifting slowly in the air.

They weren't like talons. They *were* talons.

When the talon came back down, it pounded red dirt below, shaking us and throwing dust into the air.

Behind Wik, the green wall moved. A section parted with a

wet sound, revealing a smooth, liquid dome, tiers and tiers high. I stepped back as far as I could without falling farther. Tried to make sense of the whole from its pieces.

The yellow orb, flecked with browns and greens each the size of a bone eater followed my movement. A dark iris grew larger and smaller as it tried to focus on me, on Wik.

Kirit shouted from atop the ridge. The iris found her. One small edge of a monstrous jaw far below us grated against another. Supported on a pile of broken dirt and bone, the creature's mouth moved back and forth, producing a grinding sound louder than anything, even thunder. A city roar was a whisper in comparison.

I covered my ears again, saw Kirit cower and tumble towards us. Wik still faced the other direction, towards the sunrise. He hadn't seen what we saw. Didn't see Kirit fall. He didn't see the giant yellow eye behind him, the corner nearest us seeping salty water, which now slowly blinked.

Wik pointed a shaking hand to the horizon.

I yanked him away from the eye, the jaw. We both lifted Kirit and retreated the way we'd come, but found we couldn't climb back up the leathery ridge.

"Move," I whispered. "Now."

We slid away down another slope. The giant valley of bones we'd fallen into was only the beginning. We slipped farther, finding more skulls, a scapula.

In the distance, the familiar sound of a bone eater's screech pierced the air. That stopped the three of us in our tracks. We stood back to back, searching the morning for a serrated beak, the giant claws. None plied the midden for as far as we could see.

When the dust of our fall cleared, I turned to look where Wik had been pointing, above.

The distant shadows we'd seen on the horizon before were

clearer now. The sun edged their forms in golden light: three enormous, dark shapes bristling against the bruised sky. Each kept a distance from the others that was nearly equal to their distance from us.

All three moved slowly across the horizon, one monstrous foot, then the other, inexorable.

Our own bones felt each step.

The creatures' thick necks lifted heads that swept back and forth, then dropped to the ground as bone eaters swooped near their heads and in their wake. Broad, curved backs supported ridges of bone that rose to brush the clouds, separating into towers and spires at their peaks.

Only three spires on one of the backs pierced the clouds above. They were small, even at a distance, compared to what we knew.

I pulled Kirit's and Wik's arms gently, moving them back to the nearest incline, and away from the red, dusty ground. We were safer up high. We needed to climb.

Nothing in our songs, our carvings, or engraved on the plates we'd found in the clouds prepared us for what we were seeing.

"The city," I whispered. "It's alive."

34

JUSTICE

Climbing single-handedly, and keeping well away from the city's eye, I led our scramble up another leathery ridge, Wik pushed me from behind and pulled Kirit along.

Each step threw dust in the air and filled our noses with thick scents that reminded me of trash-filled lower tiers and thrown-down garbage, but much, much worse. Strongest of all was the city's own stink.

The last thing any of us wanted was to fall in a pile of refuse that had collected on the city and surrounded its edges. What we wanted most was to be far above it.

If only we had a cheap fiber rope. I calculated how many of Aliati's tethers we'd need to climb back above the clouds and stifled a laugh that threatened to become a sob.

Finally, we crested the ridge and could see the bone wall again, and across the creature's shoulder too, almost to its flank. A long expanse of bone, too steep to scale without tethers, grips, or pitons, ran until it disappeared in the haze. We couldn't climb here either.

"It's going to get dark again soon," Wik said. The sun was just grazing the bone range that disappeared into the clouds. When the sun passed above the clouds, it would seem like a second sunset. "We should find shelter." He pointed at a flock of bone eaters that dipped their long necks and dug in the midden heaps with their beaks. One lifted a large chunk of flesh covered with feathers—the body of another bone eater—and flew it to the city's mouth. When it dropped the carrion, the city's tongue slowly emerged and dragged the morsel in.

They carry the dead away . . .

The song came unbidden, sounding almost giddy as I remembered it.

They eat the stars.
They crack the bones.
They feed the clouds below.

Bone eaters fed the city, not the clouds. Aliati and Djonn would love to know this. Moc too. I hoped to be able to tell them.

Far above, a cloud-hung meadow sheltered almost everyone I cared about. I shook my head to focus my thoughts and reeled, dizzy, with the motion.

Wik had a different worry. "We don't want one of those to surprise us and catch us, alive or dead." The moment Wik said "or dead," he looked like he wished he hadn't. Still, I couldn't have agreed more.

"Do you think that's what happened to the others? The guards?" Kirit said.

Who'd been near us in the sky? Dix, almost certainly. She was as close to the cloud base as I had been. I kept expecting to find her, or what was left of her, as we walked. "I saw several guards fall," I said, seeing again the spinning sky, the plummeting wings.

"And Hiroli had Ciel. I hope they stayed above the cloud base," Wik said. His forehead wrinkled as he frowned. "Maybe Ciel's all right."

I thought back to the fall. I hadn't seen Wik or Kirit when I tumbled, nor before that, when I struggled with Dix. "How did you fall? You were both higher than me, chasing blackwings."

Kirit laughed quietly. "We saw Dix attack you. We weren't going to leave you there. We were coming to help. Then the wind disappeared."

They could have flown away and been free, but they hadn't. Now they were stuck here too.

With a sound like a swath of wet silk being pulled across bone, the city extended its tongue again near one of the bone eaters' offerings and pulled it close. When it opened its mouth, other bone eaters took wing, bringing more food.

The sound of the city digesting its meal was too much for us. We set out again, moving down an incline to another ravine, trying to get closer to where the bone ridge began, while staying far from the city's head.

The sun passed above the clouds. In the dim half-light, Wik tripped over a pile of refuse gathered along the city's neck.

This was more than trash and deadfalls from the towers above. Mud-covered, rusting metal, some of it pitted and filled with rainwater, had accumulated on the ridge. Some holes were big enough to bathe in. A long section of what looked like wall or balcony, made from mud-colored blocks, stuck from a pile of bird bones. The trash rose and fell with the city's breath.

From this height, we could still see shapes on the horizon; other cities, moving.

"How long do you think the city's sat here, letting the bone eaters feed it?"

"Too long," Wik said. His gaze took in the depth of the trash, the height of the bone ridge. "I doubt it could move now, with the towers it supports being so high."

The city rumbled, as if in reply. We could not keep our footing. Soot and dirt rained down on us from the towers above.

"This isn't safe," I said when the rumbling stopped.

Wik agreed. "We need to go back up, now." He pointed to the farthest spur of bone. "Maybe there's a way up over there." Dark marks speckled a bone ridge in the distance, the height of which would eventually become the towers, the city. It looked more accessible than any ridge we'd seen yet.

Our landscape had altered from sky and tower to a geography of claw and tongue, joint and limb.

"I'm willing to walk there," Kirit said. "Even if it takes a moon." She began checking our weapons: four arrows left, and a bone knife. Two mostly repairable wingsets. One broken. Then she checked my wound.

"I dreamed about exploring the city, you know. About flying beyond the towers." I hissed as she resecured my bandage. "I wanted to know more."

"Dream smaller next time," Wik said.

Kirit laughed. "Your curiosity has always been endless trouble, Nat." Her teasing expression sobered. "Hold still if you want to be able to climb the ridge and get back to your family."

I couldn't let myself hope for that. Not yet.

As Kirit worked, I stared at the city's flank. It had curled one foreleg over its shoulder. Claws extended like sideways towers across its skin. On one yellowed ridge, three dark figures moved. "Look!"

"Birds," Kirit said.

"I don't think so." The creatures didn't move like birds. I squinted, rubbed my eyes and looked again. Whatever it was walked in the opposite direction from the towers, away from the city. But the dark forms tugged at the edge of my vision.

"Let's take a look?" There was a ridge just below that would give us a better view.

A dust-filled crease, muddy from the rain, offered an easy, if twisting, path down.

Wik frowned. "We can't waste time here. The city needs us, and we have a long way to go."

"The sooner we get back up, the sooner we know Elna is all right," Kirit agreed. A flicker of pain crossed her face. "And everyone else." She turned on the ball of her foot.

I knew they were right. More than anything, I wanted to see my family safe, and my city whole again. But when I made to follow Kirit towards the wall, I couldn't shake the vision of the dark figures walking away. Wik looked back too, now.

"Just a moment, to be sure," I said. Wik finally agreed with a nod. Kirit followed us, grumbling, looking back over her shoulder towards the bone ridge.

Around a bend in the city's skin, we found the remains of two blackwings. One had died naturally, if a fall was natural. The other had a deep cut across her throat.

"Someone else is alive here," Wik said. "Or was." He went through their robes and took their weapons. Kirit shouldered a water sack. I took their packs and another mostly whole wingset. Pale and shaken, we ate their food: a gryphon one had shot down before she died. We drank their water.

Then we moved again, faster, towards where we'd last seen the shadow-figures. Overhead, a bone eater flapped its giant wings and circled away. Kirit shivered.

"My theory," Kirit said as she watched the bird's shadow grow smaller on the ground, "is that, once we find out who is out there, if we get up high enough, we'll be able to launch ourselves into a decent gust. But we'll need to be very high. Possibly as high as the clouds." She was still thinking of the climb, barely tolerating the ground.

We all looked back towards the city, tilting our heads to see the bone wall silhouetted against the thick clouds.

When we came out of the crease, we could see the city's leg much more clearly. The dark figures we'd watched before had moved, but not far. I shaded my eyes against the sunlight emerging from the other side of the clouds.

I could make out details on the distant figures now. Two wore wings, but they were half furled and cockeyed. One figure limped and carried something in their arms. The other figure walked beside them. Then sun hit them all just right, and I caught a glimpse of white wings in the arms of the limping figure, seemingly immaculate against the city's skin.

"Ciel," I breathed. She lived. But someone was carrying the fledge away, towards the edge of the city and the dusty expanse beyond.

"We're going after her. Now," I said. This time, Wik and Kirit matched my pace without argument. The climb had to wait.

ʕ ʕ ʕ

In the gaining light, we left the shelter of the crease and moved as quickly as we could towards the city's shoulder. Before, when the sun had passed above the cloud, we'd closed some of the distance. Now we could see the black wings on the person carrying Ciel and the robes of their companion. The heat slowed us all. Those we pursued stumbled down the city's right shoulder, stopping to rest more often than we did.

We didn't stop for anything. Even when it began to rain momentarily as the sun appeared fully beneath the cloudline again, we kept going. An arc of color painted across the sky, something that would have captured our attention a week ago. Now we walked until it disappeared.

The city's dust became muddy and rain pooled in a dimple on the city's shoulder. The water smelled sour but tasted fine when Wik sipped it. We filled our water sacks. We walked on. The sun slipped lower, the rain stopped and the city began to steam. The stench grew. We kept going.

Ciel and those who carried her reached the bent elbow of

the city. When they set her down on the ground, we saw her struggle and roll, her feet and hands bound.

"We're coming, Ciel," Kirit said.

I'd never wished for wings and a fast breeze more. My ankles creaked, and my legs felt every step. And we were slow, painfully so. But we were gaining on Ciel's captor. We could see the way they bent and spoke to the fledge now, while Ciel knelt, sick, on the ground. When the sun struck the figure, the few beads left in their dark hair glittered. Hiroli. She waved her hands in the air over her head, yelling.

Ciel collapsed, and Hiroli grabbed her by the arm and dragged her.

The blackwing with them followed, limping.

Wik, Kirit, and I began to run, first in the heat and then in the cool of the next sunset, this one truly on the horizon. While we ran, our breath coming jagged, our feet bruised, the horizon changed color: purples, oranges, yellows. Eventually it faded, and we ran first through the dark, then by moonlight.

I could hear Wik's breathing, his dry cough getting worse. Kirit wheezed. I heard a rattle in my chest too. "We can't keep this up." I'd run in the tiers sometimes, and on the meadow, but never this far.

"We have to," Kirit said, each word costing her breath. "We can't lose Ciel."

No. We couldn't lose her again. She would say she was brave, that she could fight. But she needed us.

"She's Spire-born; she was raised to fight," Wik said. He'd been the one who wanted her to hide when Dix came, wanting her to be a child a little longer. Now he held on to a different kind of hope.

"We won't lose her," I said.

By the time the sun rose again after the long night, and the city began to heat up, we were stumbling. Kirit's limp had become a drag. We could barely keep our heads up. Red sky and gold rays edged the city, slowly illuminating the claw and leg. The full stretch of gray, dust-speckled skin glowed in the sun, and nowhere did we see them now. Hiroli, Ciel, and the blackwings had disappeared in the night.

We searched the horizon. Nothing. Wik knelt, while Kirit lay on her back, staring at the clouds above. I tried to sit, but nearly toppled to my side. I braced myself on my arm while my leg muscles twitched from exertion.

Wik shared out the rest of the blackwing's food and water from his carry-sack. "We need to eat. And find more water. We'll die at this pace." We huddled together as best we could, in the shadow of the bend in the city's leg.

When the sun finally rose above the clouds, we began to walk again in the direction we thought they'd gone, but when it passed again below the cloudline and heated the ground, Kirit sat down, dizzy. Though Wik convinced her to drink, she could go no farther that day.

I walked a short distance away to relieve myself, then returned as the shadows grew longer. Wik handed me the water sack and said, "I'll take first watch." I drank the last sips of water and settled down to sleep and dreamed of falling, until the shouting woke me.

Kirit and Wik stood before our resting place, throwing trash at a dark-winged bone eater seemingly the size of the city's biggest claw. The creature bore down on them, its serrated beak clacking. Sunrise's orange glow silhouetted the bird's enormous wings and head.

Struggling to my feet, I raised my voice to join theirs. Then I charged at it, every muscle screaming pain. The bird startled as if nothing had ever run *at* it before. Bending its knees, it pushed its body into the sky as the sun began to set. We watched the bone eater disappear.

In the dimming light, the horizon looked flat and bleak. Far away, ripples that might be water, or might be heat, formed and disappeared, a hallucination. I saw no lights glinting, no smoke climbing into the sky. Wherever our ancestors had come from, they hadn't left anyone behind to greet us, or to help us.

A small mote appeared in the air, descending, its path erratic. It looked like one of the giant bugs we'd seen swooping the midden heaps around the city, but it was too high for that. Slowly it drew closer and resolved into a whipperling, trying to fly straight with a damaged wing, feathers askew. It spiraled to the ground just over the ridge. I hurried after it, hoping.

When I reached the bird, it lay on the ground, breast pulsing, trying to right itself, but its wing would no longer move. "Maalik?" I lifted his body gently in both hands. Weakly, he nipped at my finger.

Footsteps sounded behind me; a shadow covered my shoulder. "Look at his leg," Wik said.

Tucked beneath Maalik's body, a silk cord. Two cracked and battered bone chips.

"How?" I looked up into the sky.

Wik followed my gaze. "If Aliati or Beliak sent Maalik once the meadow collapsed, he might have tried to follow us. Gotten caught in the fall?"

Maybe. I lifted the message chip. Beliak's sigil was cut into one side. My hand shook as I flipped the message over. "We are well. Guards are handled."

That was all. A signal smuggled into the air. I stroked the bird's head and cupped my hand to hold water that Wik poured. Maalik dipped his beak in, head hanging over my palm. "He's exhausted."

"He's a very lucky bird. He must have followed us the whole way to Mondarath."

I tucked Maalik into my robe. "If he recovers, perhaps he can find his way back again."

"Perhaps," Wik said. He helped me tie the message chips to my wrist. I ran my thumb across the carved letters, then returned my attention to the horizon.

Even at day's end, the city's skin steamed this close to the ground. We walked down the city's leg, hoping to find another glimpse of Hiroli and Ciel.

As we'd scrambled across the landscape, our footwraps had shredded on the city's tough skin. Our feet were blistered, our calves ached. My hair stuck damply to my neck and face, with no wind to dry my sweat.

I caught myself rubbing a patch in my robe, sliding my thumb over the quilting. Elna's stitches. The fabric grew shiny from contact with my skin.

Wik paced, head down, a frown deepening the lines on his face.

Kirit stared down the distance, daring the horizon to give up.

The air finally cooled that night as the moon rose. In the deep shadows and etched silver light, we found Dix. She hung from a bone spur jutting from the city's elbow, one wingstrap caught. The skin of her face had been scraped raw in her fall, and her feet were swollen.

My breath caught. I raised my hand to block the moonlight so I could look up at her. Wik and I scaled the bone spur. We cut her wingstraps and lowered her down. She did not wake. Her chest barely rose and when it did it made an ugly rattle. Around where she'd fallen, three of the brass plates lay, their etched faces reflecting the moon. We gathered them up and put them in Wik's satchel.

We left Dix in the shade of the bone spur to be forgotten, and we kept walking.

Staring towards the end of the city's leg, Wik frowned. "We

could walk this way for days and nights and not find them. At some point, we need to think about saving ourselves. Some point very soon."

Kirit looked at him, angry. "We're not leaving her down here."

"We'll find her," I agreed, determined. I didn't want to linger on the ground any more than Wik did. I knew that what he was thinking was practical. But I wouldn't turn my back on Ciel a second time. Not until I was sure there was nothing more I could do.

Late that night, just before the next moonset, we passed above a cesspool that had collected beside the city's leg. Not even the bone eaters would go near the foul liquid seeping from the city's side.

"Lucky we didn't land in that," Wik said. We'd walked for half a night without saying anything between us. Since just after we'd found Dix. Now he coughed, making a face at the stench. Covered his mouth and didn't speak again until we were past the cesspool.

The city hadn't moved for a very long time. A river of filth trailed away from its body, towards a rippling blue haze in the distance. The stench was beyond reckoning. No one spoke, to avoid having to open their mouths.

Beyond the worst of the smell, we found the last guard who'd been traveling with Hiroli. His weapons were gone, and his wings. If he'd carried food and water, there was none with his body now.

"She's growing desperate," Kirit said.

We all knew what Hiroli was willing to do to survive. We scanned the horizon for Ciel. Hoping to find her alive. Finally, Wik pointed over the hillside, then began moving. We followed close on his heels.

"Light," he shouted. "A campfire."

35

HORIZON

The fire Wik saw was a tiny flicker in the dark expanse of the city's leg. They'd traveled closer to us than before, but much lower down the city's side. Close to the ground.

"It will be a trick to get back up that ridge," Wik whispered. His voice was hoarse with exhaustion.

Behind us, Kirit stumbled on the city's uneven surface. We were headed now towards the expanse of ground between our city and the ones farther away. She didn't like it. Neither did I.

But Hiroli was leaving the city and taking Ciel with her, and none of us would leave Ciel behind.

"From the look of things, Hiroli's had to backtrack around a flight of bone eaters," Wik said. "Her new path takes her near the city's head. She's slowing."

We picked up the pace, moving through the dark, using our bone hooks and wing battens to feel our way. Slowly, we gained on them, dreading what we'd find when we got there.

↖ ↖ ↖

Hiroli's voice rose as she pulled Ciel farther down the ridge. The fledge stumbled, but managed to stay on her feet in the orange light of sunrise. They slid into the deep valley nearest the city's head. The bonefall clattered as they kicked pieces of bone loose.

A bone eater flew from the pit, alarmed, a femur in its beak. It flapped away noisily.

"Ciel!" I chased them down, readied the bow we'd taken off the blackwings, ignoring the pain. Wik and Kirit slid beside me. We ran across the city's skin, stumbling on rough patches. I tripped and jarred my arm. Gasped, but kept going. Feet pounded behind me as Wik and Kirit caught up with me.

Below, Hiroli waited for us.

"Stop where you are." I drew the bowstring awkwardly with my good hand. Tried to hold the weapon steady.

Hiroli looked at me and laughed. "Nat Brokenarm now. Mighty Hunter." Her voice cracked. "We're going to find a new city," she yelled, pointing at the horizon. "Just as our ancestors did." Dried spit crusted the corners of her mouth.

"That's skytouched," Kirit said. "We need to go up, not away."

Hiroli held Ciel by the robe at arms' length. "You've seen the magnificent creatures out there. We could climb one that's not half dead and begin again. Those above could join us, and survive."

"You want to climb another city?" Kirit said, trying to comprehend, while Wik slowly edged towards Hiroli in the shadows of the ridge. "What about the towers? What about Naza?"

Hiroli pointed at the horizon, where the cities paced. Stars pricked the dark sky behind them. "Look at them! Much more potential than this." She tapped the thick skin with her silk-wrapped foot.

Ciel raised her head. Her eyes were glazed with thirst and hunger. Hiroli's own lips were split and pale. They were out of water.

"Come with us, then, and warn those above us." I kept my voice calm, trying to give Wik an angle to get closer to her. There *was* time to warn the towers, I realized, as long as the bone eaters kept feeding the city. But I vowed Hiroli would not be with us when we did.

For now, I had to keep talking. To hold her attention. "We

have water. We'll eat. Then we'll all go up together. You'll need more people than just you and Ciel to go. You'll starve."

Wik had slowly edged to Hiroli's right, but couldn't get any closer. Ciel's feet kicked off the ground as Hiroli lifted her.

"You are a terrible liar, Councilor." She shook Ciel. "You won't take me with you. You want to be the one to lead." She began to drag Ciel towards the ground again, walking backwards. "I will lead us to the new city. I'll make the Laws. We'll let people come who can follow our Laws." She murmured to herself, "I'll lead."

"Come back, Hiroli," Wik said, coaxing. "Or leave Ciel with us. Then you can do whatever you want."

Hiroli didn't see the next drop, beside the city's mouth. She nearly lost her footing. At the last minute, she stepped forward, pushing Ciel before her.

Ciel stumbled. Hiroli growled and raised her hand as if to slap the fledge, then grabbed Ciel's hair and twisted it in her fist. "We'll have order in the new city." Her voice was eerily calm now. Kirit was right. Skytouched. Cloudtouched. Ground-touched.

"Stop this!" I shouted, loud enough to halt Hiroli in her tracks. She looked at me, as if just seeing me again. Smiled. "Councilor. You could join me. You and Wik."

I shook my head slowly. "Never. We'll go back up into the clouds, and rise above them again."

Her face darkened. "Dissent," she muttered. As she focused on me, Kirit tried to flank her other side, but when she and Wik got too close, the former blackwing jerked at Ciel's hair again. Ciel grabbed at Hiroli's wrists, scratching the skin hard enough to break it, but did not fight further when Hiroli shook her again. She slumped, exhausted.

Hiroli held her free hand out, motioning to the edge. "Don't make me throw the fledge down!"

In the great expanse behind Hiroli, a crack opened to a narrow slit of yellow and black, surrounded by white sclera and thick skin. Hiroli did not see it because her back was to the eye, but Ciel did. She froze. Hiroli jerked her arm.

"City save us," said Wik.

"The city can't save us," I said, changing my grip on the bow. "We have to save ourselves."

Fire shot through my arm as I readied my arrow but I hesitated. This was an unfamiliar bow, and I was injured. What if I couldn't hold it? I could harm Ciel. I could hit the city. But Kirit and Wik had no shot. I did.

Hiroli smiled, her face utterly calm, and terrifying.

We cannot lead out of fear, Ezarit had said. And I was afraid. So very afraid.

But not acting was worse. I felt the breeze against my cheek, blowing towards Hiroli. Saw the meager wind's arc and how it flowed. Even if I could not ride that breeze, I knew it. I understood it.

I drew hard and let the arrow fly. It pinned Hiroli's hand against the city's lip.

The city roared, lifting her off her feet, trying to shake her loose.

Ciel bit Hiroli's other hand. When Hiroli shrieked and let her go, Ciel dropped to the ground and ran across the bonefall, towards us. She stumbled, then kept running. Wik scooped her up and began to climb over the city's leg, away from the mouth, the eye.

Below us, the city's jaw opened slowly and the thick, gray tongue emerged. The stench bowled us back, and we scrambled unsuccessfully to climb the beast's shoulder again.

Hiroli writhed, trying to free her hand. She shouted for us to help.

We retreated to safety, then looked back.

The gray tongue had wrapped Hiroli and smothered her screams. She disappeared into the city's mouth and the jaws ground closed.

"Hurry, before the city decides it's still hungry." I started forward, and the others followed me around the immense claws and across the hot, red ground. We stopped when we were far enough from its head to avoid its tongue.

"Did she mean what she said?" Ciel asked, her breath rasping. "Is the city dying? Moc's up there. And everybody."

We looked back across the ground at the enormous shoulder ridges, at the towers and spires rising from its spine, too heavy. Towers that our ancestors had grown higher in order to rise, to be safe. Towers that were now crowded with our family, our friends, our people.

But the city chewed and shifted, sated for now. Its eye followed us.

"She meant it," I said. "But it might take a long time to die, especially if it has food."

The towers' shadow grew long against the red dirt as the sun came below the clouds again, drenching us with sweat. We felt the city's regular breathing and its heartbeat through our feet We could hear it chew.

I remembered the rolling quake from our first night on the ground. If the city died, it could roll again. And that time, the weight on its back could pull it right over. The towers might come crashing down.

The image left me breathless.

We would not let that happen. Stopping the process felt impossible, but we'd already done the impossible. We'd fallen through the clouds and lived.

"I don't think a whipperling note could get people to understand. We have to find another way to tell them." I looked up then, into the gray expanse of cloud, missing the dome of stars, the bats that flew the night. I missed the familiar and the beautiful. The blue sky, filled with birds, the bone white towers, ferns and lichen in the meadow. The glow of littlemouths in the cave. Ceetcee's smile. Beliak's laugh. Elna's songs.

Kirit closed her eyes. "Who will believe us, in enough time to make a difference? How will we convince them to leave on the word of Lawsbreakers?" she said.

I thought of everyone above whom we'd left. Whom we couldn't reach. "The northwest will believe us. They know us. And they can help."

The moon rose, brightening the horizon to dark blues, rippled with silver. "But they won't believe us if we don't return," Wik said. "We have to go back up before we can change things."

I sank to a sitting position, looking at the steep bone wall, thinking of something Ceetcee had told me long ago. "Things are already changing. The towers rose up. The blackwings are in disarray. Dix and Hiroli are no longer a threat to the city. We have the plates, and we rescued the artifex. We did that."

"The city needs much more from us," Wik said.

"They'll know. We'll find a way to make them believe." Ciel sounded hopeful. "Moc's up there. He'll be mad if he doesn't get to see this." She hummed "Nest of Thieves," but stopped partway through. "We're going to need more songs."

New songs, a new way of living.

"We go back up?" Wik asked. He put a hand on Kirit's shoulder. She nodded.

The city believed the clouds were dangerous, that fallen meant lost. But we'd fallen from the clouds. And we'd lived.

Our new horizon balanced ground and sky, cloud and bone.

Between the unreachable clouds and the immovable earth, stars shone against the darkness. They were as beautiful below as they had always been above.

"We'll lead the city to safety." I stood with my companions, beside the bone wall, below the clouds. Above us, the people we loved waited, caught between the soaring city we could no longer see and the dying city below. "We'll rise once more."

ACKNOWLEDGMENTS

To my first readers: Chris Gerwel, E. C. Myers, Lauren Teffeau, Kelly Lagor, Nicole Feldringer, Laura Anne Gilman, Jaime Lee Moyer, Sara Mueller, Sarah Pinsker, A. C. Wise, A. T. Greenblatt, and Siobhan Carroll, who encourage me whether I run short or long. To Stephanie Feldman and Siobhan for the brainstorming road trip. We should do that again.

To Natalie, Bear, Celia, Jodi, Arkady, Alex, Ilana, Oz, Jim, Ann, Nanita, T, Amy, and Sylvie, for balance. To Jennifer, Wendy, Sara, Nancy, Dan, Jeff, Claudia, Jack, and Mike in Fells Point, for community. To Charlotte and Terry, Becky, and Mark; Shveta, Jack Hart; Aliette, Chris, Eric, Blair; Stacey, Dan, Juliette, and Lydia; and Melissa, Josh, and Noa, for friendship. To Susan, Beth, Raq, Nanita, and the rest of my family, for being here.

To my wonderful editor, Miriam Weinberg, and to Russ Galen, with thanks.

To Jason Tuell and Nicole Feldringer for nattering with me about clouds. To Dominick D'Aunno for the altitude discussions. All mistakes are my own doing.

To everyone at Tor who touched this book, including cover artist Tommy Arnold, creative director Irene Gallo, copy editor Ana Deboo, production editor Lauren Hougen, everyone in PR and marketing, including Alexis, Diana, and especially Patty and Ksenia, and to the folks who work the presses, too, for making these dreams real.

As always, to a place near Worton, Maryland, for teaching me how to fly.

And to you, reading this book: may the wind always take you where you want to go.